THE NAUGHTIEST GIRL COLLECTION

THE NAUGHTIEST GIRL

Enid Blyton

THE NAUGHTIEST GIRL
COLLECTION

The Naughtiest Girl in the School

The Naughtiest Girl Again

The Naughtiest Girl is a Monitor

*Hodder
Children's
Books*

HODDER CHILDREN'S BOOKS

The Naughtiest Girl in the School first published by George Newnes in 1940
The Naughtiest Girl Again first published by Hodder and Stoughton in 1942
The Naughtiest Girl is a Monitor first published by Hodder and Stoughton 1945
This edition published in 2016 by Hodder and Stoughton

10

Text copyright © Hodder and Stoughton
Enid Blyton's signature is a registered Trade Mark of Hodder and Stoughton

A CIP catalogue record for this book
is available from the British Library.

ISBN 978 1 444 91060 5

Typeset in Sabon by Avon DataSet Ltd, Bidford-on-Avon, Warwickshire
Printed and bound in Great Britain
by Clays Ltd, St Ives plc

The paper and board used in this book
are made from wood from responsible sources

Hodder Children's Books
An imprint of
Hachette Children's Group
Part of Hodder and Stoughton
Carmelite House
50 Victoria Embankment
London EC4Y 0DZ

An Hachette UK Company
www.hachette.co.uk

www.hachettechildrens.co.uk

Contents

1 The naughty spoilt girl

'You'll have to go to school, Elizabeth!' said Mrs Allen. 'I think your governess is quite right. You are spoilt and naughty, and although Daddy and I were going to leave you here with Miss Scott when we went away, I think it would be better for you to go to school.'

Elizabeth stared at her mother in dismay. What, leave her home? And her pony and her dog? Go and be with a lot of children she would hate? Oh no, she wouldn't go!

'I'll be good with Miss Scott,' she said.

'You've said that before,' said her mother. 'Miss Scott says she can't stay with you any longer. Elizabeth, is it true that you put earwigs in her bed last night?'

Elizabeth giggled. 'Yes,' she said. 'Miss Scott is so frightened of them! It's silly to be afraid of earwigs, isn't it?'

'It is much sillier to put them into somebody's bed,' said Mrs Allen sternly. 'You have been spoilt, and you think you can do what you like! You are an only child, and we love you so much, Daddy and I, that I think we have given you too many lovely things, and allowed you too much freedom.'

'Mummy, if you send me to school, I shall be so naughty there that they'll send me back home again,' said Elizabeth, shaking her curls back. She was a pretty girl with laughing blue eyes and dark brown curls. All her life she had done as she liked. Six governesses had come and gone, but not one of them had been able to make Elizabeth obedient or good-mannered!

'You can be such a nice little girl!' they had all said to her, 'but all you think of is getting into mischief and being rude about it!'

And now when she said that she would be so naughty at school that they would have to send her home, her mother looked at her in despair. She loved Elizabeth very much, and wanted her to be happy – but how could she be happy if she did not learn to be as other children were?

'You have been alone too much, Elizabeth,' she said. 'You should have had other children to play with and to work with.'

'I don't like other children!' said Elizabeth sulkily. It was quite true – she didn't like boys and girls at all! They were shocked at her mischief and rude ways, and when they said they wouldn't join in her naughtiness, she laughed at them and said they were babies. Then they told her what they thought of her, and Elizabeth didn't like it.

So now the thought of going away to school and living with other boys and girls made Elizabeth feel dreadful!

'Please don't send me,' she begged. 'I really will be good at home.'

'No, Elizabeth,' said her mother. 'Daddy and I *must* go away for a whole year, and as Miss Scott won't stay, and we could not expect to find another governess quickly before we go, it is best you should go to school. You have a good brain and you should be able to do your work well and get to the top of the form. Then we shall be proud of you.'

'I shan't work at all,' said Elizabeth, pouting. 'I won't work a bit, and they'll think I'm so stupid they won't keep me!'

'Well, Elizabeth, if you want to make things difficult for yourself, you'll have to,' said Mother, getting up. 'We have written to Miss Belle and Miss Best, who run Whyteleafe School, and they are willing to take you next week, when the new term begins. Miss Scott will get all your things ready. Please help her all you can.'

Elizabeth was very angry and upset. She didn't want to go to school. She hated everybody, especially silly children! Miss Scott was horrid to say she wouldn't stay. Suddenly Elizabeth wondered if she *would* stay, if she asked her very, very nicely!

She ran to find her governess. Miss Scott was busy sewing Elizabeth's name on to a pile of brown stockings.

'Are these new stockings?' asked Elizabeth, in surprise. 'I don't wear stockings! I wear socks!'

'You have to wear stockings at Whyteleafe School,' said Miss Scott. Elizabeth stared at the pile, and then she suddenly put her arms round Miss Scott's neck.

'Miss Scott!' she said. 'Stay with me! I know I'm sometimes naughty, but I don't want you to go.'

'What you *really* mean is that you don't want to go to school,' said Miss Scott. 'I suppose Mother's been telling you?'

'Yes, she has,' said Elizabeth. 'Miss Scott, I *won't* go to school!'

'Well, of course, if you're such a baby as to be afraid of doing what all other children do, then I've nothing more to say,' said Miss Scott, beginning to sew another name on a brown stocking.

Elizabeth stood up at once and stamped her foot. 'Afraid!' she shouted. '*I'm* not afraid! Was I afraid when I fell off my pony? Was I afraid when our car crashed into the bank? Was I afraid when – when – when—'

'Don't shout at me, please, Elizabeth,' said Miss Scott. 'I think you are afraid to go to school and mix with obedient, well-mannered, hard-working children who are not spoilt as you are. You know quite well that you wouldn't get your own way, that you would have to share everything, instead of having things to yourself as you do now, and that you would have to be punctual, polite, and obedient. And you are afraid to go!'

'I'm not, I'm not, I'm not!' shouted Elizabeth. 'I shall go! But I shall be so naughty and lazy that they won't keep me, and then I'll come back home! And you'll have to look after me again, so there!'

'My dear Elizabeth, I shan't be here,' said Miss Scott, taking another stocking. 'I am going to another family, where I shall have two little boys to teach. I am going the day you go to school. So you can't come back home because I shan't be here, your father and mother will be away, and the house will be shut up!'

Elizabeth burst into tears. She sobbed so loudly that Miss Scott, who was really fond of the spoilt, naughty girl, put her arms round her and comforted her.

'Now don't be silly,' she said. 'Most children simply *love* school. It's great fun. You play games, you go for walks, all together, you have the most lovely lessons, and you will make such a lot of friends. You have no friends now, and it is a dreadful thing not to have a single friend. You are very lucky.'

'I'm not,' wept Elizabeth. 'Nobody loves me. I'm very unhappy.'

'The trouble is that people have loved you too much,' said Miss Scott. 'You are pretty, and merry, and rich, so you have been spoilt. People like the way you look, the way you smile, and your pretty clothes so they fuss you, and pet you, and spoil you, instead of treating you like an ordinary child. But it isn't enough to have a pretty face and a merry smile – you must have a good heart too.'

Nobody had spoken to Elizabeth like this before, and the little girl was astonished. 'I *have* got a good heart,' she said, tossing her curls back again.

'Well, you don't show it much!' said Miss Scott. 'Now run away, please, because I've got to count all these stockings, and then mark your new vests and bodices.'

Elizabeth looked at the pile of stockings. She hated them. Nasty brown things! She wouldn't wear them! She'd take her socks to school and wear *those* if she wanted to! Miss Scott turned to a chest-of-drawers and began to take out some vests. Elizabeth picked up two brown stockings and pinned them toe to toe. Then she tiptoed to Miss Scott and neatly and quietly pinned them to her skirt.

She skipped out of the room, giggling. Miss Scott carried the vests to the table. She began to count the stockings. There should be six pairs.

'One – two – three – four – five,' she counted. 'Five. Dear me – where's the sixth?'

She looked on the floor. She looked on the chair. She was really vexed. She counted the pile again. Then she went to the door and looked for Elizabeth. The little girl was pulling something out of a cupboard on the landing.

'Elizabeth!' called Miss Scott sharply, 'have you got a pair of brown stockings?'

'No, Miss Scott,' said Elizabeth, making her eyes look round and surprised. 'Why?'

'Because a pair is missing,' said Miss Scott. 'Did you take them out of this room?'

'No, really, Miss Scott,' said Elizabeth truthfully, trying not to laugh as she caught sight of the stockings swinging at Miss Scott's back. 'I'm sure all the stockings are in the room, Miss Scott, really!'

'Then perhaps your mother has a pair,' said Miss Scott. 'I'll go and ask her.'

Off marched the governess down the landing, the pinned brown stockings trailing behind her like a tail. Elizabeth put her head into the cupboard and squealed with laughter. Miss Scott went into her mother's room.

'Excuse me, Mrs Allen,' she said, 'but have you one of Elizabeth's new pairs of stockings? I've only five pairs.'

'No, I gave you them all,' said Mrs Allen, surprised. 'They must be together. Perhaps you have dropped them somewhere.'

Miss Scott turned to go, and Mrs Allen caught sight of the brown stockings following Miss Scott. She looked at them in astonishment.

'Wait, Miss Scott,' she said. 'What's this!' She went to Miss Scott, and unpinned the stockings. The governess looked at Mrs Allen.

'Elizabeth, of course!' she said.

'Yes, Elizabeth!' said Mrs Allen. 'Always in mischief. I really never knew such a child in my life. It is high time she went to school. Don't you agree, Miss Scott?'

'I do,' said Miss Scott heartily. 'You will see a different and much nicer child when you come back home again, Mrs Allen!'

Elizabeth was passing by, and heard what her mother and her governess were saying. She hit the door with the book she was carrying and shouted angrily.

'You won't see me any different, Mother, you won't,

you won't! I'll be worse!'

'You couldn't be!' said Mrs Allen in despair. 'You really *couldn't* be worse!'

2 Elizabeth goes to school

For the rest of her time at home Elizabeth was very naughty and also very good.

'I'll try being very, very good and obedient and polite and sweet, and see if Mother changes her mind,' she thought. So, to the surprise of everyone, she became thoughtful, sweet-tongued, good-mannered, and most obedient. But it had quite the wrong effect, because, instead of saying that she would keep her at home now, her mother said something quite different!

'Well, Elizabeth, now that I know what a really nice girl you can be, I'm not so afraid of sending you to school as I was,' she said. 'I thought you would get into such trouble and be so unhappy – but now that I see how well you really can behave, I am sure you will get on nicely at school. I am very pleased with your behaviour!'

And you can guess what happened after that. Elizabeth at once became naughtier than she had ever been before!

'If being good makes Mother feel like that, I'll see what being naughty does!' she thought.

So she emptied the ink-bottle over the cushions in the drawing-room. She tore a hole in one of the nicest curtains. She put three black beetles into poor Miss Scott's toothbrush mug, and she squeezed glue into the ends of both Miss Scott's brown shoes, so that her toes would stick there!

'Well, all this makes it quite certain that Elizabeth needs

to go to school!' said Miss Scott angrily, as she tried to get her feet out of her sticky shoes. 'I'm glad to leave her! Naughty little girl! And yet she can be so sweet and nice when she likes.'

Elizabeth's things were packed and ready. She had a neat brown trunk, with 'E. Allen' painted on it in black. She had a tuck-box too, with a big currant cake inside, a box of chocolate, a tin of toffee, a jam sandwich, and a tin of shortbread.

'You will have to share these things with the others,' said Miss Scott, as she packed the things neatly inside.

'Well, I shan't, then,' said Elizabeth.

'Very well, don't!' said Miss Scott. 'If you want to show everyone what a selfish child you are, just take the chance!'

Elizabeth put on the outdoor uniform of Whyteleafe School. It was very neat, and she looked nice in it. But then Elizabeth looked nice in anything!

The outdoor uniform was a dark blue coat with a yellow edge to the collar and cuffs, a dark blue hat with a yellow ribbon round it, and the school badge at the front. Her stockings were long and brown, and her lace shoes were brown too.

'My goodness, you do look a real schoolgirl!' said her mother, quite proudly. Elizabeth wouldn't smile. She stood there, sulky and angry. 'I shan't stay at school long,' she said. 'They'll soon send me back!'

'Don't be silly, Elizabeth,' said her mother. She kissed the little girl goodbye and hugged her. 'I will come and see you at half-term,' she said.

'No, Mother, you won't,' said Elizabeth. 'I shall be home long before that!'

'Don't make me sad, Elizabeth!' said Mrs Allen. But

Elizabeth wouldn't smile or say she was sorry. She got into the car that was to take her to the station, and sat there, very cross and straight. She had said goodbye to her pony. She had said goodbye to Timmy, her dog. She had said goodbye to her canary. And to each of them she had whispered the same thing.

'I'll soon be back! You'll see – they won't keep the naughtiest girl in the school for long!'

Miss Scott took her to the station and then up to London in the train. She went with Elizabeth to a big station where trains whistled and chuffed, and people ran about in a hurry.

'Now we must find the right platform,' said Miss Scott, hurrying too. 'We have to meet the teacher there, who is in charge of the girls going by this train.'

They came to the right platform and went through to where a big group of girls stood with a teacher. They were all dressed in dark blue coats and hats, with yellow hat-bands like Elizabeth. The girls were of all ages, some big, some small, and most of them were chattering hard.

Two or three stood apart, looking shy. They were the new ones, like Elizabeth. The teacher spoke to them now and again, and they smiled gratefully at her.

Miss Scott bustled up to the teacher. 'Good morning,' she said. 'Is this Miss Thomas? This is Elizabeth Allen. I'm glad we are in good time!'

'Good morning,' said Miss Thomas, smiling. She held out her hand to Elizabeth. 'Well, dear,' she said, 'so you are going to join the happy crowd at Whyteleafe School!'

Elizabeth put her hand behind her back and would not shake hands with Miss Thomas. The teacher looked surprised. The other children stared. Miss Scott blushed red, and spoke sharply to Elizabeth.

'Elizabeth! Shake hands at once!'

Elizabeth turned her back and looked at a train puffing nearby. 'I'm so sorry she's behaving so rudely,' said Miss Scott, really upset. She spoke in a low voice to Miss Thomas. 'She's an only child – very, very spoilt – rich, pretty – and she doesn't want to come away to school. Just leave her alone for a bit and I expect she'll be all right.'

Miss Thomas nodded. She was a merry-looking young woman, and the girls liked her. She was just going to say something when a man came hurrying up with four boys.

'Good morning, Miss Thomas,' he said. 'Here is my batch! Sorry I can't stop, I've a train to catch! Goodbye, boys!'

'Goodbye, sir,' said the four boys.

'How many boys have you at Whyteleafe this term?' asked Miss Scott. 'As many as girls?'

'Not quite,' said Miss Thomas. 'There are some more boys over there, look, in the charge of Mr Johns.'

Miss Scott liked the look of the boys, all in dark blue overcoats and blue caps with yellow badges in front. 'Such a good idea,' she said, 'to educate boys and girls together. For a child like Elizabeth, who has no brothers, and not even a sister, it is like joining a large family of brothers and sisters and cousins, to go to a school like Whyteleafe!'

'Oh, they'll soon knock the corners off your Elizabeth,' smiled Miss Thomas. 'Look – here comes our train. We have our carriages reserved for us, so I must find them. The boys have two carriages and the girls have three. Come along, girls, here's our train!'

Elizabeth was swept along with the others. She was pushed into a carriage with a big label on it, 'Reserved for Whyteleafe School'.

'Goodbye, Elizabeth; goodbye, dear!' cried Miss Scott. 'Do your best!'

'Goodbye,' said Elizabeth, suddenly feeling very small and lost. 'I'll soon be back!' she shouted.

'Gracious!' said a tubby little girl next to her, 'a term's a long time, you know! Fancy saying you'll soon be back!'

'Well, I shall,' said Elizabeth. She was squashed in a heap by the tubby little girl and another girl on the other side, who was rather bony. She didn't like it.

Elizabeth felt sure she would never, never learn who all the different girls were. She felt a little afraid of the big ones, and she was horrified to think there were boys at her school! Boys! Nasty, rough creatures – well, she'd show them that a girl could be rough too!

The little girl sat silently as the train rattled on and on. The others chattered and talked and offered sweets round the carriage. Elizabeth shook her head when the sweets were offered to her.

'Oh, come on, do have one!' said the tubby little girl, whose sweets they were. 'A sweet would do you good – make you look a bit sweeter perhaps!'

Everybody laughed. Elizabeth went red and hated the tubby little girl.

'Ruth! You do say some funny things!' said a big girl opposite. 'Don't tease the poor little thing. She's new.'

'Well, so is Belinda, next to you,' said Ruth, 'but she does at least *say* something when she's spoken to!'

'That will do, Ruth,' said Miss Thomas, seeing how red Elizabeth had gone. Ruth said no more, but the next time she offered her sweets round she did not offer them to Elizabeth.

It was a long journey. Elizabeth was tired when at last the train drew up in a country station and the girls poured out of the carriages. The boys came to join them, and the children talked eagerly of all they had done in the holidays.

'Come along now, quickly,' said Mr Johns, pushing them out of the station gate. 'The coach is waiting.'

There was an enormous coach outside the station, labelled 'Whyteleafe School'. The children took their places. Elizabeth found a place as far away as possible from the tubby little girl called Ruth. She didn't like her one bit. She didn't like Belinda either. She didn't like anyone! They all stared at her too much!

The coach set off with a loud clank and rumble. Round the corner it went, down a country lane, up a steep hill – and there was Whyteleafe School at the top! It was a beautiful building, like an old country house – which, indeed, it once had been. Its deep red walls, green with creeper, glowed in the April sun. It had a broad flight of steps leading from the green lawns up to the school terrace.

'Good old Whyteleafe!' said Ruth, pleased to see it. The coach swept round to the other side of the school, through a great archway, and up to the front door. The children jumped down and ran up the steps, shouting and laughing.

Elizabeth found her hand taken by Miss Thomas. 'Welcome to Whyteleafe, Elizabeth!' said the teacher kindly, smiling down at the sulky face. 'I am sure you will do well here and be very happy with us all.'

'I shan't,' said naughty Elizabeth, and she pulled her hand away! It was certainly not a very good beginning.

3 Elizabeth makes a bad beginning

It was half-past one by the time the children arrived, and they were all hungry for their dinner. They were told to wash their hands quickly, and tidy themselves and then go to the dining-hall for their dinner.

'Eileen, please look after the three new girls,' said Miss Thomas. A big girl, with a kindly face and a mass of fair curls, came up to Belinda, Elizabeth, and another girl called Helen. She gave them a push in the direction of the cloakrooms.

'Hurry!' she said. So they hurried, and Elizabeth soon found herself in a big cloakroom, tiled in gleaming white, with basins down one side, and mirrors here and there.

She washed quickly, feeling rather lost in such a crowd of chattering girls. Helen and Belinda had made friends, and Elizabeth wished they would say something to her instead of chattering to one another. But they said nothing to Elizabeth, thinking her rude and strange.

Then to the dining-hall went all the girls and took their places. The boys clattered in too.

'Sit anywhere you like today,' said a tall mistress, whose name, Elizabeth found, was Miss Belle. So the children sat down and began to eat their dinner hungrily. There was hot soup first, then beef, carrots, dumplings, onions and potatoes, and then rice pudding and golden syrup. Elizabeth was so hungry that she ate everything put before her, though at home she would certainly have pushed away the rice pudding.

As it was the first day the children were allowed to talk as they pleased, and there was such a noise as they told one another what they had done in the holidays.

'I had a puppy for Easter,' said one girl with a laughing face. 'Do you know, my father bought a simply enormous Easter egg, and put the puppy inside, and tied up the egg with a red ribbon? Goodness, didn't I laugh when I undid it!'

Everybody else laughed too.

'I had a new bicycle for my Easter present,' said a round-faced boy. 'But it wasn't put into an egg!'

'What did you have for Easter?' said Eileen to Elizabeth in a kindly tone. She was sitting opposite, and felt sorry for the silent new girl. Belinda and Helen were sitting together, telling each other about the last school they had been to. Only Elizabeth had no one to talk to her.

'I had a guinea-pig,' said Elizabeth, in a clear voice, 'and it had a face just like Miss Thomas.'

There was a shocked silence. Somebody giggled. Miss Thomas looked rather surprised, but she said nothing.

'If you weren't a new girl, you'd be jolly well sat on for that!' said a girl nearby, glaring at Elizabeth. 'Rude creature!'

Elizabeth couldn't help going red. She had made up her mind to be naughty and rude, and she was going to be really bad, but it was rather dreadful to have somebody speaking like that to her, in front of everyone. She went on with her rice pudding. Soon the children began to talk to one another again, and Elizabeth was forgotten.

After dinner the boys went to unpack their things in their own bedrooms, and the girls went to theirs.

'Whose room are the new girls in, please, Miss Thomas?' asked Eileen. Miss Thomas looked at her list.

'Let me see,' she said, 'yes – here we are – Elizabeth Allen, Belinda Green, Helen Marsden – they are all in Room Six, Eileen, and with them are Ruth James, Joan Townsend and Nora O'Sullivan. Ask Nora to take the new girls there and show them what to do. She's head of that room.'

'Nora! Hi, Nora!' called Eileen, as a tall, dark-haired girl, with deep blue eyes went by. 'Take these kids to Room Six, will you? They're yours! You're head of that room.'

'I know,' said Nora, looking at the three new girls. 'Hallo, is this the girl who was rude to Miss Thomas? You just mind what you say, whatever-your-name-is, I'm not having any cheek from *you!*'

'I shall say exactly what I like,' said Elizabeth boldly. '*You* can't stop me!'

'Oho, can't I?' said Nora, her blue Irish eyes glaring at Elizabeth. 'That's all *you* know! Get along to the bedroom now, and I'll show you all what to do.'

They all went up a winding oak staircase and came to a wide landing. All around it were doors, marked with numbers. Nora opened the door of Number Six and went in.

The bedroom was long, high and airy. There were wide windows, all open to the school gardens outside. The sun poured in and made the room look very pleasant indeed.

The room was divided into six by blue curtains, which were now drawn back to the walls, so that six low white beds could be seen, each with a blue eiderdown. Beside each bed stood a wide chest of drawers, with a small mirror on top. The chests were painted white with blue wooden handles, and looked very pretty.

There were three washbasins in the room, with hot and cold water taps, to be shared by the six girls. There was also a tall white cupboard for each girl, and in these they hung their coats and dresses.

Each bed had a blue rug beside it on the polished brown boards. Elizabeth couldn't help thinking that it all looked rather exciting. She had only shared with Miss Scott before – now she was to share with five other girls!

'Your trunks and tuck-boxes are beside your beds,' said Nora. 'You must each unpack now, and put your things away tidily. And when I say tidily I *mean* tidily. I shall look at your drawers once a week. On the top of the chest you are allowed to have six things, not more. Choose what you like – hairbrushes, or photographs, or ornaments – it doesn't matter.'

'How silly!' thought Elizabeth scornfully, thinking of her own untidy dressing-table at home. 'I shall put as many things out as I like!'

They all began unpacking. Elizabeth had never packed or unpacked anything in her life, and she found it rather exciting. She put her things neatly away in her chest of drawers – the piles of stockings, vests, bodices, blouses, everything she had brought with her. She hung up her school coat and her dresses.

The others were busy unpacking too. Whilst they were doing this two more girls danced into the room.

'Hallo, Nora!' said one, a red-haired girl with freckles all over her face. 'I'm in your room this term. Good!'

'Hallo, Joan,' said Nora. 'Get on with your unpacking, there's a lamb. Hallo, Ruth – I've got you here again, have I? Well, just see you're a bit tidier than last term!'

Ruth laughed. She was the girl who had handed round her sweets in the train, and she was plump and clever. She ran to her trunk and began to undo it.

Nora began to tell the new girls a little about the school. They listened as they busily put away their things in their drawers.

'Whyteleafe School isn't a very large school,' began Nora, 'but it's a jolly fine one. The boys have their lessons with us, and we play tennis and cricket with them and we have our own teams of girls only, too. Last year we beat the boys at tennis. We'll beat them this year, too, if only we can get some good players. Any of you new girls play tennis?'

Belinda did but the others didn't. Nora went on talking, as she hung up her dresses.

'We all have the same amount of pocket-money to spend,' she said. 'And it's plenty too. Two pounds a week.'

'I shall have a lot more than that,' said Belinda in surprise.

'Oh no, you won't,' said Nora. 'All the money we have is put into a big box, and we each draw two pounds a week from it, unless we've been fined for something.'

'What do you mean – fined?' asked Helen. 'Who fines us? Miss Belle and Miss Best?'

'Oh no,' said Nora. 'We hold a big meeting once a week – oftener, if necessary – and we hear complaints and grumbles, and if anyone has been behaving badly we fine them. Miss Belle or Miss Best come to the Meeting too, of course, but they don't decide anything much. They trust us to decide for ourselves.'

Elizabeth thought this was very strange. She had always thought that the teachers punished the children – but at Whyteleafe it seemed as if the children did it! She listened in astonishment to all that Nora was saying.

'If there's any money over, it is given to anyone who particularly wants to buy something that the Meeting approves of,' went on Nora. 'For instance, suppose you broke your tennis racket, Belinda, and needed a new one, the Meeting might allow you to take the money from the box to buy one – especially if they thought you were a very good player.'

'I see,' said Belinda. 'It sounds a good idea. Look, Nora – here are the things out of my tuck-box. What do I do with them? I want to share them with everybody.'

'Thanks,' said Nora. 'Well, we keep all our cakes and sweets and things in the playroom downstairs. There's a big cupboard there, and tins to put cakes into. I'll show you where. Elizabeth, are your tuck-box things ready? If so, bring them along, and we'll put them into the cupboard to share at tea-time.'

'I'm not going to share,' said Elizabeth, remembering that she hadn't been naughty or horrid for some time. 'I shall eat them all myself.'

There was a horrified silence. The five girls stared at Elizabeth as if they couldn't believe their ears. Not share her cakes and sweets? Whatever sort of a girl was this?

'Well,' said Nora, at last, her merry face suddenly very disgusted. 'You can do what you like, of course, with your own things. If they're as horrid as you seem to be, nobody would want to eat them!'

4 Elizabeth gets into trouble

As Nora was about to lead the way down to the playroom, she glanced at the chests of drawers to see that they were tidy on the top. To her surprise she saw that Elizabeth had put about a dozen things on her chest!

Nora stopped and looked at them. There were two hairbrushes, a mirror, a comb, three photographs, a bottle of scent, two small vases, and a clothes-brush.

'Look here!' said Nora, to the others, 'this poor child can't count up to six! She's got eleven things on her chest. Poor Elizabeth! Fancy not being able to count six.'

'I *can*,' said Elizabeth fiercely. 'One, two, three, four, five, six.'

Everybody squealed with laughter. 'She *can* count!' said Nora. 'Well, Elizabeth, count your things, and take five away – or can't you do taking-away? There are eleven things on your chest – take away five – and it will leave six – which is the number I told you to have.'

'I'm not going to take any away,' said Elizabeth rudely.

'Aren't you?' said Nora, in surprise. 'Well, if you won't – I will!'

The angry Irish girl picked up a hairbrush, the three photographs, and the mirror. She went to a box under the window, took a key from her pocket and unlocked it. She put the five things inside and locked the box.

'That's what happens when people can't count,' she

said. Elizabeth stared at her in a rage.

'Give me my things back,' she said. 'I want those photographs at once! They are of Mummy and Daddy and my pony too.'

'Sorry,' said Nora, putting the key into her pocket. 'You can have them back when you apologize, and tell me that you know how to count.'

'I shan't,' said Elizabeth.

'Just as you please,' said Nora. 'Now come on, everybody, and let's take the eatables down to the playroom.'

'I don't want to bring mine,' said Elizabeth.

'I want to leave them here.'

'Well, if you do, they'll go into that box along with the photographs,' said Nora firmly. 'The rule is that all eatables go downstairs.'

Elizabeth stood sulking, looking at her cake, her jam sandwich, her chocolate, toffee, and shortbread. Then she picked up her tuck-box and followed the others. She did not want them to go into that box! She had seen enough of Nora to know that that young lady was very determined!

They clattered down the oak staircase. At one side of the hall was an open door, leading into a very large room lined with cupboards and bookcases. It was full of boys and girls.

Some were talking, some were playing games, some were putting away cakes into tins. They were all busy and happy, and called out greetings to Nora as she came into the room.

There was a gramophone going in one corner. Elizabeth stopped to listen to it, for she loved music. It was playing a tune that her mother played at home, and suddenly the little girl felt as if she wanted her mother badly.

'But, never mind!' she thought to herself. 'I shan't be here long! I don't expect they'll keep me more than a week if I go on being awfully naughty.'

'Here are some empty tins,' said Nora, handing some down from a shelf. 'Catch, Helen. Catch, Elizabeth. Here's a big one for you, Belinda, to take in that enormous cake!'

Soon they were all putting away their things. Nora took slips of paper from a pile and wrote their names on. 'Stick your name on your tin,' she said, licking hers and sticking it to the side of her tin.

'I'd like to see the classrooms,' said Belinda. Ruth said she would show her round the whole school, and off she went with Belinda and Helen. Elizabeth followed a little way behind, curious to see what a school was like, for she had never seen inside one before.

The dining-hall she had already seen – a great high room, with big windows. Tables ran down the middle of it. It was only used for meals.

Then there were the classrooms, big, sunny rooms all over the place, with neat desks and chairs, and a bigger desk for the teacher. There were blackboards everywhere, just like the one that Miss Scott had used for Elizabeth.

'This is *our* classroom,' said Ruth to the new girls. 'I expect we'll all be in Miss Ranger's class. She's pretty strict, I can tell you! Nora's in a higher class, of course. She's older. She's a jolly good sort, don't you think so?'

'Yes,' agreed Helen and Belinda at once. But Elizabeth thought differently. She pursed up her mouth and said nothing.

'This is the gym,' said Ruth, and the three new girls looked in wonder at the great room, with its ropes and climbing-ladders, and bars and poles. Elizabeth suddenly felt excited. She loved climbing and swinging and jumping. She hoped she could do some gym before she left.

There were many other bedrooms like her own, and then there was the part of the house put aside for Miss Belle and Miss Best and the other teachers.

'You'll each have to go and see the heads after tea,' said Ruth. 'They're good sorts.'

By the time the four girls had gone over the lovely grounds and had seen the cricket fields, the tennis-courts, and the flower-filled gardens, it was time for tea. A bell rang loudly, and the girls looked cheerful.

'Good! Tea!' said Ruth. 'Come on. Wash first, all of you, and do your hair. Yours looks awful, Elizabeth.'

Elizabeth did not like her dark curls being called 'awful'. She went up to her bedroom and did her hair neatly, and washed her hands. She was very hungry, and thought with pleasure of her currant cake and jam sandwich.

'I've got the most gorgeous chocolate cake you ever saw!' said Belinda to the others. 'It just melts in your mouth! You must all have a piece.'

'And I've got some home-made shrimp-paste that's too delicious for words,' said Ruth. 'You wait till you taste it.'

Chocolate cake and home-made shrimp-paste seemed even more delicious to Elizabeth than currant cake and jam sandwich, which suddenly seemed rather ordinary. She ran downstairs wondering if she would have *two* pieces of Belinda's gorgeous chocolate cake.

Tea was laid in the dining-room. The long tables were spread with white cloths, and plates with big slices of brown bread and butter were set all the way down. There were some large plain cakes here and there, and some big pots of plum jam.

The children put their tuck-boxes on a bare table, and placed on some empty plates there the cake or sandwich, jam or paste they meant to share at tea. These plates they took to their own table.

Once again they were allowed to sit where they liked. Elizabeth put out her sandwich and her currant cake and took her place too. Grace was said and then the boys and girls began to chatter quietly.

Suddenly Nora banged on the table. She was at the head of it. Everyone at her table stopped speaking.

'I nearly forgot to say something,' said Nora. 'Elizabeth Allen does not wish to share her things with anyone, so don't ask her for a piece of her cake, will you? She wants it all herself.'

'All right!' said the other children, and they stared at Elizabeth in surprise. Elizabeth went on eating her bread and butter. Next to her was Ruth, opening a large pot of shrimp-paste that smelt simply delicious. She passed it round the table – but did not offer Elizabeth any.

Nobody offered her anything at all. Belinda counted how many there were at the table – eleven – and then cut her cake into ten big pieces. Ten was enough, because she missed Elizabeth out! Elizabeth watched the others munching the chocolate cake, which looked and smelt marvellous, and longed for a piece.

She cut her currant cake. It looked quite nice. She suddenly felt that she really couldn't eat it all by herself, she *must* offer it to the others too. She didn't mind being thought naughty, but being thought mean was different.

'Will you have a piece of my cake?' she asked Ruth.

Ruth stared at her in surprise. 'How you do change your mind!' she said. 'No thanks. I've had enough.'

Elizabeth offered her cake to Belinda. Belinda shook her head. 'No, thank you,' she said. Elizabeth held out her plate to Helen, but Helen simply made a face at her and turned away.

Nobody would have any of Elizabeth's cake or of her sandwich either. Everyone else had either cut up half or all their cakes, and had finished up their pots of jam or paste. Only Elizabeth's cake and sandwich stood almost untouched on their plates.

A bell rang. Miss Thomas stood up and spoke to the girls and boys. 'You may go out to play,' she said, 'but the new children must stay behind in the playroom, and see the headmistresses.'

So Helen, Elizabeth, and Belinda went to the playroom, and also two boys named Kenneth and Ronald. They set the gramophone going. Belinda did a funny dance and made them all laugh.

Then someone poked her head in at the door and called to the children.

'Miss Belle and Miss Best are waiting to see you. Go and line up outside the drawing room door – and mind you each say you're going to do your best for Whyteleafe School, and will work and play hard!'

The girl disappeared. The new children went to line up outside the drawing room door. It opened and Miss Best appeared. 'Come in,' she said to Belinda, and in Belinda went. The door shut.

'Well, *I'm* not going to say I shall work hard and play hard,' said Elizabeth to herself. 'I'm just going to warn them that I won't stay here and I'll be so bad they'll have to send me away. I *won't* stay at this horrid school!'

The door opened and Belinda came out, smiling. 'You're to go in next, Elizabeth,' she said. 'And for goodness' sake behave yourself!'

5 Elizabeth is naughty

Elizabeth pushed open the door and went into the big drawing room. It was a lovely room, with a few beautiful pictures on the walls, and glowing cushions on the chairs and the couches. The two mistresses were sitting on chairs near the window. They looked up as Elizabeth came in.

'Well, Elizabeth! We are very glad to see you at Whyteleafe School,' said Miss Belle. She was young and pretty, but Miss Best was older, and, except when she smiled, she had rather a stern face.

'Sit down, Elizabeth,' said Miss Best, smiling her lovely smile. 'I hope you have made a few friends already.'

'No, I haven't,' said Elizabeth. She sat down on a chair. Miss Best looked at her in surprise, when she answered so shortly.

'Well, I expect you will soon make plenty,' said the headmistress. 'I hope you will be very happy with us, Elizabeth.'

'I shan't be,' said Elizabeth in a rude voice.

'What a funny little girl!' said Miss Belle, and she laughed. 'Cheer up, dear – you'll soon find things are very jolly here, and I am sure you will do your best to work hard, and make us proud of you.'

'I'm not going to,' said Elizabeth, going red. 'I'm going to be as bad and naughty and horrid as I can possibly be, so there! I don't want to go to school. I hate Whyteleafe

School! I'll be so bad that you'll send me home next week!'

The little girl glared at the two mistresses as she said all this, expecting them to jump up in anger. Instead they both threw back their heads and laughed and laughed!

'Oh, Elizabeth, what an extraordinary child you are!' said Miss Belle, wiping away the tears of laughter that had come into her eyes. 'You look such a good, pretty little girl too – no one would think you wanted to be so bad and naughty and horrid!'

'I don't care how you punish me,' said Elizabeth, tears coming into her own eyes – but tears of anger, not of laughter. 'You can do all you like – I just shan't care!'

'We never punish anyone, Elizabeth,' said Miss Best, suddenly looking stern again. 'Didn't you know that?'

'No, I didn't,' said Elizabeth in astonishment. 'What do you do when people are naughty, then?'

'Oh, we leave any naughty person to the rest of the children to deal with,' said Miss Best. 'Every week the school holds a Meeting, you know, and the children themselves decide what is to be done with boys and girls who don't behave themselves. It won't bother *us* if you are naughty – but you may perhaps find that you make the children angry.'

'That seems funny to me,' said Elizabeth. 'I thought it was always the teachers that did the punishing.'

'Not at Whyteleafe School,' said Miss Belle. 'Well, Elizabeth, my dear, perhaps you'd go now and tell the next child to come in, will you? Maybe one day Whyteleafe School will be proud of you, even though you are quite sure it won't!'

Elizabeth went out without another word. She couldn't help liking the two headmistresses, though she didn't want to at all. She wished she had been ruder to them. What a funny school this was!

She spoke to Helen outside the door. 'You're to go in now,' she said. 'The Beauty and the Beast are waiting for you!'

'Oh, you naughty girl!' said Helen, with a giggle. 'Miss Belle and Miss Best – the Beauty and the Beast! That's rather clever of you to think of that, Elizabeth!'

Elizabeth had meant it to be very rude. She did not know enough of other children to know that they always loved nicknames for their masters and mistresses. She was surprised that Helen thought her clever – and secretly she was pleased.

But she stuck her nose in the air and marched off. *She* wasn't going to be pleased with anything or anybody at Whyteleafe School!

She wandered round by herself until the supper-bell went at seven o'clock. She felt hungry and went into the dining-hall. The children were once more opening their tins of cakes, and a lively chatter was going on. It all looked very jolly.

There were big mugs on the table and big jugs of steaming hot cocoa here and there. There were piles of bread again, butter, cheese, and dishes of stewed fruit. The children sat down and helped themselves.

Nobody took any notice of Elizabeth at all, till suddenly Helen remembered what she had called Miss Belle and Miss Best. With a giggle she repeated it to her neighbour, and soon there was laughter all round the table.

'The Beauty and the Beast,' went the whisper, and chuckles echoed round. Elizabeth heard the whispers and went red. Nora O'Sullivan laughed loudly.

'It's a jolly good nickname!' she said. 'Belle means Beauty, and Best is very like Beast – and certainly Miss Belle is lovely, and Miss Best isn't! That was pretty smart of you, Elizabeth.'

Elizabeth smiled! She really couldn't help it. She didn't want to – she wanted to be as horrid as possible – but it was really very pleasant to have everyone laughing at her joke.

'It's strange, though,' she thought. 'I meant to be horrid and rude, and the others just think it's funny. I guess Miss Belle and Miss Best wouldn't think it was funny, though!'

Nobody offered Elizabeth any of their goodies, and she did not like to offer hers, for she felt sure everyone would say no. The meal went on until half-past seven, and then after grace was said the children all got up and went to the playroom.

'When's your bedtime?' said Nora to Elizabeth. 'I expect it's eight o'clock. You'd better see. The times are on the notice-board over there. My bedtime is at half-past eight, and when I come to bed I expect all the rest of you to be safe in bed.'

'I don't want to go to bed at eight o'clock,' said Elizabeth indignantly. 'I go to bed much later than that at home.'

'Well, you shouldn't, then,' said Nora. 'No wonder you're such a crosspatch! My mother says that late hours make children stupid, bad-tempered, and slow.'

Elizabeth went to see the times for going to bed. Hers was, as Nora had said, at eight o'clock. Well, she wouldn't go! She'd be naughty!

So she slipped out into the garden and went to where she had seen two or three big swings. She got on to a swing and began to push herself to and fro. It was lovely there in the evening sunshine. Elizabeth quite forgot that she was at school, and she sang a little song to herself.

A boy came into the place where the swings were, and stared at Elizabeth. 'What are you doing here?' he said. 'I bet it's your bedtime!'

'Mind your own business!' said Elizabeth at once.

'Well, what about you going off to bed, and minding *yours*!' said the boy. 'I'm a monitor, and it's my job to see that people do what they're told!'

'I don't know what a monitor is, and I don't care,' said Elizabeth rudely.

'Well, let *me* tell you what a monitor is,' said the boy, who was just about Elizabeth's size. 'It's somebody put in charge of other silly kids at Whyteleafe, to see they don't get *too* silly! If you don't behave yourself I shall have to report you at the Meeting! Then you'll be punished.'

'Pooh!' said Elizabeth, and she swung herself very hard indeed, put out her foot and kicked the boy so vigorously that he fell right over. Elizabeth squealed with laughter – but not for long! The boy jumped up, ran to the swing and shook Elizabeth off. He caught hold of her dark curls and pulled them so hard that the little girl yelled with pain.

The boy grinned at her and said, 'Serves you right! You be careful how you treat me next time, or I'll pull your nose as well as your hair! Now – are you going in or not?'

Elizabeth ran away from him and went indoors. She looked at the clock – quarter-past eight! Perhaps she would have time to go to bed before that horrid Nora came up at half-past.

So she ran up the stairs and went to Bedroom Number Six. Ruth, Joan, Belinda, and Helen were already there half undressed. Their curtains were pulled around their cubicles, but they were talking hard all the same. Elizabeth slipped into her own cubicle.

'You're late, Elizabeth,' said Ruth. 'You'll get into trouble if you're caught by a monitor.'

'I have been,' said Elizabeth. 'But *I* didn't care! I was on the swing and I put out my foot and kicked him over!'

'Well, you're very silly,' said Ruth. 'You will get into trouble at the Meeting if you don't look out. And that's not pleasant.'

'I don't care for any silly Meeting,' said Elizabeth, jumping into bed. She remembered that Nora had put her three photographs into the locked box, and she jumped out again. She went to the box and tried to open it – but it was still locked. Nora came in at that moment and saw Elizabeth there.

'Hallo, kid,' she said. 'Do you want your things back? Well, apologize and you can have them.'

But Elizabeth was not going to say she was sorry. She made a rude face at Nora, and flung herself into bed.

'Well, you *are* a sweet child, aren't you!' said Nora mockingly. 'I hope you get out at the right side of your bed tomorrow!'

Then there was a creak as Nora sat on her bed to take off her stockings. A clock struck half-past eight downstairs. 'No more talking now,' said Nora. 'Sleep tight, all of you!'

6 Elizabeth joins her class

Elizabeth wondered where she was when she awoke the next morning, but she soon remembered. She was at that horrid school!

A bell rang. Nora sat up in her bed and spoke to the others. 'That's the bell for getting up,' she said. 'Stir yourselves! You've got half an hour.'

Elizabeth thought she wouldn't get up. She lay there warm in her bed, and looked up at the white ceiling. Nora's voice came sharply to her.

'Elizabeth Allen! Are you getting up or are you not?'

'Not,' said Elizabeth cheekily.

'Well, I'm in charge of you five, and it's my job to get you down to breakfast in good time,' said Nora, poking her nose round the curtain. 'Get up, you lazy creature!'

'Are you a monitor?' asked Elizabeth, remembering the boy of the evening before.

'I am,' said Nora. 'Come on, get up, Elizabeth, and don't make yourself such a nuisance.'

Elizabeth still lay there. Nora nodded to plump Ruth, and the two went beside Elizabeth's bed. Together they stripped all the clothes off the lazy girl, and then tipped up the mattress. Elizabeth gave a shriek and slid on to the floor. She was very angry.

She rushed at Nora – but Nora was big and strong, and caught hold of the angry girl's arms at once. 'Don't be silly now,' she said. 'Get dressed and hurry up or I'll give you what for! Monitors do that sometimes, you know!'

Elizabeth felt that she couldn't bear to test Nora's threat. She washed very sulkily, dressed, cleaned her teeth and did her hair. She was just going downstairs when Nora, who had gone into everyone's cubicle to see if they were tidy, called her back.

'Elizabeth! Come and put your chest of drawers tidy! Do you want me to put the rest of your things into the locked box?'

Elizabeth went back and tidied her things. It was quicker to do that than argue with Nora. She wondered if Nora would notice that she had put socks on instead of the long brown stockings!

But Nora didn't notice. She was in too big a hurry to get down to breakfast in time, and besides, she didn't dream that anyone would wear socks instead of stockings at Whyteleafe School!

But a great many of the other children noticed Elizabeth's bare legs at once, and giggled. Miss Thomas noticed them too, and called to Elizabeth.

'You've put the wrong things on, Elizabeth. You must change your socks for stockings afterwards.'

But Elizabeth didn't! When she went up to make her bed afterwards, she didn't change at all. Nora saw that she hadn't and spoke to her.

'For goodness' sake put stockings on, Elizabeth. Really, I shouldn't have thought anyone could be quite so silly as you seem to be!'

'I'm not silly,' said Elizabeth. 'I prefer socks. Stockings make my legs too hot. And I'm going to keep my socks *on*.'

Ruth spoke to Nora. 'Nora, Elizabeth is really babyish,'

she said. 'And the babies at Whyteleafe are allowed to wear socks, aren't they? I've seen them in the Kindergarten, with their dear little bare legs. Well, why not let Elizabeth keep her socks, to show that she is really only a baby, though she's getting on for eleven? You can easily explain that to Miss Thomas.'

'That's a good idea,' said Nora, with a laugh. 'All right, Elizabeth – keep your socks on, and we'll explain to everyone that we're letting you because you're really not much more than a baby!'

The girls went out of the room laughing. Elizabeth put on her bedspread and stood thinking. She didn't think she wanted to keep her socks on now! If only the younger children wore them, because they were the babies of the school, she didn't want to. The babies would laugh at her, and so would the others.

Elizabeth tore off her shoes, grabbed her socks and pulled them off in a temper. She took out her stockings and pulled them on. Bother, bother, bother! Now she would have to wear stockings after all!

She flew downstairs to the gym, where she had been told to go after making her bed and tidying her cubicle. All the others were there. Elizabeth had felt sure that they would all make remarks about her stockings being on after all – but nobody took any notice of her at all.

Hymns were sung and prayers said. Miss Best read part of a Bible chapter in her rather stern voice. Then she called the names of all the girls and boys to see that they were there.

Elizabeth had a good look round. The boys and girls were in separate rows. There were a good many masters and mistresses. The matron of the school, who looked after the children when they were ill, stood on the platform with some of the other mistresses, a fat, jolly-looking person, dressed like a nurse, in apron and cap. The music-master played the piano for the singing, and again when the children marched out.

He made up a fine marching tune, and Elizabeth liked it very much for she loved music. She wondered if she was supposed to learn music at Whyteleafe. Miss Scott had taught her at home, but Miss Scott was not musical and Elizabeth had not enjoyed her lessons at all.

Out marched the children to their classrooms. 'You are in Miss Ranger's class,' said Ruth, poking Elizabeth in the back. 'Come with me and I'll show you.'

Elizabeth followed Ruth. She came to a big sunny classroom, and into it poured six boys and nine girls, all about Elizabeth's age.

'Bags I this desk,' squealed Ruth. 'I like to be by the window!'

She put her things into the desk. The other children chose their desks too, but the new ones were told to wait till Miss Ranger came. Ruth sprang to hold the door open as soon as she heard Miss Ranger's rather loud voice down the passage.

In came Miss Ranger. 'Good morning, children!'

'Good morning, Miss Ranger,' said everyone but Elizabeth.

'All the old children can sit, but the new ones must stand whilst I give them their places,' said Miss Ranger. She gave Elizabeth a desk at the back. Elizabeth was glad. It would be a good place to be naughty in! She meant to be bad in class that very morning. The sooner that everyone knew how naughty she meant to be, the sooner she would be sent home.

Books were given out. 'We will take a reading lesson first,' said Miss Ranger, who wanted to make sure that the new children could read properly. 'Then dictation – then arithmetic!'

Elizabeth could read beautifully, spell well, and she liked arithmetic. She couldn't help feeling that it was rather fun to do lessons with a lot of people instead of by herself! When her turn came she read very nicely indeed, though she had a great many difficult words in her page.

'Very good, Elizabeth,' said Miss Ranger. 'Next, please.'

Elizabeth got all her dictation right. She thought it was very easy. Miss Ranger took a red pencil and marked 'VERY GOOD' on Elizabeth's page. Elizabeth looked at it proudly – and then she suddenly remembered that she had meant to be naughty!

'This won't do!' she said to herself. 'I can't get Very Goods like this – they'll never send me home. I'd better be naughty.'

She wondered what to do. She looked at Ruth by the window, and wondered if she could flip her rubber at her and hit her. She took her ruler, fitted her rubber against the end of it, bent it back and let it go. Whizzzzzz! The rubber flew across the schoolroom and hit Ruth on the left ear!

'Ooooh!' said Ruth, in surprise. She looked round and saw Elizabeth's grinning face. Others began to giggle when they saw Ruth's angry look.

Elizabeth grew bolder. She folded up a bit of paper, and flipped it at Helen, who sat in front. But Helen moved her head, and the pellet of paper flew past her and landed on Miss Ranger's desk. She looked up.

'Playtime is for things like this,' she said. 'Not lesson-time. Who did that?'

Elizabeth didn't answer. Miss Ranger looked up and down the rows. 'WHO DID THAT?' she said again. The boy next to Elizabeth poked her hard with his ruler.

'Own up!' he whispered. 'If you don't we'll all be kept in.'
So Elizabeth owned up. 'I did it,' she said.

'Well, Elizabeth, perhaps you would like to know that I don't allow behaviour like that in *my* class,' said Miss Ranger. 'Don't do it again.'

'I shall if I want to,' said Elizabeth. Everybody looked at her in amazement. Miss Ranger was surprised.

'You must be very bored with these lessons to want to flip paper about,' she said. 'Go outside the room and stay there till you feel it would bore you less to come back than to stand outside. I don't mind how long you stand there, but I do mind anybody being bored in my class. Now, children, get out your paint-boxes, please.'

There was a clatter as the desks were opened and paint-boxes were taken out. Elizabeth loved painting and was very good at it. She wanted to stay. She sat on in her desk and didn't move.

'Elizabeth! Go outside, please,' said Miss Ranger. There was no help for it then – up Elizabeth got and went outside the door.

'You may come back when you think you can really behave yourself, and not disturb my class,' said Miss Ranger.

It was very dull standing outside the door. Elizabeth wondered if she should wander away and have a swing. No – she might meet the Beauty and the Beast! Ha ha! She was being naughty all right!

But it *was* dull standing so long outside a door and hearing happy talking coming from inside, as the children painted blue and pink lupins that Miss Ranger had brought in. Elizabeth couldn't bear it any longer. She opened the door and went in.

'I can behave myself now,' she said, in a low voice to Miss

Ranger. Miss Ranger nodded, without a smile.

'Take your place,' she said. 'There's no time for you to do any painting – you can do a few more sums!'

'Sums again!' thought Elizabeth angrily. 'Well – I'll just be bad as soon as ever I can think of something really naughty again!'

7 *The first school Meeting*

That evening, after tea, the first Meeting was held. The whole school attended it, and Miss Belle, Miss Best, and Mr Johns came too. They sat at the back and did not seem to be taking a great deal of notice of what was going on.

'But all the same, they never miss a word!' said Ruth to Belinda, who was feeling just a little scared of this first important Meeting.

The two head children of the school, a grave-looking girl called Rita, and a merry-eyed boy called William, sat at a large table in the gym, where the Meeting was held. They were the Judges. Twelve other children, six boys and six girls, big and small, sat round a table just in front of the two Judges. They were called the Jury. All the others sat on forms around.

At first Elizabeth had thought she would not go to the Meeting. Then she had felt rather curious about it, and decided to go just this one time. She had seen a notice on the notice-board that said, 'Please bring all the money you have,' and she had brought hers in her purse – though she was quite determined not to give it up if she were asked to do so.

All the children stood up when the two Judges and the two mistresses and master came into the room – all but Elizabeth! However she got up in a great hurry when she felt Ruth's hard fingers digging into her back to make her move! She glared round at Ruth, and was just going to speak angrily to her when there was the sound of a hammer being rapped on a table.

'Sit, please,' said one of the Judges. Everyone sat. Elizabeth saw that there was a wooden hammer or mallet on the table in front of the Judges, and also a large notebook and some sheets of paper. There was a large box as well, like a big money-box. It all looked important and exciting.

'The twelve children round the smaller table are the monitors,' whispered Ruth to Elizabeth. 'They are chosen by us all every month.'

Elizabeth saw that Nora was at the Jury table, and so was the boy she had kicked the day before. She didn't know any of the others, except Eileen, the girl who had been kind to her yesterday.

The girl Judge rose in her seat and spoke clearly to the school. 'This is our first Meeting this term,' she said. 'We have very little to do today, because school only opened yesterday, but we must just make our Rules clear to the new children, and we must also take in the money. We do not need to choose new monitors because we elected those at the last Meeting of the Easter term. You see them at the Jury table. They will remain monitors for one month unless any Meeting decides to choose others instead. As you know, monitors are chosen for their common sense, their loyalty to the school and its ideas, and their good character. They *must* be obeyed, because you yourselves have chosen them.'

The girl Judge stopped and looked down at a paper she held, on which she had written notes to remind her of what she wanted to say. She looked round at the listening children.

'We have very few rules,' she said. 'One rule is that we place all the money we get into this box, and we draw from it two pounds a week each. The rest of the money is used to buy anything that any of you especially want – but you have to state at the weekly Meeting what you need the money for, and the Jury will decide if you may have it.'

One or two of the children clinked their money as if they would like to put it into the box at once. The Judges smiled. 'You'll be able to give your money in a minute,' said the girl Judge. 'Now, to go on with our Rules. The second rule is that if we have any complaint at all, we must bring it to the Meeting and announce it there, so that everyone may hear it, and decide what is to be done with it.

'Any bullying, unkindness, untruthfulness or disobedience may be brought before the Meeting, and we will decide what punishment shall be given. Please be sure you understand the difference between a real complaint and telling tales, because telling tales is also punished. If you are not sure of the difference, ask your monitor before you bring your complaint to the Meeting.'

The girl Judge sat down. The boy Judge got up, and beamed round the listening company. 'We will now take the money,' he said. 'After that we will hand out the two pounds to everyone, and then see if anybody wants extra this week. Thomas, take the box round, please.'

Elizabeth was quite sure she was *not* going to give up her money. She quickly pushed her purse under her and sat on it hard.

Thomas came round with the box. Money clinked into it – pound coins and fifty pences, five pounds and even a ten pound note or two went into the big box.

The box came to Elizabeth. She passed it on without putting her money into it. But Thomas the monitor noticed it at once. 'Haven't you any money at all?' he asked.

Elizabeth pretended not to hear. Thomas said no more,

but went on taking the box round. Elizabeth was pleased. 'I did what I wanted to them and they couldn't stop me!' she thought.

Thomas took the box up to the Judges. It was very heavy now. He put it on their table and said something to them in a low voice.

William, the boy Judge, rapped on his table with the hammer. Everyone stopped chattering.

'Elizabeth Allen did not put her money into the box,' he said. 'Elizabeth, have you no money?'

'Yes, I have,' answered Elizabeth defiantly. 'But I'm going to keep it.'

'Stand up when you speak to me,' ordered the Judge. Elizabeth felt Ruth's hard fingers poking her again and she stood up. Ruth saw the purse on the floor, and quickly picked it up.

'Why do you want to keep your money to yourself?' asked William. 'Are you so very selfish?'

'No,' said Elizabeth. 'But I think it's a silly idea.'

'Listen,' said William patiently. 'In this school we don't like to think that some of us have heaps of money to spend and others have hardly any. We all get the same, and if you want anything extra you can always have it if the Meeting agrees.'

'Well, I'm not going to stay at this school very long,' said Elizabeth, in a rude, defiant voice. 'And I shall want some money to go home by train – so I'm not going to give it to *you*.'

There was a buzz of surprise and horror. The Judges and the Jury stared at Elizabeth as if she was something very strange indeed.

The two headmistresses and the senior master looked up

with great interest, wondering what the Judges would say. William and Rita spoke together in low voices. Then they banged on the table with the hammer. Everyone was silent at once.

William spoke in a grave voice. 'We think Elizabeth is wrong and silly,' he said. 'Her parents are paying a lot of money to keep her in this fine school, and even if she goes home in a short while, her term's fees still have to be paid. Also we think she is very feeble not to try and see if she likes Whyteleafe.'

'If I'm not sent home, I'll *run* away,' said Elizabeth, angry at being spoken of like this.

'That can't be allowed,' said William at once. 'You would worry your parents and everyone here, just because you are a selfish, silly girl. Ruth, is that Elizabeth's money I see you waving at me? Bring it here.'

Elizabeth made a snatch at her money, but it was too late. Ruth took the bag to the table and emptied six pound coins, two fifty pences, and five twenty pence pieces into the money-box. Elizabeth blinked her eyes. She wanted to cry, but she wasn't going to.

'Elizabeth, we can't allow you to keep your money in case you are foolish enough to use it for running away,' said Rita, in a kind but stern voice.

One of the Jury stood up. It was a tall boy called Maurice. 'I should like to say that the Jury think that Elizabeth Allen must not have any money at all to spend this week, because of her behaviour,' he said.

All the Jury put up their hands to show that they agreed.

'Very well,' said the Judge. 'Now, Elizabeth, we shan't say any more to you today, because you are a new girl, and must be given a chance to settle down. I hope you will have a good report at next week's Meeting. We shall be very pleased if you do.'

'Well, I shan't, then,' said Elizabeth, in a furious voice. 'You just wait and see what I'll do.'

'Sit down,' said William, losing his patience with the defiant little girl. 'We've had enough of you for one meeting. Nora, give out the money to everyone, please.'

Nora gave two pounds to everybody, except Elizabeth. The little girl sat sulking on her form, hating everybody. How dared they take her money? She would pay Ruth out for taking her purse like that!

When everyone had their money, the Judges knocked for silence again. 'Does anyone want extra money this week for anything?' asked William.

A small boy stood up. 'I should like sixty pence extra,' he said.

'What for?' asked William.

'I've been told I must give some money to the school Club, to help towards a new gramophone,' he said.

'Well, take it out of your two pounds,' said William. 'Sit down. Sixty pence extra not granted.'

The boy sat down. A girl got up. 'May I have ninety pence extra to pay for an electric light bulb I broke by accident in the playroom?' she asked.

'Who's your monitor?' asked Rita. One of the Jury stood up, a girl called Winnie.

'Was it a proper accident, Winnie, or just fooling about?' asked Rita.

'It was a proper accident,' said Winnie. 'Elsie was trying to open a tin, and the opener flew out of her hand and broke the light bulb.'

'Give her ninety pence out of the box, then,' ordered

Rita. Winnie took the money and gave it to the girl, who was very pleased.

'Any more requests?' asked William. Nobody said anything. 'Any complaints or grumbles?' asked Rita.

Elizabeth suddenly felt uncomfortable. Would Nora complain about her? Would that boy she had kicked, who was a monitor, complain too? Goodness, this Meeting was lasting much too long!

8 The first week at school

Nobody made any complaints at all. Elizabeth couldn't help feeling glad. 'All the same, they'll have plenty of complaints to make about me next week!' she thought. 'I'll just show them that I mean what I say!'

Somebody had a grumble. It was a small boy called Wilfred. He stood up, looking rather shy.

'I have a grumble,' he said.

'Go on, then,' said William, the Judge.

'Please,' he said, 'I learn music, and one of the times put down for my practice is half of cricket-time on Tuesday. Could I have it changed, because I do hate missing cricket?'

'Certainly,' said William. 'Mr Johns, do you think that could be changed?'

'I'll see to it,' said Mr Johns, from the back of the room. 'I'll speak to the music-master and have it put right for Wilfred.'

'Thank you,' said William and Wilfred together. There were no more grumbles. William hammered on the table.

'The Meeting is over,' he said. 'The next will be held at the same time on the same day next week. Everyone must attend.'

The children jumped up, talking loudly, and went out to their various tasks. Some had lessons to prepare for the next day. Some had pets to feed. Some wanted to practise cricket or tennis. Everyone seemed to have something to do.

All except Elizabeth. She seemed to have no one to talk to,

no one to walk with. She knew it was her own fault, but she didn't like it. She wandered off by herself and came to a little room where someone was playing the piano softly and beautifully.

Elizabeth loved music with all her heart. She crept into the little music-room and sat down to listen. Mr Lewis, the music-master, was there, playing to himself. When he finished, he turned round and saw Eizabeth.

'Hallo!' he said. 'Did you like that?'

'Yes, I loved it,' said Elizabeth. 'It sounded to me like the sea.'

'It was supposed to be the sea on a summer's day,' said Mr Lewis. He was an old man, with gentle eyes and a small grey beard. 'It was written by a man who loved to put the sea into his music.'

'I wish I could learn to play it,' said Elizabeth. 'I really do wish I could. Am I supposed to be learning music at this school, do you know?'

'What's your name?' asked the music-master, taking out a small notebook and opening it. 'Mine is Mr Lewis.'

'Mine is Elizabeth Allen,' said Elizabeth.

'Yes – here's your name,' said Mr Lewis. 'You *are* down for music lessons with me. That's fine. We shall get on well together, and perhaps by the end of the term you will be able to play this sea-piece you like so much.'

'I'd like that,' said Elizabeth, 'but I shan't be here long. I hate school.'

'Dear me, what a pity,' said Mr Lewis. 'Most children simply love it – especially Whyteleafe School. Well, if you think you won't be here long perhaps I had better cross your name off my list. It seems a waste of time to have any music lessons if you mean to go.'

'Well – I might as well have one or two lessons,' said Elizabeth. 'I suppose I couldn't have one now, could I?'

Mr Lewis looked at his watch. 'Yes,' he said. 'I've got twenty minutes. Fetch your music and we'll see what you can do.'

Elizabeth was happy for the first time when she sat down at the piano with the music-master by her side. She played one of her favourite pieces. Mr Lewis jerked his foot in time to the music and nodded his head when she had finished.

'Yes, Elizabeth,' he said, pleased. 'You will be one of my best pupils. I must ask you to change your mind about leaving us soon – it will be a pleasure to me to teach you that sea-piece.'

Elizabeth felt pleased and proud. But she shook her head. 'I'm afraid I shan't stay,' she said. 'They've taken my money away so that I can't run away, but I'm going to be so horrid that they'll have to *send* me away!'

'What a pity!' said Mr Lewis. He looked at his watch again. 'Play me something else,' he said. 'I've a little more time.'

At the end of the lesson Mr Lewis showed Elizabeth the name of the sea-piece he had played. 'There is a most beautiful recording of it,' he said. 'Why don't you ask for some money to buy it at the next Meeting? Everyone would love the record in the playroom, and I know they haven't got it.'

'I'd love to get it,' said Elizabeth. 'Then I could hear it whenever I wanted to. But I know the Meeting wouldn't give *me* any money! Why, they've even not let me have the two pounds everyone else has.'

'Dear dear,' said Mr Lewis, smiling. 'You must really be a *very* bad little girl – and yet you play my piano like an angel!'

'Do I really?' said Elizabeth in delight – but the music-master had gone, leaving Elizabeth to put away her music and shut the piano.

Elizabeth soon found out that there were many pleasant things that the children of Whyteleafe were allowed to do. Every other day they were allowed to go down to the village in twos, to buy sweets, toys, books, and anything they wanted. They were also allowed to go to the cinema once a week, provided that they paid for themselves.

They could go riding every day, and this Elizabeth simply adored, for there were rolling hills and commons around the school, on which it was perfectly lovely to gallop. Elizabeth rode very well indeed, for she had had her own pony for years.

Then, on two evenings a week, the music-master gave a little concert to those children who really loved music. The concert was from half-past seven to eight, after supper, and Mr Lewis gathered round him about twelve boys and girls who loved to hear the beautiful music he drew from his piano. Sometimes he played the violin too, and Elizabeth longed to learn to play it when she heard Mr Lewis drawing the bow across the strings of his fine violin.

On another evening there was a small dance, beginning at half-past seven, for an hour. Elizabeth loved dancing too, and when she saw the notice on the notice-board, she was pleased.

No wonder the children were happy at Whyteleafe! There seemed always something lovely to look forward to, something exciting to do. Helen and Belinda, the other new girls, soon settled down well, made firm friends with one another, and were very happy. The two new boys also made friends. Once Joan tried to make friends with Elizabeth, but the little girl made a rude face and turned away.

As the days went on, Elizabeth kept to her plan. She took every chance of being naughty and rude, till everyone was tired of her. She spent most of the mornings outside the door of the classroom because Miss Ranger could not have her in the room as she disturbed the class so much.

One morning she caught the school cat and put it inside Miss Ranger's desk before anyone entered the room. When Miss Ranger opened the lid, the cat jumped out, and Miss Ranger squealed in fright. Everyone giggled. They knew it was Elizabeth, of course.

Another time Elizabeth put the classroom clock ten minutes fast, and Miss Ranger stopped the lesson too soon. When Miss Ranger found out, she was angry.

'As you all have missed ten minutes of your arithmetic lesson,' she said, 'I am going to give you two extra sums to do for your preparation time this afternoon.'

The class was angry with Elizabeth. 'You wait till the next Meeting!' said Ruth. 'There'll be some fine complaints about you there!'

'I don't care,' said Elizabeth. And she didn't.

One afternoon after tea Elizabeth wanted to go and see the village of Whyteleafe. She went to Nora, her monitor, and asked her for permission to go and look at the shops in the village.

'Yes, you can go,' said Nora. 'But get someone to go with you. We are only allowed to go in twos.'

Elizabeth went to Ruth. 'Will you come with me to the village?' she asked. 'I want to look at the shops.'

'No thanks,' said Ruth. 'I don't want to go with anyone like *you*! I don't know how you might behave in the road. I might be ashamed of you.'

'I know how to behave in the road,' said Elizabeth crossly.

'Well, you don't know how to behave at school!' said Ruth, and walked away.

Elizabeth asked Belinda. But Belinda shook her head. 'I don't want to go,' she said.

Helen wouldn't go either, nor would Joan. Elizabeth didn't like to ask any of the boys, because they always laughed at her when they saw her coming.

'Here's the bold bad girl!' they said to one another. And soon poor Elizabeth began to be known as the Bold Bad Girl!

Elizabeth went back to Nora. 'Nobody will go with me,' she said.

'It serves you right,' said Nora. 'You can't go if nobody will go with you. We are not allowed to go alone.'

'Well, *I'm* going alone!' said Elizabeth to herself. And she slipped out of the school door, down the steps, round to the right, and through the big archway! Down the hill she ran to see the village.

She had a lovely time looking into all the shops. She looked longingly into the sweet shop and wished she had some money to buy some toffee. She looked into a music shop and wondered if they had the record of the sea-piece she loved. She looked into the toy shop and good gracious! Coming out of it was Rita, the head girl of Whyteleafe School!

Now what was naughty Elizabeth to do?

9 Rita has a job for Elizabeth

Elizabeth had no time to run away. Rita came out of the shop almost on top of her. She smiled at the little girl and then she saw that she was alone. Her smile faded, and she looked stern.

'Surely somebody is with you?' she asked.

'No,' said Elizabeth.

'But, Elizabeth, you know by now that no one is allowed in the village by herself,' said Rita. 'You must always come with somebody. Why didn't you?'

'Because nobody would come with me,' said Elizabeth. 'I did ask a whole lot of them.'

'Well, you had better come with *me* now,' said Rita. 'I am alone, because the girls of the top class are allowed to shop by themselves. So walk along with me.'

Elizabeth was just going to say that she didn't want to, when she saw what lovely kind eyes Rita had. Rita was looking at her, and Elizabeth thought she was the kindest-looking girl she had ever seen – even nicer than Eileen. So she walked along by Rita in silence.

'You know, Elizabeth, it is strange that no one would go with you,' said Rita. 'Doesn't anybody at all like you?'

'No,' said Elizabeth. 'Don't you remember, Rita, that I told you I was going to be as horrid as could be so that I could go home? Well, everybody thinks I *am* very horrid, so nobody wants to talk to me or walk with me.'

'And are you *really* horrid?' asked Rita.

Elizabeth looked up. She was surprised that Rita should talk to her kindly, after having found her out in disobedience. But Rita did not look angry, only very understanding and wise.

Elizabeth thought for a moment. Was she really horrid? She remembered all the governesses she had had. She remembered that Miss Scott wouldn't stay with her. Perhaps she really and truly *was* a horrid girl.

'I don't know,' she said at last. 'I believe I am horrid really, Rita. I make myself horrider than I truly am – but all the same, I believe I can't be very nice.'

'Poor little Elizabeth!' said Rita. 'I wonder what has made you grow so horrid? You look such a nice little girl, and when you smile you are quite different. I do feel sorry for you.'

A lump suddenly came into Elizabeth's throat, and tears into her eyes. She blinked the tears away angrily. Now Rita would think she was a baby!

'Don't feel sorry for me,' she said. 'I *want* to be horrid, so that I can go home.'

'Couldn't you try to be nice for a change, and just give yourself a chance?' asked Rita.

'No,' said Elizabeth. 'I shan't be sent home if I am nice. I simply must be as bad as I can be.'

'But you will make yourself very unhappy,' said Rita. 'And you will make other people unhappy too.'

'Shall I?' said Elizabeth in surprise. 'Well, I don't mind making myself unhappy, if I can get what I want in the end – but I don't want to make other people unhappy. I think I *am* a horrid girl, but Rita, I wish you'd believe me when I say that I really don't mean to make the others unhappy.'

'Well, listen, Elizabeth,' said Rita, walking all the time back towards the school, 'there is someone in your room who isn't very happy. Have you noticed it? You might at least do what you can to make things nicer for her.'

'Who is it?' asked Elizabeth in surprise.

'It is Joan,' said Rita. 'She hasn't a happy home, and she comes back to school very miserable each term. She worries about her father and mother

all the time, because they don't seem to want her or to love her. They never come to see her at half-term.'

'Oh,' said Elizabeth, remembering that Joan usually did look rather sad. 'I didn't know.'

'Nobody knows except me,' said Rita. 'I live near Joan at home, so I know. I am telling you this, Elizabeth, because if you really *do* mean what you say about not wanting to make other people unhappy, you can just try to make things better for Joan. She hasn't any friend, any more than you have – but for a different reason. She is afraid of making friends in case anyone asks her to stay with them for the holidays – and she knows her mother wouldn't bother to ask any friend back to stay with Joan. And Joan is very proud, and can't bear to take kindnesses she can't return. Now – there's a job for you to do! Can you do it?'

'Oh yes, Rita,' said Elizabeth at once. Although she was spoilt, she had a tender heart, and when she saw that someone was in trouble, she would always go to help them. 'Thank you for telling me. I won't tell anyone else.'

'I know you won't,' said Rita. 'It *is* such a pity that you mean to be bad, Elizabeth, because I can see you would be splendid if you would give yourself a chance.'

Elizabeth frowned. 'It's no good,' she said. 'I'm going to do what I meant to do – get sent home as soon as ever I can. And I can't be sent home if I'm good.'

'Well, come and talk to me any time you think you would like to,' said Rita, as they walked in at the school gates. 'And I say, Elizabeth – don't go alone into the village again, will you? Can you promise that?'

Elizabeth was just going to say no, she wouldn't promise, when she thought of how kind and gentle Rita had been – and she felt she *must* promise.

'I promise, Rita,' she said, 'and – and thank you for being so nice. You make it rather difficult for me to be as horrid as I want to be.'

'*That*'s a good thing!' said Rita, with a laugh, and the tall head girl walked away to her own room.

Nora met Elizabeth as she walked to the playroom. '*Did you go to the village?*' she asked.

'Yes, I did,' said Elizabeth.

'Who went with you?' asked Nora.

'Nobody,' answered Elizabeth defiantly.

'Then I shall report you at the next Meeting,' said Nora angrily.

'Report me all you like!' said Elizabeth, in a don't-care tone. '*I* shan't mind!'

'You'll mind all right when the time comes, Miss Don't-Care,' said Nora.

Elizabeth went to the playroom and put a record on the gramophone. She looked through the pile of records to see if the sea-piece was there that she loved. But it wasn't. She wondered how much it would cost. But what was the use of wondering that? She would never have any money now to buy anything! This horrid, horrid school!

Joan Townsend came into the playroom. People were used to her quiet ways, and nobody took much notice of her.

They called her the Mouse, and often asked her where she kept her bit of cheese!

Elizabeth looked up and thought that Joan did indeed look very sad. 'Has the afternoon post come yet?' asked Joan.

'Yes,' said Helen. 'Long ago. Nothing for you, Joan.'

'Perhaps she hoped to hear from her mother or father,' thought Elizabeth. 'I hear from Mummy often, and Miss Scott has written twice – but I don't remember Joan getting a single letter!'

She was just going to say something to Joan when the supper-bell rang. The children all trooped into the dining-hall. Elizabeth tried to sit next to Joan but she couldn't. She noticed that Joan hardly ate anything.

After supper there was a concert in the music-master's room. Elizabeth ran up to Joan and spoke to her. 'Joan! Come and hear Mr Lewis playing tonight. He's going to play a lovely thing to us – my Mummy plays it at home, and I know it very well.'

'No thanks,' said Joan. 'I've got a letter to write.'

Elizabeth stared after her as Joan went to the playroom. Joan always seemed to be writing letters – but none ever came for her. Elizabeth ran to tell Mr Lewis she was coming to his little concert, and then she ran and peeped in at the playroom. Joan was there alone – but she was not writing letters.

She sat with her pen in her hand, and two big tears dropped on to the writing-pad on the desk below. Elizabeth was horrified. She hated to see anyone crying. She stepped into the room – but Joan turned and saw her coming. She wiped her tears away at once and spoke fiercely to Elizabeth.

'What are you spying on me for, you horrid thing? Can't

you leave anybody alone? You're always making a nuisance of yourself.'

'Joan, I only wanted to . . .'

'Yes, I know what you wanted!' said Joan, just as fiercely. 'You wanted to see me crying, and then laugh at me and tell all the others I'm a baby! You say you want to be as horrid and nasty as you can – but just you try telling the others you saw me crying!'

'Oh please, Joan! I wouldn't do that, I really wouldn't!' said Elizabeth, full of dismay to think that Joan should think such a thing of her. 'Joan, please listen . . . I'm not quite as horrid as I make myself be. Oh, do please let me be friends with you.'

'No,' said Joan, who was almost as obstinate as Elizabeth, when she was unhappy. 'Go away. Do you suppose I'd let the naughtiest girl in the school be my friend? I don't want *any* friend. Go away.'

Elizabeth went. She felt dreadful. How could she help Joan if Joan wouldn't believe that she was not quite as horrid as she pretended to be? She thought of Joan's unhappy, freckled face, and although the music-master played really beautifully that evening, for once Elizabeth did not listen in delight – for once she was thinking of somebody else, and not herself!

'If only Joan would let me help her,' thought Elizabeth. 'Rita wouldn't have told me if she hadn't thought I could do it. I wish I could have a chance of showing Rita I can really do something for somebody.'

Elizabeth's chance came that very night. When she and the other five girls in her room were in bed, and Elizabeth was almost asleep, she heard a sound from the end bed, where Joan slept. Joan was sobbing quietly under the bedclothes!

Elizabeth was out of bed at once, although she knew that the rule was that no one was to leave her own cubicle till morning. But Elizabeth didn't care for rules, anyhow – and she meant to go to Joan, even if Joan pushed her away as fiercely as before!

10 Joan's secret

Elizabeth slipped by Nora's bed, and by Belinda's. She came to Joan's, at the end beside the wall. She slipped in between the curtains and went to sit on Joan's bed.

Joan stopped crying at once and lay quite stiff and still, wondering who it was on her bed. Elizabeth whispered to her.

'Joan! It's me, Elizabeth. What's the matter? Are you unhappy?'

'Go away,' said Joan, in a fierce whisper.

'I shan't,' said Elizabeth. 'It makes me unhappy myself to hear you crying all alone. Are you homesick?'

'Go away,' said Joan, beginning to cry softly again.

'I tell you I shan't,' said Elizabeth. 'Listen, Joan. I'm unhappy too. I was so bad at home that no governesses would stay with me – so my mother had to send me away to school. But I love my mummy, and I can't bear to be sent away from home like this. I want my dog – and my pony – and even my canary – so I do know how *you* feel if you are homesick.'

Joan listened in surprise. So that was why Elizabeth was so horrid – partly because she was unhappy too, and wanted to be at home.

'Now, Joan, tell me what's the matter with *you*,' begged Elizabeth. 'Please do. I won't laugh, you know that. I only want to help you.'

'There's nothing much the matter,' said Joan, wiping her eyes. 'It's only that – I don't think my mother and father love me – and I do love them so much. You see – they hardly ever write to me – and they never come to see me at half-term – and it's my birthday this term, and everyone knows it – and I shan't get a present from them or a birthday cake or anything – I know I shan't. And it makes me feel so dreadful.'

'Oh, Joan!' said Elizabeth, and she took the girl's hand in hers and squeezed it. 'Oh, Joan. That's awful. When I think how my mummy spoilt me – and gave me everything I wanted – and fussed me – and I was cross and impatient all the time! And here are you, just longing for a little tiny bit of everything I had. I feel rather ashamed of myself.'

'Well, so you ought to be,' said Joan, sitting up. 'You don't know how lucky you are to be loved and fussed. Goodness! I should be really thrilled and frightfully happy if my mother wrote to me even once a fortnight and yours has sent you cards and letters almost every day. It makes me jealous.'

'Don't be jealous,' said Elizabeth, beginning to cry herself. 'I would share everything with you if I could, Joan; I really would.'

'Well, you can't be quite so horrid as everyone thinks you are, then,' said Joan.

'I think I am rather horrid, but I do make myself much worse,' said Elizabeth. 'You see, I mean to be sent back home as soon as possible.'

'That will make your mother very unhappy,' said Joan. 'It is a great disgrace to be expelled from school, sent away never to come back. You are very odd – you love your mother, and she loves you, and you want to go back to her – and yet you are willing to make her very unhappy. I don't understand you. I'd do anything in the world for my mother, and she doesn't love me at all. I try to make her proud of me. I do everything I can for her, but she doesn't seem to bother about me. *You're* as bad as you can be, and I expect your mother will love you all the same. It isn't fair.'

'No – it doesn't seem fair,' said Elizabeth, thinking hard. She was glad her mother wasn't like Joan's. She made up her mind to be very nice to her mother when she went back home, to make up for making her unhappy by her behaviour at school.

'You see, Elizabeth, the other girls see me waiting for letters every day, and they laugh at me behind my back, and think my parents must be very strange people,' said Joan. 'And I do hate that too. Last term I sent some letters to myself, just so that I should have some – but the others found out and teased me dreadfully.'

'It's a shame,' said Elizabeth. 'Joan, don't worry so. Perhaps things will come right. Couldn't we be friends, please? Just whilst I'm here. I don't mean to be here for long, but it would be nice to have somebody for a friend for a little while.'

'All right,' said Joan, and she took Elizabeth's hand. 'Thank you for coming to me tonight. I'm so glad you're not as horrid as I thought. I think you're *very* nice!'

Elizabeth slipped back to her own bed, her heart feeling warm and glad. It was good to have a friend. It was lovely to be thought very nice. No boy or girl had ever said that of Elizabeth before!

'I won't let the others laugh at Joan!' thought Elizabeth fiercely. 'She's my friend now! I shall look after her – she's just a timid mouse.'

To the astonishment of everyone the two girls soon

became fast friends. They went down to the village together. Joan spent some of her two pounds on sweets, which she shared with Elizabeth. Elizabeth helped Joan with her sums during preparation in the afternoon, for Joan was bad at arithmetic and Elizabeth was quick.

Joan asked Elizabeth many questions about her father and mother. She was never tired of hearing how wonderful they were, and the presents they gave Elizabeth, and the fuss they made of her.

'What are they like to look at?' asked Joan.

'I could show you their photographs, but Nora locked them up in her box, by the window,' said Elizabeth.

'Well, fancy letting them stay there, when all you've got to do is to say you're sorry and that you know how to count,' said Joan, remembering what had happened. 'Goodness – I wouldn't let *my* mother's picture stay in that dirty old box!'

'I shan't apologize to Nora,' said Elizabeth sulkily. 'I don't like her – interfering creature.'

'She's not,' said Joan. 'She's a good sort. Sometimes I think you are an awful baby, Elizabeth. Only a baby would talk like that.'

'Oh! So you think I'm a baby, do you?' cried Elizabeth, flaring up in a rage, and tossing her curls over her shoulder. 'Well, I'll just show you!'

Nora was coming into the bedroom at that very moment. She was astonished to find Elizabeth flinging herself almost on top of her, shouting loudly: 'Nora! I'm sorry about those things you put in the box. I know how to count and I'll show you I can put six things on my chest of drawers.'

'Good gracious! Don't deafen me,' said Nora. 'All right – you can have them back.'

Nora unlocked the box, took out all Elizabeth's things, and gave them to her.

'You're an awful goose, you know,' she said, half-scolding, half-kindly. She had been pleased to see that Elizabeth had really tried to make friends with someone at last.

Elizabeth proudly put her photographs on her chest and showed them to Joan. The bell went for tea and they had to go downstairs before Elizabeth had finished saying all she wanted to. As they passed the hall letter-rack, Elizabeth glanced up to see if there were any letters for her.

'Goody! A letter from Mother – and one from Daddy too – and this looks like one from Granny!' said Elizabeth. She took them down. Joan had no letters at all.

'Hallo, Joan! Still glooming over the letter-rack as usual!' called Helen's voice. 'I'm sure I don't know what you'd do if ever you did find a letter there one day! Jump through the roof, I should think!'

Joan went red and turned away. Elizabeth saw that she was hurt, and she jumped round on Helen.

'I suppose you think you're funny!' she shouted. 'Well perhaps you'd like to know that Joan had four letters and a card this morning, and she *didn't* jump through the roof. She's not quite such a cuckoo as you are!'

Helen was so astonished to hear Elizabeth sticking up for anyone that she couldn't say a word. Elizabeth made a rude face at her, tucked her arm through Joan's, and walked off with her.

Joan turned to Elizabeth. 'What an awful story you told!' she said. 'I didn't have any letters today and you know I didn't.'

'Yes, I know,' said Elizabeth. 'It *was* a story – but I really couldn't help it, Joan. You looked like a timid mouse that's been clawed at by a cat, and I felt like a dog that wanted to bark something horrid at the cat!'

Joan threw back her head and laughed. 'You do say the funniest things, Elizabeth!' she said. 'I never know what you will say or do next.'

Nobody ever did know what Elizabeth would take into her head to do or say. The days were slipping by now, and another week had almost gone. Elizabeth enjoyed her work, for she had a good brain and things came easily to her. She enjoyed the riding lessons, the gym, the painting, the walks, the concerts, and above all, her music lessons. She liked cricket, and she was getting quite good at tennis.

She had to keep reminding herself that she mustn't enjoy these things. She must really be naughty, or she wouldn't be sent home in disgrace. So every now and again she was very naughty indeed.

One morning she did every single thing wrong in her class. She wrote badly and spelt every word wrong. She got all her sums quite wrong. She spilt ink over her neat geography map. She whistled and hummed till she drove Miss Ranger quite mad.

Miss Ranger had been told to be patient with naughty Elizabeth, and she tried to be. But even the children became angry with her, although at first they giggled and laughed and thought she was funny.

'I shall report you at the Meeting tomorrow,' said a boy at last. He was a monitor, and had the right to report anyone. 'I'm sick of you. You disturb everyone.'

'And I shall report you too!' said Nora that afternoon. 'Three times you've not gone to bed at the right time this week. Last night you even came up later than I did! And look at this – you've spilt ink over your blue bedside rug.

That will have to be cleaned.'

'Well, *I'm* not going to clean it,' said Elizabeth rudely. 'I'll make it a bit worse, just for fun!' And the naughty little girl tipped up some more ink over another part of the rug.

Nora stared at her in disgust.

'You're too silly for words,' she said. 'Well, you'll be sorry at the Meeting tomorrow!'

'Pooh! That's all *you* know!' said Elizabeth.

11 *The Meeting punishes Elizabeth*

The Meeting the next day was at the same time as before. All the children went, and once again the two Judges, Rita and William, sat at the big table, and the twelve monitors, the Jury, sat at the smaller table.

Other teachers were there too, this time, besides Miss Belle and Miss Best. They sometimes came to hear what was being done at the Meeting, although they never interfered.

Rita hammered on the table for quiet. Elizabeth sat looking sulky. She knew quite well that she would be scolded and punished, and she kept telling herself that she didn't care. But one week at Whyteleafe School had made her see that it really was a splendid school and she couldn't help feeling rather ashamed of her behaviour.

'Well, it can't be helped. They won't send me home unless I behave badly,' she kept saying to herself.

'Has anyone any more money to put into the box?' asked William. He looked at a sheet of paper. 'Jill Kenton and Harry Wills have received money this week and have already put it in. Has anyone else any?'

Nobody had. 'Nora, give out the two pounds to everyone, please,' ordered William.

Nora began to give out the money. She even gave it to Elizabeth, who was most surprised. She had quite thought that, owing to her behaviour, she would get no money at all. She made up her mind to buy some peppermints and some toffee and share them with Joan. She whispered this to her friend, who was sitting beside her.

'Thank you,' whispered back Joan. 'I shall want most of my money to buy stamps this week, so I shall love to share your sweets!'

'Does anyone want extra money?' asked William. George got up and spoke.

'We need a new cricket ball for a practice game,' he said. 'We lost ours in the shrubbery.'

'You must look for it again before you get the money,' said William. 'Come to me tomorrow.'

George sat down. Queenie got up. 'Could I have some money to buy a birthday present for somebody?' she asked. 'It's my old nurse's birthday this week, and I'd like to send her something. One pound will do nicely.'

One pound was given to Queenie.

'I'd like a new garden spade,' said John Terry, standing up. 'I'm afraid it will cost rather a lot, though.'

Mr Warlow, the games master, got up and spoke for John.

'I should just like to say that in my opinion John deserves a new spade,' he said. 'He is the best gardener in the school, and I believe the peas we had for dinner today were due to his hard work.'

John's spade was passed at once. 'Give him the money,' said William. 'How much is it, John?'

'I'm afraid it is five pounds,' said John. 'I've asked at three shops and the price is the same in each.'

Five pounds was handed out. John sat down, blushing with pleasure.

Other things were asked for. Some were granted and some were refused. Then came the complaints and grumbles.

'Any reports or complaints?' asked Rita, knocking on the table for silence.

'I want to report Harry Dunn for cheating,' said a monitor firmly.

There was a buzz at once. Everyone knew Harry Dunn, a sly-faced boy in the class above Elizabeth's. He sat on his form, looking red.

'Cheating is awful!' said William, shocked. 'We haven't had a proper case of that here for three terms.'

'Don't give him any money to spend for the rest of the term!' called someone.

'No. That's a silly punishment for cheating,' said William at once. 'It wouldn't stop him and would only make him angry.'

There was a loud discussion about Harry. Rita banged on the table with her hammer.

'Quiet!' she said. 'I want to ask Harry something. Harry, what lesson do you cheat in?'

'Arithmetic,' said Harry sulkily.

'Why?' asked William.

'Well, I missed five weeks last term, and I got behind in my arithmetic,' said Harry. 'My father doesn't like me to be bad at arithmetic, and I knew I'd be almost bottom if I didn't cheat. So I thought I'd better cheat, and copy Humphrey's sums. That's all.'

'Yes – he did miss five weeks last term,' said a monitor. 'He had mumps, I remember.'

'And his father does get wild if he isn't near the top in arithmetic,' said another monitor.

'Well, it seems to me that we'd better ask Mr Johns if he'd be good enough to give Harry extra help in arithmetic this term, so that he can catch up what he missed,' said William.

'Then he won't need to cheat. Mr Johns, I can see you at the back this evening – do you think it would help Harry if you gave him extra time?'

'Rather!' said Mr Johns. 'I've already suggested it to Harry – and now that this has happened I think he'll be glad of extra help in arithmetic, won't you, Harry?'

'Yes, thank you, sir,' said Harry.

But William hadn't finished with Harry.

'We can't let you sit with the others in your class until we know you won't cheat again,' he said. 'You had better put your desk apart from the others until you have caught up with the arithmetic you've missed – and then you can go back, if you will come and tell me that you won't cheat again.'

'All right, William,' said Harry. He hated the idea of being set apart because he was a cheat – and he made up his mind he would soon know as much as anyone else – and then he'd beat them with his own brains, and never cheat again.

'Cheating is only done by stupid or lazy people,' said William. 'Now – any more complaints?'

Then it was Elizabeth's turn to go red and look sulky! Up got Nora at once.

'I have a serious complaint to make,' she said. 'It is about Elizabeth Allen again. I am the monitor in her bedroom, and I can't make her go to bed at the right time. Not only that – she is awfully rude and horrid. I don't think she cares how she behaves at all.'

'Anything else?' asked Rita, staring in disgust at Elizabeth.

'Yes – she has poured ink twice over her bedside rug, and refused to clean it,' said Nora.

'Well, we will send it to the cleaner's and Elizabeth can pay for it,' said Rita. 'It costs two pounds to get those rugs cleaned – so I am afraid you will have to give up your two pounds, Elizabeth.'

Elizabeth really didn't like to be rude to Rita. So she meekly took out her two pounds and passed them back to Nora, who put them into the money-box.

'About the going late to bed,' said William, 'that's easily dealt with. In future Elizabeth's bedtime will be altered, and she will go at half-past seven, instead of eight.'

'But I shall miss the concerts and the dancing,' said Elizabeth in dismay.

'That's your own fault,' said Rita sternly. 'If you are sensible, we will alter your bedtime next week – but *only* if you are sensible.'

'And now about the rudeness and horridness,' said William. 'I'm not sure we can blame Elizabeth for that. You know, we've usually found that rude children are caused by silly parents, who spoil them and let them say and do what they like. I should think Elizabeth's *parents* are to blame for her present rude behaviour. They haven't taught her good manners.'

Elizabeth leapt up at once, her face full of anger. 'Mummy and Daddy *have* taught me good manners!' she said. 'They've beautiful manners themselves, and Mummy is never rude to anyone.'

'Well, we shall only believe that when we see that you are following their example!' said William. 'Whenever you are rude this week we shall each say to ourselves: "Poor Elizabeth! She can't help it! She wasn't brought up properly!" '

'I'll show you I've got good manners!' shouted Elizabeth. 'I'll just show you, you horrid boy!'

Everyone began to laugh at the angry little girl. William banged on the table with his hammer. 'Silence! Elizabeth wants to show us that she has good manners. Go on, Elizabeth, shout a little more and call us names. Then we shall see exactly what your good manners are.'

Elizabeth sat down, boiling. So they thought her mother and father didn't know how to bring children up with good manners, did they? Well, nobody would be more polite than she would be, next week! They would have to say they were wrong!

Kenneth, the monitor in Elizabeth's class, got up next. 'Please, William and Rita,' he said, '*could* you do something about Elizabeth's behaviour in class? It is simply impossible. She spoils all our lessons, and we are getting very tired of it. I guess Miss Ranger is too.'

'This is really dreadful,' said Rita. 'I had no idea Elizabeth was so bad. I am very disappointed. Has *no*body a good word to say for her?'

No one spoke. No one said a word. And then everyone got a surprise, for up got Joan Townsend, the Mouse! She was blushing red, for she hated to speak in public.

'I – I – I should like to speak for Elizabeth,' she said. 'She can be very kind. She isn't really as horrid as she pretends to be.'

Joan sat down with a bump, as red as fire. Elizabeth looked at her gratefully. It was good to have a friend!

'Well, it's something to hear *that*!' said William. 'But it isn't enough. What are Elizabeth's favourite lessons?'

'Music, painting, and riding,' shouted Elizabeth's class.

'Well, Elizabeth, until you can behave in the lessons you don't seem to like, you must miss those you *do* like,' said William, after consulting with Rita for a while. 'You will miss riding, music, and painting this week, and you will not go down to the village at all. We hope there will be better reports next week, so that we can give you back the things you love. We simply can't let you spoil lessons for the rest of your class.'

Elizabeth could not stand the Meeting for one moment more. She stood up, pushed a chair aside, and rushed out. 'Let her go,' she heard Rita say, in a sorry sort of voice. 'She's being awfully silly – but she's really not as bad as she makes out!'

Poor Elizabeth! No money to spend – an early bedtime – no concerts, no dancing, no riding, painting, or music! The little girl sat on her bed and wept. She knew it was all her own fault, but it didn't make things any better. Oh when, when would she be able to leave this horrid school?

12 Elizabeth has a bad time

Joan went to find Elizabeth as soon as the Meeting was over. She guessed she would be in their bedroom. Elizabeth dried her eyes as soon as she heard Joan coming. She wasn't going to let anyone see her crying!

'Hallo!' said Joan. 'Come down to the playroom. It's raining or we could go and have a game of tennis.'

'Joan, it was decent of you to speak up for me,' said Elizabeth. 'Thanks awfully. But don't do it again, because, you see, I want *everyone* to think I'm too bad for this school, so that I'll be sent home.'

'Oh, Elizabeth, do get that silly idea out of your head!' said Joan. 'I'm quite sure that the school won't send you home, and you'll only go on getting yourself into more and more trouble. Do be sensible.'

'Do you really think they won't send me home, how*ever* badly I behave?' said Elizabeth in dismay. 'But surely no school would want to keep a really bad child?'

'Whyteleafe School has never expelled anyone yet,' said Joan. 'So I don't expect they'll start on *you*. You'll just have a perfectly horrid time, instead of having a lovely one. You'd have much more chance of going home if you went to Rita and said you'd be good if only she would do her best to get you home because you were so unhappy here.'

'Really?' said Elizabeth, astonished. 'Well, I didn't think of that. Perhaps I'll go to Rita. I'll see. I am really getting a bit tired of remembering to be bad. There are so many nice things to do here, that I can't help enjoying myself sometimes.'

'I think you're a silly goose,' said Joan. 'Come on down. It will soon be seven o'clock, and you know you've got to go to bed directly after supper for a whole week, instead of at eight o'clock.'

Elizabeth frowned. 'I've a good mind to go at eight o'clock, just to spite them!' she said.

'Oh, don't be foolish,' said Joan. 'Do you suppose the Meeting cares if you go to bed at seven or eight? You'll only be hurting yourself, not anyone else, if you're silly.'

'Oh,' said Elizabeth, seeing for the first time that she was spoiling things for herself far more than she was spoiling them for other people. She sat and thought for a minute.

'Listen, Joan,' she said, 'I'll do as I'm told this week. See? I'll obey the orders of the Meeting, and go to bed early, and miss all the things I love – and at the end I'll go to Rita and tell her I'm so unhappy that I simply *must* go home, and I'll see what she says. I'm sure she could tell Miss Belle and Miss Best and they could write to Mummy for me.'

'Well, you do that,' said Joan, getting a bit tired of Elizabeth's curious ideas. 'Now do come on – bother – there's the supper-bell, and we've wasted all this time!'

They had supper – and then poor Elizabeth had to go straight upstairs to bed. Nora popped in to see that she had obeyed the orders of the Meeting and felt quite surprised to see Elizabeth under the sheets.

'Good gracious!' she said. 'You are learning to be sensible at last! Now just you listen to me, Elizabeth – the Meeting hates punishing anyone as much as they have punished you this week – so be good and sensible and obedient, and you'll find that everything will be all right at the next Meeting.

By the way, I'll take up your bedside rug – the cleaner comes tomorrow, and I'll see that it's put ready for him to take.'

'Thank you, Nora,' said Elizabeth, in a very good voice.

The week that followed was not a pleasant one for Elizabeth. She had to see the others go out riding without her. She had to sit indoors and copy out sums instead of going out sketching with the painting class. Worst of all she had to tell Mr Lewis that she couldn't have her music lessons that week.

Mr Lewis was disappointed. 'Well, aren't you a little silly?' he said, patting her on the shoulder. 'What a pity! And we were going to do something rather exciting this week too – I've got Richard Watson to learn a duet, and I thought you and he could play it together. Duets are fun.'

'Oh dear,' said Elizabeth in dismay. 'I've never played a duet, and I've always thought it would be fun. Could you wait till next week, do you think, Mr Lewis? I might get all my punishments taken off by that time.'

'I should hope you *would*!' said the music-master. 'Now, Elizabeth, although you are going to miss your lessons with me this week, there is no need for you to miss your practice. Take this duet and try to learn your part by yourself – and next week I'll have Richard alone too, and we'll all have a go at it. Practise your other pieces too, and don't forget your scales.'

'I won't forget,' promised Elizabeth, and she ran off. Richard Watson was a big boy, and Elizabeth couldn't help feeling rather proud to think that Mr Lewis had chosen her to play a duet with him. She knew that Richard Watson played the piano and the violin beautifully.

Elizabeth turned over a new leaf that week. Nobody could have worked harder in class than she did. She only got one sum wrong the whole of the week. She didn't get a single mistake in dictation. Even the French mistress, Mademoiselle, was pleased with her because she learnt a French song so quickly.

'Ah, but you are a clever little girl!' she said to Elizabeth. 'Will you not help this poor little Joan to learn her piece? Always she makes mistakes, and is at the bottom of my class.'

'Yes, I'll help Joan,' said Elizabeth eagerly. 'I can easily teach her the song.'

'You have a good heart,' said Mademoiselle. Elizabeth went red with pleasure. The other children stared at her. They couldn't understand this strange girl who was so bad and horrid one week, and so good and helpful the next!

Elizabeth helped Joan to learn the song. She and Joan went off to a corner of the garden and Elizabeth sang each line of the song in her clear voice, and made Joan sing it after her. It wasn't long before Joan knew it perfectly.

'You are very decent to me, Elizabeth,' said Joan gratefully. 'I wish I was going to have a birthday cake on my birthday – I'd give you the biggest piece of all!'

'When is your birthday?' asked Elizabeth.

'It's in two weeks' time,' said Joan. 'And I do hate it so, because I know I shan't get a single card, and my parents are certain not to remember it. Everyone else seems to have a big cake, and presents and cards.'

'I think it's a shame,' said Elizabeth warmly. '*I* shall give you a present, anyhow – that is if only the Meeting will give me my two pounds! I shan't pour ink on my rug again, anyway – that was an awful waste of two pounds. I could have bought toffees with that. I haven't had a sweet for ages!'

'I'll buy some this afternoon and share them with you,' said Joan. 'I want most of my money for stamps, but I shall have a few pence over for sweets. It's a pity you can't go down to the village with me and choose the sweets. It would be fun to go together.'

'It would,' agreed Elizabeth. 'But I'm not going down till I'm allowed to. For one thing I promised Rita I wouldn't go alone – and for another thing, I'm jolly well not going to have the Meeting taking away my good times any more!'

They went indoors. On the way they met three of the boys, going out to practise bowling.

'Hallo, Bold Bad Girl!' said one of them. Elizabeth went red, and tried to rush at them. But Joan held her arm firmly.

'Don't take any notice,' she said. 'They only want to see you get angry – and after all, you do deserve the name, you know!'

The boys went off to the cricket field, grinning. Elizabeth felt very angry. She still had not got used to the good-natured teasing that went on all around her. She wished she could tease back, or laugh, as the other children did.

Miss Ranger was delighted with Elizabeth that week. The little girl really had a fine brain, and was fond of a joke. She could say clever things that made Miss Ranger and the class laugh heartily. She had only to look at a page once or twice and she knew it by heart! She liked her work and did everything well.

'Elizabeth, you are a lucky little girl,' said Miss Ranger. 'Lessons come easily to you, and you should be able to do something fine in the world when you grow up. Whyteleafe School and your parents will be proud of you one day.'

'Whyteleafe School won't,' said Elizabeth firmly. 'I shan't be here long enough. Half a term is as long as I shall stay, and I may go home before that.'

'Well, we'll see,' said Miss Ranger. 'Anyway, it is a

pleasant change to see the other side of you this week, and not the unpleasant rudeness of last week.'

Elizabeth practised hard at the piano all the week. She wanted to show Mr Lewis that she could play that duet with Richard! Over and over she played the pages of the music, trying to get the right time, and to play softly and loudly at the proper moments.

One morning she got a letter from her mother enclosing some stamps. 'Now that you have to buy your own stamps I thought perhaps it would help you if I sent you some,' wrote her mother. 'Then you can spend all your money on the things you like.'

Elizabeth counted the stamps. There were twelve first class ones and twelve second class ones. She divided them in half and went to find Joan.

'Joan! Here are some stamps for you! Now you needn't spend all your money on them,' said Elizabeth.

'Oh, thanks,' said Joan, delighted. 'What a bit of luck! Your mother must be a darling to think of things like that. I'll go straight down and buy some toffee.'

She did – and the two girls sucked it happily after tea that day, as they wandered round the school garden. They came across John Terry busy gardening with his new spade. He showed it to the girls, and they admired it. Elizabeth told John about the garden she had at home.

'You sound as if you know a lot about gardening,' said John. 'Not many girls do. I suppose you wouldn't like to come and help me sometime, would you, Elizabeth? There's a lot to do, and in the summer-time not many people come and help.'

'I'd love to,' said Elizabeth proudly. Fancy clever John Terry asking her to help him! 'I'll come whenever I can.'

'You do look happy, Elizabeth,' said Joan, staring at her friend's bright eyes. 'I don't believe you want to leave Whyteleafe at all.'

'Well, I do, then,' said Elizabeth, quite fiercely. 'I don't change my mind as quickly as all that! You'll soon see. I'll ask Rita to get me sent back home before half-term!'

13 The third Meeting

The third Meeting came. Everyone went to the gym as before, and took their places. Some of the teachers sat at the back as usual. Rita and William came in last of all and the children rose and stood until their two Judges sat down.

Joan was sitting next to Elizabeth. She was hoping very much that Elizabeth would not say anything silly, and so spoil her week's good work and behaviour. Elizabeth wished the Meeting was over. She was not used to having her behaviour discussed and dealt with, and she didn't like it at all. But she knew that everyone was treated the same, and she saw that it was quite fair.

Money was put into the box. One girl, Eileen, had had a whole ten pounds sent to her by her grandmother, and she put it into the box very proudly. She was glad to feel that she could add so much to the spending money of the school.

The two pounds were given out to everyone. Elizabeth took hers gladly – now she would be able to buy some sweets for Joan.

'Does anyone want anything extra this week?' asked William, rattling the money-box.

Eileen wanted a pound to get her watch mended, and it was granted at once. Nobody else said anything.

'Nothing else?' asked Rita, looking round.

Elizabeth suddenly found herself standing up. 'I don't

expect you will let me have it,' she said, 'but I would very much like something – it isn't only for myself, but it would be nice for everyone else too.'

'What is it you want?' asked Rita.

'Well, there's a lovely sea-piece that Mr Lewis plays,' said Elizabeth eagerly. 'He says there is a beautiful recording of it, and I *would* so much like it. I'm sure everybody would love it too. I know I could buy it with my two pounds, but I owe Joan Townsend a lot of sweets, and I'd like to buy her some this week.'

William and Rita looked at the twelve monitors below them at the small table. 'What do you think about it?' Rita asked them. 'You might discuss it for a moment.'

The Jury discussed it for a few minutes. Then Nora stood up.

'We think the money might be granted to Elizabeth,' said Nora. 'We have heard her practising like anything every morning this week before breakfast, and we think she deserves a reward.'

'An extra two pounds is granted, then,' said William. 'Give the money to Elizabeth, Nora.'

Elizabeth was given another two pounds. She was really delighted. She thought the monitors were very decent to have granted her wish. She forgot that she had hated them all last week!

The Meeting passed on to complaints and reports. One boy, Peter, was reported for scribbling over one of the cloakroom walls.

'A disgusting habit!' said William severely. 'You will spend your next two playtimes cleaning off the scribble with soap and hot water, and then you will buy some yellow distemper from the school stores out of your two pounds, and repaint that bit of wall yourself. I shall come to see it at the end of the week.'

Peter sat down, very red. Never again in his life would he scribble on walls. He was not angry at his punishment for he knew that it was just – he must remove the mess he had made, and make the wall good.

'We *all* see the walls,' said William, 'and we certainly don't want to see your silly scribbles on them.'

Then there was a report on Harry, who had cheated the week before. Mr Johns had sent in a written note to William about him. William read it to the Meeting.

'I have to report that Harry is rapidly catching up with the rest of his class in arithmetic,' wrote Mr Johns. 'After another week, he will be as good as the rest. As he will then have no reason to cheat, I propose that at the next Meeting Harry is told he may sit with the others again, and not apart.'

'What about letting Harry sit with the rest of his class *this* week?' asked one of the monitors. 'He's had a week of sitting apart, and it's not very nice.'

'No,' said William firmly. 'He cheated before because he didn't know as much as the others – and if we let him go back too soon, he'll be tempted to cheat again. We don't want it to become a habit. Harry, next week we hope to put you back in your old seat with the others.'

'Yes, William,' said Harry. He made up his mind to work so hard at his arithmetic that he would be top of the class before the end of the term – then the Meeting, and Mr Johns, would know he had no reason to cheat at all!

'And now for the Bold Bad Girl, Elizabeth Allen,' said William. Everyone laughed. Elizabeth laughed too. It sounded funny, not horrid, when William called her by those names. 'Nora, what report have you to give?'

Nora stood up. 'An excellent report,' she said. 'Elizabeth has obeyed all the orders of last week's Meeting, and as far as I know has obeyed them cheerfully and well.'

'Thank you,' said Rita. Nora sat down. Rita opened a note. It was written by Miss Ranger.

'Here is a report to me from Miss Ranger,' said Rita. 'This is what she says: "It has been a pleasure to have a girl like Elizabeth in my class this week. She has worked well, could easily be top of her class, and has been very helpful to others who cannot work as quickly as she can. She has been as good this week as she was bad last week!"' Rita looked up. She smiled her lovely smile at Elizabeth, and William smiled too.

'This is very good, Elizabeth,' said Rita. 'I too have noticed a great difference in you this week.'

'Have you?' asked Elizabeth, pleased to think that Rita had taken any notice of her. 'Rita, did you notice that my manners were better? Because I'd like you to think that my mother and father have taught me good manners and brought me up properly. I don't like people to think they haven't.'

'Well, we take back what we said about your parents being at fault,' said Rita. 'But you really must see, Elizabeth, that if a boy or girl is rude or horrid, it often means that their parents are to blame for not having taught them any better.'

'I do see that,' said Elizabeth. 'Well, you'll see my father and mother at half-term, and then you'll know that they couldn't possibly be nicer.'

'Oh – so you have made up your mind to stay with us, then?' asked Rita, with a sudden smile

of amusement. She couldn't help liking Elizabeth, for the little girl said such funny things, and was so serious about everything.

'Oh no, I haven't,' said Elizabeth at once. 'But I see now

that you wouldn't let me go home if I behave too badly – you'll only be angry with me and *make* me stay just to show me I can't get my own way. But, Rita, if I do try hard to be good, and do everything I ought to, will you please ask Miss Belle and Miss Best to let me go home? They can ask my parents at half-term to take me away. My mother wouldn't want me to stay anywhere where I was unhappy.'

William and Rita looked at Elizabeth in surprise, very puzzled to know what to do with such a strange little girl.

Rita spoke to William, and the Jury discussed things together too. But nobody could decide anything at all. Rita hammered on the table and everyone was quiet.

'Well, Elizabeth,' said Rita, 'we simply don't know what to say to you. We've never been asked such a thing before. We think we'd better ask Miss Belle and Miss Best to help us. Please, Miss Belle and Miss Best, could you advise us what to do best for Elizabeth?'

The two headmistresses came up to the platform, and Rita got them chairs. Mr Johns came too, and sat with them. It was not often that the masters and mistresses came on to the platform at the weekly Meetings, and it seemed to make things much more important and serious.

'Well, first,' said Miss Belle, 'I think we should all discuss this thing together – and as it is not very pleasant to discuss a person when she is present, and Elizabeth may find it a little awkward to hear us, I suggest that she shall be given the chance to leave the room until we have finished. What do you think about it, Elizabeth?'

'I'd rather go out of the gym and wait till you say what's decided,' said Elizabeth. 'But please, Miss Belle, I shall be awfully naughty again if . . .'

'Don't say anything more, Elizabeth, my dear,' said

Miss Best hurriedly. She didn't want the children to feel annoyed with Elizabeth. She knew it was very difficult to be fair if people were feeling angry.

Elizabeth went out of the gym. She went to a music-room nearby and began to practise her part of the duet. She hoped that she would be able to have her music lessons the next week, then she could play the piano with Richard.

The Meeting began to discuss Elizabeth and what to do with her. Everyone had a say, and everyone was listened to.

'We don't want her, she's a nuisance,' said one girl. 'Why not let her go?'

'We *do* want her,' said Miss Belle. 'I think we can help her a great deal.'

'She's been spoilt,' said William. 'It's always difficult for spoilt children to fit in anywhere. They think the world's made for them and them alone.'

'But you can't think how *kind* Elizabeth is really,' said Joan eagerly. 'I'm her only friend, and I know more about her than anyone. She really has a good heart. Mademoiselle said she had too.'

'That is quite true,' came Mademoiselle's voice from the back of the gym. 'This little Elizabeth is a good child at heart, and a clever one. But she is so-o-o-o-o obstinate.'

Everyone laughed at Mademoiselle's long 'so-o-o-o-o'.

'It's so silly to think that Elizabeth *can* be simply splendid, but means to be awful if we don't give her what she wants,' said William. 'Fancy *wanting* to leave Whyteleafe School! I've never, never known anyone want to do *that* before.'

The discussion went on. Nobody could imagine how Elizabeth could want to leave such a fine school as Whyteleafe, where the children were so happy, and where they ruled themselves. Miss Belle, Miss Best, and Mr Johns smiled at one another when they heard the excited children blaming Elizabeth for wanting to leave Whyteleafe.

'I think I can see the answer to your problem,' said Miss Belle, at last. 'Shall we say this to Elizabeth – that she may certainly leave us after the half-term if she is really unhappy, and can say so honestly to the Meeting? She does not need to be rude or naughty or disobedient any more, but may be good, hard-working and enjoy herself all she likes – because we are *quite* willing to let her go, if she really wants to, in a few weeks' time!'

'Oh – I see,' said Rita, her eyes shining. 'You mean that Elizabeth can't possibly come and say she is unhappy, after enjoying herself at Whyteleafe till half-term! So she won't want to go after all – but we're offering her what she wants, so she needn't be bad any more?'

'That's right,' said Miss Belle. 'If Whyteleafe School is all you say it is, and I am very proud to hear it – then I think we can safely say that you children and the school will be able to keep Elizabeth here of her own free will. We shall see Elizabeth at her best – and we can all help her to be good and happy.'

Everyone stamped their feet and agreed. It seemed comical to them – they were going to tell Elizabeth she could leave when she wanted to – but when the time came they were sure she wouldn't want to! What a good idea! They all made up their minds to be as nice as possible to Elizabeth so that she simply *couldn't* say she was unhappy, when half-term came!

'Call Elizabeth in,' said Miss Best. 'We'll tell her.'

14 A lovely week

Elizabeth was called back to the gym by Nora. She stopped playing the piano and went back to her place in the gym.

She wondered what the Judges were going to say. They looked serious, but not angry. Rita knocked on the table.

'Quiet,' she ordered. 'Elizabeth, we have all discussed what you want us to do. And we have decided that if you come to us at the Meeting at half-term, and tell us honestly that you are unhappy here, and want to go home, Miss Belle and Miss Best will advise your parents to take you away.'

'Really!' said Elizabeth in delight. 'Oh, thank you, Rita. I *am* pleased. Now I don't need to be horrid and rude any more. I can wait till half-term, but I warn you that at the very last Meeting before that I shall ask to go home. I hate being at school.'

Elizabeth wondered why everyone roared with laughter when she said that. She looked round in surprise. Even Joan was laughing.

'Well, Elizabeth, that's settled, then,' said Rita. 'Please be as nice as you know very well how to be until half-term – and then, if you wish, you can certainly go home, if your parents will take you away.'

'I know they will, if I'm unhappy,' said Elizabeth. 'Thank you, Rita. I promise to be really good now.'

'Very well,' said William. 'All your punishments are lifted from now on. Your bedtime will be as before, at eight o'clock.

You can take riding and painting and all your favourite lessons.'

'Good!' said Elizabeth, beaming. She felt very pleased with herself. She had got what she wanted! She could go home at half-term!

'I'm glad it's not before then,' thought the little girl. 'I do want to learn that duet with Richard. And I want to give Joan a present for her birthday. And I want to do some more riding – oh yes, and buy that record too! How everyone will love to hear it when I first put it on.'

Elizabeth was very happy. She beamed round at everyone, not listening to anything else that was said at the Meeting. There was very little else to discuss, anyway, and very soon the gym was empty, and the children ran off to their various tasks or hobbies.

'Well, Elizabeth, I've got you till half-term, anyway!' said Joan, tucking her arm into Elizabeth's. 'That's something.'

'Well, make the most of me!' said Elizabeth with a laugh. 'For you won't have me afterwards. I jolly well mean to go back home to my pony, and my dog. I mean to show my parents that I just *won't* be sent away to school!'

A lovely week began for Elizabeth then. After supper that night there was a little dance, and the boys and girls had great fun. When eight o'clock struck Elizabeth and the others of her age went upstairs to bed, leaving the older ones to go on dancing.

The next day she and Joan went down to the village to buy sweets, and the gramophone record that Elizabeth wanted. The music-shop didn't have it, but they said they would send for it to the town over the hill, and get it for Elizabeth. They would send it up to the school for her.

Joan bought some chocolate and a book. Elizabeth bought

some toffee, and two packets of lettuce seeds. She hadn't forgotten that she was going to help John Terry with his gardening! Dear me, what a lot of things there were to do!

'You can have the first lettuce that grows from these seeds,' she promised Joan.

'Well, you'll have to stay till the end of the term then,' laughed Joan. 'Lettuces don't grow quite so quickly as you think, Elizabeth.'

'Oh,' said Elizabeth, disappointed. 'Well – *you'll* have to cut the first lettuce then, after I'm gone. Have a toffee?'

It was fun to eat toffees and talk to a friend. It was fun to feel the lettuce seeds rattling in their packets. It was lovely to think of going riding that afternoon and having a music lesson after tea. Perhaps Richard would be there, and they would play their duet.

The riding lesson was glorious. Twelve boys and girls were taken out on the hills by the riding master. Elizabeth had been used to her pony and she rode well, enjoying the jog-jog-jog, and sniffing the fresh early summer breezes. This was much better fun than cantering along on her old pony at home.

That afternoon the postman brought a parcel for Elizabeth. She undid it – and inside she found a large chocolate cake, sent to her by her Granny!

'Oh, I say! Look at this!' cried Elizabeth. 'We can all share it at tea-time!'

'My word, Elizabeth, you're rather different from when you first came!' said Nora, staring at the excited girl as she put her cake into her tin in the playroom. 'You wouldn't share a *thing* then!'

Elizabeth blushed. 'Don't remind me of that, Nora,' she begged. 'I'm ashamed of it now. All I hope is that you won't all say no when I offer you some of this cake!'

Well, nobody did say no! Elizabeth counted the number of people at her table – eleven. She cut the cake into twelve pieces. They were very large. Elizabeth offered the plate round and soon there were only two pieces left.

'Thanks, Elizabeth! Thanks, Elizabeth!' said everyone, taking a piece. They were delighted to have it, because by now everyone's tuck-box was empty, and no more goodies had come yet from their homes, for no one had had a birthday.

'Your Granny must be jolly generous!' said Nora. 'This is the finest cake I've ever tasted.'

Elizabeth was proud and pleased. She took the plate to Miss Ranger and offered her one of the two pieces that remained on it. Miss Ranger took it and nodded.

'Thank you, Elizabeth,' she said. Then Elizabeth helped herself to the last piece and settled down happily to eat it. This was better than keeping everything to herself! It was lovely to share. She looked round at all the contented faces, and liked to see the girls and boys eating *her* cake.

'Miss Scott would be surprised at me,' thought Elizabeth suddenly. 'She wouldn't know me! What a horrid girl I must have seemed to her.'

After tea Elizabeth got her music and raced off to Mr Lewis. Richard was there too, a big, serious boy with long clever fingers. He meant to be a musician when he grew up. He looked at Elizabeth and didn't smile.

'I suppose he doesn't think girls can play at all,' thought Elizabeth. She was right. Richard was disgusted to find that he was expected to play a duet with a girl – and Elizabeth too, that Bold Bad Girl! What would *she* know of music?

They began. Elizabeth had practised so hard that she

knew her part wonderfully well. She took the lower part, the bass, and Richard had the more difficult part, the treble, where the higher notes were.

'I shall count the first few bars,' said Mr Lewis. 'Now – *one* two three four, *one* two three four, *one* two three four . . .'

He soon stopped, for the two children found their own time, and the duet went with a swing. Mr Lewis let them play it all the way through and then he smiled.

'Very good,' he said. 'You have a feeling for each other's playing. Now, Richard, wasn't I right when I said I had found someone you need not be afraid of playing with?'

But Richard was as obstinate in his way as Elizabeth was in hers. He looked at the little girl's flushed face and did not answer. Elizabeth was disappointed.

Mr Lewis laughed. 'Thank you, Richard,' he said. 'You may go – but come back in half an hour's time, and I will give you your lesson then. I am going to give Elizabeth hers now. Can you manage to practise together sometimes?'

'I suppose so,' said Richard ungraciously.

'Well, don't if you don't want to!' said Elizabeth, flaring up. 'I play my part just as well as you play yours. You made two mistakes.'

'And you made three!' said Richard.

'Now this won't do,' said Mr Lewis, patting Richard on the back. 'You can choose which you would rather do, Richard – play the duet with Harry, or with Elizabeth. I can find someone else for her, you know – but she's the best, after you.'

'Well – I'll have Elizabeth,' said Richard. 'Harry plays the piano as if his fingers were a bunch of bananas.'

Elizabeth went off into a peal of laughter. It tickled her to think of a bunch of bananas playing the piano. Richard laughed too.

'I'll practise with Elizabeth, sir,' he said to Mr Lewis. 'She's really jolly good.'

Elizabeth glowed with pride, because Richard was one of the bigger boys. She settled down to her music lesson happily. Mr Lewis made her play over the duet with him, and pointed out places where she went wrong. Elizabeth used to get cross when Miss Scott pointed out her mistakes, but with Mr Lewis it was different. She thought he was very clever indeed, and she could listen all day long to his playing!

'I've ordered that gramophone record, Mr Lewis,' she said. 'The shop is getting it for me.'

'I'll come and hear it when it arrives,' promised Mr Lewis. 'Now let's get on with tackling the sea-piece on *our* piano, Elizabeth. You want to learn it, don't you – but it won't be easy. Perhaps you could play it for me at the school concert at the end of the term, if you're good enough.'

'Oh, I'd love to,' said Elizabeth, pleased, and then she stopped and looked disappointed. 'Oh, but I can't. I forgot. I shall be going home at half-term.'

'Really?' said Mr Lewis, who knew all about it. 'Still being the Bold Bad Girl? Dear, dear, what a pity!'

'Isn't there a concert at half-term?' asked Elizabeth, her voice trembling.

'Afraid not,' said Mr Lewis. 'Come along – get on with your scales now. Don't worry about not being able to play that sea-piece. I can easily get someone else to learn it for me.'

'Let me learn it, anyhow,' said Elizabeth. 'Even if I can't play it for you at a concert, I can still learn it for myself, because I love it.'

'Good,' said Mr Lewis. 'All right. I'll play it for you now, and you must listen hard.'

So Elizabeth listened and was happy. She was happy all the day, and she couldn't help being surprised at herself.

'It *is* a nuisance!' thought funny Elizabeth. 'I really can't go about being happy like this – whatever shall I say to the Meeting at half-term?'

15 Two tricks – and a quarrel

The week slipped by quickly. Elizabeth practised her pieces, and loved her music lessons. She and Richard practised their duet together, and had such fun that they asked Mr Lewis for an even harder piece.

'I'm glad you chose me to play with you instead of Harry,' said Elizabeth to Richard. 'I do love the way you play, Richard. You are as good as Mr Lewis.'

'No, I'm not,' said Richard. 'But some day I shall be far, far better, Elizabeth. Some day you will come to London to hear me play at a great big concert! And some day you will hear the music *I* make up, played all over the world!'

It didn't seem like boasting when Richard spoke like this. Elizabeth didn't mock at him or laugh at him. She believed him, and although he was sometimes very moody and bad-tempered she grew to like him very much.

'I always hated boys before,' thought Elizabeth, surprised at herself. 'I do seem to be changing. I'd better be careful, or I *will* be different when I leave here, just as Miss Scott said!'

So, to show that she really did still hate boys she played a trick on Harry. She knew that he would have to go to the music-room to fetch some music he had left behind. Elizabeth took a sponge, filled it so full of water that it dripped, and then, climbing on a chair, she balanced the wet sponge on the top of the door.

She arranged the sponge so that anyone who opened the

door would move the sponge, which would at once drop down on to the surprised person's head!

Then Elizabeth hid in a cupboard in the passage outside, and waited for Harry. He soon came along, rushing to fetch his forgotten music before the bell rang. He pushed open the door – and down fell the sponge on top of his head, squelch, squash!

'Oooh!' said Harry, in the greatest astonishment. 'Whatever is it?'

He soon found out! He took the sponge off his neck and threw it down on the floor in a rage. '*Now* I've got to go and change my coat!' he said. 'Who did that?'

Nobody answered, of course. But as Harry knew quite well that people who set traps for others usually like to hide somewhere near to see what happens, he guessed that the joker was in the passage cupboard!

He stole up to the cupboard, and flung the door open. Inside was Elizabeth, trying her best not to laugh loudly. Her handkerchief was stuffed into her mouth and tears of laughter were trickling down her cheeks.

'Oh, it's *you*, is it?' said Harry, hauling her out. 'It's the Bold Bad Girl! Well, I'll just stuff this wet sponge down your neck, see!'

But he didn't have time to, because the bell rang and he had to run. 'I'll pay you out for that!' he yelled. But Elizabeth only laughed mockingly.

'I hate boys!' she shouted. 'They're silly! Ha ha! I tricked you properly, Harry!'

But Harry soon paid Elizabeth back for her trick. He waited until the painting class, and then, when Elizabeth was quite lost in her work, bending over her painting, he stole up behind her. In his hand was a large sheet of paper.

He neatly pinned it to Elizabeth's back. The little girl felt something and shook herself – but the paper was safely on, and she didn't know it. She went on with her painting.

Harry went back to his place, giggling. The class was nearly over, and if Miss Chester, the art mistress, did not notice what he had done, there was a good chance of Elizabeth going about with the paper on her back.

Everyone saw the paper and giggled. On it was printed in big letters: 'I'M THE BOLD BAD GIRL! BEWARE! I BARK! I BITE! I HATE EVERYBODY!'

Joan was not in that painting class or she would have told Elizabeth what Harry had done. All the others thought it was very funny, especially as Elizabeth was known as the Bold Bad Girl.

The bell rang. Everyone cleared up their things. Miss Chester began to prepare for the next class, and did not notice Elizabeth's paper. The children went out of the artroom, and went to their own classrooms.

Once in her classroom all the others there saw the paper; they nudged one another and giggled. Joan was holding the door for Miss Ranger to come in, and did not see what everyone was laughing at. Soon Elizabeth noticed that the class was giggling at her, and she grew red.

'What are you all laughing at?' she demanded angrily. 'Is my hair untidy? Have I a smudge on my nose?'

'No, Elizabeth,' answered everyone in a chorus.

Then Miss Ranger came in, and the class settled down to work. They worked hard until break, when the school had fifteen minutes play out of doors, and could have biscuits and milk if they wished.

Harry looked to see if the paper was still on Elizabeth's back. It was! He ran round to all his friends, pointing it out. All the boys kept behind Elizabeth, reading the paper and giggling.

'She's the Bold Bad Girl,' they whispered. 'Look at the notice!'

Every time that poor Elizabeth turned round she found somebody behind her, giggling. She grew so furious that she called out she would slap anyone who giggled behind her again.

Joan came out at that moment, and Elizabeth called to her. 'Joan! What's the matter with everyone today? They keep going behind my back and giggling. I hate it!'

Joan knew more of the ways of children than Elizabeth did. She guessed at once that someone had pinned a notice to Elizabeth's back.

'Turn round,' she said. Elizabeth turned round, and Joan saw the notice: 'I'M THE BOLD BAD GIRL! BEWARE! I BARK! I BITE! I HATE EVERYBODY!'

Joan couldn't help giggling herself. 'Oh, Elizabeth!' she said. 'Do look what you've been going round with all morning! It's too funny! No wonder everyone laughed.'

She unpinned the paper and showed it to Elizabeth. The little girl, who was not used to being teased, went red with rage. She tore the paper into half and faced the laughing children.

'Who pinned that on me?' she asked.

'I didn't, Bold Bad Girl!' shouted someone. Everybody laughed. Elizabeth stamped her foot.

'Look out!' cried John. 'She barks! She bites! She'll show her teeth next!'

'I suppose the person who pinned that on me doesn't *dare* to own up!' shouted Elizabeth.

'Oh yes, I dare!' grinned Harry, nearby. 'I pinned it on

you, my dear girl – in return for the wet sponge!'

'*Don*'t call me your dear girl!' cried Elizabeth in a rage. 'You're a hateful boy, and a cheat, cheat, cheat! How *dare* you pin a notice on me like that! Take that!'

The furious little girl slapped Harry hard in the face. The boy stepped back in surprise.

'Stop that,' commanded Nora, coming up at that minute. 'Elizabeth! That sort of behaviour won't do. Apologize to Harry. He's too much of a gentleman to slap you back, as you deserve.'

'I won't apologize,' cried Elizabeth. 'Nora, I want you to report Harry at the next Meeting – and if you don't I *shall*!'

'Come with me,' said Nora to Elizabeth. She saw that Elizabeth was really upset, and needed to be quietened. 'You can tell me about it in the playroom. There's nobody there.'

Holding the torn bits of paper in her hand Elizabeth followed Nora, trembling with anger. Nora made her sit down and tell her what had happened.

Elizabeth pieced the bits of paper together and Nora read what Harry had written. She stopped herself smiling, but she really thought it was very funny.

'And why did Harry play this trick on you?' asked Nora.

'Just because I played a trick on him!' said Elizabeth. 'I put a wet sponge on the music-room door and it fell down on his head!'

'And why shouldn't Harry play a trick on you, then, if you play tricks on him?' asked Nora. 'You know, you wet his coat, and he was late for his class because he had to change it. If you weren't quite so silly, Elizabeth, you would see that the joke he played on you was quite as funny as the one you played on him. After all, you *know* that we call you the Bold Bad Girl!'

'You're not to,' said Elizabeth.

'Well, we certainly shall if you go on behaving so fiercely,' said Nora.

'Will you report Harry at the Meeting?' said Elizabeth.

'Certainly not,' said Nora. 'We don't report jokes!'

'Then *I* shall report him!' said Elizabeth.

'Elizabeth, that would be telling tales, not reporting,' said Nora firmly. 'You mustn't do that. Don't spoil this good week of yours by being silly. And, you know, I really *should* report *you*!'

'Why?' asked Elizabeth defiantly.

'Because I heard you call Harry a cheat, and you slapped him hard,' said Nora. 'It is very mean to call him a cheat when you know he isn't now. We try to help one another at Whyteleafe, and it was hateful of you to remind Harry and everyone else of something he's ashamed of.'

Elizabeth went red. 'Yes,' she said. 'That *was* hateful of me. I wish I hadn't. And I wish I hadn't slapped Harry now. I knew he wouldn't slap me back. Oh, Nora – I really have tried to behave decently, and now I've spoilt it all!'

'No, you haven't,' said Nora, getting up, pleased that Elizabeth's temper had gone. 'Little things like this can always be put right. Harry is a good-tempered boy. Go and say you're sorry and he won't think any more about it.'

'I don't like saying I'm sorry,' said Elizabeth.

'Nobody does,' said Nora. 'But it's a little thing that makes a big difference. Go and try it, and see if I'm not right!'

16 An apology – and another Meeting

Elizabeth went to find Harry. She noticed that everyone turned away as she came, and she was sad.

'They were all so friendly to me,' she thought. 'And now I've been silly again, and they don't like me any more. I do wish I didn't lose my temper.'

She didn't want to say she was sorry. She felt sure Harry would say something horrid, or would laugh at her. All the same, Elizabeth was truly sorry that she had called Harry a cheat. It was most unfair when the boy was doing his best to make up for his cheating. And Elizabeth was just a little girl, although she did such funny things when she was in a rage.

Harry was playing with about eight other boys and girls in a corner of the garden. Elizabeth stopped and looked at them. They turned their backs on her. It was horrid.

'Harry!' she called.

'I don't want to speak to you,' said Harry.

'But Harry, I want to say something to you in private,' said Elizabeth, almost in tears.

'Say it in public, then, in front of everyone,' said Harry. 'It can't be anything important.'

'All right, then,' said Elizabeth, going up to the group of children. 'I've come to say I'm sorry for calling you a cheat, when I know you're not now – and – and I'm sorry for slapping you, Harry. Nora has explained things to me, and I feel different now.'

The children stared at her. They all knew how hard it was to apologize, especially in front of others, and they admired the little girl.

Harry went up to her. 'That's decent of you,' he said warmly. 'You've got an awful temper, Elizabeth, but you're a good sort all the same.'

Everybody smiled. Everybody was friendly again. What a difference a little apology made! Elizabeth could hardly believe it. She suddenly felt that everything was perfectly all right, and she wanted to skip for joy.

'Come and see my rabbits,' said Harry, slipping his arm through Elizabeth's. 'I've got two, called Bubble and Squeak, and they've got three babies. Would you like one?'

Elizabeth had always longed for a rabbit. She stared at Harry in delight. 'Oh *yes!*' she said. 'Let me buy one from you.'

'No, I'll *give* you one,' said Harry, who was a very generous boy, and was eager to make Elizabeth forget all about the quarrel. 'I've got a little old hutch you can have for it. It will be ready to leave its mother about half-term.'

'Oh!' said Elizabeth, disappointed. 'I shan't be here after that. I shall be going home, you know. I can't have the rabbit!'

The bell rang for school again, so she couldn't see the baby rabbit. She didn't want to, now, either, because she wouldn't be able to have it. What a pity she couldn't have it now, and give it back to Harry at half-term!

She asked Harry and Richard to come and listen to the new gramophone record that evening. It had come, and was, as Mr Lewis said, very lovely. The three children sat and listened to it. They played it five times. They were all fond of music, and Harry played quite well although his fingers were, as Richard had said, rather like a bunch of bananas! But he couldn't help that!

'You know, Elizabeth, we have a marvellous concert at the end of the term,' said Harry, putting the record on for the sixth time, and letting the sea-piece flood the room again. 'It's a pity you won't be here for it. You could have played at it, and your parents would have been jolly proud of you.'

Elizabeth had a quick picture in her mind of herself playing the lovely grand piano at the concert, and her mother and father sitting proudly to listen to her. For the first time she really wished she was staying on at Whyteleafe School.

'But it's no good,' she said to herself quickly. 'I've made up my mind, and that's that! I shan't stay a minute longer than half-term.'

After supper that night Mr Lewis gave one of his little concerts. About nine children were in the music-room listening, all music-lovers. Mr Lewis had asked Elizabeth to bring her new record for them all to hear, and the little girl proudly put it on Mr Lewis's fine gramophone.

It was such fun to sit around listening. When two of the children thanked Elizabeth for getting two pounds to buy such a fine record, Elizabeth nearly burst with pride and pleasure.

'It really is fun to share things,' she thought. 'I simply loved all the others listening to *my* record. How could I ever have thought it was horrid to share things? I didn't know much!'

Joan was not such a music-lover as Elizabeth was, but she came to the concerts to be with Elizabeth. Joan was much happier now that she had a friend – though, as she said, it was rather like being friends with a thunderstorm! You never quite knew what Elizabeth was going to do next.

Elizabeth looked forward to the next school Meeting. She knew now that it was the most important thing of the whole school week. She was beginning to see that each child was one of a big gathering, and that, because its behaviour brought good or ill to the school as a whole, each child must learn to do its best so that the whole school might run smoothly and happily.

This was a difficult thing for a spoilt only child to learn – but Elizabeth was not stupid, and she soon saw what a fine thing it was for the children to rule themselves and help each other. But she also saw that they would not be able to do this as well as they did, if they had not had excellent teachers, able to teach and guide the classes in the best way.

'I see why everyone is so proud of Whyteleafe School now,' said Elizabeth to herself. 'I'm beginning to feel proud of it myself!'

Elizabeth enjoyed the next Meeting very much. Nora had said that she had nothing bad to report of her, and so Elizabeth had nothing to fear. She sat listening to the reports, complaints, and grumbles, and beamed with delight when she heard that Harry had been second in his class in arithmetic, and was now to be allowed to sit with the others again.

'Thank you,' said Harry to William. 'I shall never in my life cheat again, William.'

'Good,' said William. Everyone knew that Harry meant what he said and they were as pleased about it as Harry himself. The boy was different to look at now, too – his sly face had gone, and his eyes looked straight at everyone. He and everyone else had seen and known his fault, and he and the whole school had conquered it – there was nothing to be ashamed of now!

There was a report that Peter had carefully cleaned and

newly distempered the wall which he had spoilt by scribbling.

'See that you don't have to waste your two pounds on buying distemper again,' said William to Peter.

'I certainly won't,' said Peter heartily. He had had to go without his weekly visit to the cinema, and had missed all his sweets for a week. He wasn't going to let *that* happen again!

There was a complaint about a small girl called Doris. The monitor who complained of her was very angry.

She stood up and made her report. 'Doris has two guinea-pigs,' she said. 'And on two days last week she forgot to feed them. I think they ought to be taken away from her.'

'Oh no, please don't,' begged Doris, almost crying. 'I do love them, really I do. I can't think how I came to forget, Rita. I've never forgotten before.'

'*Has* she ever forgotten before?' asked William.

'I don't think so,' answered the monitor who had reported Doris.

'Then it was probably just a mistake, which will never happen again,' said William. 'Doris, pets trust us completely for their food and water, and it is a terrible thing to forget about them. You must write out a card and pin it over your chest of drawers to remind you. Print on it: "Feed my guinea-pigs". Take it down after three weeks, and see that you remember without being reminded. If you forget again your guinea-pigs will be taken away and given to someone who will remember them.'

'I'll never forget again,' said small Doris, who was very much ashamed that everyone should know she had forgotten her beloved guinea-pigs.

Nora reported that Elizabeth was behaving well, and said no more. Another monitor complained that somebody had been picking and eating the peas out of the school garden.

But John Terry immediately got up and said that the boy who had taken the peas had gone to him, and had apologized and paid him a pound for the peas he had eaten.

'Then we'll say no more about that,' said William.

When the Meeting was over, Elizabeth went out to the garden to see Harry's rabbits. Harry was not there and the little girl looked at the furry babies running round the big hutch.

As she was standing there looking, she suddenly remembered something. She had meant to ask for extra money at the Meeting – and she had forgotten!

And what was the extra money for? It was to buy Joan a nice birthday present! Now Elizabeth would have to save her two pounds and buy it with that. She was cross with herself, for she had meant to ask for two pounds to buy Joan a little red handbag she had seen in the draper's shop.

Joan had said nothing to anyone but Elizabeth about her coming birthday. She hoped no one would notice it, because she knew she would have no cake to share with her friends, and no presents or cards to show. She became a timid Mouse once more, as her birthday came near, ashamed because nobody ever remembered her.

But a surprise was coming to Joan! And, of course, it was that Bold Bad Girl, Elizabeth, who planned it!

17 Elizabeth has a secret

During the next week, a registered letter came for Elizabeth from her Uncle Rupert. She opened it – and stared in delight. There was a ten pound note inside!

'Ten pounds!' said Elizabeth, in surprise. 'Ooooh! How kind of Uncle Rupert!'

She read her uncle's letter. He said that he had just heard that she had gone to school, and had sent her some money to buy some nice things to eat.

'A whole ten pound note!' said Elizabeth, hardly believing her eyes. 'I can buy heaps of things with that! I can buy Joan a *lovely* present!'

She went off to her bedroom to put the money into her purse. Plans began to form in her mind – wonderful plans!

'Oh!' said Elizabeth, sitting on her bed, as she thought of the plans. 'What fun! I shall go down to the village and order a fine birthday cake for Joan! She will think it comes from her mother, and she will be so pleased!'

Elizabeth went on thinking. 'And I shall order the new book that Joan wants, and send that through the post too – and I'll put a card in "With love from Mother!" Then Joan won't be unhappy any more.'

The little girl thought these were marvellous plans. She didn't stop to think that Joan would find out sooner or later that the cake and the book were *not* from her mother. She just longed to give her friend a fine surprise.

She couldn't ask Joan to come down to the village with her, in case Joan found out what she was doing. So she asked Belinda.

'All right,' said Belinda. 'I want to buy some stamps, so I'll go after tea with you. Don't spend your two pounds all at once, Elizabeth!'

All that day Elizabeth thought about the cake and the presents for Joan. She thought about them so much in the French class, that Mademoiselle got cross with her.

'Elizabeth! Three times I have asked you a question, and you sit there and smile and say nothing!' cried the French mistress, who was very short-tempered.

Elizabeth jumped. She hadn't heard the questions at all. 'What was it you asked me, Mam'zelle?' she asked.

'This girl! She thinks she will make me repeat myself a hundred times!' cried Mademoiselle, wagging her hands about in the funny way she had. 'You will listen to me properly for the rest of the lesson, Elizabeth, or else you will come to me for an extra half-hour after tea.'

'Gracious!' thought Elizabeth, remembering that she wanted to go shopping after tea. 'I'd better stop dreaming and think of the French lesson.'

So for the rest of the lesson she did her best, and Mademoiselle smiled graciously at her. She liked Elizabeth, and found her very amusing, though she sometimes wanted to shake her when she said, 'Well, you see, Mam'zelle, you needn't bother about whether I shall be top or bottom in exams, because I'm not staying after half-term.'

'You are the most obstinate child I have ever seen,' Mademoiselle would say, and rap loudly on her desk, half-angry and half-smiling.

After tea Elizabeth went to get her money and to find

Belinda. Helen said she would come too, so the three of them set off.

'What are you going to buy, Elizabeth?' asked Helen curiously.

'It's a secret,' said Elizabeth at once. 'I don't want you to come into the shops with me, if you don't mind, because I really have got some secrets today. It's to do with somebody else, that's why I can't tell you.'

'All right,' said Helen. 'Well, we are going to have strawberry ice-creams in the sweet-shop. You can join us there when you have finished your shopping. Don't be too long.'

Helen and Belinda went off to the sweet-shop, and sat down at a little marble-topped table there to enjoy their ice-creams. Elizabeth disappeared into the baker's shop.

The baker's wife came to see what she wanted. 'Please, do you make birthday cakes?' asked Elizabeth.

'Yes, miss,' said the woman. 'They are one pound fifty, two pounds, or, for a very big one with candles on, and the name, five pounds.'

'Would the five pound one be big enough for heaps of children?' asked Elizabeth, feeling certain that Joan would like to share the cake with everyone.

'It would be big enough for the whole school!' answered the woman, smiling. 'It's the size people often order for Whyteleafe School.'

'Oh, good,' said Elizabeth. 'Well, will you make a cake like that for Friday? Put eleven candles on it, all different colours – and put "A happy birthday for my darling Joan" on it. Will there be enough room for all that, do you think?'

'Oh yes,' said the woman. 'I'll decorate it with sugar flowers, and make it really beautiful, and it shall have two layers of thick cream inside.'

'I'll pay now,' said Elizabeth. 'Oh, and will you please send it to Miss Joan Townsend, Whyteleafe School, on Friday morning, early?'

'Any message inside, miss?' asked the baker's wife, writing down the name and address.

'No,' said Elizabeth. She took the ten pound note out of her purse, and was just giving it to the shop woman, when Nora came into the shop. She smiled at Elizabeth. Then she looked round the shop. 'Are you alone?' she asked. 'Surely you didn't come down to the village by yourself?'

'Oh no, Nora,' said Elizabeth. 'I came with Helen and Belinda. They're waiting for me at the ice-cream shop.'

The little girl paid for the cake, and received five pounds change. Nora stared at the money, and looked puzzled. Elizabeth waved goodbye and went out.

She went to the bookshop and ordered the book she knew Joan wanted. It was a book all about birds and cost one pound. Elizabeth asked the shopman to send it by post, and to put inside a little card that she gave him. On the card she had written: 'With love, from Mother'.

'Now Joan will think her mother has sent her a fine cake *and* a present!' thought Elizabeth, pleased to think of Joan's surprise. 'I'll buy some birthday cards now.'

She bought three nice ones. In one she wrote 'With love, from Daddy', in the second she wrote 'With love, from Mother', and in the last she wrote 'With love, from Elizabeth', and added a row of kisses. She bought stamps for them, and put them safely in her pocket, ready to post on Thursday.

Then she went to buy the handbag she had seen in the draper's shop. She had four pounds left by that time, so she bought the red bag, paid for a red comb and a red handkerchief to put inside, and put the change into the little purse belonging to the bag! There was fifty pence change, and Elizabeth thought it would be fun to put that in too.

Then she went to the ice-cream shop. Helen and Belinda were there, tired of waiting for her.

'You *have* been a time, Elizabeth,' said Helen. 'Whatever have you been doing? You can't possibly be so long spending only two pounds!'

And then, for the first time, Elizabeth remembered that all money had to be put into the school money-box, and asked for! And she had spent a whole ten pound note that afternoon, and hadn't even put a penny into the box.

She frowned. Goodness, now what was she to do? How *could* she have forgotten?

'Well, perhaps it's a good thing I *did* forget,' said Elizabeth to herself. 'If I'd put the money into the big money-box, and asked for ten pounds to spend on somebody's birthday, I'm sure Rita and William wouldn't have given me so much. It *is* an awful lot to spend all at once – but I did so want to give Joan a fine birthday!'

All the same, Elizabeth was rather worried about it. She had broken a rule – but she couldn't mend the broken rule because she had spent all the money! It was no use saying anything about it. The thing was done. And anyway Joan would have the finest surprise of her life!

But Elizabeth had a very nasty surprise on her way back to school with Helen and Belinda. Nora ran up to them and said, 'Elizabeth! I want to speak to you for a minute. Helen, you and Belinda can go on by yourselves. Elizabeth will catch you up.'

'What is it, Nora?' asked Elizabeth in surprise.

'Elizabeth, where did you get that money from that I saw you spending in the baker's shop?' asked Nora.

'My uncle sent it to me,' said Elizabeth, her heart sinking when she knew that Nora had seen the money.

'Well, you knew the rule,' said Nora. 'Why didn't you put it into the money-box? You knew you could have out what you wanted, if you really needed it for something.'

'I know, Nora,' said Elizabeth, in a small voice. 'But I forgot all about that till I'd spent the money. Really I did.'

'Spent *all* the money!' cried Nora in horror. 'What! A whole ten pounds! Whatever did you spend it on?'

Elizabeth didn't answer. Nora grew angry. 'Elizabeth! You *must* tell me! Whatever could you have spent ten pounds on in such a little time? It's a real waste of money.'

'It wasn't,' said Elizabeth sulkily. 'Please don't ask me any more, Nora. I can't tell you what I spent the money on. It's a secret.'

'You're a very naughty girl,' said Nora. 'You break a rule – and spend all that money – and then won't tell me what you spent it on. Well – you can tell the next Meeting, if you won't tell *me*!'

'I shan't tell them,' said Elizabeth. 'It's a secret – and a secret I can't possibly tell. Oh dear! I always seem to be getting into trouble, and this time I really didn't mean to.'

Nora would not listen to any more. She sent Elizabeth to catch up Helen and Belinda. Poor Elizabeth! She simply did not know what to do. She couldn't tell her secret, because then she would have to own up that she was buying things for Joan, and pretending that they came from Joan's mother. And the Meeting would be angry with her just when she was being good and enjoying herself!

'Well – never mind – Joan will have a good birthday, anyhow,' said Elizabeth, thinking of the cake and the book. '*How* surprised she will be!'

18 Joan's wonderful birthday

'Joan, you will soon be eleven!' Elizabeth said at breakfast the next day, as she chopped the top off her boiled egg. 'Gracious! You *are* getting old.'

Joan went red and said nothing. She hated anyone to talk about her birthday, because she knew there would be no cards or present or cake for her. She was such a timid little mouse that she had no friends at all, except Elizabeth – and Joan was always feeling astonished that the bold Elizabeth should be *her* friend!

'I wonder if you'll have a cake?' went on Elizabeth, knowing perfectly well that Joan was going to, because she herself had ordered it! 'I wonder what it will be like?'

Joan scowled at Elizabeth. She really felt angry with her. 'How silly Elizabeth is, talking about my birthday, and if I'm going to have a cake, when she knows quite well that I don't want anything at all said about it,' thought Joan. She frowned at Elizabeth and signed to her to stop – but Elizabeth happily went on talking.

'Let me see – it's Friday that's your birthday, isn't it, Joan? I wonder how many cards you'll have?'

'Joan didn't have a single one last year, and she didn't have a cake either,' said Kenneth. 'I don't believe she's got a father and mother.'

'Well, I have, then,' said Joan, feeling quite desperate.

'Funny they never come and see you, not even at half-term, then,' said Hilda, who liked to see Joan getting red.

'You be quiet,' said Elizabeth suddenly, seeing that things were going too far. 'What *I'm* surprised at is that *your* parents bother to come and see a girl like *you*, Hilda! If I had a daughter like you, I'd go to the end of the world and stay there.'

'That's enough, Elizabeth,' said Nora, who pounced on Elizabeth very often since the little girl had refused to tell her her secret. Elizabeth said no more. She longed to say quite a lot, but she was learning to control her tongue now. Miss Scott would indeed not have known her!

Nothing more was said about Joan's birthday just then, and after breakfast, as the girls were making their beds, Joan went up to Elizabeth.

'Please, Elizabeth,' she said, 'for goodness' sake don't say any more about my birthday. You make things much worse if you do – think how I shall feel when everyone watches to see what cards and presents come for me by the post, and I haven't any! You are lucky – you have two grannies, and two grandpas, and uncles and aunts – but I haven't a single uncle, aunt, or granny! So it's no wonder I don't get many treats.'

'You *are* unlucky, Joan,' said Elizabeth, in surprise. 'Really you are. Well – I won't say any more about your birthday to the others, if you don't like it.'

But she longed to, all the same, for she kept hugging her delicious secret – Joan would have a wonderful cake, with eleven candles on, and cards, *and* presents too!

Nora was not kind to Elizabeth that week. She did not say any more to Elizabeth about her secret, but she had quite made up her mind to report her at the next Meeting. She thought Elizabeth was very deceitful and mean not to give up her money as everyone else did, and not to tell her what she had spent it on.

'After all, we gave her a fine chance to be as decent as possible, at the last Meeting,' said Nora to herself. 'We really did – and the funny thing is, *I* felt sure that Elizabeth would be worth that chance, and would do her best to keep our rules, and help the school, as we all try to do. But I was wrong. I don't feel as if I like Elizabeth a bit now.'

When Thursday came Elizabeth posted the three birthday cards she had bought. She could hardly go to sleep that night for thinking of Joan's pleasure in the morning! It really was lovely to give a surprise to someone.

Friday came. Elizabeth leapt out of bed, ran to Joan's bed, hugged her and cried, 'Many happy returns of the day, Joan! I hope you'll have a lovely birthday! Here's a little present for you from me!'

Joan took the parcel and undid it. When she saw the red handbag inside, she was delighted – and she was even more thrilled when she found the comb, the handkerchief, and the fifty pence piece. She flung her arms round Elizabeth and squeezed her so hard that Elizabeth almost choked!

'Oh, thank you, Elizabeth!' she cried. 'It's perfectly lovely. I did so badly want a handbag. I only had that little old purse. Oh, how I shall love using it! It's the nicest present I have ever had.'

There was another surprise for Joan before she went down to breakfast. Hilda slipped into the bedroom with a lace-edged handkerchief for Joan. She had felt rather ashamed of herself for teasing Joan the day before, and had taken one of her best hankies to give for a present.

Joan was thrilled – in fact, she was so thrilled that a bright idea came into Elizabeth's head. She flew down to the playroom to see if Harry was there. He wasn't – but she could hear him practising in the music-room.

'Harry! Harry!' cried Elizabeth, rushing up to him, and startling him so much that his music fell to the floor. 'Will you do something for me?'

'Depends what it is,' said Harry, picking up his music.

'Harry, it's Joan Townsend's birthday,' said Elizabeth. 'You know you said you'd give me one of your rabbits, don't you, and I said it wasn't any good, because I was going at half-term – well, would you *please* give it to Joan instead, because you can't *think* how pleased she is to have presents!'

'Well—' said Harry, not quite sure about it.

'Go on, Harry, do say yes – be a sport!' begged Elizabeth, her blue eyes shining like stars. It was very difficult to refuse Elizabeth anything when she looked like that. Harry nodded.

'All right,' he said. 'What shall I do – bring the baby rabbit in at breakfast-time?'

'Oooh!' said Elizabeth, with a squeak of delight. 'Yes! Do! Say, "Shut your eyes, Joan, and feel what I've brought you!" and then put it into her arms. What a surprise for her!'

'Well, I'll go and get it now,' said Harry, putting his music away. 'But she'll have to look after it herself, Elizabeth. It will be her rabbit.'

'I'll look after it for her,' said Elizabeth, feeling delighted at the thought of mothering a baby rabbit each day. 'Hurry, Harry!'

Elizabeth went back to the bedroom. The breakfast-bell rang as she was tidying her chest of drawers. She slipped her arm through Joan's, and they went downstairs together. They stopped at the letter-rack. There was one card for Elizabeth from Mrs Allen – and in Joan's place were three envelopes, in which were the cards that Elizabeth had bought!

Joan took them down, going red with surprise. She opened them. She took out the first card and read it: 'With love, from Mother'. She turned to Elizabeth, her eyes shining.

'She's remembered my birthday!' she said to Elizabeth, and her voice was very happy. She was even more surprised when she found a card marked 'With love from Daddy', and she was delighted with Elizabeth's card.

'Fancy! Three cards!' said Joan, so happy that she didn't notice that the writing on the envelopes was the same for all three. She went into breakfast, quite delighted.

And on her chair was an enormous cardboard box from the baker, and a small neat parcel from the bookshop; Joan gave a cry of astonishment. 'More presents! Who from, I wonder?'

She opened the little parcel first, and when she saw the book about birds, and read the little card, her eyes filled suddenly with tears. She turned away to hide them. 'Look,' she whispered to Elizabeth, 'it's from my mother. Isn't it lovely of her to remember my birthday! I didn't think she would!'

Joan was so happy to have the book, which she thought came from her mother, that she almost forgot to undo the box in which was the enormous birthday cake.

'Undo this box, quickly,' begged Elizabeth.

Joan cut the string. She took off the lid, and everyone crowded round to see what was inside. When they saw the beautiful cake, they shouted in delight.

'Joan! What a fine cake! Oooh! You *are* lucky!'

Joan was too astonished to say a word. She lifted the cake out of the box, on its silver board, and stood it on the breakfast-table. She stared at it as if it was a dream cake. She couldn't believe it was really true.

'I say!' said Nora. 'What a cake! Look at the candles – and the sugar roses! And look at the message on it – "A happy birthday for my darling Joan!" Your mother has been jolly generous, Joan – it's the biggest birthday cake I've seen.'

Joan stared at the message on the cake. She could hardly believe it. She felt so happy that she thought she would really have to burst. It was all so unexpected and so surprising.

Elizabeth was even happier – she looked at her friend's delighted face, and hugged herself for joy. She was glad she had spent all Uncle Rupert's ten pound note on Joan. This was better than having a birthday herself – much, much better. Something that Miss Scott had often said to her flashed into her head.

'It is more blessed to give than to receive,' Miss Scott had said, when she had tried to make Elizabeth give some of her toys to the poor children at Christmas-time.

'And Miss Scott was quite right!' thought Elizabeth, in surprise. 'I'm getting more fun out of giving these things, than if I was receiving them myself!'

'Everybody in the school must share my birthday cake,' said Joan in a happy, important voice, and she lifted her head proudly, and smiled around.

'Thanks, Joan! Many happy returns of the day!' shouted everybody. And then Harry came in and cried, 'Joan! Shut your eyes and feel what I've got for you!'

In amazement Joan shut her eyes – and the next moment the baby rabbit was in her arms. She gave a scream and opened her eyes again. She was so surprised that she didn't hold the rabbit tightly enough – and it leapt from her arms and scampered to the door, through which the teachers were just coming to breakfast.

The rabbit ran all round them, and the masters and mistresses stopped in astonishment.

'Is this a rabbit I see?' cried Mademoiselle, who was afraid of all small animals. 'Oh, these children! What will they bring to breakfast next?'

'I'm so sorry,' said Harry, catching the rabbit. 'You see, it's Joan's birthday, and I was giving her one of my rabbits.'

'I see,' said Miss Best. 'Well, take it out to the hutches now, Harry, and Joan can have it again after breakfast.'

'Oh, Elizabeth ! I'm so happy!' whispered Joan, as they sat down to their eggs and bacon. 'I can't *tell* you how happy I am!'

'You needn't tell me,' said Elizabeth, laughing. 'I can see how happy you are – and I'm glad!'

19 Joan gets a shock

Joan had a wonderful birthday. She laughed and chattered in a way that no one had ever seen before. The little girl become quite pretty with happiness, and when she cut her birthday cake, and gave a piece to everyone in the school, her face was a picture!

'Nobody could possibly look happier,' thought Elizabeth, eating the delicious cake. 'Goodness! That baker certainly did make Joan's cake well. It's gorgeous!'

That evening, after supper, Elizabeth asked Joan to come and help her plant the lettuce seeds she had bought, but Joan shook her head.

'I can't,' she said. 'I'd love to, Elizabeth – but I've got something important to do.'

'What is it?' asked Elizabeth, rattling the seeds in her packets.

'Well – I've got to write and thank my mother and father for their cards, and the lovely cake and the book,' said Joan. 'I *must* do that tonight.'

'Oh,' said Elizabeth in dismay. She turned away, biting her lip and frowning. 'Good gracious!' she thought. 'I didn't think of Joan writing to say thank you. Whatever will her mother think when she gets Joan's letter, thanking her for things she hasn't sent? Will she write and tell Joan she doesn't know anything about them – and what will poor Joan do then?'

Elizabeth went out to the garden, thinking hard. Now she *had* made a muddle! Why hadn't she thought of Joan writing to her mother? It was silly of her. Joan was going to be very unhappy – and perhaps angry – when she found out the truth.

'Perhaps it wasn't such a good idea after all,' said Elizabeth to herself. 'Bother! Why do I do things without thinking first? I wonder if Joan's mother will be angry with me for pretending those cards and the book and the cake were from Joan's parents. I don't feel happy about it any more. I feel dreadful.'

She went to give John Terry the seeds. He was delighted.

'Good!' he said. 'Just what I wanted. I plant a new row of lettuce every week, Elizabeth, and then we have new lettuces growing in different sizes, so that each week I have a fresh row to pull. Did you like the lettuces we had for tea yesterday? Those were out of the frames. I was rather proud of them.'

'They were simply lovely, John,' said Elizabeth, still busy thinking about Joan. She simply couldn't imagine what would happen and she felt worried.

She helped to plant the lettuce seeds, but John scolded her because she sowed them so thickly. 'I thought you knew something about gardening!' he said. 'Do you want the lettuces to come up like a forest?'

'Sorry, John,' said Elizabeth. 'I was thinking about something else.'

'You haven't been naughty, I hope?' asked John, who liked Elizabeth, and was always pleased when she came to help him in his garden. 'I hope you won't get ticked off at the Meeting again. You've had enough of that!'

'I'm afraid I *shall* be!' said Elizabeth, sighing. She was

worried about that too – she was sure Nora would report her for spending a whole ten pounds – and whatever would she say about it? She wasn't going to give away her secret, and let everyone know that it was she, and not Joan's parents, who had sent the cake and the book. Things were suddenly getting very difficult.

Joan was very happy for two days – and then she got a letter from her mother that took away all her happiness.

Elizabeth was with Joan when she found the letter at teatime in the letter-rack. 'Oh! Mother has written very quickly to answer my letter,' said Joan happily, and she took the letter down. She tore it open and stood reading it.

Then she turned very pale and looked with wide, miserable eyes at Elizabeth.

'Mother says – Mother says – she didn't send me a card – she forgot,' said Joan in a trembling voice. 'And – and she says she didn't send me a cake – or that book – and she can't understand why I'm writing to thank her. Oh, Elizabeth!'

Elizabeth didn't know what to do or say. She put her arm round Joan and took her to the playroom. No one was there, for everyone had gone in to have tea. Joan sat down, still very white, and stared at Elizabeth.

'I don't understand it,' said poor Joan. 'Oh, Elizabeth, I was so very happy – and now I feel dreadful! Who could have sent those things – if it wasn't my mother?'

Still Elizabeth couldn't say a word. How could she say *she* had done it? Her kindness now seemed like a cruel trick. Poor Joan!

'Come in and have some tea,' said Elizabeth at last, finding her voice. 'You look so pale, Joan. Come and have some tea – it will do you good.'

But Joan shook her head. 'I'm not hungry. I couldn't eat

anything,' she said. 'Let me alone. You go in to tea without me. I want to be alone – *please*, Elizabeth. You are kind and sweet to me, but I don't want anybody just now. I'm going out for a walk. I'll be better when I come back.'

Joan slipped out of the playroom. Elizabeth stared after her, unhappy and worried. Joan had gone out alone – without anyone, which wasn't allowed. Elizabeth simply didn't know *what* to do. So she went in to tea, very late, and was scolded by Nora.

'You're late, Elizabeth,' snapped Nora. 'You'll have to go without cake today.'

Elizabeth slipped into her place and said nothing. As she ate her tea, she noticed that the room was getting very dark indeed.

'There's a good old storm blowing up,' said Harry. 'My goodness – look at that rain!'

'Splendid!' said John. 'I badly need it for my broad beans and peas!'

But Elizabeth did not think it was splendid. She was thinking of poor Joan, out for a walk all alone in the storm. A roll of thunder sounded, and lightning flashed across the window.

'Joan hadn't even got a hat on,' said Elizabeth to herself. 'She'll be soaked! If only I knew which way she had gone I'd go and meet her with a mackintosh. Oh dear, everything's going wrong!'

She could hardly eat any tea. When the meal was over, she ran to the playroom and then to the bedroom to see if Joan was back. She wasn't. Elizabeth looked out of the window. She felt very ashamed and guilty.

'I meant to be so kind – and all I've done is to give Joan a dreadful shock, make her very unhappy, and now she's out in this dreadful thunderstorm!' thought Elizabeth.

For a whole hour Elizabeth watched for Joan to come back. The thunder gradually rolled itself away and the lightning stopped. But the heavy rain went on and on, lashing down on the new leaves of the trees, and making a noise like the waves breaking at sea.

At last Joan came back. Elizabeth saw a small dripping figure coming in through the garden-door. She rushed to Joan at once.

'Joan! You're simply soaked through! Come and change at once.'

Water dripped off Joan's dress, for the rain had been tremendous. The little girl was soaked through to the skin. She was shivering with cold.

'Oh, poor Joan,' said Elizabeth, dragging her friend upstairs. 'You'll catch a dreadful cold. Come on, you must change into dry things straight away.'

On the way up, the two girls met the matron of the school, who looked after them when they were ill, and who bandaged their arms and legs when they hurt themselves. She was a fat, jolly woman, and everyone liked her, though she could be very strict when she liked. She stopped when she saw Joan.

'Good gracious!' she said. 'Wherever have you been to get into that state, you silly child?'

'She's been out in the rain,' said Elizabeth. 'She's awfully cold, Matron. She's going to put on dry things.'

'I've got some of Joan's things airing in my hot cupboard,' said Matron. 'She'd better come along with me. Gracious, child, what a sight you look!'

Joan went with Matron. She was hurriedly stripped of her soaking clothes, and Matron rubbed her down well, with a rough towel. Joan said nothing at all, but stood looking so sad and miserable that Matron was worried.

'I think I'd better take your temperature,' she said. 'You don't look right to me. Put this warm dressing-gown round you for a minute. I'll get the thermometer.'

She sent Elizabeth away. The little girl went off to the music-room to practise, feeling very upset. She practised her scales steadily, and somehow it comforted her. She went to look for Joan at supper-time, but she was nowhere to be seen.

'Haven't you heard?' said Belinda. 'Joan's ill! She'd got a high temperature, and she's in bed in the San.'

The San, or Sanatorium, was where any boy or girl was put when they were ill. It was a cheerful, sunny room, built apart from the school. So Joan was there, ill! Elizabeth's heart sank. She felt that it was all her fault.

'Cheer up! She'll be all right tomorrow, I expect,' said Belinda, seeing Elizabeth's dismayed face.

But Joan wasn't all right. She was worse! The doctor came and went with a grave face. It was dreadful.

'I know what would make Joan better,' thought Elizabeth, in despair. 'If only her mother could come and see her, and love her a bit – Joan would be quite all right! Her chill would go, and she'd be happy again.'

Elizabeth sat and wondered what she could do. Then an idea came into her head. She would write to Joan's mother! She would tell her of the presents she had given to Joan pretending that they were from Joan's mother. She would tell her how much Joan loved her mother, and wanted her to think of her and remember her – and she would beg her to come and see Joan because she was ill!

Elizabeth jumped up. She ran to Joan's writing-paper,

which she kept on a shelf in the playroom. In it she found the letter from Joan's mother, and Elizabeth copied the address for herself. Then she slipped the letter back.

'Now I'll write to Mrs Townsend,' said the little girl. 'It will be the most difficult letter I've ever written – but it has got to be done. Oh dear – what an awful lot of trouble I'm going to get into!'

20 More trouble!

Elizabeth sat down to write to Joan's mother. She bit the end of her pen. She began twice and tore the paper up. It was very, very difficult.

It took her a long time to write the letter, but at last it was done, and put in the box to be posted. This is what Elizabeth had written:

Dear Mrs Townsend,

I am Elizabeth Allen, Joan's friend. I am very fond of Joan, but I have made her unhappy, and now she is ill. I will tell you what I did.

You see, Joan told me a lot about you, and how she loved you, and she said she didn't think you loved her very much because you hardly ever wrote to her, and you didn't remember her birthdays. It is awful not to have your birthday remembered at school, because most people have cards and a cake. Well, I had ten pounds from my Uncle Rupert, and I thought of a good idea. At least, I *thought* it was a good idea, but it wasn't. I ordered a big birthday cake for Joan, with a loving message on it – and I got cards and wrote in them "With love, from Mother", and "With love, from Daddy", and sent them. And I got a book and pretended that was from you too.

Well, Joan was awfully happy on her birthday because she thought you had remembered her. You can't think how happy she was. Then she wrote to thank *you* for the things. I quite forgot she would do that – and of course you wrote back to tell her that you hadn't sent them. Joan got a dreadful shock, and she went out for a walk by herself and a thunderstorm came. She was soaked through, and now she is very ill.

I am very unhappy about it, because I know it is all my fault. But I did really mean to make Joan happy. What I am writing for is to ask you if you could come and see Joan, and make a fuss of her, because then I think she would be so glad that she would soon get better. I know you will be very angry with me, and I am very sorry.

Elizabeth Allen

That was Elizabeth's letter, written with many smudges because she had to stop and think what she wanted to say, and each time she stopped she smudged her letter. She licked the envelope, stamped it, and left it to be posted. What would Joan's mother say? If only she would come and see Joan and put things right for her; it would be lovely – but goodness, she would be very, very angry with Elizabeth!

Elizabeth missed Joan very much. The next day she went to ask Matron if she might see Joan, but Matron shook her head.

'No,' she said. 'The doctor says no one must see her. She is really ill.'

Elizabeth went to find John. He was putting sticks in for his peas to climb up. Every spare moment he spent in the school garden. That was the nice part of Whyteleafe School – if you had a love for something, you could make it your hobby and everything was done to help you.

'John,' said Elizabeth, 'Joan is ill. Do you think you could spare me some flowers for her?'

'Yes,' said John, standing up straight. 'You can pick some of those pink tulips if you like.'

'Oh, but they are your best ones, John,' said Elizabeth. 'Aren't you keeping them for something special?'

'Well, Joan's being ill is something special,' said John. 'Pick them with nice long stalks. Slit the stalks at the end before you put them into water – the tulips will last a long time then.'

Elizabeth just had time to pick the tulips, find a vase, and run to Matron with it before the school bell went. Matron promised to give the flowers to Joan. Elizabeth shot back to the classroom, and was only just in time.

'Don't forget it's the school Meeting tonight,' Belinda said to Elizabeth at the end of school that morning.

'Bother!' said Elizabeth in dismay. She had forgotten all about it. 'I don't think I'll come. I know I'm going to get into trouble.'

'You *must* come!' said Belinda, shocked. 'Are you afraid to?'

'No,' said Elizabeth fiercely. 'I'm *not* afraid to! I'll be there!'

And she was, sitting angrily on a form beside Harry and Helen, knowing perfectly well that Nora was going to report her as soon as possible.

'Well, if she does, I shan't give Joan's secret away,' thought Elizabeth. 'They can punish me all they like – but if they do I'll start being naughty again! Worse than ever!'

Of course Nora reported Elizabeth almost at once. She stood up and spoke gravely to Rita and William, the two Judges.

'I have a serious report to make,' said Nora. 'It is about

Elizabeth. Although we gave her every chance to be good and helpful last week, I am sorry to say that she has been mean and deceitful. She went down to the village this week, and took with her a ten pound note to spend, instead of putting it into the money-box to share out. She spent the whole ten pounds and would not tell me anything about it.'

Everyone stared at Elizabeth in surprise.

'Ten *pounds*!' said Rita. 'Ten pounds – spent in one afternoon. Elizabeth, is this true?'

'Quite true,' said Elizabeth sulkily.

'Then it's too bad!' cried Eileen. 'We all put our money into the box and share it out – and we gave Elizabeth extra money for a record – but she puts *her* money into her own purse, the mean thing!'

Everybody thought the same. The children began to talk angrily. Elizabeth sat silent, looking red and sulky.

Rita hammered on the table. 'Quiet!' she said. Everyone was silent. Rita turned to Elizabeth. 'Stand up, Elizabeth,' she said. 'Please tell me what you spent the ten pounds on – you can at least let us judge whether or not you spent the money well.'

'I can't tell you what I spent it on,' said Elizabeth, looking pleadingly at Rita. 'Don't ask me, Rita. It's a secret – and not my own secret, really. As a matter of fact, I quite forgot that I ought to put my money into the box, and then ask for what I wanted. I really *did* forget.'

'Do you think we would have allowed you to spend the money on what you bought?' asked Rita.

'I don't know,' said Elizabeth, rather miserably. 'All I know is that I wish I hadn't spent it on what I did! I was quite wrong.'

Rita felt sorry for Elizabeth. 'Well,' she said, 'you used the money wrongly and you know it – if you had only kept our rule, we should have known whether or not to let you have the money to spend as you did. Don't you see what a good idea our money-box is, Elizabeth?'

'Yes, I really do, Rita,' said Elizabeth, glad that Rita was speaking kindly to her.

'Well, now listen, Elizabeth,' said Rita, after talking with William for a while, 'we will be as fair as we can be to you about this, but you must trust us and tell us what you wanted the money for, first. If we think it was for a very good purpose, we shall say no more about it, but ask you to remember the rule another time.'

'That's very fair of you, Rita,' said Elizabeth, almost in tears. 'But I can't tell you. I know now that I did something wrong with the money – but there's somebody else mixed up in the secret, and I simply can't say any more.'

'Who is the other person in the secret?' asked Rita.

'I can't tell you that either,' said poor Elizabeth, who had no wish to bring Joan in. After all, it wasn't Joan's fault at all, that this had happened.

'Have you told anybody about this secret?' asked Rita.

'Yes, one person,' said Elizabeth. 'It's a grown-up, Rita.'

'What did the grown-up say when you told her?' asked William.

'She hasn't said anything yet,' said Elizabeth. 'I told her the secret in a letter, and she hasn't answered my letter yet. I only wrote it yesterday.'

William, Rita, and the monitors spoke together for a little while. Everyone was puzzled to know what to do. It was a very serious matter, and somehow it had to be dealt with.

'The Beauty and the Beast aren't here tonight,' said Nora,

looking towards the back of the room. 'They are worried about Joan Townsend being ill. Only Miss Ranger and Mr Johns are here. If the others were here we could ask them for advice again – but somehow I feel I'd like to settle it without asking Miss Ranger or Mr Johns.'

'I think I know what we'll do,' said William at last. 'We'll leave the matter until Elizabeth has had an answer to her letter.'

'Good,' said Rita. She hammered on the table. 'Elizabeth,' she said, 'we are going to leave the matter until you have had an answer to your letter. Will you please come to me and tell me when you have?'

'Yes, Rita,' said Elizabeth gratefully. 'I think the person I wrote to will be very, very angry with me, and I wish I could tell you all about it, but I can't.'

'Well, it seems to me as if Elizabeth is being punished quite enough without us saying anything more,' said William. 'We'll leave it for a day or two. Then please go to Rita, Elizabeth, and tell her what answer you have received.'

Elizabeth sat down, glad that things were not worse. She thought the children were very fair and just. She hadn't even been punished!

When the two pounds were given out to everyone, Elizabeth put hers back into the box.

'I won't have it this week,' she said. 'I'll do without it.'

'Good girl,' said William. There was a nicer feeling in the room at once. Everyone felt that Elizabeth had tried to make up a bit for her mistake.

After the Meeting, Elizabeth went to ask how Joan was. The Matron came to the door of the San and shook her head.

'She's not any better,' she said. 'She's worrying about something, the doctor says – and she even says she doesn't want to see her mother, though we have asked her if she would like us to send for her!'

'Oh,' said Elizabeth, and ran away in dismay. Now Joan didn't want to see her mother – and Elizabeth had written to ask her to come!

'I always seem to do the wrong thing!' said Elizabeth to herself. 'I wish I could go and tell Rita everything – then perhaps she could help me – but I can't do that without giving Joan away. She would hate to think that anyone knew her cake didn't come from her mother after all! Oh dear! Whatever is going to happen? I wish Mrs Townsend would hurry up and write to me.'

21 Joan's mother arrives

Two days later Joan was seriously ill, and the Matron and doctor were very worried indeed.

'We must send for her mother,' said Miss Belle at once.

'The child begs us not to send for her,' said Matron in a puzzled voice. 'It is very strange. I hardly know whether it would be good for Joan to see her – she seems so much against having her mother sent for.'

'Well,' said Miss Best, 'the mother ought to come, for her own sake, if not for Joan's. She would be very angry if we did not send for her. We can tell her that Joan is behaving rather strangely about her. It may be her illness that is making her think funny thoughts.'

But Mrs Townsend arrived before she was sent for! She had received Elizabeth's odd letter, and had packed a bag, and taken a train to Whyteleafe the same day.

Elizabeth saw the taxi coming up through the archway of the school wall, but she did not know that Mrs Townsend was inside it. She did not see her get out, pay the man, and ring the bell.

Mrs Townsend was shown into the headmistresses' drawing room at once. Miss Belle and Miss Best were most astonished to see her.

'I've come about Joan,' said Mrs Townsend. She was a small, sad-looking woman, beautifully dressed, and with large eyes just like Joan's. 'How is she?'

'Not any better, I'm afraid,' answered Miss Belle. 'But how did you know she was ill?' she asked in surprise.

'I had a letter from a girl called Elizabeth Allen,' said Mrs Townsend. 'A very strange letter – about Joan's birthday. Did she tell you anything about it?'

'No,' said Miss Belle, even more surprised. 'I know nothing about it. May we see the letter?'

Mrs Townsend gave the two mistresses Elizabeth's smudgy letter. They read it in silence.

'So that is what Elizabeth wanted the money for!' said Miss Best, her lovely smile showing for a moment. 'Well! Children are always surprising – but Elizabeth is the most astonishing child we have ever had – so naughty and yet so good – so defiant, and yet so kind-hearted and just!'

'I understand now why Joan keeps saying that she doesn't want you to be sent for, Mrs Townsend,' said Miss Belle. 'She is ashamed, poor child, because she thought you had sent her those presents – and now she finds you didn't – and she is bewildered and hurt.'

'I think perhaps I ought to explain a few things to you,' said Mrs Townsend. 'I must explain them to Joan too.'

'Yes, please tell us anything that will help us with Joan,' said Miss Best.

'Well,' said Joan's mother, 'Joan had a twin, a boy called Michael. He was the finest, loveliest boy you ever saw, Miss Best. His father and I couldn't help loving him more than we loved Joan, because we both wanted a boy, and we didn't care much for girls. He was brave and bonny and always laughing – but Joan was always rather a coward, and beside Michael she seemed sulky and selfish.'

'Don't you think that might have been because you made such a fuss of the boy, and perhaps rather left Joan out?'

asked Miss Belle. 'She may have been jealous, and that does strange things to a child.'

'Yes – you may be right,' said Mrs Townsend. 'Well, when they were three, both children fell ill – and Michael died. And because we loved him so much, we both wished that – that . . .'

'That Joan had been taken and Michael had been left to you?' said Miss Best gently. 'Yes, I understand, Mrs Townsend – but you did a great wrong to poor Joan. You have never forgiven her for being the only child left. Does Joan know she had a twin?'

'She soon forgot,' said Mrs Townsend, 'and we didn't tell her as she grew older. I don't think she knows even now that she ever had a brother.'

'Well, Mrs Townsend, I think you should tell Joan this,' said Miss Best firmly. 'She loves you very much and is miserable because she can't understand why you don't seem to love her.'

'I *do* love her,' said Mrs Townsend. 'But somehow it is difficult to show it to Joan. When I got this strange little letter, telling me how somebody tried to buy Joan presents, pretending to be me, I felt dreadful. I felt I must come and see my poor little Joan at once.'

'Come and see her now,' said Miss Belle. 'Tell her what you have told us. Joan will understand, and once she is sure of your love, she will not mind how little you show it! But it shouldn't be difficult to love a child like Joan – she is so gentle and kind.'

'And what about Elizabeth?' asked Mrs Townsend. 'I must speak to her. I think she must be a very kind child, to try to make Joan happy.'

'Go and see Joan first,' said Miss Best. So Mrs Townsend

was taken to the San. She opened the door and Matron beckoned her in, seeing at once that she was Joan's mother.

'She is asleep,' she whispered. 'Come over here and sit by the bed till she wakes.'

Mrs Townsend sat beside the bed. She looked at Joan. The little girl was thin and pale, and her sleeping face was so unhappy that her mother couldn't bear it. She leant over Joan and kissed her gently on the cheek.

Joan awoke and stared up. Her large eyes grew larger as she saw her mother. She looked at her for a moment and then spoke. 'Are you really here? Was it you who kissed me?'

'Of course,' said Mrs Townsend, with tears in her eyes. 'Poor little Joan! I was so sorry to hear you were ill.'

Joan's mother put her arms round her little girl and hugged her. Joan flung her arms round her mother's neck in delight.

'Oh, Mother! I didn't want you to come! But now I'm so happy!'

'I'm sorry I didn't remember your birthday, darling,' said Mrs Townsend. 'I think we've got a few things to say to one another. Why didn't you want me to come?'

'Because – because – oh, because I didn't think you would be pleased that somebody pretended to be you and sent me things,' said Joan. 'I was afraid of seeing you.'

'Now listen, Joan; I want to tell you something,' said Mrs Townsend, sitting on the bed and cuddling Joan beside her. And she began to tell the little girl of her lost brother. 'You see, I grieved so much for him, that I almost forgot I had a little daughter to make up for him,' said Mrs Townsend in a trembling voice. 'You have always been so quiet and timid, too, Joan – you never asked for things, never pushed yourself forward. So I never knew that you minded so much. You didn't say a word.'

'I couldn't,' said Joan. 'But I'm very happy now, Mother. This is the biggest surprise of my life. I understand things now! I do wish you had told me before. But it doesn't matter. Nothing matters now that I've got you close beside me, and I know you really do love me, and won't forget me again.'

'I will never forget you,' said Mrs Townsend. 'I didn't think you minded at all – but now that I know what you have been thinking, I shall be the kind of mother you want. But you must hurry up and get better, mustn't you?'

'Oh, I feel much, much better already,' said Joan. And indeed she looked quite different. When Matron came in, she was surprised to see such a happy-looking child.

'I shall want lots of dinner today!' said Joan. 'Because Mother is going to have it with me, Matron, and she wants to see how much I can eat!'

As they were eating their dinner together they talked about Elizabeth. 'I guessed that it was Elizabeth who sent those things, when you said it wasn't you,' said Joan. 'It was just the sort of mad, kind thing she *would* do! You know, Mother, she's the first real friend I've had, and *I* think she's splendid, though the first weeks she was here she was really the naughtiest, rudest girl in the school. The sad thing is – she's made up her mind to go at half-term, so I shan't have her very much longer.'

'I want to see Elizabeth,' said Mrs Townsend. 'She wrote me such a funny, sad letter. If it hadn't been for her letter, and what she did for your birthday, we shouldn't have come to understand one another as we now do, Joan! And although she thinks she did a very wrong thing, somehow or other it has come right, because she really did mean to be kind.'

'Matron! Do you think Elizabeth might come and see me whilst my mother is here?' asked Joan, when Matron came in to take her temperature.

'We'll see what your temperature is doing,' said Matron, pleased to see the empty plates. She slipped the thermometer into Joan's mouth. She waited a minute and then took it out again.

'Good gracious! Just below normal!' she said. 'You *are* getting better quickly! Yes – I think Elizabeth might come. I'll send for her.'

Elizabeth was practising her duet with Richard when the message came. One of the school maids brought it.

'Mrs Townsend is in the San with Joan and says she would like to see you,' said the maid. 'Matron says you can go for twenty minutes.'

Elizabeth's heart sank. So Mrs Townsend had come to the school! She had got her letter – and now she was here, and wanted to see Elizabeth!

'I don't want to go to the San,' said Elizabeth. 'Oh dear – isn't there any excuse I can make?'

'But I thought Joan was your friend?' said Richard in surprise.

'She is,' said Elizabeth, 'but you see – oh dear, I can't possibly explain. Things have just gone wrong, that's all.'

The little girl put her music away, looking glum. 'Cheer up!' said Richard. 'Things aren't so bad when you go and face them properly!'

'Well, I'll face them all right,' said Elizabeth, throwing her curls back. 'I wonder what's going to happen to me *now*?'

22 Rita talks to Elizabeth

Elizabeth went to the San. Matron was just coming out, smiling.

'How is Joan now?' asked Elizabeth.

'*Much* better!' said Matron. 'We shall soon have her out and about again now.'

'Oh, good,' said Elizabeth. 'Can I go in?'

'Yes,' said Matron. 'You can stay for twenty minutes, till afternoon school. Talk quietly, and don't excite Joan at all.'

Elizabeth went in. She shut the door quietly behind her. Joan was lying in a white bed under a big sunny window, and Mrs Townsend was sitting beside her.

'And is this Elizabeth?' asked Mrs Townsend with a welcoming smile. Elizabeth went forward and shook hands, thinking that Mrs Townsend didn't look very angry after all. She bent over and kissed her friend.

'I'm so glad you're better, Joan,' she said. 'I do miss you.'

'Do you really?' said Joan, pleased. 'I've missed you too.'

'Come here, Elizabeth,' said Mrs Townsend, drawing Elizabeth to her. 'I want to thank you for your letter. I was so surprised to get it – and I know it must have been hard to write.'

'Yes, it was,' said Elizabeth. 'I was awfully afraid you would be angry with me when you got it, Mrs Townsend. I meant to make Joan so happy on her birthday – and I didn't think she'd find out it wasn't you who sent the things! I know it was a silly thing to do, now.'

'Never mind,' said Joan's mother. 'It has made things come right in the end!'

'Have they come right?' asked Elizabeth in surprise, looking from Joan to her mother.

'Very right,' said Mrs Townsend, smiling. 'Joan will tell you all we have said, one day, and you will understand how they went wrong. But now I want to tell you that I am very, very glad Joan has such a kind little friend. I know she will be much happier at Whyteleafe now that she has you. It is so horrid to have no friends at all.'

'Oh, Elizabeth, I *do* so wish you were staying on at Whyteleafe,' sighed Joan, taking her friend's hand. 'Couldn't you possibly, possibly stay?'

'Don't ask me to, Joan,' said Elizabeth. 'You know I've made up my mind to go, and it's feeble to change your mind once you've made it up! I've said I shall go, and if the Meeting says I can, I shall go back with my parents when they come to see me at half-term.'

'Do you think *you* will be able to come and see me at half-term?' asked Joan, turning to her mother.

'Yes, I will,' answered Mrs Townsend. 'I hope by then that you will be up and about, and we will go to the next town, and spend the day there, Joan.'

'Oh, good,' said Joan happily. It was the first time her mother had ever come to take her out at half-term, and the little girl was delighted. 'I shall get better quickly now, so that I shall be ready for you at half-term!'

A bell rang in the school. Elizabeth got up quickly. 'That's my bell,' she said. 'I must go. Goodbye, Mrs Townsend, and thank you for being so nice about my letter. Goodbye,

Joan. I'm so glad you're happy. I'll come and see you again if Matron will let me.'

She ran off. Mrs Townsend turned to Joan. 'She's a very nice child,' she said. 'How funny that she should have been so naughty at first – and what a pity she wants to leave! She's just the sort of girl that Whyteleafe School would be proud of.'

Elizabeth thought of Rita as she sat in class that afternoon, doing her painting. 'I told Rita I would go to her as soon as I had an answer to my letter,' she thought. 'Well – I haven't *exactly* had an answer – and yet I *do* know the answer, because Mrs Townsend came herself and told me!'

She wondered if she should go to Rita after tea. What should she tell her? She didn't know!

She need not have worried herself. Miss Belle and Miss Best had sent for Rita that day, and had told her about Elizabeth, and her odd letter to Joan's mother.

'She spent the money her uncle gave her on buying that big birthday cake for Joan, and other presents and cards,' said Miss Belle. 'That is where the money went, Rita!'

'But then why didn't Elizabeth say so?' asked Rita, puzzled.

'Because if she explained that, the school would know Joan's unhappiness at being forgotten by her mother,' said Miss Best. 'If Elizabeth had been longer at Whyteleafe School, she would have gone to you, Rita, or to one of the monitors she trusted, and would have asked their advice – but she has been here such a short time, and is such a headstrong, independent child, that she takes matters into her own hands – and gets into trouble!'

'All the same, she has the makings of a very fine girl in her,' said Miss Belle. 'She is fearless and brave, kind and clever, and although she has been the naughtiest, rudest girl we have ever had, that only lasted for a little while.'

'Yes,' said Rita. 'I liked her almost from the beginning, although she has been very difficult. But she really is the sort of girl we want at Whyteleafe. I'm afraid now, though, that she will go home, for we have promised that she shall, if she wants to.'

'You must send for her and have a talk with her, Rita,' said Miss Best. 'She was supposed to come and tell you when she had an answer to her letter to Mrs Townsend, wasn't she? Well – we know the answer now – and it is not an answer that can be explained fully to a school Meeting. Have a talk with Elizabeth, and then decide what to do. I think you will feel that although Elizabeth did wrong, the kindness that was at the bottom of it more than makes up for the upset she caused!'

'Yes, I think so too,' agreed Rita, who had been very interested in all that Miss Belle and Miss Best had told her. She was glad to know that Elizabeth had spent the ten pounds on somebody else, glad that it was only kindness that had caused such a disturbance! She went out to look for Elizabeth.

It was after tea. Elizabeth was running to see if Matron would let her sit with Joan again. She bumped into Rita round a corner.

'Good gracious! What a hurricane you are!' said Rita, her breath bumped out of her. 'You're just the person I want to see. Come to my study.'

Rita had a little room of her own, a study all to herself, because she was head girl. She was very proud of it, and had made it as nice as she could. Elizabeth had never been in it before, and she looked round in pleasure.

'What a dear little room!' she said. 'I like the blue carpet

– and the blue tablecloth – and the pictures and flowers. Is this your very own room?'

'Yes,' said Rita. 'William has one too. His is just as nice as mine. He is coming here in a minute. Have a sweet, Elizabeth?'

Rita took down a tin from her small cupboard and offered it to Elizabeth, who at once took a toffee. Elizabeth wondered what Rita and William were going to say to her. There was a knock at the door, and William strolled in.

'Hallo,' he said, smiling at Elizabeth. 'How's the Bold Bad Girl?'

Elizabeth laughed. She liked William calling her that, though she had hated the name not so very long ago.

'Elizabeth, William and I know now what you spent that ten pounds on, and why you did it,' said Rita. 'And we want to say that we quite see that you couldn't tell the Meeting.'

'And *we* shan't tell the Meeting either,' said William, sitting down in Rita's cosy arm-chair.

'But won't you have to?' asked Elizabeth in surprise.

'No,' said William. 'Rita and I are the judges of what the Meeting can be told, and what need not be explained, if we think best. We shall simply say that we have had a satisfactory answer and explanation, and that the matter is now finished.'

'Oh, thank you,' said Elizabeth. 'It wasn't really myself I was thinking of, you know, it was Joan.'

'We know that now,' said Rita. 'You tried to do a right thing in a wrong way, Elizabeth! If you had been at Whyteleafe a little longer, you would have done things differently – but you haven't been here long enough.'

'No, I haven't,' said Elizabeth. 'I do see that I have learnt a lot already, but I haven't learnt enough. I wish I was wise like you and William.'

'Well, why not stay and learn to be?' said William with a laugh. 'You are *just* the sort of girl we want, Elizabeth. You would make a fine monitor, later on.'

'Me! A monitor!' cried Elizabeth, most astonished. 'Oh, I'd never, never be a monitor! Good gracious!'

'It may sound funny to you now, Elizabeth,' said William. 'But in a term or two you would be quite responsible and sensible enough to be made one.'

'I'd simply *love* to be a monitor, and sit in the Jury!' said Elizabeth. 'Whatever would Mummy say – and Miss Scott, my old governess, would never, never believe it. She said I was so spoilt I would never do anything worth while!'

'You *are* spoilt!' said Rita, smiling. 'But you would soon get over that. What about staying on, Elizabeth, and seeing what you can do?'

'I'm beginning to feel it would be nice,' said Elizabeth. 'But I can't change my mind. I said I meant to go home at half-term, and I'm going to. It's only feeble people that change their minds, and say first one thing and then another. I'm not going to be like that.'

'I wonder where you got that idea from?' said William. 'I mean, the idea that it's feeble to change your mind once it's made up? That's a wrong idea, you know.'

'Wrong?' said Elizabeth, in surprise.

'Of course,' said William. 'Make up your mind about things, by all means – but *if* something happens to show that you are wrong, then it is feeble *not* to change your mind, Elizabeth. Only the strongest people have the pluck to change their minds, and say so, if they see they have been wrong in their ideas.'

'I didn't think of that,' said Elizabeth, feeling puzzled.

'Well, don't puzzle your head too much about things,'

said William, getting up. 'I must go. Think about what we have said, Elizabeth. The next Meeting will be your last one, if you are leaving us – and we shall keep our word to you and let you go if you want to. You can tell your parents when they come to see you at half-term, and Miss Belle and Miss Best will explain everything to them. But we shall be sorry to lose the naughtiest girl in the school!'

Elizabeth left the study, her head in a whirl. She did like William and Rita so much. But she couldn't change her mind – she would be so ashamed to climb down and say she had been wrong.

23 Elizabeth fights with herself

The next day or two were very pleasant. Elizabeth was allowed to see Joan whenever she liked, and she took her some more flowers from John. She also took her a jigsaw puzzle from Helen, and a book from Nora.

Joan was looking very pretty and very happy. Her mother had gone, leaving behind her a big box of velvety peaches, a tin of barley sugar, and some books. But best of all she had left Joan a promise that never, never would she let Joan think she was forgotten again!

'It's all because of *you*, Elizabeth,' said Joan, offering her friend a barley sugar to suck. 'Oh, Elizabeth – do please stay on at Whyteleafe. Don't make me unhappy by leaving, just as I've got to know you!'

'There are plenty of other people for you to make friends with,' said Elizabeth, sucking the barley sugar.

'I don't want them,' said Joan. 'They would seem feeble after you, Elizabeth. I say – have you been looking after my rabbit for me?'

'Of course,' said Elizabeth. 'Oh, Joan, it's the dearest little thing you ever saw! Really it is. Do you know, it knows me now when I go to feed it, and it presses its tiny woffly nose against the wire to welcome me! And yesterday it nuzzled itself into the crook of my arm and stayed there quite still till the school bell rang and I had to go.'

'Harry came to see me this morning and he said he wishes

you were not leaving, because he wants to give us two more baby rabbits, to live with my tiny one,' said Joan. 'He said they could be between the two of us.'

'Oh,' said Elizabeth, longing for the two rabbits. 'Really, if I'd known what a nice place Whyteleafe School was, I'd never have made up my mind to leave it!'

She had to go then, because it was time for her music lesson. She rushed to get her music. Richard was in the music-room, waiting for her with Mr Lewis.

The two were getting on well with their duets. Richard was pleased with Elizabeth now, for he knew that she really loved music, as he did, and was willing to work hard at it. They played two duets very well indeed for Mr Lewis.

'Splendid!' he said. 'Elizabeth, I'm pleased with you. You've practised well since your last lesson, and got that difficult part perfect now. Now – play Richard your sea-piece that you love so much.'

Elizabeth was proud to play to Richard, for she thought him a wonderful player. She played her best. Mr Lewis and Richard listened without a word or a movement till she had finished.

'She ought to play that at the school concert at the end of the term,' said Richard, when the piece was ended. 'It's fine!'

Elizabeth glowed with pleasure. She liked praise from Richard even more than praise from the music-master.

'That's what *I* suggested to her,' said Mr Lewis, sitting down at the piano and playing some beautiful chords. 'But she doesn't want to.'

'I *do* want to!' cried Elizabeth indignantly. 'It's only that I'm leaving soon.'

'Oh – that silly old story again,' said Richard in disgust. 'I thought better of you, Elizabeth. You can stay here if you want to – but you're just too jolly obstinate for words. Your music may be good – but I don't think much of your common sense.'

He stalked off without another word, his music rolled under his arm. Elizabeth felt half angry, half tearful. She hated being spoken to like that by Richard.

'I expect Richard is disappointed with you because I know he hoped that you and he would play the duets in the concert this term,' explained Mr Lewis. 'He'll have to play them with Harry now – and though Harry likes music, he's not a good player.'

Elizabeth finished her music lesson without saying very much. She was thinking hard. She was in a muddle. She wanted to stay – and she wanted to go, because her pride told her to keep her word to herself and leave.

She went out to do some gardening when her lesson was over. She and John had become very friendly indeed over the garden. Elizabeth did not mind working hard with John, and he was pleased.

'So many of the others like to pick the flowers, and trim the hedges when they feel like it,' he said, 'but hardly anybody really works *hard*. When the tiny plants have to be bedded out, or the kitchen garden has to be hoed, who is there that offers to do it? Nobody!'

'Well, aren't I somebody?' demanded Elizabeth. 'Don't I come?'

'Oh yes – but what's the use of *you*?' said John. 'You're leaving soon, aren't you? You can't take a real interest in a garden that you won't ever see again. If you were going to stay I would make all my plans with you – I believe Mr Johns would let you take part-charge of the garden with me. It really would be fun.'

'Yes – it would,' said Elizabeth, looking round the garden. 'Are you the head of the garden, John?'

'Yes – under Mr Johns,' said John. 'Nobody needs to garden unless they like, you know – but if it's anyone's hobby, as it is mine, they are allowed to spend most of their spare time here. I've had charge of the garden for two years now, and it's pretty good, don't you think so?'

'Oh yes, I do,' said Elizabeth, looking round it. 'It's lovely. I could think of lovely things for it too, John. Don't you think a row of double pink hollyhocks would be nice, looking over that wall?'

'Fine!' said John, standing up from his hoeing. 'Fine! We could get the seeds now and plant them – and we could set out the new little plants this autumn, ready to flower next summer. Let's ask for money for the seeds at the next Meeting, shall we?'

'Well – you can, if you like,' said Elizabeth. 'I'm afraid it will be my last Meeting, John.'

'Your last Meeting!' said John scornfully, and he dug his hoe into the hard ground as if he were digging it into a Meeting. 'What a feeble goose you are, Elizabeth.'

'Feeble!' cried Elizabeth angrily. 'I like *that*! Just because I'm keeping my word and sticking to what I said, you call me feeble.'

'Well, it *is* feeble to give up everything you like so much here – your gardening – your riding – your friend – and your music – just because you're too proud to climb down and change your mind,' said John. 'I'm disappointed in you.'

Elizabeth stamped off in a rage. She hated to be called feeble. It was the one thing she had always thought that she wasn't.

She went to the swings. There was no one else there.

Elizabeth sat on the highest swing and began to sway to and fro. She thought very hard.

'Now let's get things clear in my own mind,' said Elizabeth to herself. 'First of all – I didn't want to come here, and I vowed to myself, to Mummy and Miss Scott that I'd get sent home as soon as possible. Well, I got the Meeting to say I *could* leave at half-term, and I was jolly pleased. I'd got what I wanted!'

Elizabeth swung high, and the swing creaked as it went to and fro.

'Yes – I'd got what I wanted,' said Elizabeth. 'I needn't even stay a term at this horrid, hateful school. That was what I called it.

'And now I find it isn't horrid or hateful. I can't help being happy here. The others seem to like me now that I've given up being so awful. I have a friend who is longing for me to stay and will be unhappy when I go. I've disappointed Richard, who wants to play with me at the concert. I've disappointed Mr Lewis. John is angry with me because I don't like his garden enough to stay – though really I do like it awfully. And Harry wants to give me those lovely rabbits.'

She swung even higher as her thoughts sped along.

'And why am I going? Now I'll just be really honest with myself. I'm *not* going because I'm unhappy. I'm very happy now. I'm going simply because I can't bear to change my mind and say I'm wrong. I'm too proud to say I'll stay, when I've said I'll go. I'm not strong enough to change my mind, and own up I'm wrong!'

Elizabeth slowed down the swing and put her feet on the ground. She frowned and looked at the grass. She had never thought so hard in her life. She spoke to herself sternly.

'Elizabeth Allen, you're feeble! Richard is right and Harry

is right. You're feeble! You're a coward! You don't dare to
stand up at the next Meeting and say you're too happy to
leave! You aren't strong enough to change your mind! You're
proud and silly! Elizabeth Allen, I'm ashamed of you!'

Elizabeth spoke these words to herself more sternly than
anyone had ever spoken to her. She stopped for a moment,
thinking deeply.

'But *am* I really so silly? *Am* I really so feeble? Can I really
spoil my happiness here, and Joan's too, by being so stupid
and proud? No, I can't! I'm stronger than I thought. I *can*
change my mind! I will change my mind! What did William
say? He said that only the strongest people could change
their minds when they saw they were wrong – it was the
feeble ones who *couldn't*!'

She began to swing again. 'Well, I'm strong!' she sang, as
she swung. 'I can change my mind! I can say I'm wrong!
Elizabeth Allen, you're not such a poor thing as I thought!
Just wait till the next Meeting – and I'll give them the biggest
surprise they've ever had!'

The little girl laughed as she swung. She felt very happy.
She was no longer obstinate and proud. She was strong
enough to change her mind.

'I wish the next Meeting would come soon!' she said to
herself. 'What a shock I shall give them!'

24 A surprise for the school

The last Meeting before half-term met at the same time as usual in the gym. Everyone was there except Joan, who was in the San, rapidly getting better.

Elizabeth sat on her usual form, between Harry and Belinda, feeling rather excited. What a surprise she was going to give everyone!

The ordinary business of the Meeting went through as usual. Money was taken from the box, but none was put in. Most of the children were expecting money from their parents when they saw them at half-term, and the next week the box would be very full again!

A few complaints were made, and one or two reports. Doris, who owned the guinea-pigs, beamed when her monitor reported that she had not forgotten her pets once.

'And,' said the monitor, 'they look the finest guinea-pigs I've ever seen now.'

'Good,' said Rita. 'See that they keep like that, Doris!'

Then Elizabeth's turn came, at the end of the reports. Rita knocked on the table with the mallet, and everyone was silent.

'I haven't much to say about Elizabeth Allen this week,' said Rita. 'But I must just say this – both William and I know now why Elizabeth spent so much money and what she spent it on. We are quite satisfied about it, and we hope that the Jury and the rest of you will accept our word when we say that we can only say that we are satisfied, and not tell you any more. Elizabeth was wrong to do what she did, but she was right not to tell us about it. Now the matter has come right, and we have no more to say.'

'Wait, Rita,' said William. 'We *have* more to say! This is the Meeting at which we were to ask Elizabeth if she wanted to leave us – it is our half-term Meeting. Well – we are keeping our word to you, Elizabeth. If you want to go, and you have made up your mind to do so, we give you our permission. Miss Belle and Miss Best will tell your parents, and if they agree, you may go back with them when they see you tomorrow.'

Elizabeth stood up. Her cheeks were flaming red, and her voice was not quite the same as usual.

'I've got something to say,' she said. 'It's not very easy – and I don't quite know how to say it. But anyway, it's this – I'm not going!'

'Not going!' cried everyone in surprise, turning to look at Elizabeth.

'But why not?' asked Rita. 'You said you had made up your mind to go, and that you never changed your mind.'

'Well, William said that only feeble people never change their mind if they know they are wrong,' said Elizabeth. 'And I know I was wrong now. I only made up my mind to be as naughty as possible because I was angry at being sent to school when I didn't want to go, and I vowed I'd go back home as soon as possible, just to show I'd have my own way. Well, I like Whyteleafe. It's a lovely school. And I want to stay. So I've changed my mind, and though you've said I can have what I want, and it's very nice of you, I don't want it now! I want to stay – that is, if you'll let me after all I've done!'

Everyone began to talk at once. Harry thumped Elizabeth on the back. He was very pleased. John nodded at her in delight. Now she could help

him with the garden! Richard actually left his place and came to whisper to her.

'You're a good sort,' he said. 'You can play the game as well as you play the piano.'

William banged with the mallet. 'Richard, go back to your place!'

Richard went back, grinning. Belinda and Helen smiled at Elizabeth, trying to catch her eye. Everyone seemed as pleased as could be.

'Elizabeth!' said William, 'we are very pleased with you. You've made a lot of silly mistakes, but you have made up for them all – and we admire you for being able to change your mind, admit you were wrong, and say so to us all! You are the sort of person we want at this school. We hope you will stay for years, and do your very best.'

'I will,' said Elizabeth, and she meant it. She sat down, looking happy and excited. It was lovely that everyone was pleased. She wasn't the Bold Bad Girl any more – she was Elizabeth Allen, the sort of person that Whyteleafe School wanted. She was proud and happy.

The Meeting ended soon after that – and Elizabeth sped off to the San to find Joan. Joan was sitting up in a chair, reading.

'Hallo!' she said. 'What happened at the Meeting? Anything exciting?'

'Well – the Meeting said I could go home with my parents tomorrow,' said Elizabeth. 'So I got my own way, you see.'

'Oh, Elizabeth – I *shall* miss you so!' said Joan.

'You won't!' said Elizabeth. 'Because, you see, I'm not

going! I'm staying on! I've changed my mind, Joan. I love Whyteleafe, and I won't leave it for years and years and years! Oh, what fun we'll have together! We'll be monitors one day – think of that! Shan't we be grand?'

'Good gracious!' said Joan, so delighted that she hopped out of her chair, and flung her arms round her friend. 'I can't believe it! Oh, I do feel so glad.'

Matron came into the room and looked horrified to see Joan out of her chair.

'What are you doing?' she said sternly. 'I shan't let Elizabeth come in here if that's the way you behave, Joan!'

'But, Matron, I was so pleased because Elizabeth is staying on instead of leaving,' said Joan, sinking back into her chair.

'Dear me! Fancy being pleased because a bad girl like this is staying with us!' said Matron, with a twinkle in her eye.

The girls laughed. They liked Matron – she was cheerful and friendly, though strict. She gave Joan some medicine, and went out.

'We shall have a lovely half-term now,' said Joan. 'My mother's coming to take me out. Is yours coming too?'

'Yes, I had a letter this morning,' said Elizabeth. 'Oh, Joan – let's ask our mothers to take us out together! That would be much more fun than going alone.'

'Yes, we will,' said Joan happily. 'I am sure I shall be well enough tomorrow to get up properly. Now you'll have to go, Elizabeth. That's the supper-bell.'

'Well, I'll see you tomorrow,' said Elizabeth. 'What fun we'll have! Oh, I *am* glad I'm not going home with my mother tomorrow. I wonder what she'll say when she hears that I want to stay on. Every letter I've written to her I've told her that I want to leave!'

Mrs Allen was *very* much astonished when she saw

Elizabeth the next day. The little girl looked so bright and happy – her mouth was no longer sulky, and there was no sign of a frown at all! Elizabeth flung herself into her mother's arms and hugged her.

'It's lovely to see you, Mummy,' she said. 'Do come and see everything – the playroom, and my classroom, and our bedroom – it's Number Six – and the garden – and everything!'

Her mother followed Elizabeth round, marvelling at the change in her little girl. *Could* this really be Elizabeth – this good-mannered, polite, happy child? Everyone seemed to like her. She had lots of friends, especially the gentle Joan, who seemed to be Elizabeth's special friend.

'Well, Elizabeth, you're quite a different child!' said her mother at last. 'Oh, look – there is Miss Best. I must just have a word with her.'

'Good morning, Miss Best,' said Mrs Allen. 'Elizabeth has just been showing me round – and really, she does seem so happy and jolly. What a change you have made in her! I feel quite proud of her!'

'She has made a change in herself,' said Miss Best, smiling her lovely smile. 'You know, Mrs Allen – she was the naughtiest girl in the school – yes, she really was! It was difficult to know what to do with her – but she knew what to do with herself. One of these days she will be the *best* girl in the school, and how proud you will be of her then!'

'Then you want to stay on, Elizabeth?' said her mother in astonishment. 'Well, I *am* glad! What a surprise!'

Mrs Townsend arrived to see Joan at that minute, and Elizabeth ran to see if Joan was ready. She had been kept in bed to breakfast, but was to get up afterwards and allowed to go in her mother's car. She was tremendously excited.

'It's the first time I've ever had a half-term treat like this!' she chattered excitedly, as Elizabeth helped her to dress quickly. 'And it's all because of *you*, Elizabeth!'

'Oh, rubbish!' said Elizabeth. 'Hurry up, Joan. What a time you take with your stockings. We're going to have lunch at a hotel – fancy that! I hope there will be strawberry ice-creams, don't you?'

Joan was ready at last, and the two girls went to find their mothers, who had already made friends. Then they settled down in Mrs Townsend's car, for she said she would drive them all.

'Now we're off for our treat!' said Elizabeth happily, as the car sped through the archway. She looked back at the beautiful building.

'Goodbye for a little while!' she said. 'I'm coming back to you, and I'm glad it's not goodbye for ever!'

We must say goodbye too, though maybe we will see Elizabeth again, and follow her exciting adventures at Whyteleafe School. Goodbye, Elizabeth – naughtiest girl in the school!

1 Back at Whyteleafe

Elizabeth was excited. The long summer holidays were almost over, and it was time to think of going back to school. Her mother, Mrs Allen, was busy getting all her things ready, and Elizabeth was helping her to pack the big trunk.

'Oh, Mummy, it's fun to think I'll see all my friends again soon!' said Elizabeth. 'It's lovely to be going back to Whyteleafe School once more. The winter term ought to be great fun.'

Her mother looked at Elizabeth and laughed.

'Elizabeth,' she said, 'do you remember what a fuss you made about going away to school for the first time last term? Do you remember how you said you would be so naughty and disobedient that you would soon be sent back home again? I'm glad to see you so happy this term – looking forward to going back.'

'Yes, I was stupid and silly,' said Elizabeth, going red as she remembered herself a few months back. 'Goodness, when I remember the things I said and did! Do you know, I wouldn't even share the cakes and things I took back? And I was so awfully rude and naughty in class – and I just wouldn't go to bed at the right time or do anything I was told. I was quite, quite determined to be sent back home!'

'And after all you weren't sent back, because you found you wanted to stay,' said Mrs Allen, with a smile. 'Well, well

– I hope you won't be the naughtiest girl in the school *this* term.'

'I don't expect I shall,' said Elizabeth. 'I shan't be the best either – because I do fly into tempers, you know, and I don't think before I speak. I'm sure to get into trouble of some sort! But never mind, I'll get out of it again, and I'll really do my best this term.'

'Good girl,' said her mother, shutting down the lid of the trunk. 'Now look, Elizabeth – this is your tuck-box. I've put a tin of toffees in, a big chocolate cake, a tin of shortbread, and a large pot of blackcurrant jam. That's all I can get in. But I think it's enough, don't you?'

'Oh, yes, thank you, Mummy,' said Elizabeth joyfully. 'The others will love all those. I wonder if Joan's mother will give her a tuck-box this term.'

Joan was Elizabeth's friend. She had been to stay with Elizabeth in the summer holidays and the two had had a lovely time together. Then Joan had gone back home again for a week or two before school began. Elizabeth was looking forward to seeing her friend again – what fun to sleep in the same dormitory together, to sit in the same form, and play the same games!

Elizabeth had told her mother all about Whyteleafe School. It was a school for boys and girls together, and the children ruled themselves, and were seldom punished by the masters or mistresses. Every week a big school Meeting was held, and all the children had to attend. The head boy and girl were the Judges, and twelve monitors, chosen by the children themselves, were the Jury. Any grumbles or complaints had to be brought to the Meeting, and if any child had behaved wrongly, the children themselves thought out a suitable punishment.

Poor Elizabeth had suffered badly at the weekly meetings, for she had been so naughty and disobedient, and had broken every rule in the school. But now she had come to see that good behaviour was best not only for herself but for the whole school too, and she was very much looking forward to everything. Perhaps this term she could show just how good she could be, instead of just how naughty!

She was to leave the next day. Everything was packed up. She had a new lacrosse stick and a new hockey stick, for both games were played at Whyteleafe. Elizabeth was very proud of these. She had never played either game before, but she meant to be very good indeed at them. How she would run! What a lot of goals she would shoot!

Her mother took her up to London to catch the train that was ready to take her and the other girls and boys to the school. Elizabeth danced on to the London platform, and cried out in delight to see all her friends waiting there.

'Joan! You're here first! Oh, how do you do, Mrs Townsend? Have you come to see Joan off?'

'Yes,' said Mrs Townsend. 'How do you do, Mrs Allen? I'm glad to see the naughtiest girl in the school looking so delighted to be going back to Whyteleafe again!'

'Oh, don't tease me,' said Elizabeth. 'I'm not the naughtiest girl any more! Oh, look – there's Nora! Nora, Nora! Did you have good holidays?'

Nora, tall and dark, turned and waved to Elizabeth. 'Hallo, kid!' she said. 'So you're coming back again, are you? Dear, dear, we shall have to make a whole set of new rules for you, I expect.'

Mrs Townsend laughed. 'There you are, Elizabeth!' she said. 'Everybody will tease you. They will find it hard to forget how naughty you were in your first term at Whyteleafe!'

'Look! There's Harry!' cried Joan. 'Harry! You know those rabbits you gave Elizabeth and me last term? Well, they're grown up now, and they've got babies of their own. I've got two of them with me to take back to school for my own pets.'

'Good!' said Harry. 'Hallo, Elizabeth! How brown you are! Hi, John – here's Elizabeth! You'd better start planning your winter gardening with her.'

John Terry came up. He was a tall, strong boy, about twelve years old, so fond of gardening that he was head of the school garden, under Mr Johns, a master. He and Elizabeth had planned all kinds of things for the winter term.

'Hallo, Elizabeth!' he said. 'Have you brought that gardening book you promised? Good! We'll have some fun this term, digging, and burning up rubbish!'

The two of them talked eagerly for a minute or two, and then another boy came up, dark-haired and serious-faced. He took Elizabeth's arm.

'Hallo, Richard!' said Elizabeth. 'You are a mean thing – you said you'd write to me and you didn't! I bet you haven't practised once during the holidays!'

Richard smiled. He was a splendid musician for his age and could play both piano and violin beautifully. He and Elizabeth shared a great love for music, and the two of them had been twice encored when they played duets at the school concert.

'I went to stay with my grandfather,' he said. 'He has a really marvellous violin, and he let me use it. I just didn't think of anything but music all the time I was on holiday. Thanks for your card. The writing was so bad I could only read your name at the end – but still, thanks all the same!'

'Oh!' began Elizabeth indignantly, and then she saw the

twinkle in Richard's eye, and laughed. 'Oh, Richard, I hope Mr Lewis lets us learn duets again this term!'

'Say goodbye to your people now,' said Miss Ranger, coming up to the little group. 'The train is just going. Find places as quickly as you can.'

Miss Ranger was Elizabeth's form-mistress. She was strict, very just, and quite a jolly person. Elizabeth and Joan were delighted to see her again. She smiled at them and went on to the next group.

'Do you remember how Miss Ranger sent you out of the room last term for flipping your rubber at people?' said Joan, with a giggle, as the two of them jumped into a carriage. Elizabeth laughed. She turned to her mother.

'Goodbye, Mummy darling!' she said. 'You needn't worry about me *this* term! I'll do my best, not my worst!'

The engine whistled loudly. Every boy and girl was now safely on the train. The mothers, fathers, uncles, and aunts waved goodbye. The train pulled out of the station and London was soon left behind.

'Now we're really off!' said Elizabeth. She looked round the carriage. Belinda was there, and Nora. Harry had got in, and John Terry too. John was already pulling out a bag of sweets. He offered them round. Everybody took one, and soon chatter and laughter filled the carriage, as the children told about their holidays.

'Is there anybody new this term, I wonder?' said Joan. 'I haven't seen anyone yet.'

'Yes – there are two or three newcomers,' said John. 'I saw a boy down the other end of the train, and a couple of girls. I should think they'd be in your form. I didn't like the look of the boy much – sulky-looking creature!'

'What are the girls like?' asked Joan. But John hadn't

noticed. 'Anyway, we shall soon see what they're like when we arrive,' said Joan. 'I say, Elizabeth, what have you got in your tuck-box? My mother has given me a huge box of chocolates, a ginger cake, a tin of golden syrup, and a jam sponge sandwich.'

'Sounds good!' said Elizabeth. The children began to talk about their tuck-boxes, and the time flew past as the train roared on its way.

At last the long journey was over and the train came to a stop at a little country platform. The boys and girls jumped down from their carriages and ran to take their places in two coaches.

'Let's look out for the first glimpse of Whyteleafe School!' said Elizabeth, as the coaches rumbled off. 'Oh, look – there it is! Isn't it lovely!'

The children stared up the hill on the top of which was their school. All of them were glad to see it again. Here and there the creeper up the walls was beginning to turn red, and the windows shone in the autumn sun.

Through an enormous archway rumbled the coaches, and up to the front door. Elizabeth remembered the first time she had arrived there, five months before, at the beginning of the summer term. How she had hated it! Now she was glad to jump down the coach steps with the other children and race into the school.

She looked round for the new girls and boy. She saw them standing rather forlornly together, wondering where to go. Elizabeth took Joan's arm. 'Let's go and look after the new ones,' she said. 'They're looking a bit lost.'

'Right!' said Joan, and they went up to the three children. They were all about eleven or twelve years old, though the boy was big for his age.

'Come with us and we'll show you where to wash, and where to go for dinner,' said Elizabeth. They all looked at her gratefully. Rita, the head girl, came by just then, and beamed at Elizabeth.

'So you've taken the newcomers under your wing,' she said. 'I was just coming to see about them. Good! Thanks, Elizabeth and Joan!'

'That's the head girl,' said Elizabeth to the boy and two girls. 'And look – that's William, our head boy. They're both fine. Come on. I'll show you the cloakrooms and we can all wash.'

Off they all went, and were soon washing and drying themselves in the big cloakroom downstairs. Then into the dining-hall they went, hungry as hunters. How glad they were to smell a good stew, and see the carrots and onions floating in it!

'It's grand to be back again!' said Elizabeth, looking happily round, and smiling at all the faces she knew. 'I wonder what adventures we'll have this term.'

'Perhaps we shan't have any,' said Joan. But she was wrong. Plenty of things were going to happen that term!

2 Settling down

Everyone soon settled down. Except for a few new children, the girls and boys were the same as the term before. Some had gone up into a higher form, and felt rather grand for the first few days. The new boy and two new girls were all in Elizabeth's form.

Miss Ranger took down their names: 'Jennifer Harris, Kathleen Peters, Robert Jones.'

Jennifer was a jolly-looking girl, with straight hair cut short, and a thick fringe. Her brown eyes twinkled, and the other girls felt that she would be good fun.

Kathleen Peters was a pasty-faced girl, very plain and spotty. Her hair was greasy-looking, and she had a very unpleasant expression, almost a scowl. Nobody liked her at all, those first few days.

Robert Jones was a big boy for his age, with a rather sullen face, though when he smiled he was quite different.

'I don't like Robert's mouth, do you?' said Joan to Elizabeth. 'His lips are so thin and pursed up. He doesn't look very kind.'

'Oh well, we can't help our mouths!' said Elizabeth.

'I think you're wrong there,' said Joan. 'I think people make their own faces, as they grow.'

Elizabeth laughed. 'Well, it's a pity poor Kathleen Peters didn't make a better face for herself,' she said.

'Sh!' said Joan. 'She'll hear!'

The first week went by slowly. New books were given out, and lovely new pencils and pens. The children were given their places in class, and Joan and Elizabeth sat next to one another, much to their delight. They were by the window and could see out into the flowery garden.

Any child who wanted to could help in the garden. John Terry was willing to give anyone a patch, providing they would promise to keep it properly. These little patches, backing on to an old sunny wall, were interesting little spots. Some children liked to grow salads, some grew flowers, and one child, who loved roses better than anything, had six beautiful rose-trees and nothing else.

Elizabeth didn't want a patch. She wanted to help John in the much bigger garden of which he was in charge. She was longing to make plans with him about it. She had all kinds of ideas about gardens, and had read her gardening book from end to end twice during the holidays.

The children were allowed to have their own pets, though not dogs or cats, as these were too difficult to deal with, and could not be kept in cages. Some children had rabbits, some had guinea-pigs, a few had fantail pigeons that lived in a big pigeon-house on a pole, and one or two had canaries or goldfish. It was fun having pets. Not all the children kept them – only those who were fond of animals or birds. The pets were kept in a big airy shed not far from the stables where the horses were kept that the children were allowed to ride.

Hens and ducks were kept, of course, and although these belonged to the school, any child who wished could help to care for them and feed them. There were three beautiful Jersey cows in the meadow, too, and one girl and boy milked these every day. They had to be up early in the morning, but they didn't mind at all. It was fun!

Jennifer Harris had some pets. They were small white mice, and she was very fond of them indeed. They were kept in a big cage, and she cleaned it out every day, so that it was spotless. No one else had white mice at that time, and Elizabeth and Joan went with Jennifer to see them.

'Aren't they sweet?' said Jennifer, letting a mouse run up her sleeve. 'Do you see their pink eyes? Elizabeth, would you like to let that one run up your sleeve? It's such a lovely feeling.'

'Well, I don't think I will, thank you,' said Elizabeth politely. 'It may be a lovely feeling to you, but it might not be for me.'

'Hallo! Are these your white mice, Jennifer?' asked Harry, coming up. 'I say, aren't they lovely? Golly, you've got one peeping out from your neck – did you know?'

'Oh yes,' said Jennifer. 'Take it, Harry. It will run up your sleeve and come out at your neck, too.'

Sure enough it did! It ran up the boy's sleeve, and soon its tiny nose was peeping out behind his collar. Joan shivered.

'I really don't think I could bear that,' she said.

The bell rang and the mice were hurriedly put back into their cage. Joan went to have a last peep at her two rabbits. They were fat and contented. She shared them with Elizabeth and was very fond of them indeed.

Teatime and supper-time the first week were lovely, because the children were allowed to take what they liked from their tuck-boxes. How they enjoyed the cakes, sandwiches, sweets, chocolates, potted meat, and jams they brought back with them! Everybody shared, though the new boy, Robert, didn't look too pleased about it, and Elizabeth noticed that Kathleen Peters did not offer any of her sweets round, though she shared her potted meat readily enough.

Elizabeth remembered how selfish she had been about sharing her own things at the beginning of her first term, so she held her tongue and said nothing.

'I can't very well blame other people for a thing I've done myself,' she thought. 'I'm jolly glad I'm different now!'

The big happening of each week was the school Meeting. The whole school attended, and any of the masters and mistresses who wished to. The two headmistresses, Miss Belle and Miss Best, always came, and Mr Johns usually came too. But they sat at the back, and did not take any part in the Meeting unless the children called upon them for help.

It was a kind of school Parliament, where the children made their own rules, heard grumbles and complaints, judged one another, and punished bad behaviour.

It was not pleasant to have one's faults brought before the whole school and discussed, but on the other hand it was much better for everyone to know their own failings and have them brought out into the open, instead of fearing them and keeping them secret, so that they grew bigger. Many a child had been cured for always of such things as cheating or lying by having the sympathy and help of the whole school.

The first school Meeting was held about a week after school began. The girls and boys filed into the gym, where a big table had been placed for the twelve monitors, who were the Jury. These had been chosen at the last Meeting of the summer term, and would remain monitors for a month, when they could either be chosen again, or others put into their place.

Everyone had to stand when William and Rita, the head boy and head girl, came into the gym. They sat down and everyone else sat too.

William knocked on the table with a small wooden hammer, and the children were quiet.

'There isn't much to say today,' said the head boy. 'I expect the new children have been told why we hold this big Meeting every week, and what we do at it. You see at this table our twelve monitors, and you all know why they are chosen. We chose them ourselves because we can trust them to be sensible, loyal and kind, and therefore you must obey them and keep the rules they make.'

Then Rita spoke. 'I hope you have all brought your money with you. As the new children probably know, any money we have is put into this big box, and out of it we take two pounds for every person each week. Out of that you must buy anything you need, such as stamps, sweets, ribbons, shoelaces, and so on. If you want any more than two pounds you must say why, and it will be given to you if it is deserved. Now will you please get your money ready. Nora, take round the box.'

Nora got up. She took the big box and handed it down each row. The children all put in their money. The new boy, Robert Jones, looked most annoyed.

'I say,' he said, 'you know I've got a whole ten pounds from my grandfather. I don't see why I should put it into the box. I shan't see it again!'

'Robert, some of us have too much money and some of us have too little,' explained William. 'It sometimes happens that we have a birthday and get lots of money, and sometimes we haven't any at all. Well, by putting all our money into the big box each week, we can always have two pounds to spend – the same for everyone, you see, which is quite fair – and if we need anything beyond that, we can always get it if the Jury give permission. So put in your money.'

Robert put his ten pound note in, and did not look at all pleased. His face looked even more sulky than usual!

'Cheer up!' whispered Elizabeth, but he gave her such a scowl that she said no more. Nora took the box back to the table. It was very heavy now.

Two pounds were given out to everyone, and the money went into pockets and purses. Rita and William had the same as everyone else.

'Any extra money wanted this week?' asked William, looking round the school.

Kenneth stood up. 'Could I have an extra fifty pence?' he asked. 'I borrowed a book out of the school library and I can't find it, and I've been fined fifty pence.'

'Take it out of your two pounds,' said William, and the Jury nodded in agreement. 'I don't see why the school's money should pay you for being careless, Kenneth! There are too many books lost. Pay the school library fifty pence, and you can have it back when you find the book. No extra money granted!'

A girl stood up. 'My mother is abroad and I have to write to her each week, of course, but the letters have to have a forty pence stamp on. Could I possibly have a little extra money allowed for that?'

The Jury discussed the matter. They agreed that it was hard luck on Mary to have to spend so much money on one letter each week.

'Well, you can have twenty pence extra each week,' said Rita, at last. 'That means you pay the usual amount for a stamp, and the school money pays the rest. That's quite fair.'

'Oh yes,' said Mary gratefully. 'Thank you.' Twenty pence was given to her, and she put it into her purse.

'I think that's all the business for this week,' said Rita,

looking at her notes. 'You all understand that any bad behaviour, such as unkindness, disobedience, cheating, bullying, and so on, must be brought before this Meeting each week. But I hope that the new children will understand that this does not mean telling tales. Perhaps their monitor will explain everything to them.'

'Yes, I will,' said Nora.

'Now – any complaints or grumbles before we go?' asked William, looking up. But there were none. So the Meeting broke up, and the children filed out of the gym. Elizabeth was rather silent as she went. She was remembering the bad time she had had last term at the Meeting. How defiant and rude she had been! She could hardly believe it now.

She went off with Joan to feed the rabbits. One was so tame that it would lie quite peacefully in Elizabeth's arms, and she loved that.

'Isn't everything peaceful this term?' said Joan. 'I hope it goes on like this, don't you?'

But it wasn't going to be peaceful for long!

3 Elizabeth makes an enemy

It was two of the new children who disturbed the peace of the form. When Robert had settled down and found his feet, the other boys and girls found that he was spiteful and unkind. And they discovered, too, that Kathleen Peters, the white-faced, spotty girl, was so quarrelsome that it was really very difficult to be nice to her.

On the other hand, Jennifer Harris was great fun. She was a wonderful mimic and could imitate the masters and mistresses marvellously, especially Mam'zelle. Mam'zelle wagged her hands rather a lot, and her voice went up and down when she spoke. Jennifer could put on a face exactly like Mam'zelle's, and talked and wagged her hands in a manner so like her that she sent the class into fits of laughter.

'Jenny's fine,' said Elizabeth. 'But I simply can't bear Robert or Kathleen. You know, I think Robert's cruel, Joan.'

'Why do you think that?' asked Joan. 'Has he been unkind to you?'

'No – not to me,' said Elizabeth. 'But I heard someone squealing yesterday and I saw little Janet running away from him, crying. I called out to know what was wrong, but she wouldn't tell me. I believe Robert had been pinching her or something.'

'I shouldn't be surprised,' said Joan.

Belinda Green heard what they were saying and came up.

'I think Robert's a bully,' she said. 'He's always running

after the smaller ones, and jumping out at them, and giving them sly pinches.'

'The hateful thing!' cried Elizabeth, who always hated any unfairness. 'Wait till I catch him! I'll jolly well report him at the very next Meeting!'

'Well, be sure to get your facts right,' said Belinda, 'or Robert will say you are telling tales, and then you won't be listened to.'

Robert came up at that moment and the three of them said no more. Robert bumped hard into Elizabeth as he passed and nearly sent her into the wall.

'Oh, I didn't see you!' he said, with a grin, and went on down the room. Elizabeth went red with rage. She took a step after Robert, but Joan pulled her back.

'He only did it to make you annoyed,' she said. 'Don't be annoyed!'

'I can't help being,' said Elizabeth furiously. 'Rude, clumsy thing!'

It was time to go into class then, and there was no time to do anything more. Robert was in Elizabeth's class, and she glared at him as she sat down. He made an extraordinary face at her – and they were enemies from that moment.

When Robert got nearly all his sums wrong, Elizabeth smiled with pleasure. 'Serves you right!' she said in a loud whisper. Unfortunately Miss Ranger heard it.

'Is there any need to gloat over bad work done by somebody else?' she said coldly – and then it was Robert's turn to grin with delight.

Each of them was pleased when the other did badly – though Elizabeth got more laughs out of Robert than he did out of her, for she was a clever girl and found lessons easy. Robert was much slower, though he was bigger and taller.

At games they did all they could to defeat each other. They were very often on opposite sides, and if Robert could give Elizabeth a whack over the hand with his lacrosse stick, or a blow on the ankle with his hockey stick, he would. Elizabeth was not an unkind girl, but she found herself lying in wait for Robert, too, and giving him a hard blow whenever she could.

Mr Warlow, the games master, soon noticed this, and he called the two of them to him.

'You are playing a game, not fighting a battle,' he told them gravely. 'Keep your likes and dislikes out of hockey and lacrosse, please, and play fairly.'

Elizabeth was ashamed, and stopped trying to hurt Robert – but Robert took an even greater delight in giving Elizabeth a bruise whenever he could, though now he was careful to do it when Mr Warlow was not watching.

'Elizabeth, you really are stupid to make an enemy of Robert,' said Nora one day. 'He is much bigger than you are. Keep out of his way. You'll lose your temper one day and put yourself in the wrong. That's what he's hoping for.'

But Elizabeth would not listen to advice of that sort. 'I'm not afraid of Robert!' she said scornfully.

'That isn't the point,' said Nora. 'He's only doing all this to annoy you, and if only you'd take no notice of him, and not try to pay him back, he'd soon get tired of it.'

'He's a hateful bully!' said Elizabeth.

'You're not to say things like that unless you have real proof,' said Nora, at once. 'And if you *have* real proof, then you must make a complaint at the Meeting. That's the place to accuse people of things. You know that quite well.'

Elizabeth made a sulky face and went off by herself. Why couldn't Nora believe her? Oh, well – Nora wasn't in her form and didn't know that hateful Robert as well as she, Elizabeth, knew him.

The next afternoon, after tea, Elizabeth went round to play with the rabbits. On the way she heard somebody calling out in a pleading voice:

'Please don't swing me so high! Please don't!'

Elizabeth peeped round at the swings. She saw a small boy on one, about nine years old. Robert was swinging him, and my goodness, wasn't he swinging him high!

'I feel sick!' cried the boy, whose name was Peter. 'I shall *be* sick! I shall fall off. Let me down, Robert, let me down! Don't swing me any more!'

But Robert took no notice of the small boy's shouting. His thin lips were pursed together, and with an unkind gleam in his eyes, he went on pushing the swing – high, high, higher!

Elizabeth was so angry that she had to blink her eyes to see clearly. She ran to Robert.

'Stop!' she cried. 'You're not to do that! You'll make Peter ill.'

'Mind your own business,' said Robert. 'He asked me to give him a swing and I'm giving him one. Go away, you interfering girl. You're always poking your nose where it isn't wanted.'

'Oh, I'm not!' cried Elizabeth. She tried to catch hold of the swing as it came down, to stop it, but Robert was too quick for her. He gave her a push and sent her spinning into a bush. Then he sent the swing even higher than ever.

'I'll go and tell somebody!' cried Elizabeth, picking herself up.

'Tell-tale, tell-tale!' chanted Robert, giving the swing another push. Elizabeth lost her temper completely and rushed at the aggravating boy. She caught hold of his hair

and pulled at it so hard that she pulled a whole handful out!
Then she slapped his face and gave him such a punch in his
middle that he doubled himself up with a groan.

Elizabeth stopped the swing and helped the trembling
Peter off the seat. 'Go and be sick if you want to,' she said.
'And don't let Robert swing you any more.'

Peter staggered off, looking rather green. Elizabeth turned
to face Robert, but just then three or four children came
up, and neither child felt inclined to go on with the quarrel
in public.

'I'll report you at the very next Meeting!' cried Elizabeth,
still in a great temper. 'You just see! You'll be punished all
right, you cruel, unkind boy!'

She went off, raging. Robert looked round at the interested
children who had come up. 'What a temper that girl has got!'
he said. 'Look here – she pulled my hair out!'

He picked up some of his dark hairs and showed them to
the others. They looked surprised.

'You must have been doing something awful to make
Elizabeth lose her temper like that,' said Kenneth.

'I was only giving someone a swing,' said Robert.
'Elizabeth interfered, as usual. I wish she'd leave me alone.
No wonder she was called the naughtiest girl in the school
last term!'

'We pinned a notice on her once, called her the Bold Bad
Girl!' said somebody, with a laugh, as he remembered how
angry Elizabeth had been. 'Did you hit Elizabeth, Robert? If
you did, you're mean. Girls are awfully annoying sometimes,
but if you're a boy, you can't hit them.'

'I didn't touch her,' said Robert, though he knew quite
well that if the others hadn't come up at that moment he
would certainly have gone for Elizabeth and slapped her

hard. 'She just went up in smoke and flew at me, the horrid girl!'

Elizabeth rushed off to tell Joan all that had happened. Joan listened gravely.

'Robert really is a horrid bully,' she said. 'He'll have to be stopped. But oh, Elizabeth, I do think it's rather a pity you lost your temper like that! You have got such a hot temper, you know!'

'Well, *anyone* would have lost their temper if they had seen Robert swinging that poor wretched little Peter almost over the top of the swing-post!' said Elizabeth, still boiling with rage. 'He was quite green.'

'You don't suppose the Meeting will think it's telling tales if you report Robert, do you?' asked Joan doubtfully. 'If I were you, I'd ask Nora first.'

'I'll do no such thing!' cried Elizabeth. 'I'm the best judge of this! I saw what happened, didn't I? All right then – I'll report Robert at the Meeting tomorrow, and then we'll just see what the Jury say. He'll get a dreadful shock – and he'll deserve it, too.'

Elizabeth was angry all day, and when the next day came she could hardly wait for the evening to come, to report Robert. Then he would see what happened to boys who did mean, unkind things!

Robert did not seem to be at all upset at the idea of Elizabeth reporting him. He made faces at her whenever he saw her, which made her very angry indeed.

'You'll get a shock at the Meeting tonight!' said Elizabeth. But there was a shock waiting for Elizabeth too!

4 What happened at the Meeting

The time for the weekly Meeting came. Elizabeth sat down on the form next to Belinda and Joan, longing for the moment to come when she could make a complaint about Robert. Robert sat not far away, his sullen face unsmiling, but there was a gleam in his eye when he turned to look at Elizabeth.

'I shouldn't be surprised if Robert doesn't make a complaint about you too, Elizabeth,' whispered Joan. 'He looks as if he's got something up his sleeve.'

'I don't care,' said Elizabeth. 'Wait till the Meeting hears what *I've* got to say!'

William and Rita came in, with the headmistresses and Mr Johns. The children stood up. The head girl and boy sat down, and the Meeting began.

Money was collected, though there was not very much that week. Kenneth had had a birthday and had five pounds to put into the box. Janet had a pound. Everyone was given their two pounds, and Mary got her twenty pence extra for her weekly stamp.

'Have you found the lost library book yet?' asked William, looking at Kenneth. 'We said you could have back your fifty pence fine if you did.'

'No, I haven't found it,' said Kenneth. 'I've hunted everywhere.'

'Anybody want any extra money?' asked Rita, jingling the box to see how much there was in it.

'I suppose I couldn't have any extra?' asked Ruth, standing up. 'I lost all my two pounds last week. It was a dreadful blow because I badly wanted some stamps.'

'How did you lose it?' asked Rita.

'There was a hole in my pocket,' said Ruth. 'It fell out through that, goodness knows where.'

'Did you know there was a hole in your pocket?' asked Rita.

Ruth hesitated. 'Well,' she said, 'I did know there was one coming, as a matter of fact. It was just a tiny little hole. I didn't know it had got big enough to lose money.'

'Who's your monitor?' asked William. 'Oh, you are, Nora. Do you think it was Ruth's fault?'

'Well,' said Nora, 'quite truthfully, Ruth isn't awfully good at mending her clothes when she ought to. She lost a lovely pocket-knife last term, through a hole in a pocket – didn't you, Ruth?'

'Yes,' said Ruth, looking rather uncomfortable. 'Yes, I did. I know I should have mended that hole. I'm untidy and careless about things like that. I jolly well won't get a hole again, though. I think I shouldn't have asked for extra money, as it was my own fault.'

She sat down. The Jury began to talk to one another. A girl sitting on one of the forms stood up. It was Eileen, a kindly girl with a mass of fair curls.

'May I say something?' she asked. 'I think that as Ruth has owned up that it was her own fault, and as she really is very generous with her money when she has it, couldn't she have an extra two pounds, just for once?'

'We are just discussing that,' said Rita. 'This is what we are going to do. We will let you have a pound, Ruth, not two pounds, because we all believe you aren't quite so silly as to let a thing like this happen a third time, and you have been very honest about it. Come and take an extra pound.'

'Oh, thank you,' said Ruth, going to the table. 'I had to borrow some stamps from Belinda, and now I can pay her back without using this week's two pounds. I'll be more careful in future, Rita!'

'Any more money wanted?' asked William, knocking on the table with his hammer, for the children had begun to talk to one another. Everyone was quiet.

'It's my Granny's birthday this week,' said a small girl, getting up. 'I want to send her a card. Could I have extra money to buy it with, and for the stamp, too?'

'No,' said William. 'That should come out of your two pounds. Not granted. Any more requests?'

There were none. Elizabeth knew that the time for complaints or grumbles would come next, and she went red with excitement. William said a few words to Rita about something and then knocked for silence again.

'Any complaints or grumbles?' he asked. Elizabeth stood up – and so did Robert – but Robert was just half a second before her.

'You first, Robert,' said William. 'Sit down and take your turn next, Elizabeth.'

Elizabeth didn't sit down. She didn't mean to let Robert speak first.

'Oh, please, William!' she said. 'I have such a serious complaint to make.'

'Well, it will keep,' said William. 'Sit down.'

'But William, it's about Robert,' began Elizabeth again, her voice rising.

'Elizabeth, do as you're told,' ordered Rita. 'You will have plenty of time to say all you want to.'

There was nothing for it but to sit down. Elizabeth was very angry. She glared at Robert, who didn't look at her at all, but stood patiently waiting to speak.

'Well, Robert, what have you to say?' asked William.

'I hope this isn't telling tales,' began Robert in a rather apologetic voice, 'but I really must complain about Elizabeth Allen's behaviour to me. I have always tried to be fair to her . . .'

'Oooooh!' cried Elizabeth indignantly. 'You know you haven't! You've . . .'

'Silence, Elizabeth!' ordered William sharply. 'You can say all you want to say in a minute. Don't interrupt. Go on, Robert.'

Elizabeth was boiling with rage. Joan put her hand on her friend's arm to try and calm her, but Elizabeth shook it off. Just wait till she had her turn to speak!

'I've always tried to be fair to her,' went on Robert in a very polite voice. 'But really, I can't let her pull my hair out and slap me in the face.'

There was an astonished silence. Everyone looked at Elizabeth. Robert went on, pleased at the surprise he had caused.

'I've got some of the hairs she pulled out in this envelope to show you, William, in case you don't believe me. And there are two or three children who will tell you it really happened. Of course, as she's a girl, I couldn't hit her back. I know she was supposed to be the naughtiest girl in the school last term, and . . .'

'You can leave that out, Robert. It has nothing to do with this,' said William at once. 'We have always found Elizabeth to be just and fair and kind so far, no matter how naughty she once was. Will you please tell us *why* Elizabeth did these extraordinary things?'

'She didn't want me to swing somebody,' said Robert. 'She's always interfering with me, whatever I do. She laughs if I make a mistake in class. Well, never mind about that. I was just swinging Peter, and he was squealing with excitement, and she came and pulled out my hair, slapped me and punched me.'

'Thank you,' said William. 'Sit down. Elizabeth, perhaps you would like to tell us if these complaints are true. Did you pull out Robert's hair and slap him?'

Elizabeth stood up, her cheeks as red as fire and her eyes flashing. 'Yes, I did!' she said. 'And he deserved it! I wish I'd pulled out more of his hair. I wish . . .'

'That's enough, Elizabeth,' said Rita, at once. 'If you can't control yourself enough to tell us properly what happened, there's no use in your saying anything.'

Elizabeth knew she was being silly. She tried her hardest to be sensible. 'Please, Rita, I'll tell my story properly,' she said. 'Then you'll see why I got so angry, and perhaps you'll say I was right to lose my temper with Robert. I was going to see my rabbits, when I heard somebody squealing out. It was Peter on the swing, and he was shouting to Robert not to swing him so high, because he was frightened.'

'Go on,' said William gravely.

'Well, I rushed over to stop the swing, and Robert sent me right over,' said Elizabeth, feeling her temper rise again as she told what had happened. 'I got up and flew at Robert to stop him swinging Peter again, because he was quite green and I thought he would fall off. And oh, William and Rita, that's not the only time that Robert has bullied the younger ones. He's a real bully, unkind and mean.'

There was a silence again. Everyone in the school knew quite well that a very serious thing had happened. Which of the two children was right? Bullying was hateful. Bad temper and fighting were wrong.

Joan was very upset. She knew quite well that Elizabeth had made up her mind to be good and do as well as she could this term, and now here was the hot-tempered girl flying into trouble almost at once! It was just no good trying to stop her. If Elizabeth saw something unfair she would rush at it in a temper and try to put it right that way. Joan couldn't see how this matter could be put right.

William and Rita spoke together in low voices. The Jury discussed the matter, too. Robert sat on his form, not even red in the face. He did not look at Elizabeth.

William knocked for silence. 'We would like to ask the boys and girls who saw the affair to report on it,' he said. 'Who saw it?'

Three children stood up. They said shortly that they had seen the hairs that Elizabeth had pulled out and had seen how red Robert's face was where it had been slapped.

'Did Robert hit back at all?' asked Rita.

'Not that we saw,' said Kenneth, and sat down, feeling sorry for Elizabeth.

'And now we will ask Peter to tell us what happened,' said William in a kindly tone. 'Stand up, Peter, and answer my questions.'

The small nine-year-old Peter stood up. His knees shook beneath him, and he felt dreadful to have the eyes of the whole School on him.

'Was Robert swinging you high?' asked William.

Peter looked across at Robert. Robert gave him a strange look. Peter spoke in a trembling voice. 'Yes – he was swinging me quite high.'

'Were you frightened?' asked William.

'N-n-n-no,' said Peter.

'Did you squeal for help?' asked Rita.

'No,' said Peter, with a look at Robert. 'I was just – just squealing for fun, you know.'

'Thank you,' said William. 'Sit down.'

Elizabeth leapt up. 'Robert must have made Peter promise to say all that!' she cried. 'Ask if there are any other young ones who would like to complain about Robert, Rita.'

Rita looked round where the younger children sat.

'Is there anyone who has a complaint to make about Robert?' she asked. 'If he has been unkind to you, or ill-treated you in any way, speak now.'

Elizabeth waited for half a dozen children to stand up and speak. But there was a complete silence! Nobody spoke, nobody complained. What a very strange thing! *Now* what was going to happen?

5 Elizabeth is very cross

The complaints to the school Meeting were so serious that the two Judges and the Jury took a long time to discuss them. In the meantime the rest of the children also discussed the matter among themselves. Not many of them were for Robert, for he was not liked, but on the other hand most of the boys and girls felt that Elizabeth had no right to lose her temper so fiercely.

'And after all,' whispered one child to another, 'she *was* the naughtiest girl in the school last term, you know.'

'Yes. We used to call her the Bold Bad Girl,' said another child. 'But she was quite all right after the half-term. She really did turn over a new leaf.'

'And I know quite well that she meant to do her very best this term,' said Harry. 'I've heard her say so heaps of times. She lost her temper with me last term, but she said she was sorry and has been absolutely decent to me ever since.'

So the talk went on, whilst Elizabeth and Robert sat up straight, hating one another, each longing to hear that the other was to be punished.

Meanwhile, the Judges and Jury were finding things very difficult. Some of the Jury felt quite certain that Robert was a real bully – and yet not even Peter would complain, so maybe there was not much truth in what they thought. All the monitors on the Jury were fair-minded and just, and they knew quite well that they must never judge anyone unless they had real, clear proof of wrong-doing.

Again, all the Jury knew quite well how bad Elizabeth had been the term before, and yet how marvellously she had managed to conquer herself and turn over a new leaf. They could not believe that she would fight Robert just for nothing. It was all very difficult. They did not feel that they wanted to punish Elizabeth in case by any chance Robert *did* turn out to be a bully.

At last William knocked with his wooden mallet for silence. The whole school sat up, eager to know what had been decided. Elizabeth was still fiery red in the face, but Robert looked quite pale and cool.

'We find this matter very difficult to decide,' said William in his pleasant voice. 'It is quite clear that Elizabeth did lose her temper badly, and flew at Robert, but it isn't quite as clear that Robert was bullying Peter. After all, we must take Peter's word for that. He should know! But we know enough of Elizabeth to realize that she is a very just person, and it is quite plain that she thought Robert was doing something very unkind.'

There was a pause. The school listened hard. William thought for a moment and then went on:

'Very well. Elizabeth may have been mistaken, but she really believed that Robert was being unkind. So she lost her temper and flew at him to stop him. That is where you were wrong, Elizabeth. Hot temper makes you see things all muddled instead of clearly, so when you see something you disapprove of, you *must* try to keep your temper, so that you can judge things properly and not get them all exaggerated and twisted. You spoke as if you hated Robert just now, and that does *you* as much harm as it does Robert.'

'I do hate him!' burst out Elizabeth angrily.

'Well, to go on with this,' went on William, 'we have decided that unless we get much plainer proof that Robert is a bully, we can't very well either judge him or punish him. And as we are sure you really did think he was doing something mean, we shan't punish you either, Elizabeth, but you must say you are sorry to Robert for behaving so badly to him.'

The whole school thought this was a good decision. Nobody wanted Elizabeth badly punished, for they really did like the hot-headed girl. The school came to the conclusion that she must have been mistaken about Robert and therefore she really should apologize, and let the matter end there.

Elizabeth said nothing. She sat on the form, looking sulky. Robert looked pleased. This was grand! William and Rita spoke together for a moment or two, and then said a few more words to close the matter.

'Well, that is our decision, Elizabeth and Robert. You will apologize, Elizabeth, and you will accept the apology graciously, Robert. Elizabeth, guard your temper – and, Robert, see that no charge of bullying is ever made against you. If it should be, you would not be judged lightly.'

Then William spoke of other things for a few moments and broke up the meeting, for the time was getting late. The children were dismissed and filed out of the gym, all looking rather solemn. Bad temper and bullying! These were things not often dealt with at the Meeting.

Robert swaggered out, hands in pockets. He felt important and pleased. He had won *that* battle. Now Elizabeth had got to say she was sorry. Serve her right!

But Elizabeth had no intention of saying she was sorry. Joan looked in dismay at the angry face of her friend as she marched into the common-room.

'Elizabeth! There's Robert over there. For goodness' sake go and apologize now, and get it over,' she begged the angry girl.

'But I'm *not* sorry!' said Elizabeth in a loud voice, tossing back her dark curls. 'Not a bit! I'm glad I flew at Robert. How can I say I'm sorry if it's an untruth?'

'Well, you can apologize,' said Joan. 'That's only good manners. Just go up and say, "I apologize, Robert." You don't need to say anything more.'

'Well, I'm not going to,' said Elizabeth. 'The Judges and the Jury were wrong for once! Nobody can make me apologize.'

'Elizabeth, no matter what you feel, you should be loyal to William and Rita,' said Joan, troubled. 'It isn't what you feel yourself that matters – it's what all the others feel to be right. You're one against a whole lot.'

'Well, I may be, but I'm the one who happens to be right,' said Elizabeth in a trembling voice. 'I know Robert is a bully.'

'Elizabeth, do what the Meeting says, and then we'll watch and see if we can't catch Robert at his horrid tricks,' begged Joan. 'Do it to please me. You'll make me so unhappy if you don't – and the whole school will think badly of you if you're afraid to apologize.'

'I'm not afraid!' said Elizabeth, with her eyes flashing angrily.

Joan smiled a little smile to herself. She turned away from Elizabeth. 'You *are* afraid,' she said. 'You're afraid of hurting your own silly pride.'

Elizabeth marched straight up to Robert. 'I apologize,' she said stiffly.

Robert gave a polite bow. 'I accept your apology!' he said. Elizabeth stalked off by herself. Joan ran after her.

'Leave me alone,' said Elizabeth crossly. She went into a music practice-room and sat down at the piano. She played a piece she knew, very loudly and fiercely. Mr Lewis, the music-master, looked into the room in surprise.

'Good gracious, Elizabeth!' he said. 'I've never heard that piece sound so angry before. Get up, and let me play you something *really* fierce – something with a thunderstorm or two in it.'

Elizabeth got up. Mr Lewis took her seat and played a stormy piece of music, with the wind and the sea, streaming clouds, roaring trees in it – and then the storm died down, the rain sprinkled softly, the wind ceased, the sun shone, and the music became calm and smooth.

And as she listened, the little girl felt soothed and softened too. She loved music so much. Mr Lewis glanced at her and saw that she looked peaceful instead of troubled. He played a little longer and then the bell went for Elizabeth's bedtime.

'There you are,' said Mr Lewis, shutting the piano. 'After the storm, the calm. Now go off to bed, sleep well, and don't worry your head too much about anything.'

'Thank you, Mr Lewis,' said Elizabeth gratefully. 'I do feel better now. I was all hot and bothered about something, but now I feel happier. Goodnight!'

6 Jenny's white mice

Elizabeth did not sleep very well that night. She tossed and turned, thinking of the Meeting, of 'that hateful Robert', as she called him to herself, of the apology she had had to make – and she made plans to catch Robert when he was being unkind to any of the younger ones.

'Yes – I'll watch and wait and catch him properly,' said Elizabeth to herself. 'He *is* a bully, I know he is – and sooner or later I'll catch him!'

Elizabeth was heavy-eyed and tired the next day. She did her lessons badly, especially French, and Mam'zelle was cross with her.

'Elizabeth! How is it that you did not learn your French verbs yesterday?' scolded Mam'zelle. 'That is not good. You sit there, half asleep, and you pay no attention at all. I am not pleased with you.'

Robert grinned to himself, and Elizabeth saw him. She bit her lip to stop herself from being rude to both Robert and Mam'zelle.

'Well, have you no tongue?' asked Mam'zelle impatiently. 'Why did you not learn your verbs, I said?'

'I *did* learn them,' said Elizabeth truthfully. 'But somehow I've forgotten them this morning.'

'Then you will please learn them sometime today and remember them!' said Mam'zelle, her dark eyes flashing. 'You will come and say them to me when you know them.'

'All right,' said Elizabeth sulkily. But Mam'zelle would not let that pass. She rapped on the desk and spoke sharply.

'You will not say "All right" to me in that rude way! You will say "Very good, Mam'zelle."'

'Very good, Mam'zelle,' said Elizabeth, knowing quite well that Robert was enjoying her scolding immensely, and wishing that she could pull some more hairs out of his dark head.

After that the lesson went on smoothly, for Elizabeth was determined not to give Robert any more chances to crow over her. But she did not do so well as usual in anything, for as soon as she had a moment to think, she began to plan how she might catch Robert being unkind to someone.

Belinda and Joan and Nora had a little talk together, whilst Elizabeth was having her music lesson that day.

'We'll have to keep Elizabeth away from Robert for a few days if we can,' said Joan. 'She just hates him, and, you know, she has such a quick temper that she's quite likely to fly at him again if he makes a rude face at her.'

'After a few days she won't feel so badly about it all,' said Nora. 'We'll try and get her to come down into the town with us, or to garden with John, or something like that – the less she sees of Robert the better. I can't say I want to see very much of him myself!'

So for the next few days Elizabeth found that she was always being rushed off somewhere.

'Come and help me to choose a new ribbon, Elizabeth!' Joan would beg. 'I really must get one.' And down to the town the two would go.

'Elizabeth, come and practise catching the ball at lacrosse with me,' Nora would say. 'You're getting quite good. A little more practice and you'll be first-rate.'

Then Elizabeth would beam with pride and go to fetch her lacrosse stick.

'Elizabeth, John wants you and me to go and help him to pile up rubbish for a bonfire!' Belinda would call. 'Coming?'

And off Elizabeth would go again, so that she hardly saw Robert at all, except in class. But she did not forget what she had planned to do, and when she had a chance she watched to see if any of the smaller children were being bullied.

But she saw nothing of the sort. Robert went about his own business and seemed to keep right away from the younger ones. He knew quite well that Elizabeth was watching for him to do something bad again, and he wasn't going to give her the chance to catch him. She would soon get tired of that.

Robert was immensely fond of horses, and rode as often as he could. He was not allowed to look after them, because only the bigger boys and girls were allowed to do that, but he spent as much time as he could hanging round the stables, and talking to the brown-eyed horses, who put their heads out over the stable doors when they saw him. Robert took no interest in the other pets at all, much to the annoyance of the other children, who always loved to show off their pets to anyone.

So, what with Robert going out riding and the other girls taking Elizabeth off with them as often as they could, the two enemies had few chances to meet and quarrel. It was only in class that they could show their dislike of one another.

Robert was so anxious not to give Elizabeth any chance of jeering at him that he worked extra hard, and took enormous care with his homework. Miss Ranger, the form-mistress, was surprised and pleased to find Robert making such progress with everything, and she praised him.

'Robert, you are doing very well,' she said. 'I shouldn't be surprised if you are top of the class one week this term, if you work like this!'

Robert went red with pleasure. He was really a lazy boy, and had never been anywhere near the top of his form, even at his old school. Elizabeth was annoyed to hear Miss Ranger say this. Why, she, Elizabeth, could easily be top of the form if she wanted to! She would work like anything and just show Robert he couldn't get to the top whilst she was in the form!

So she worked very hard too; but both children were working hard for the wrong reason – to spite one another! So they did not enjoy their work at all, which was a great pity.

Then for a time both Robert and Elizabeth forgot their quarrel in the interest of something else. Jennifer's white mice made a great disturbance, and Jenny nearly got into serious trouble!

Her white mice had a family of nine small baby mice, most adorable creatures with soft white fur, woffly noses, pink eyes, and tiny tails. Jenny loved these very much indeed, and it was quite a sight to see the little girl with half a dozen mice running up and down her sleeves.

'Jenny, put them back, the bell's gone,' said Elizabeth one morning. 'Hurry! You'll be late, and Miss Ranger isn't in a very good temper this morning.'

'Oh, golly, I can't find them all,' said Jenny, feeling all over her body for the baby mice. 'Wherever have they gone? Is there one down my back, Elizabeth?'

'Oh, Jenny, how can you let them do that!' cried Elizabeth. 'No, there isn't one down your back. They must be all there in the cage now. Do come on. I shan't wait for you if you're a second longer.'

Jenny shut the cage-door carefully and latched it. Then she ran off with Elizabeth, and they arrived in their classroom panting, just as Miss Ranger also arrived.

They took their places. The lesson was geography, and the class were learning about Australia and the big sheep-farms there. Jenny had a seat in the first row, just in front of Elizabeth and Joan.

And, in the middle of the lesson, Elizabeth saw the nose of a white mouse peeping out at the back of Jenny's neck! Jenny felt it too. She wriggled, put up her hand and pushed the mouse down. It disappeared.

Elizabeth so badly wanted to giggle that she did not dare to look up at all. When she *did* look up, she saw the mouse peeping out of Jenny's left sleeve. It looked round at Elizabeth with pink eyes. Then it disappeared again.

Jenny found the mouse very tickly indeed. She wriggled about. She tried to make the mouse go up to her shoulder where it could be comfortable and go to sleep. But it wasn't at all sleepy. It was a very lively mouse indeed. It ran all round Jenny, sniffing here and there at shoulder straps and tapes, and Jenny couldn't stop wriggling.

Miss Ranger noticed her. 'Jenny! What in the world is the matter with you this morning? Do sit still.'

'Yes, Miss Ranger,' said Jenny. But a second later the mouse went under her left arm-hole, where Jenny really was very ticklish indeed, and the little girl gave a giggle and another wriggle. Miss Ranger looked up.

'Jennifer! You are behaving like a child in the kindergarten! And Elizabeth, what is the matter with *you*?'

There was nothing the matter with Elizabeth except that she simply could *not* help laughing at Jenny, because she knew so well why Jenny was wriggling. The mouse popped its head out of Jenny's neck and stared at Elizabeth and Joan. The two girls tried to stop their giggles, but the more they tried to stop, the worse they got.

'This class is a disgrace this morning,' said Miss Ranger impatiently. 'Come up here to the board, Jennifer, and point out some things to me on the map. If you can't *sit* still, perhaps you can stand still!'

Jenny got up and went to the board. The mouse was pleased to find it was having a ride, and it scampered all round Jenny's back. Jenny put her hand behind her and tried to stop it.

'Jenny! What *is* wrong?' asked Miss Ranger. By this time the whole class knew about Jenny's mouse, and everyone was bending over their books, red in the face, trying their hardest not to giggle. A little squeal came from Kenneth, and Miss Ranger put down her book in despair.

'There is some joke going on,' she said. 'Well, let me share it. If it's funny, we'll all have a good laugh. If it isn't, we'll get on with the lesson. Now, what's the joke?'

Nobody told her. Jenny looked at the class with pleading eyes, begging them silently not to give her away. The mouse also looked out of Jenny's sleeve. Miss Ranger was really puzzled.

And then the mouse decided to explore the world a bit! So out it ran, jumped on to Miss Ranger's desk, and sat up to wash its whiskers.

The class went off into shouts of laughter. Miss Ranger looked down in the greatest astonishment. She had not seen where the mouse had come from.

'How did this mouse come here?' she asked.

'It jumped from my sleeve, please, Miss Ranger,' said Jenny. 'I was playing with my white mice when the bell rang, and I suppose I didn't put them all back into the cage. This one was still up my sleeve.'

'So that's the joke!' said Miss Ranger, beginning to smile. 'Well, I agree it's a good joke, and no wonder everyone laughed. But it's not a joke to be repeated, Jenny. It's funny this time – but if it happens a second time, I shan't think it is at all funny. You quite understand that, don't you? White mice are very nice in their cage, but not at all suitable running round people's necks in a classroom.'

'Oh yes, I do understand that, Miss Ranger,' said Jenny earnestly. 'It was quite an accident. May I put the mouse up my sleeve again?'

'I'd much rather you didn't,' said Miss Ranger. 'I feel this lesson will not be very successful as long as that mouse is in the room. Take it back to its cage. It will have plenty to tell all its brothers and sisters.'

So off went Jenny, and the class settled down again. But the laughter had done everyone good, especially Elizabeth. She felt almost her old happy self again after that!

7 Kathleen in trouble

Elizabeth enjoyed the games in the winter term very much indeed. She didn't know which she liked best, hockey or lacrosse!

'I almost think I like lacrosse best,' she said to Joan. 'The catching is such fun.'

'If you go on playing well, you'll be in the next match,' said Joan. 'I heard Eileen say so!'

'Did you really and truly?' said Elizabeth joyfully. 'Oh, I say! Nobody else out of our form has been in a school match yet. If only I could be!'

Somebody else in the form was extremely good at lacrosse too – and that was Robert! He had never played the game before, but he was very quick on his feet, and could catch marvellously. The game was played with a hard rubber ball which had to be thrown from one player's net to another, caught, and sent hurtling at the goal-net. The job of the other side was to knock the ball away, or make the player who had the ball toss it to someone else, when the enemy might perhaps be able to get it.

As soon as Robert saw that Elizabeth was becoming good enough to play in a school match, he made up his mind that he would be better than she was, and take her place in the match.

He knew that only one person would be chosen from their form, for only one was lacking in the numbers that made up the team. What sport it would be if he could play better than Elizabeth! So that was another thing for him to do – practise catching the ball whenever he could get someone to throw to him. But he wouldn't let Elizabeth guess that he was trying to be better than she was – no, he would let her think he wasn't trying very hard, else she would begin to practise as well.

In the meantime, school life went on much as usual. Elizabeth began to work very hard with John in the school garden. They cut down all the old summer flowers, and piled them in heaps on the place where they had their bonfires. They dug over the beds, and made themselves very hot and tired but very happy. They each made out plans for the spring and gave them to each other, and John actually said that Elizabeth's plan was better than his.

'It's not very *much* better,' said John, looking at the two plans carefully, 'but I do like one or two of your ideas very much, Elizabeth. For instance, your idea of having crocuses growing in the grass on that bank over there is lovely.'

'Well, your idea of having rambler roses over that ugly old shed is lovely too,' said Elizabeth. 'I say, John, won't it look marvellous!'

'I wonder if the school Meeting will allow us extra money this week for the crocus corms,' said John. 'We should want about five hundred crocuses to make any sort of a show. Let's ask, shall we?'

'Well, *you'd* better ask, not me,' said Elizabeth, her face going sulky. 'You know what happened at the last Meeting, John. It was horrid to me.'

'No, it wasn't, Elizabeth,' said John, leaning on his spade and looking at Elizabeth across the trench he was digging. 'I think the Meeting was quite fair. Don't be silly. You can be such a sensible girl, and yet you're such an idiot sometimes.'

'I shan't help you in the garden if you call me an idiot,' said Elizabeth.

'All right,' said John. 'I'll get Jenny. She's jolly good.'

But Elizabeth did not walk away in a rage as she felt inclined to do. She took up her spade and began to dig so hard that the earth simply flew into the air. She wasn't going to let Jennifer take her place!

John burst out laughing. 'Elizabeth! You'll dig down to Australia if you're not careful! And really I'd rather you didn't cover me with earth whilst you're doing it.'

Elizabeth looked up and laughed too.

'That's better!' said John. 'You'll get a face like Kathleen Peters if you aren't careful!'

'I hope not!' said Elizabeth. 'That's another person I don't like, John. She's so quarrelsome, and she seems to think we are always saying or thinking nasty things about her – and honestly, we just don't bother about her half the time.'

'Well, don't start making an enemy of her too,' said John, beginning to dig again. 'Friends are better than enemies, Elizabeth, old thing, so make those instead.'

'Well, nobody could make a friend of Kathleen!' said Elizabeth. 'Honestly they couldn't, John. You're not in her form, so you don't know what a tiresome person she is.'

It was quite true that Kathleen was tiresome. She was always grumbling about something, and she spent the whole of her two pounds each week on sweets, which she never shared with anyone else.

'No wonder she's spotty!' giggled Belinda unkindly. 'She's eating sweets all the time – and her mother sends her heaps too, only she never tells us, in case we might expect her to share them. Let her keep them! I don't want any!'

Kathleen was not only tiresome with the boys and girls,

always trying to quarrel, and accusing them of saying nasty things about her, but she was always in trouble with the mistresses and masters too. If anyone found fault with her, she would argue back and try to make out that she was right.

Mam'zelle was not so patient with her as were the others. When Kathleen dared to say that Mam'zelle hadn't told her what homework to do the day before, the hot-tempered French mistress flared up at once.

'And now, this Kathleen again!' she cried, wagging her hands at the ceiling. 'She thinks I am a goose, a cuckoo, a donkey! She thinks I do not know how to give homework! She thinks I am not fit to teach French to her!'

This was really rather funny, and the class sat up, enjoying the fun. When Mam'zelle got cross it was marvellous!

'But, Mam'zelle,' said foolish Kathleen, who simply would not stop arguing with anyone, 'you did say . . .'

'Ah! I did say something then!' cried Mam'zelle. 'Truly, you think I did say something? Ah, my Kathleen, that is so, so kind of you! Perhaps if you think a little harder you will remember that I did give you some homework to do – though, of course, that is no reason why you should do it.'

'But you DIDN'T give me any,' said Kathleen.

Belinda nudged her. 'Shut up, Kathleen,' she said. 'You *were* given some – but you didn't write down what you had to do.'

'Belinda! It is not necessary that you should interfere,' said Mam'zelle. 'Ah, this class! It will turn my hair white as snow!'

Mam'zelle had hair as dark as a raven's wing, and the class did not feel that anything would turn it white. They sat staring from Mam'zelle to Kathleen, wondering what was going to happen next. It ended in Kathleen being sent by herself to the common room to do the homework she had not done.

'That girl will drive me mad,' thought Mam'zelle to herself, 'with her spots and her greasy hair and pale face. How she whines!'

The other mistresses were not quite so impatient, and Miss Ranger was really rather worried about Kathleen. The girl always looked so miserable – which, of course, was no wonder, because she was always arguing or quarrelling with someone.

Jennifer Harris enjoyed the scene with Mam'zelle very much. She watched all Mam'zelle's actions, listened carefully to the rise and fall of her excited voice, and then practised the whole scene by herself. First she was the whining Kathleen, then she was impatient Mam'zelle, and so on. It really made a very funny scene.

Jenny was most anxious to try it on the others to make them laugh. So the next evening, when most of her form were in the common-room, playing the gramophone, reading books, and writing letters, she began to mimic Mam'zelle.

The boys and girls looked up, interested. Belinda switched off the gramophone. Kathleen was not there.

In a moment or two the clever girl had the whole room roaring with laughter. She wagged her hands like Mam'zelle, and when she came out with 'I am a goose, a cuckoo, a donkey!' exactly as Mam'zelle had said it, the children giggled in delight.

Jenny mimicked Kathleen's rather whining voice marvellously. It really might have been Kathleen speaking! But then Jenny went a bit too far. She said things that Mam'zelle had not said.

'Ah, truly, Kathleen, I do not like your spots, I do not like your greasy hair, I do not like your manners!' said Jenny, with a funny accent just like Mam'zelle's. And at that moment Elizabeth noticed something – Kathleen was in the room! No one had seen her come in. How long had she been there?

Elizabeth nudged Jenny, but Jenny took no notice. She was enjoying herself far too much. Everyone was listening to her, amused and admiring.

'Jenny! Shut up!' hissed Elizabeth. 'Kathleen's come in.'

Jenny stopped at once. All the children looked round, and felt rather uncomfortable when they saw Kathleen. Belinda started up the gramophone. Somebody began to whistle the tune. Nobody liked to look at Kathleen.

Elizabeth sat down in a corner, wishing that Jenny hadn't said quite such awful things in Mam'zelle's voice. Suppose Kathleen really thought that Mam'zelle had said them after she had been sent to the common room to do her forgotten homework? She stole a quick look at Kathleen.

At first it seemed as if Kathleen was going to turn off the gramophone and say something. But she thought better of it, and sat down with a jerk in a chair. She got out her notepaper, and sat chewing the end of her pen. Her pale face was as white as usual, and her eyes were small and angry. She looked spiteful and mean.

'I guess she won't easily forgive Jenny for that,' thought Elizabeth. 'We ought to have stopped Jenny, because she went too far – but really, she's so awfully funny. I wonder if Kathleen will complain about it at the next Meeting. I shouldn't be surprised.'

Kathleen didn't say a word about the affair to anyone. She spoke to no one at all that evening. Her bed was next to Elizabeth's in the dormitory, and when Kathleen did not reply when everyone called goodnight as usual, Elizabeth poked her head between the white curtains to speak to her, for she was sorry about the whole thing.

Kathleen did not see her. The girl was sitting on her bed, looking earnestly at her face in her hand-mirror. She looked really sad, and Elizabeth knew why. Poor Kathleen was thinking how plain and ugly she was! She had always known it herself – but it was dreadful to know that everyone else knew it too, and laughed about it.

Elizabeth drew back her head and said nothing. Would Kathleen have the courage to repeat at the Meeting all that Jenny had said about her? Surely she couldn't do that!

Kathleen had her own plans. She was going to pay Jenny out in her own way. She got into bed and lay thinking about them. Jenny had better look out, that's all!

8 Another school Meeting

Things were not very pleasant the next two or three days. There seemed to be rather a lot of bad feeling about. For one thing, Kathleen simply would not speak to Jenny at all, which was not very surprising considering what she had overheard Jenny saying.

But besides not speaking to her, Kathleen began to speak *against* her. Jenny was always very hungry, and she ate very well indeed – and Kathleen called her greedy.

'It makes me sick to see the way that greedy Jenny eats,' she said to Belinda, after tea the next day. 'Honestly, she ate seven pieces of bread-and-butter, and three buns, besides an enormous piece of birthday cake that Harriet gave her.'

Belinda said nothing. She did not like rows – but Elizabeth overheard and flared up at once in defence of Jenny.

'That's a mean thing to say, Kathleen!' she said. 'Jenny *isn't* greedy! She's always terribly hungry at mealtimes – well, I am too, I must say – but I've never seen Jenny gobbling just for the sake of eating, or taking more than her share if there wasn't enough for everyone. And how awful of you to *count* how many pieces of bread-and-butter she had!'

'I shall count again,' said Kathleen, 'and you'll be surprised to find I'm right. Jenny is greedy. It's disgusting!'

'Kathleen! What about you and your sweets then!' cried Elizabeth. 'You're greedy over them – why, you never offer anyone any!'

'Stop it now, you two,' said Belinda, feeling uncomfortable. 'I don't know what's the matter with our form this term – somebody always seems to be quarrelling!'

Kathleen went off. Elizabeth took out her paint-box to paint a map, and set it down on the table with a crash. Her face was as black as thunder.

'Elizabeth! I wonder you haven't broken that box in half!' exclaimed Belinda. 'My word, I wish you could see your face!'

'I think you might have stuck up for Jenny,' said Elizabeth, stirring her paint water so crossly that it slopped over on the table. 'I wouldn't let anyone say a word against a friend of mine without sticking up for them.'

'Well, you've made things much worse by sticking up, than I have by saying nothing,' said Belinda. 'I don't know what's come over you lately – you're really bad-tempered!'

'No, I'm not,' said Elizabeth. 'Things have gone wrong, that's all. Anyway, I won't let that spotty-faced Kathleen say mean things about old Jenny. Jenny's a sport. Golly, how I laughed about that white mouse the other day! Miss Ranger was nice about that, wasn't she?'

About a quarter of an hour later, Jenny came into the common room looking furious. She sat down in a chair with a bump. Belinda looked up from her sewing.

'My goodness! Another thunderstorm beginning!' she said. 'What's up, Jenny? One look at you and even the milk would turn sour!'

'Don't be funny,' said Jenny. 'It's that horrible Kathleen! She told Kenneth that I borrowed his bike yesterday without asking him. And I didn't. I took Harry's and I *did* ask him! Mine had a puncture!'

'Well, really, Kathleen's going a bit too far!' said Elizabeth indignantly. 'That's twice she's said nasty things about you today. I'll tell her what I think of her when I see her!'

'She's in the passage outside, still telling Kenneth about me,' said Jenny. 'Go and say what you want to – it will do her good!'

'No, don't, Elizabeth,' said Belinda. 'You are such a little spitfire. Don't interfere.'

But Elizabeth had already marched out of the room. She saw Kathleen and went up to her.

'Look here, Kathleen,' she said, 'if you don't stop saying unkind and untrue things about Jenny, I'll report you to the next Meeting!'

'And what about the unkind and untrue things that Jenny said about me in front of you all!' said Kathleen in a low and trembling voice. 'How dared she mock me like that!'

'Well, they might have been unkind, but they weren't untrue,' said Elizabeth. Then she was sorry she had said that. But it was too late to unsay it. Kathleen turned away and went off without saying another word.

She was really afraid that Elizabeth might report her, and she made up her mind that she had better not speak against Jenny. But she would do all kinds of little things to annoy her and get her into trouble – and she would do them to that interfering Elizabeth, too.

'I'll be very, very careful so that nobody guesses it's me,' thought Kathleen to herself. 'I'll hide their books – and make blots on their homework – and do things like that. I'll soon pay them out!'

The next school Meeting came along quickly. The children took their places as usual, and the Meeting began. A nice lot of money was put into the box, for three children had had birthdays and had many postal orders sent to them. That was lucky!

'We are rich today,' said William, jingling the box. 'Give out the ordinary money, Eileen – and twenty pence extra to Mary as usual. Now – any requests for extra money?'

Leonard, one of the bigger boys, stood up. 'May I have five pounds to pay for mending a window, please?' he asked. 'I broke one yesterday in the common room.'

'By accident, or were you fooling about?' asked William.

'I was playing with an old cricket ball,' said Leonard.

'Well, you know quite well that we made a rule last term not to bring balls into the common room,' said William. 'It only means broken windows.'

'I quite forgot that rule,' said Leonard. 'I *should* like the money, though – five pounds is a lot to have to pay. I'm sorry about it, William.'

The Jury discussed the matter. They quite saw that five pounds was a lot of money when each boy and girl only had two pounds each week. On the other hand, Leonard had broken a rule that he himself had helped to make last term, and why should the school money pay for his fooling about?

The matter was decided at last. William banged with his hammer and the children were quiet.

'Was anybody else fooling about with you?' asked William. Leonard stood up again.

'Well, yes,' he said, 'but it was when I threw the ball that the window got broken.'

'The Jury think that the five pounds shouldn't come out of the school box,' said William, 'but they also think that you shouldn't have to pay it all. You'd better discuss it with the children who were playing about with you at the time, and divide the payment between you. That's fair.'

A boy got up. 'I was fooling about too,' he said. 'I'll pay my share. I agree that it's fair.'

Two others got up, a boy and a girl. 'We will pay our share too,' they said.

'Right,' said William. 'Four into five pounds – one pound twenty five pence each. That won't ruin any of you. And please remember that as you all help to make the few rules we have, it's up to you to keep them.'

John nudged Elizabeth. 'Ask for the money for our crocuses,' he whispered. 'Go on. I'm not going to! It was your idea.'

'I'm sure the Meeting won't let me have anything after what they said last week,' said Elizabeth in a fierce whisper.

'Coward!' said John, with a grin. That was quite enough to make Elizabeth shoot to her feet at once. She could never bear to be called a coward!

Kathleen looked at her rather anxiously. She was half afraid that Elizabeth was going to complain about her to the Meeting.

'What do you want, Elizabeth?' asked Rita. 'Extra money?'

'Yes, please,' said Elizabeth. 'John and I have got some fine plans for the school garden and we both think it would be lovely to have yellow and purple crocuses growing in the grass on that sloping bank near the gates. John says we'd want at least five hundred crocus bulbs. Please may we have the money to buy them, Rita?'

William and Rita spoke together for a moment and the Jury nodded their heads at one another. Everyone thought the money could be given.

'Yes, you can have what you want,' said William. 'The whole school will enjoy seeing the crocuses in the early spring, and it is quite fair that the money should come out of the school box. Find out how much the bulbs will be, Elizabeth, and we shall be very pleased to give you the money. Also, I would like to say that the whole school appreciates the way that you and John work at our garden.'

Elizabeth blushed with pleasure. This was quite unexpected. She sat down with a word of thanks. John grinned in delight at her. 'What did I tell you?' he whispered. 'You can always trust William and Rita to be absolutely fair!'

'Any complaints or grumbles?' asked Rita. A small boy got up promptly. He was a cheeky-looking child, and had his complaint all ready.

'I should like to make a complaint about Fred White,' he said. 'He's always borrowing my things and never giving them back.'

'That's telling a tale, not making a proper complaint,' said William at once. 'Go to your monitor to decide silly little things of that sort. Who is your monitor?'

'I am,' said a boy called Thomas.

'Well, please explain carefully the difference between telling tales and making a genuine complaint,' said William. 'We only decide serious things at this Meeting.'

'Any more complaints?' asked Rita. A boy called William Peace got up. He was in the form below Elizabeth, a serious-faced boy.

'I have a small complaint to make,' he said. 'I learn the violin and I see that my practice-times have been altered to the times when my form goes for a Nature ramble. I belong to the Nature Society, and I hate to miss the rambles. May the time of one of them be altered?'

'It would be quite easy,' said William. 'Discuss it with Mr Lewis, the music-master, and see if there is anyone who can change practice-times with you.'

'Thank you,' said the boy, and sat down. There were no more complaints. Kathleen did not get up and say anything at all, though the others in her form were almost sure that she would complain about Jenny. They did not know that the girl was going to punish Jenny in her own way.

'The Meeting is dismissed,' said William, and the school filed out, chattering as soon as the children got to their various common-rooms. Elizabeth went to John.

'It's good that we can have the money for the crocuses, isn't it?' she said, with her eyes shining. 'We'll go down to the town tomorrow, John, and see how much they are. I'm longing to plant them, aren't you? October is the right month. They will look so lovely in the springtime.'

'Elizabeth, I wish you knew how much nicer you look when you are all happy and smiling like that,' said John. 'It is so horrid when you frown and sulk.'

'You're always lecturing me, John!' said Elizabeth. But she was glad all the same that John was pleased with her. Alas! He was not going to be pleased with her for long!

9 Kathleen plays some tricks

Kathleen did not change her mind about paying back Elizabeth and Jenny. She began to play all kinds of mean little tricks on them, and she played them so cleverly that they did not guess she had done them.

She slipped into the classroom after tea when there was no one there and went to Jenny's desk. She knew that Jenny had written out her French homework very carefully indeed, and she had seen her put the book back into her desk.

Kathleen took out the book and opened it at the place where the work had been done. She dipped a pen in the ink – and then she made three large blots on the page by shaking the pen hard!

She looked at it. The page was dreadful. Jenny would get into trouble, no doubt about that! She waited until the blots were dry and then shut the book. She slipped it into the desk and ran back to the common room. She saw Jenny there and gave her a sly look. 'Ah, wait, Jenny! You'll have a shock tomorrow,' thought Kathleen.

Elizabeth was in the room too, putting one of her favourite gramophone records on. Kathleen wondered what she could do to her. She sat and thought for a while, then quietly got up. She slipped out of the room and put on her coat. It was dark outside, and she went out of the garden door into the school grounds.

She went to where Elizabeth kept her spade, fork, and

trowels. John always insisted that every tool used should be cleaned till it was bright and shining, before it was put away. Elizabeth was always particular about this, for she knew that well-kept tools did good work.

Kathleen took down the garden tools. She carried them outside, and went to a place where she knew that the earth was damp and muddy. She dug the tools into the wet soil and made them very dirty indeed.

Then she carried them back to the shed and put them into a corner. She shone her torch on to them. They were brown with mud. John would be furious when he found them – and as they were the ones that Elizabeth always used, he would be sure to think that she had been careless.

'Well, I'll soon teach Jenny and Elizabeth that it doesn't pay to be horrid to me!' thought Kathleen to herself, as she went back to take off her coat. 'They deserve to be punished! They've been mean to me. Now I'm being mean back to them. Serves them right!'

She went back to the common room. She couldn't help feeling rather victorious somehow, and she longed for the next day to come, so that she might see her two enemies getting into trouble.

The first one to get into trouble was poor Jenny. Mam'zelle asked Kenneth to collect the French books and Jenny gave hers up without even opening it. Mam'zelle set the class some translation to do, and then opened the French exercise books to correct them.

When she came to Jenny's and saw the three enormous blots across the page, blotting out some of the sentences, she threw up her hands in horror.

'What is this?' she cried. 'Whose book is this?' She looked quickly at the name, and gazed across at Jenny in astonishment.

'Jennifer Harris! How can you give in work like this! It is shocking!'

Jenny looked up in surprise. What *could* be the matter with her work? She had done it quite carefully. 'Why, Mam'zelle!' she said. 'Is there something wrong?'

'Jenny, my child, you do not belong to the kindergarten!' cried Mam'zelle, holding up the book for Jenny to see. 'Look at this page! Is it not disgraceful? You know that you should have written out all this work again – work from this form cannot be given in covered with blots. I am truly ashamed of you!'

Jenny stared in the greatest surprise at her book. She knew quite well she hadn't made any blots at all. It couldn't be her book!

'That's not my book, Mam'zelle,' she said. 'It can't be. I didn't make any blots at all. I would never give in work like that.'

'Jenny, I am not blind as a bat!' cried Mam'zelle, beginning to get excited. 'I read your name here, see – Jennifer Harris. It is most certainly your book. And if you did not make these blots, how did they come? Blots do not make themselves, as you very well know.'

'I simply can't imagine how they came,' said poor Jenny, really puzzled now. 'Honestly I can't, Mam'zelle, I'm most awfully sorry. I'll do the work again.'

'And you will be more careful in future,' said Mam'zelle, calming down. Jenny was upset and puzzled. She supposed that in some way she must have made the blots without noticing them, just as she shut the book. She did not see Kathleen looking at her with a spiteful gleam in her eyes. Kathleen was delighted at the success of her trick. She would play a few more on Jenny very soon!

There was half an hour that afternoon for any child to go for a walk, practise lacrosse, or do gardening. Elizabeth chose to go to the garden. There was one piece she hadn't quite been able to finish digging the day before. She could just finish it in the time.

So off she skipped, and called out to John who was already digging hard. But John did not look at all pleased with her.

'Elizabeth, you did do some digging and forking yesterday, didn't you?' he called.

'Rather!' said Elizabeth, stopping beside him. 'I used nearly all my tools, I was so busy. What's the matter, John? You look cross.'

'I *am* cross,' said John. 'Go and get your tools and you'll see why.'

Elizabeth couldn't *think* what he meant. She rushed off to the shed – and stopped in surprise and dismay when she saw her tools. They were all muddy and dirty! Not one of them shone bright and silvery. What a very extraordinary thing!

She went outside, carrying them with her. 'John!' she said. 'I'm quite sure I cleaned them as usual yesterday when I put them away.'

'You can't have,' said John in a cold sort of voice. 'Tools don't get dirty at night by themselves, Elizabeth. Have some sense.'

'I've got plenty!' cried Elizabeth. 'And my sense tells me that if I *did* clean them, which I know I did, it's not *my* fault that they're dirty now.'

'Well, don't let's argue about it,' said John. 'I'd have thought a lot more of you, Elizabeth, if you'd owned up, and said you'd forgotten just for once. It's not like you to say you did a thing, when you didn't.'

'John!' cried Elizabeth, shocked. 'How can you say such a

thing about me! I'm never afraid of owning up. You know that. I tell you I *did* clean the tools.'

'All right, all right,' said John, going on with the digging. 'I suppose they all walked out of the shed in the middle of the night and went digging by themselves and forgot to have a wash and brush-up afterwards. We'll leave it at that.'

The two children dug in silence. Elizabeth was puzzled, upset, and angry. She hated to think that John didn't believe her, and yet her common sense told her that it really did look as if she had forgotten to clean her tools. It was horrid to have John cross with her. She didn't know what to do.

'John,' she said at last, 'I really do think I cleaned the tools, but if I forgot, I'm very sorry. I've never forgotten before. I won't forget again.'

'All right, Elizabeth,' said John, lifting his honest brown eyes to hers. He smiled at her, and she smiled back. But in her secret heart she was very puzzled indeed.

Kathleen had been waiting about by the garden shed to see what would happen. She was pleased when she saw that John was cross with Elizabeth. She went away, planning to do something else to get Elizabeth into trouble. What should she do next? Perhaps in a day or two she would dirty the tools again. She had better not do that too soon, though, in case Elizabeth began to suspect a trick.

She decided to take two or three of Elizabeth's books and hide them somewhere. Miss Ranger would be cross if they couldn't be found. So once again Kathleen slipped into the classroom, and this time she went to Elizabeth's desk. She took out her geography exercise book, her arithmetic book, and her history book. She slipped out of the room with them and went to a cupboard outside. On the top were kept old maps. Kathleen stood on a chair and threw the books right on the very top, among the old maps. Nobody was about to see her. She quickly put back the chair, and went away.

And now, what should she do to Jenny? The naughty girl frowned, and thought hard. Then she smiled to herself. She would take two of the white mice and put them into Miss Ranger's desk! That would be marvellous! Miss Ranger would be quite sure to think that Jenny had put them there herself. Nobody would know who had done it.

To do this Kathleen had to wait till the next morning. She planned to get the mice before breakfast. No one would be about then. She lay in bed that night thinking of what Miss Ranger would say when she opened the desk and found the mice.

She was up early the next morning. Nora was surprised, for Kathleen was usually one of the last out of bed. 'Hallo, turning over a new leaf?' she said.

Kathleen didn't answer. She slipped downstairs five minutes before the breakfast-bell went, and ran to the big shed where the pets were kept. She went to the cage of white mice. She had with her a little box, and it took her only a second or two to pick up two of the tiny white mice and slip them into the box. Then she hurried to her classroom with them. She lifted up the lid of Miss Ranger's desk.

She opened the box – and out scurried the white mice into the desk. Kathleen shut down the lid. What a surprise Miss Ranger and Jenny were going to get!

10 *Excitement in class!*

The first lesson that morning was arithmetic. Miss Ranger explained a new kind of sum to the class, and they listened hard.

'Now get out your books and we will do a few of these sums,' said Miss Ranger, beginning to put down a few on the blackboard. 'You should all be able to do them correctly, but if anyone hasn't quite understood what I have been saying, ask me first, before you begin the sums.'

Elizabeth opened her desk to get out her arithmetic exercise book. It wasn't on the top of the pile, where she usually put it. She hunted through her desk. How funny! The book wasn't there at all. Where could it be?

'Elizabeth! How much longer are you going to have your head in your desk?' asked Miss Ranger.

'I can't find my book,' said Elizabeth.

'Well, you had it yesterday,' said Miss Ranger. 'Did you take it out of the classroom?'

'No, Miss Ranger,' said Elizabeth. 'I hadn't any arithmetic homework to do. I just put the book back when I'd finished with it yesterday morning. But it really isn't here.'

'Take some squared paper from the shelf in the cupboard,' said Miss Ranger. 'We can't wait all morning for you to find the book.' So Elizabeth took some squared paper and did her sums on that, thankful that she hadn't got into trouble. She simply could *not* imagine where her book could be! She kept on and on thinking about it.

Kathleen wondered what would happen when Elizabeth couldn't find the other books! She was also longing for Miss Ranger to open her own desk and find the mice. But Miss Ranger had no reason to open her desk in the arithmetic lesson. So the mice remained undisturbed. They had curled up in a corner and gone to sleep.

The next lesson was French, and after that came geography. Miss Ranger wanted a map drawn, and the girls got out their exercise books. And once again Elizabeth couldn't find hers.

'Well, really, Elizabeth, you are surely not going to tell me that your geography book is lost, too!' said Miss Ranger impatiently.

'Miss Ranger, I just can't understand it, but it's gone,' said Elizabeth, putting her head above the desk-lid to speak to Miss Ranger.

'It is very careless of you to lose both books,' said Miss Ranger. 'I am not pleased, Elizabeth. Perhaps I had better look through your desk myself to make quite sure that they are not there. I can't imagine that you could lose *two* of your exercise books, when you say you did not even take them out of the classroom!'

But not even Miss Ranger's sharp eye could see the missing books, and she went back to her own desk. Robert was pleased to see Elizabeth getting into trouble. As for Kathleen, she was so delighted at the success of her mean trick that she did not dare to look at either Elizabeth or Jenny in case they saw how glad she was.

'I will give you some map-paper, and you must pin the map you draw into your book, when it is found again,' said Miss Ranger. She lifted up the lid of her desk to get some blank drawing-paper – and awoke the two mice!

With squeals and squeaks they raced round the desk in fright, jumping over rubbers and books and rulers. Miss Ranger stared at them in amazement and anger.

She was about to shut down the desk and leave the mice there, when they both leapt out, ran down Miss Ranger's skirt and tore across the floor. All the girls and boys stared in the greatest astonishment.

Miss Ranger put on a very stern face and looked at the surprised Jenny.

'Jenny,' she said, 'I believe you are the only person in the school who keeps white mice as pets. Do you really think it is a funny joke to put the poor little things into my airless desk in order to play a foolish trick on me?'

Jenny couldn't say a word at first. She really was too amazed to speak. *Were* they her mice? How in the world could they have got into the desk?

'Miss Ranger, of *course* I didn't put them in there!' she said at last. 'Please, please believe me. I wouldn't do such a thing to my little mice. And anyway, you were so decent to me when I came to class with one down my neck that I certainly wouldn't have been mean enough to play a trick on you after that.'

The mice fled all over the room. Jenny watched them anxiously, terrified that they would go under the door and escape – perhaps to get eaten by the school cat!

'You had better try to catch them,' said Miss Ranger. 'We can't have the whole lesson disturbed like this. I can't imagine how they could have got into my desk unless you put them there. I shall have to think about the whole thing. I am very displeased about it.'

Jenny leapt up from her seat to catch the mice. But that was easier said than done. The frightened creatures tore all over the room, hiding under first one desk and then another. Some of the girls pretended to be frightened and squealed whenever a mouse came near to their feet. Elizabeth and Belinda tried to help, but those mice were too nimble to be caught.

And then, to Jenny's great dismay, they squeezed themselves under the schoolroom door, and escaped into the passage outside! Jenny ran to the door and opened it – but the mice had disappeared! Goodness knew where they had gone! The little girl ran down the passage, looking everywhere, but the mice were nowhere to be seen.

Jenny was really fond of her mice. Tears came into her eyes and she brushed them away. But others came, and she did not like to go back to the classroom crying. So she leaned against the passage wall for a minute, trying to fight back her tears. Someone had played a mean trick on her! Someone had tried to get her into trouble! Someone had made her lose two of her pets! It was horrid, horrid, horrid!

Footsteps came down the passage – and who should come round the corner but Rita, the head girl! She was most surprised to see Jenny standing there, crying.

'What's the matter?' she asked. 'Have you been sent out of the room?'

'No,' said poor Jenny. 'It's my white mice. They're gone – and I'm so afraid the school cat will eat them.' She poured out the whole story to Rita. The head girl looked very grave.

'I don't like the idea of somebody trying to get you into trouble like this,' she said. 'You are quite, quite sure you didn't play the trick yourself, Jenny?'

'Oh, Rita – I really couldn't treat my pets like that,' said Jenny earnestly. 'Do believe me.'

'Well, the matter must be brought up at the next Meeting,'

said Rita. 'We'll have to get to the bottom of it. Now go back to your class, Jenny. Cheer up. Maybe the mice will turn up again!'

Jenny went back. Miss Ranger saw her red eyes and did not scold her any more. The bell went for the lesson to stop, and the class put away their books. Break came next. Thank goodness!

Robert bumped into Elizabeth as they went out of the classroom, and she glared at him. 'How many more books are you going to lose?' he asked.

Elizabeth tossed her head and walked off with Joan. But a thought came into her head. Could Robert have taken her books? It really was so very extraordinary that both her arithmetic book *and* her geography book should have gone! She went over to Jenny and pulled her into a corner.

'Do you think Robert has got anything to do with my losing my books and your mice being put into the desk?' she said. 'I know he'd like to get me into trouble.'

'Yes – but why should he get *me* into trouble, too?' said Jenny.

'Oh, he might think that if he played tricks only on *me*, I would guess it was him,' said Elizabeth. 'But if he played tricks on you and anybody else, we might not think it was him at all. See?'

'Well, he must be pretty horrid if he's as mean as all that,' said Jenny, troubled. 'Oh, Elizabeth, I wish I knew who it was. It's so awful having these things happen.'

It was even more horrid when the history lesson came and Elizabeth had to confess to Miss Ranger that that book had disappeared too!

'Elizabeth! This is really peculiar,' said Miss Ranger crossly. 'One book is enough to lose – but *three*! You must have taken them out of the classroom and left them somewhere. You must hunt for them well, and if you cannot find them you must come to me and buy new ones.'

'Oh, bother!' thought Elizabeth in dismay. 'They are fifty pence each. That's one fifty out of my precious two pounds. It's too bad! If Robert has hidden my books I'll pull all the hairs out of his head!'

She said this to Joan. 'No, you won't do anything of the sort,' said Joan. 'You'll report him at the Meeting and let the school judge him. After all, that's what the Meeting is for, Elizabeth – for all of us to help to untangle the difficulties of a few of us. It's much better, too, to let the Jury and the Judges decide for us, because we have chosen them as being the wisest among us. Don't take matters into your own hands, Elizabeth. You're such an impatient person – you'll only do something silly!'

'I wish you wouldn't keep talking to me like that,' said Elizabeth, taking her arm from Joan's. 'You might back me up!'

'I *am* backing you up, if you only knew it,' said Joan with a sigh. 'I would be a poor friend to you if I said, "Go to Robert and pull his hair out," even before you really know for certain whether he is playing these horrid tricks, or not.'

'Well, you've only got to see how pleased he is when I get into trouble to know that he's at the bottom of it all!' cried Elizabeth. 'Oh, if only I could catch him bullying someone again. Wouldn't I love to report him at the very next Meeting!'

Elizabeth hadn't long to wait. She caught Robert the very next day!

11 More trouble

For some time now Robert had not bullied anyone or been unkind, because he really had been afraid of being seen by Elizabeth. He knew that she was watching to catch him and he did not mean to give her any chance to report him again.

But two or three weeks had now gone by and he thought that she no longer bothered to watch. He did not know that she thought he had played the tricks on her and was watching very carefully indeed.

Robert had to go and get some water for his painting after tea. Elizabeth saw him go out of the common room and she looked at Joan.

'Joan! Do you think Robert has gone to take my books again, or do some horrid trick?' she said in a low voice. 'Let's follow him and see.'

So the two girls got up and followed Robert. He went down the passage, and ran down the stairs to the cloakroom where the water taps were. And running round the corner came small, cheeky Leslie, the boy who had complained that another was always borrowing things and not giving them back. He ran full-tilt into Robert, and made him double up in pain.

Leslie giggled. It was funny to see big Robert panting like that! Robert put out a hand and caught him, holding the boy's arm so tightly that it hurt.

'Let me go,' said Leslie.

Robert looked up and down the passage quickly. No one was about. He pulled Leslie into the wash-place and shook him hard.

'How dare you run into me like that!' he demanded. 'And I'll teach you to laugh at me, you little nuisance!'

'Robert, let me go!' begged Leslie again. He knew that Robert was a bully and he was afraid of him.

'Say "I humbly beg your pardon, and I will never, never do such a thing again!"' said Robert.

But Leslie, although he was afraid, was not a coward. He shook his head. 'I'm not going to be as humble as all that!' he said. 'You let me go, you big bully!'

Robert was angry. He shook Leslie hard again. 'You say what I told you to say, or I'll make you sit on the hot-water pipes!' he said.

Hot-water pipes ran all round the wash-place to warm it. Leslie glanced at them fearfully. But he still shook his head.

'No, I shan't beg your pardon,' he said obstinately. 'If you'd been decent to me, as any other of the big boys would have been, I'd have said I was sorry like a shot. Let me go!'

'You'll sit on the hot-water pipes first!' said Robert in a rage, and he dragged poor Leslie towards the pipes. They were not terribly hot, but hot enough to make Leslie shout.

Meantime, where were Elizabeth and Joan? They were just round the corner, listening to all that was said, and when they heard Robert pulling Leslie to the hot pipes they ran into the wash-place at once. Leslie was just shouting.

Robert pulled the little boy off the pipes as soon as he saw Elizabeth and Joan. He went red and looked very angry. To think he had been caught by those interfering girls – and one of them Elizabeth too!

'We've caught you nicely, you horrid boy,' said Elizabeth

scornfully. 'Leslie, we are going to report Robert at the next Meeting. Just see you tell the truth and back us up in what we say.'

'I'll do that all right,' said Leslie. 'I'm not a little coward like some of the others, who didn't dare to complain about Robert when they had the chance! As for Peter, you know why he didn't say that Robert was swinging him much too high, don't you? Robert went to him and threatened him with all kinds of punishment if he dared to say a word against him!'

'I did not,' said Robert angrily, though he knew perfectly well that what Leslie said was true. 'You wait till I get you alone again, that's all!'

'There you are, you see!' said Leslie. 'You would like to do exactly the same thing to me again. But you won't get the chance! I'll report you at the Meeting all right, even if Elizabeth and Joan don't!'

The small boy marched off. Elizabeth turned to Robert. She spoke fiercely. 'I know jolly well that it's you that has been playing those horrid tricks on me and on Jenny,' she said.

'I did not,' said Robert, this time speaking quite truthfully.

'Well, I don't believe you!' said Elizabeth. 'You are mean enough for anything. You're a perfectly horrid boy and I think you ought to be sent away from our school.'

'Just as *you* ought to have been sent away last term, I suppose!' said Robert mockingly. He had heard all about Elizabeth's naughtiness during the summer term. Elizabeth went red.

'Be quiet!' said Joan. 'It was a good deal because Elizabeth wanted to be kind to *me* that she was disobedient and I won't have you sneering at her for that!'

'I shall say what I like,' said Robert, and went off by himself, hands in pockets, whistling as if he didn't care about anything at all.

'Well, now that he knows we know he played those nasty tricks, he won't dare to play any more,' said Elizabeth, pleased. 'So that's something!'

But, of course, it was Kathleen who had tried to get Elizabeth and Jenny into trouble, not Robert – and she saw no reason why she should stop being horrid to the two girls whom she so much disliked. Both girls were pretty, clever, and amusing – three things that poor Kathleen was not – and she was jealous of their shining hair and bright eyes, their good brains and jolly jokes. She wanted to hurt the girls who had the things she hadn't and yet so much wanted to have.

Elizabeth told Jenny that she was sure it was Robert who had taken her mice, and put them in the desk. The mice had never been found again and Jenny had been sad ever since. Her eyes flashed when she heard Elizabeth say that it was Robert who had played the trick.

'And I suppose he blotted my French book too, so that I had to do the work again!' said Jenny angrily. 'And I shouldn't be surprised if he dirtied those garden tools of yours, Elizabeth – I could never understand that, you know.'

'Well, I guess we shan't have any more tricks played on us, because Robert will be afraid we'll tell them all to the Meeting,' said Elizabeth. 'And we will too!'

But next day another trick was played on her and on Jenny too. On Wednesdays their monitor had to look at all their drawers and their hanging-cupboards to see that they were tidy. Nora was very strict about tidiness, and the girls in her dormitory had learnt to be very neat indeed – even

Ruth, who was most untidy by nature, and found it difficult to keep any drawer neat.

'It's awful!' she complained about three times a week. 'I tidy my drawers so well – then I want a handkerchief in a hurry and can't find it, and turn the drawer upside down, and then it's all untidy again!'

Elizabeth and Jenny were quite tidy, and they always made a rule on Tuesday night to tidy everything beautifully so that their chest and cupboard were ready for Nora to inspect the next day. They had done this as usual – so on Wednesday, when Nora went to pull open their drawers and found everything in a most terrible muddle, they were too astonished to say anything.

'Jenny! Elizabeth! What *have* you been thinking of to get your things into such a disgraceful mess!' cried Nora, looking at their drawers. 'Look – everything jumbled up – crumpled, untidy – honestly I've never seen such a mess. And you are usually so tidy, both of you. What have you been doing? Didn't you remember I always looked on Wednesdays?'

'Of course we remembered,' said Jenny. 'And we tidied them last night before we went to bed. Why, you must have noticed us, Nora.'

'I didn't notice,' said Nora. 'I was at the other end of the dormitory.'

The three girls looked into the drawers. Everything was upside down. Elizabeth and Jenny knew perfectly they could never have got their things into that muddle. Somebody had played a hateful trick again, to get them into trouble.

'It's Robert!' burst out Elizabeth. 'He's always playing horrid jokes on us, Nora. He dirtied my tools, and took my books, and put Jenny's mice into Miss Ranger's desk, and . . .'

'My dear girl, it couldn't have been Robert who did this,'

said Nora. 'You know the boys never come into this part of the school. He would have been seen at once, because there is always somebody going up and down the passage outside.'

'Well, it must have been Robert,' said Elizabeth sulkily. 'If you're going to get anyone into trouble, for these untidy drawers, Nora, you ought to go and scold Robert.'

'I'm not going to scold anyone,' said Nora. 'You're neither of you so untidy as all that! I think someone *has* been mean to you. Anyway, tidy your things, for goodness' sake.'

The girls set to work. They were both angry. They did not notice how pleased Kathleen looked. 'Ah,' she thought, 'so Elizabeth and Jenny thought that it was Robert who had played tricks! Good!' Nobody would think it was she, Kathleen, who had done them all. She felt much safer now.

The next school Meeting was not until Friday night. On Thursday something happened that disappointed Elizabeth very much. The Lacrosse Match was to be on Saturday, and she had been practising very hard indeed to be good enough to play in it. Only one of her form was to be chosen for the school team, and Elizabeth felt certain she would be the one.

But when she went to look at the notice-board, on which were pinned notices of matches, rambles, and so on, she found that Robert's name was set down for the match instead of hers!

There it was – 'Robert Jones has been chosen from Form One to play in the Lacrosse Match on Saturday against Kinellan School.'

There was a lump in Elizabeth's throat. She had tried so hard! She did so badly want to play. She was very good, really she was! And now that horrid, hateful Robert had been chosen instead of her. She could really hardly believe it.

'Never mind,' said Joan. 'You'll get a chance next time, I expect.'

'I *do* mind!' said Elizabeth fiercely. 'He will crow over me now. Oh, how I hope that the school Meeting will punish him well and say he's not to play in the match!'

Robert was delighted to see his name down, but for all his pleasure he was really very anxious indeed. He knew Elizabeth and Joan were going to report him at the Meeting and he was not looking forward to that. He was a little coward at heart, and he was afraid.

So when Friday came, Robert looked rather anxious. If only the Meeting were after Saturday, so that he could play in the match first! How marvellous that he had been chosen and not Elizabeth! Serve her right, the interfering girl!

The time for the Meeting came. The children took their places, looking rather solemn, for they knew it was going to be a serious one.

12 A very serious Meeting

Even the smaller children felt rather solemn, as the whole school took their places in the big gym. Leslie had told everyone in his form that he was going to report the big boy, Robert, and some of the younger ones, who disliked Robert very much, had made up their minds that they too would tell about him if they had the chance.

'I should have told the truth about him when I was asked at the other Meeting,' said Peter. 'He did swing me much too high and made me sick – and afterwards he came to me and said he would open the door of my guinea-pigs' cage and let them escape, if I dared to say anything against him. So I didn't dare. But I wish I had now.'

William and Rita looked rather grave as they took their places at the table up on the platform. Rita had told William of the mean tricks that had been played on Jenny to get her into trouble, and the two Judges knew that they might have a rather difficult time trying to get at the bottom of things. Still, Miss Belle and Miss Best, and Mr Johns too, were at the back of the room. They could help if things got too difficult.

Robert looked pale. Elizabeth was red with excitement and so was Jenny. Joan was excited too, though she didn't show it.

The usual business was done with the box of money. The two pounds were given to everyone, and extra was allowed to two children for something they wanted. Then the Meeting got down to the real business of the evening.

'Any complaints or grumbles?' asked William, tapping on the table with his hammer.

Up jumped Elizabeth and Leslie, both together.

'Elizabeth was first,' said Rita. 'Sit down, Leslie. Your turn will come later.'

Leslie sat down. Elizabeth began to speak, her words almost tumbling over one another in her haste.

'William and Rita, I have a very serious complaint to make,' she said. 'It's the same one as Leslie was going to make. It's about Robert.'

'Go on,' said William, with a grave face.

'You will remember that I reported him for bullying Peter,' said Elizabeth. 'And because there wasn't enough proof of that, and because I lost my temper with Robert, the Meeting didn't punish Robert, and made me apologize to him. Well, listen to this!'

'Keep calm, Elizabeth,' said Rita. 'Don't get so excited.'

Elizabeth tried to speak calmly, but she did dislike Robert so much that it was difficult not to sound in a rage all the time.

'Well, William and Rita, Joan and I actually *saw* Robert bullying Leslie,' said Elizabeth. 'He made him sit on the hot-water pipes! And another thing we have found out is that he made Peter promise not to complain about being swung so high. He said he would let all Peter's guinea-pigs out of their cage if Peter dared to say anything against him at the Meeting. I was quite right – he is a horrid bully!'

'Don't call people names like that,' said Rita. 'Wait till the whole Meeting has judged, Elizabeth. Have you anything more to say?'

'Yes, I have,' said Elizabeth. 'And it's this: not only has Robert been unkind to the younger ones, but he has been perfectly horrid to me and Jenny too. He has got us into all kinds of trouble by playing mean tricks on us.'

'What tricks?' asked William, looking very worried.

'Well, he took three of my books and hid them somewhere where I can't find them,' said Elizabeth. 'He took my garden tools and dirtied them so that John scolded me. He put two of Jenny's white mice into Miss Ranger's desk and they escaped, and Jenny never found them!'

'Is that true, Jenny?' asked William.

Jenny stood up. 'It's quite true,' she said. 'I never found my poor little mice again. I don't mind a trick being played on *me*, William, but it's cruel to play it on my pets.'

'Sit down, Jenny,' said William. He spoke to Rita, and then turned to the School again.

'Leslie, stand up and say what you have to say,' he said.

The cheeky little Leslie stood up. He felt rather important. He put his hands in his pockets, and began rather cheekily: 'Well, it was like this . . .'

But William cut him short. 'Take your hands out of your pockets, stand up properly, and remember that this is a serious affair,' he said. Leslie took his hands out at once, and went red. He lost some of his cheeky look, and began to speak in a polite tone. He related exactly what had happened, and the Judges and Jury heard him patiently to the end.

'And now we should like to hear what Peter has to say,' said Rita. The small Peter got up. His knees were shaking again, for he was greatly in awe of the head boy and girl. He stammered as he spoke.

'P-p-please, William and Rita, Robert d-d-*did* swing me too high that time,' he said. 'And I was sick afterwards.'

'Then why did you tell an untruth about it when we asked you?' asked William.

'Because I was afraid to tell the truth,' said poor Peter. 'I was afraid of Robert.'

'You must never be a coward,' said William gently. 'It is much finer to be brave, Peter. If you had been brave and had told the truth, we could have stopped Robert from bullying others. Because you were afraid, you have been the cause of others being ill-treated, and you made us disbelieve Elizabeth, and made her unhappy. Remember to tell the truth always, no matter how hard it seems at the time. We shall all think much more of you if you do.'

'Yes, William,' said poor Peter, making up his mind that he would never be a coward again.

'You could have told your monitor about it, even if you were afraid to tell the Meeting,' said William. 'That is why we choose monitors – because we hope that their common sense will help us. Sit down, Peter.'

Peter sank down, glad that he hadn't to say any more. William looked at Robert, who was sitting looking sulky and unhappy.

'And now, Robert, what have you to say?' he asked. 'Serious complaints have been made against you. Are they true?'

'Only one complaint is true,' said Robert, standing up. He spoke in such a low voice that the Jury could not hear him.

'Speak up,' said William. 'What do you mean – only one complaint is true? Which complaint?'

'It is quite true that I made Leslie sit on the hot-water pipes,' said Robert, 'but anyway they weren't very hot. But I did NOT play any tricks on Elizabeth and Jenny. Not one! Not one!'

'Oooh!' said Elizabeth. 'You did, Robert! I saw how pleased you were each time I got into trouble!'

'Silence, Elizabeth!' said William. 'Robert, you say you did not play the tricks that Elizabeth described. Now you did not tell us the truth last time, when you told us about Peter and the swing. It will be difficult for us to believe you this time, because we shall all think that again you may be telling us untruths to get yourself out of trouble.'

'Well, I *am* telling the truth this time!' said Robert fiercely. 'I didn't play those tricks. I don't know who did – I jolly well know *I* didn't! I don't like Elizabeth, I think she's a horrid, interfering girl, but I'm not mean enough to play tricks like that to get her into trouble – and why should I play tricks on Jenny? I don't dislike Jenny. I tell you, somebody else is to blame for those tricks.'

Most unfortunately for Robert, there was not one person in the school, except Kathleen of course, who believed him. They all remembered that he had told an untruth before, and they felt certain that he was doing so again. William knocked on the table with his hammer, for the children had begun to whisper together.

'Silence!' he said. 'Now, we have a very serious matter to attend to. Three charges have been made against one boy. First, that he bullies smaller children than himself. Second, that he has played mean tricks to get two girls into trouble. Third, that he tells untruths. The Jury and Rita and I are going to discuss the matter to see what must be done about this, and the rest of you can also discuss it among yourselves, so that if anyone has a good idea, they may bring it forward in a few minutes.'

The school began to chatter. The Jury and the Judges talked together in low tones. They all looked extremely serious. Robert sat by himself, for the boys next to him had gone to talk to the children behind. He felt dreadful. Why, oh why had he been stupid enough to bully the younger ones? Why must he always be so unkind to the little ones? Now perhaps he would be sent home and his mother and father would be very angry and upset.

Miss Belle and Miss Best looked very serious too. Mr Johns said a few words to them, and then the three of them waited to see what the Judges would say. They never interfered with the school Meeting unless they were asked to.

After a little while Rita and William knocked on the table for silence. The whole school sat up. Surely the Judges and Jury hadn't decided so quickly! What were they going to say?

'Miss Belle, and Miss Best, and Mr Johns, we feel we would like your help today,' said William gravely. 'Would you please give us your advice?'

'Of course,' said Miss Best, and the three teachers came up on to the platform. And then began a strange talk that was going to make all the difference to Robert's school life!

13 Robert gets a chance

The whole school was now looking very solemn and serious. Not a smile was to be seen anywhere. Everyone stopped talking as the three teachers took their places on the platform, on chairs that the Jury quickly fetched for them.

'The matter had better be openly discussed,' said Miss Belle. 'Let us take one complaint at a time. First of all, this question of bullying the smaller ones. Now, have we ever had any cases of bullying since you became our Judges, William and Rita?'

'No,' said William. 'But I remember there was a case when I was much lower down in the school. Will it be in the Book?'

The Book was a record of all the complaints made by the children, and of how they had been dealt with, and what the results were. It lay on the table, a big brown volume half full of small writing. Each Judge had to enter in a report of the Meetings held, because Miss Belle and Miss Best said that sometime the Book might be a great help. Now William took up the Book and began to look back through the pages.

At last he found what he wanted. 'Here it is,' he said. 'A girl called Lucy Ronald was accused of bullying younger children.'

'Yes, I remember,' said Miss Belle. 'We found out the cause of her bullying. Read it, William, and see what it was. It may help us with Robert.'

William read it quickly to himself. Then he looked up. 'It

says here that it was found out that Lucy had been an only girl for seven years, and then she had twin baby brothers brought to live with her in her nursery,' he said. 'And her mother and father gave all their attention to them, and so did the nurse, so that Lucy felt left out. She hated the babies because she thought that her parents gave them the love they had always given to her.'

'Go on,' said Miss Belle.

'Well, she couldn't hurt the babies because they were never left alone,' said William. 'So she worked off her feelings of dislike and jealousy on other children – she always chose the smaller ones because they couldn't hit back, and because they were small like her baby brothers.'

'And I suppose the habit grew and grew until she couldn't stop it,' said Rita, interested. 'Is that how bullies are made, Miss Belle?'

'It's one of the commonest ways,' said the headmistress. 'But now, we must find out if Robert's fault is caused in the same way.'

The whole school had been listening with great interest to this discussion. Everybody knew what a bully was, and nobody liked bullies at all. The children looked at Robert to see if he was listening too. He was. He gazed at William, and didn't miss a word.

'Well,' said Mr Johns, 'we'll find out if Robert has anything to say now. Robert, have you any brothers or sisters?'

'I've two brothers, five years and four years younger than I am,' answered Robert.

'Did you like them when they were small?' asked William.

'No, I didn't,' said Robert. 'They took up everybody's time, and I didn't have a look in. Then I got ill, and nobody seemed to bother about me as they used to do, and I knew it was because of James and John, my little brothers. Well, when I got better, I just seemed to hate little children, and I began to pinch them and be unkind to them. I pretended they were James and John. I couldn't do it to them because nobody would let me, and I would have got into such a row.'

'And so a bully was made!' said Mr Johns. 'You made war on other children because you couldn't get rid of the two small brothers whom you thought took your place at home! Poor Robert! You make yourself much more unhappy than you make others.'

'Well, people have called me a bully ever since I was about five,' said Robert sullenly. 'So I thought I was one – something that couldn't be helped and that I couldn't stop!'

'Well, it can be helped, and you can stop it yourself,' said Miss Best. 'You see, Robert, once you understand how a bad habit began, and how it grows, you also understand how to tackle it. Now that we know why you became a bully, I am sure that none of us really blames you. It was just unlucky for you. You aren't really a bully – you are just an ordinary boy who took up bullying because you were jealous of two small brothers. You can stop any time, and change to something that is *really* you!'

'I remember being awfully jealous of my little sister,' said Belinda. 'I know how Robert felt.'

'So do I,' said Kenneth. 'It's a horrid feeling.'

'Well, it's quite a natural one,' said Miss Belle. 'Most of us grow out of it, but some don't. Robert just hasn't – but he will now that he sees clearly what has happened. It isn't anything very dreadful, Robert. But doesn't it seem rather silly to you that a boy of your age should be teasing and bullying Peter and Leslie just because years ago a feeling of jealousy grew up in your heart for your two young brothers?

It's time you put all that behind you, don't you think so?'

'Yes, it is,' said Robert, feeling as if a light had suddenly been lit in the darkness of his mind. 'I'm *not* really a bully. I want to be kind to people and animals. I didn't know why I was the opposite – but now that I do know it will be easy to change. I feel different about it already. I'm sorry I was so beastly to other children all these years. But I'm afraid no one will trust me now – they won't help me!'

'Yes, we will, Robert,' said Rita earnestly. 'That is the great thing about Whyteleafe School – that we are all willing to help one another. There isn't a boy or girl in this school who would refuse to help you, or to give you a chance to show that you are quite different from what you have seemed.'

'What about Elizabeth?' said Robert at once.

'Well – we'll ask her,' said Rita. 'Elizabeth, what do *you* think about it?'

Elizabeth got up. Her mind was in a whirl. So Robert the bully wasn't really a bully – he was only a boy who had got a wrong idea about himself because of something that had happened years ago. It seemed very strange. Was it true? She didn't believe that Robert would change! And what about all those horrid tricks that had been played on her and on Jenny?

'Well—' said Elizabeth, and stopped. 'Well – of course I'll help if Robert wants to try. After all, you all helped me last term when I was dreadful. But I can't forgive him for playing those mean tricks on me and Jenny. I think he should be punished for those.'

'I tell you I didn't do them!' burst out Robert.

'Somebody must have done them,' said Rita. 'If Robert didn't do them, who was it? Is the boy or girl brave enough to own up?'

Nobody said a word. Kathleen went red but looked down at the floor. She had begun to feel rather dreadful now that Robert had been accused of her tricks.

'William and Rita, you didn't believe me before when I complained about Robert,' said Elizabeth. 'And I was right. It isn't fair of you not to believe me now. I'm sure I'm right.'

The Jury and Judges talked together. They found it very hard to decide anything. Then William spoke.

'Well, Elizabeth, you may be right. We did not believe you last time – and this time we will not believe Robert. We will try to make things fair between you by saying that you may play in the match tomorrow instead of Robert. Nora says that you were disappointed that you were not chosen.'

'Oh, thank you!' said Elizabeth, thrilled.

Robert stood up. He looked unhappy.

'Very well,' he said. 'I quite see that it's my turn to give way to Elizabeth this time, as she had to apologize to me last time when I told untruths. But I do say again and again that I didn't play those tricks.'

'We won't say any more about that,' said William. 'Now, Robert, we've been talking about how we can help you. Mr Johns says that the best thing we can do for you is to let you take care of something or somebody, so that it's easy for kindness to take the place of unkindness. You love horses, don't you?'

'Oh yes!' said Robert eagerly.

'Well, although your form are not allowed to have anything to do with the horses except ride them, we are going to make another rule just for you,' said William. 'You will choose two of the horses and make them your special care. You will feed them, water them, and groom them. When your class goes riding, you may choose one of the younger children to ride the second horse, and help him all you can.'

Robert listened as if he could not believe his ears. Good gracious! Choose two horses for his own special pets – look after them each day! This was a thing he had always longed to do, for of all animals the boy loved horses best – loved them with all his heart. He felt as if he could weep for joy. He didn't care about not playing in the match now! He didn't care about anything. He felt a different boy.

'Thank you *aw*fully, William,' said Robert in a rather choky voice. 'You can trust me to take care of the horses – and you can bet I'll choose those kids that I've teased, to take out riding first!'

'We thought you'd do that,' said Rita, pleased. 'Let us know at the next Meeting how you've got on, Robert. We shall all want to know.'

'I'll go riding with you, Robert!' called a small boy's voice. It was Peter. He had listened hard to everything that had been said, and in his generous heart he wanted to help Robert. He also felt a little guilty – for he remembered how once he had been jealous of his small sister and had smacked her when no one was looking. Good gracious, he might have turned into an unhappy bully like Robert!

'The Meeting must really break up now,' said Miss Belle. 'It has taken a long time and it is past the bedtime of the younger ones. But I think we all feel tonight that we have learnt something big – and once again you children have the chance of helping one of yourselves. It is grand to be helped – but it is even grander to help!'

'The Meeting is dismissed!' cried William, and knocked on the table with his hammer.

The children filed out, rather serious, but happy and

satisfied. A difficult problem had been solved, and they were pleased.

Only one child was neither happy nor pleased. And that child, of course, was Kathleen! Robert had lost his place in the match because of her. Every child in the school was going to help him – but Kathleen had harmed him.

She was very miserable. But whatever could she do about it?

14 The day of the match

The next day was Saturday, the day of the lacrosse match. Elizabeth woke up early, and looked eagerly at the window. Was it a fine day?

It wasn't very fine. There were clouds across the sky. But at least it wasn't raining. Good! What fun it would be to play in her first match!

'Jenny!' whispered Elizabeth, as she heard the girl move in her bed. 'Jenny! It's the day of the match – and I'm playing instead of Robert!'

Jenny grunted. She wasn't sure if she was very pleased that Elizabeth should crow over Robert like that. Jenny thought Robert should certainly be punished – but crowing over him was another thing altogether.

Kathleen was awake too. She heard what Elizabeth said, and she felt guilty. She had thought that it was fine for another child to take the blame and the punishment for something she herself had done – but somehow she didn't feel like that now. Also, she was angry that Elizabeth should have the pleasure of playing in the match – for she did dislike Elizabeth so very much! What a nuisance everything was!

And what about Robert? Well, Robert also awoke early, and he remembered at once all that had happened the night before. He sat up in bed, his eyes shining, as he thought of the two horses he would choose for his own special care. He felt quite different. It didn't matter now a bit that the whole school knew he had been a bully – because they also knew it wasn't really his fault, and in a week or two he would be able to show them what he really was. What a surprise they would get!

He remembered the lacrosse match, and a little sinking feeling came into his heart as he remembered that Elizabeth was to take his place.

'I'd like to have played in the match,' he thought to himself. 'And it is jolly hard that the Meeting gave me that punishment for something I really didn't do – but I suppose they had to believe Elizabeth this time. I must put up with it and hope that the person who's really playing those tricks will be found out some time. Then everyone will be jolly sorry they punished me for nothing!'

He sat and thought for a while, his chin on his knees. 'Elizabeth is a funny girl. She's so fierce and downright, so keen on being fair and just – and yet she's been awfully unfair to me. She might know I wouldn't play mean tricks like that. I don't like her at all.'

Robert half made up his mind that he wouldn't speak to Elizabeth at all, or have anything to do with her. Then, as he thought of the lovely time he was going to have looking after the horses, his heart softened, and he couldn't feel hard even to Elizabeth! And anyway, he was going to show everyone that he could be kind just as easily as unkind.

'I know what I'll do!' he said to himself. 'I'll go and watch the match – and if Elizabeth shoots a goal I'll cheer like the rest. That will be a hard thing for me to do, but I'll do it just to show everyone I can!'

Robert got up before the others in his dormitory that morning. He slipped out and went to the stables. He would talk to the two horses he was going to care for – and he would go riding over the hills on his favourite. He felt proud and important as he unlocked the stable door and spoke to the stableman.

'Can I talk to Bessie and Captain?' he asked. 'I've got permission to look after them.'

'Yes, I've been told,' said the man. 'All right – but I'll have to oversee your work with them the first week, young man. After that, if you're all right, you can carry on.'

Robert heard running footsteps and looked out into the yard. He saw Leonard and Fanny hurrying to the cowsheds. They were going to milk the cows. They saw him and shouted:

'Hallo, Robert! Have you chosen your horses yet?'

'Rather!' said Robert. 'Come and see the two that are going to be mine! Look – this is old Bess – she's a darling. And this is Captain. Rub his nose.'

Leonard and Fanny looked at the two horses and then they looked at Robert. They stared at him so hard that Robert was puzzled.

'What's the matter?' he said. 'Have I got a smut on my nose, or something?'

'No,' said Fanny. 'But you do look different, Robert. You used to look so horrid – sort of sulky and mean – but now you're smiling and your eyes are all shiny. We're staring because it seems rather strange to see somebody change in a night! Come and see our cows! Would you like a glass of warm milk?'

The children linked their arms in Robert's and pulled him over to the cowsheds, where the patient cows stood waiting to be milked. They chattered and laughed as they went, and Robert felt warmed by their friendly talk and looks. He began to chatter too, and soon he was standing drinking a glass of warm, creamy milk from the first cow.

'This is fun!' he thought. 'I'll see Leonard and Fanny each morning when I come to see my horses. I shall soon make friends!'

In five minutes' time he was galloping over the hills by himself, enjoying the wind in his hair and the bump of the horse's back beneath him. He talked to Bess, and she pricked back her ears to listen. All horses loved Robert. He had never had a great deal to do with them before, and now it seemed to him almost too good to be true to think that he could have as much to do with them as he liked.

'After tea I'll ask young Peter if he'd like to come riding on Captain,' he planned. 'I'll soon make that kid forget all about the teasing I gave him.'

Everyone who met Robert that morning had a grin for him, or a clap on the back. The whole school was keeping its word!

Neither Kathleen nor Elizabeth met him, for both girls were busy. Elizabeth was digging with John in the garden, and Kathleen had gone with some others for a Nature ramble. Elizabeth was chattering to John about the match.

'It's a bit of luck for me that I'm playing, isn't it?' she said. 'I was so disappointed when I saw Robert's name up on the board, instead of mine.'

'I expect Robert is feeling just as disappointed now,' said John, digging hard.

'Well, it serves him right,' said Elizabeth. 'He's been jolly mean to me and Jenny. Think how he dirtied my tools one night, John – and you blamed me for it.'

'I'm sorry I blamed you wrongly,' said John. 'I only hope you are right about Robert, Elizabeth, and that *he* is not being blamed for something he hasn't done either.'

'Well, he's a horrid boy, anyhow,' said Elizabeth. 'I'm

glad he's out of the match. I bet he won't come anywhere near it. He'll be so ashamed that he's not playing after all!'

But that was just where Elizabeth was quite wrong!

The children playing the match had to change into their gym clothes immediately after lunch. The matches usually began at half-past two, so they hadn't a great deal of time. Kinellan School was arriving by bus at twenty-past two, and the Whyteleafe team had to be at the gate to meet them and welcome them.

Elizabeth could hardly eat any lunch, she was so excited. She stole a look at Robert, and saw that he was looking quite happy. Elizabeth pushed her potatoes to the side of her plate.

'Miss Ranger! I just can't eat any more. I'm so excited!'

'Well, for once you may leave what's on your plate,' said Miss Ranger, smiling. 'I know what it feels like to be playing in your very first match.'

Elizabeth rushed off with the others to change. Then she went to welcome the Kinellan team, and take them to the field. They put their clothes in the pavilion there.

'Look – almost the whole School has turned out to watch!' said Elizabeth to Nora, as she saw the children streaming up from the school.

'And there's Robert too!' said Nora, as she caught sight of Robert coming along with the others.

'Where?' asked Elizabeth in surprise. Then she saw him. Good gracious! Robert had come to watch the match he had hoped to play in! He had come to watch somebody play instead of him! The little girl could hardly believe her eyes. She suddenly felt rather small and ashamed. She knew she wouldn't have been able to do such a generous thing if she had been in Robert's place.

'I call it jolly decent of Robert to come and watch you play in his place,' said Nora. 'I think that's a big and generous thing to do. It's funny that a boy able to do a big thing like that should be mean enough to play horrid tricks. It makes me wonder if he really did do them, after all.'

Elizabeth picked up her lacrosse stick. She had felt so sure Robert wouldn't come near the match. She was quite wrong. And now suppose that, as Nora said, Robert hadn't done all the things she thought he had – suppose he was being punished unfairly? And all because of her! It wasn't a very nice feeling.

'Oh, well, never mind! I'm jolly well going to enjoy my first match!' said Elizabeth to herself, and she ran out of the pavilion into the field.

But what a disappointment – it was beginning to rain! The teams stared up into the sky in dismay. Surely the rain wasn't going to be much? Surely it would soon stop? It would be too bad if they couldn't play.

The children all crowded into the pavilion to wait. The rain fell more and more steadily. It pelted down. The clouds became lower and blacker – there really was no hope at all!

'I'm afraid the match is off,' said Mr Warlow. 'Go to the gym and we'll arrange games for the visiting team.'

The children ran helter-skelter to the school. Elizabeth ran too, sadly disappointed. It was too bad! Her very first match, and the rain had spoilt it!

A voice spoke in her ear. 'Elizabeth! Bad luck! I'm sorry!'

The girl turned – and saw that it was Robert who had spoken! He had run off to join the others, so she couldn't answer. Elizabeth stood still, astonished. *Robert!* Fancy *Robert* saying that! She simply couldn't understand it.

'Elizabeth! Do you want to be soaked to the skin?' cried

Miss Ranger's voice. 'What are you doing standing out there like that? Come along at once, you silly child!'

And into the school with the others Elizabeth went, very much puzzled, and not knowing quite what to do about it!

15 Kathleen owns up

Everybody was disappointed that the match was off, especially the players themselves.

The rain poured down all the afternoon. Mr Johns and Miss Ranger got some games going in the gym, and the visitors enjoyed themselves thoroughly.

Joan was sorry for Elizabeth's disappointment. She slipped her arm through her friend's. 'Elizabeth, never mind! There's another match next Saturday. Maybe you'll be able to play in that instead.'

'Perhaps,' said Elizabeth. 'But it really *is* bad luck that it rained today. I've been practising so hard, and really I'm getting quite good at catching the ball and shooting at goal!'

'I guess Robert was pleased that it rained so that you couldn't play,' said Joan.

'Well, Joan, that's the funny part – he was there to watch – and when it rained and we all went off the field, he came up and said it was bad luck and he was sorry,' said Elizabeth. 'I really was surprised. And somehow I felt rather mean.'

'Wait till he plays a few more tricks, then you won't feel so mean!' said Joan.

But no more tricks were played. Kathleen hadn't the heart to think of any more. She had seen somebody else publicly punished for her own wrong-doing, and she was beginning to despise herself. She hated Jenny and Elizabeth, but it was a miserable sort of feeling now, not a fierce red-hot feeling.

'I'm a dreadful person!' thought Kathleen in despair. 'I'm plain and spotty and pale. I'm dull and slow, and now I'm mean and deceitful and cowardly! That's the worst of beginning to do horrid things – they make you feel horrid yourself, and then you can't ever be happy any more. I'm not fit to be at a school like Whyteleafe, where the children are happy and jolly – and where even a boy like Robert, who's been hateful to others, can turn over a new leaf and begin again!'

Poor Kathleen! It had seemed such fun, and so clever, at first, to think out nasty little tricks to get Jenny and Elizabeth into trouble – but now that she had found that mean ways make a mean person, she hated herself.

'And it's much worse to hate yourself than it is to hate somebody else,' thought Kathleen. 'Because you can never get away from yourself. I wish I was a happy honest sort of person like Nora or John.'

Kathleen was really unhappy. She went about looking so miserable that the girls felt sorry for her.

'Don't you feel well?' asked Elizabeth.

'I'm all right,' said Kathleen, and walked off with her head drooping like a sad little dog.

'What's up, Kathleen? For goodness' sake, smile a bit!' cried Belinda. 'You're enough to turn the milk sour! Have you had bad news from home, or something?'

'No,' said Kathleen. 'I just don't feel like smiling, that's all. Leave me alone.'

Her work was so bad that Miss Ranger began to be worried. What in the world could be the matter with the girl? She looked as if she was worrying about something. Miss Ranger managed to get Kathleen alone for a few minutes, and spoke to her gently.

'Kathleen, my dear – is there anything wrong? Your work has gone to pieces this week, and you look so miserable. Can't you tell me what's wrong? I may be able to help.'

Kathleen felt the tears coming into her eyes when she heard Miss Ranger speaking to her so kindly. She turned her head away.

'Nobody can help,' she said in a funny muffled voice. 'Everything's gone wrong. And nothing and nobody can put it right.'

'My dear child, there are very few things that can't be put right, if only you will give somebody a chance to help,' said Miss Ranger. 'Come now, Kathleen – what's wrong?'

But Kathleen wouldn't tell her. She shook her head obstinately, and Miss Ranger gave it up. She could not like Kathleen, but she felt very sorry for her.

Then Kathleen made up her mind to do a very foolish thing. She would run away – right away home – but first she would tell Elizabeth and Jenny all she had done. She would confess to them, so that Robert would be cleared of blame. She could at least do that. She wouldn't despise herself quite so much if she owned up.

'Though it will be awfully difficult,' thought poor Kathleen. 'They will look at me in such a horrid way – they will call me names – and everyone in the school will know how awful I have been. But still, I shall have run away by then, so I shan't mind.'

That evening, after tea, Kathleen went up to Jenny. 'Jenny,' she said, 'I want to speak to you and Elizabeth alone. Where's Elizabeth?'

'She's in the gym,' said Jenny, surprised. 'We'll go and get her. What do you want, Kathleen?'

'I'll tell you when Elizabeth is with us,' said Kathleen.

'We'll go into one of the music practice-rooms. We'll be alone there.'

Very much puzzled, Jenny went with Kathleen to find Elizabeth. They soon found her and called her. Elizabeth went with them, surprised and rather impatient, because she had been having some fun with Belinda and Richard.

Kathleen closed the door and faced the other two. 'I've got something to say to you both,' she said. 'I've been very unhappy, and I can't bear it any more, so I'm going to go home. But before I go I want to own up to something. Don't blame Robert for all those tricks – *I* did them all!'

Elizabeth and Jenny stared at Kathleen as if they couldn't believe their ears. *Kathleen* had done all those things – hidden the books, taken Jenny's mice, dirtied the garden tools, muddled the drawers? Oh, the horrid, horrid creature!

'I knew you would look at me like that,' said Kathleen, tears beginning to trickle down her cheeks. 'I expect I deserve it. But before I go, I'd like to tell you something else. You're both pretty and jolly clever, and everyone likes you. I'm plain and pale and spotty and dull, and I can't help it. But you don't know how I'd *like* to be like you! I envy you, and I can't help disliking you because you're all the things I'm not. You were very unkind once, Jenny, when you imitated Mam'zelle and me having a quarrel, but . . .'

'I'm sorry about that,' said Jenny at once. 'I didn't know you'd come into the room. I don't wonder you wanted to pay me out for that, Kathleen. But you shouldn't have got Elizabeth into trouble, too.'

'Well, I've paid myself out, too!' said Kathleen. 'I don't like myself any more than *you* like me. I know I'm simply horrid, and that's why I'm going home. My mother loves me, even though I'm not as pretty and nice as other girls are. And she will perhaps understand and forgive me for running away.'

There was a silence. Elizabeth and Jenny simply did not know what to say. They were shocked at Kathleen's confession – and Elizabeth especially felt very angry because she had blamed Robert for things he hadn't done, and that was terrible.

'Well, Kathleen, all I can say is it's a jolly good thing you had the sense to own up,' said Jenny at last. 'I think more of you for that. But, my goodness, you're a spiteful mean person, I must say! Don't you think so, Elizabeth?'

'Yes, I do,' said Elizabeth. 'And you've made me get Robert into trouble – and I'll have all that to put right. I wish to goodness you'd never come to Whyteleafe School, Kathleen!'

'I wish it too,' said Kathleen in a low voice. 'But I shan't be here much longer!'

She opened the door and slipped away down the passage. She went to the stairs and ran up, tears pouring down her face. She had owned up – and it had been even worse than she had expected! Now she would get her things and go.

Elizabeth stared at Jenny, and the two were just going to talk about Kathleen's confession, when Joan came along. 'Hallo!' she said in surprise. 'What are you two doing here looking so fierce? What's happened?'

Elizabeth poured everything out to Joan. 'Now don't you think Kathleen is a spiteful girl?' she cried. 'I'd never have thought anyone could be so horrid.'

Joan looked thoughtful. She remembered how unhappy and lonely she herself had once been in the summer term, when everything had gone wrong. She could guess how

Kathleen felt. And how very miserable she must be to think of running away!

'Look here,' said Joan, 'don't think of how mean and spiteful Kathleen's been. Think instead of how it must feel to be plain and jealous and dull, as Kathleen is, and to be unhappy and ashamed as well! Elizabeth, you were helped last term, and I was helped too. I'm going to help Kathleen! She hasn't been mean to me, so I don't feel angry about things as you do. I just feel sorry.'

She ran out of the room. Jenny looked at Elizabeth. They both knew at once that Joan was right. They had been thinking of themselves, and not of a miserable girl who needed comfort and help. 'We'd better go along too,' said Jenny.

'Wait till Joan's had time to say a few words,' said Elizabeth. 'She's awfully good at that sort of thing, you know. I sometimes think she's almost wise enough to be a monitor!'

'Well, we certainly are *not*,' said Jenny. 'I can't imagine how this can be put right, Elizabeth. I really can't.'

Meanwhile, Joan ran up the stairs to her dormitory. Kathleen was there, putting on her hat and coat, and packing a few things into a small case. Joan went straight up to her.

'Kathleen! I've heard all about it! You were brave to own up. Wait till Jenny and Elizabeth have had time to get over it, and they'll forgive you and be friends. They are kind and generous really, you know – just give them time.'

'I can't stop at Whyteleafe,' said Kathleen, putting on her scarf. 'It's not only that I've made enemies. I feel that everybody thinks I'm so awful. Look at your hair, all shiny and nice – mine's like rats' tails! Look at your bright eyes and red cheeks, and then look at me! I'm a sort of Cinderella!'

'Do you remember how Cinderella changed one night?' said Joan, taking Kathleen's hand. 'She sat in the cinders and moped, and maybe she looked just as plain and miserable as you do. But it wasn't just beautiful clothes and a coach that made her so different all of a sudden! Don't you think she smiled and looked happy, don't you think she brushed her hair till it shone? What a silly girl you are, Kathleen! Do you know that you look sweet when you smile?'

'I don't,' said Kathleen obstinately.

'Well, you do,' said Joan. 'Your eyes light up then, your mouth turns up, and you get a dimple in your left cheek. If you smiled a lot more, you wouldn't be plain long. Nobody's ugly when they smile. Haven't you noticed that, Kathleen?'

'Perhaps you are right about that,' said Kathleen, remembering how sweet her mother always looked when she smiled and was happy. 'But I never feel very much like smiling.'

Footsteps came up the passage and Elizabeth and Jenny came into the room. They went up to Kathleen.

'We weren't very nice to you just now,' said Jenny. 'We're sorry. Don't run away, Kathleen. We'll forgive you and forget all you did to us.'

'But Robert would have to be cleared from blame,' said Kathleen, 'and that means everything going before the school Meeting. I'm sorry – but I'm not brave enough for that!'

The girls looked at one another. Yes – of course the matter would have to be discussed there!

'So I'm going!' said Kathleen. 'I'm a coward, I know. But I can't help that. Where's my case? Goodbye, all of you – don't think too unkindly of me, *please*!'

16 Kathleen runs away

Kathleen picked up her case and went out of the room. Joan ran after her and took hold of her arm.

'Kathleen! Don't be an idiot! You just can't run away from school! It's impossible!'

'It's not impossible,' said Kathleen. 'I'm doing it! Don't try to stop me, Joan. I'm going to walk down to the station to get the train.'

She shook off Joan's hand and ran down the passage. It wasn't a bit of good going after her. She had made up her mind, and nothing would stop her. The three girls stared at her.

'I feel simply awful about this,' said Jenny suddenly, in a trembling voice. 'I wish I hadn't imitated Mam'zelle and Kathleen that evening. That's what began all the trouble.'

'What are we going to do?' said Joan in a troubled voice. 'We'll have to report that Kathleen has run away. But I can't help feeling that it's no good trying to stop her in any way, because honestly I wouldn't want to face the school Meeting as she would have to do when everything comes out. She'd probably run away after that, if she didn't now! She's not a brave person at all.'

Just then Nora came by. She was surprised to see the three girls standing at the door of their dormitory, looking so worried.

'What are you here for?' she asked. 'Didn't you know that

the concert is beginning in a minute? You'd better hurry. *Why* are you all looking so solemn? Has anything happened?'

'Well, yes,' said Elizabeth. 'An awful lot has happened. We don't know what to do about it. It's dreadful, Nora.'

'Good gracious! You'd better tell me about it then, as I'm your monitor,' said Nora.

'I think we'd like to,' said Jenny. 'Don't let's go to the concert, Nora. Let's go to the common room. It will be empty now and we can tell you what's happened.'

Once a week a concert was given by those children who learnt the piano, the violin, singing or reciting, and usually most of the forms attended, for it was fun to hear their own forms playing or singing. So the common room was empty when the four girls walked into it.

Jenny told the tale. She told it from the very beginning, and although she went red when she related how she had imitated Mam'zelle and Kathleen, she did not miss out anything. She was a truthful, honest girl, willing to take her fair share of any blame. Nora listened gravely.

'Poor old Kathleen!' she said. 'She *has* made a mess of things. Well, we've got to do something about it, but I daren't say what. We must find Rita and get her to come to Miss Belle and Miss Best with us.'

'Oh, goodness! Will they have to know?' asked Elizabeth in dismay.

'Of course, idiot! You don't suppose a girl can run away from Whyteleafe without the heads knowing, do you?' said Nora. 'Come on – there's no time to be lost.'

They found Rita in her study. 'Rita! Could you come with us to Miss Belle and Miss Best?' asked Nora. 'A girl in Elizabeth's form has run away, and we think we ought to tell the whole story to the heads.'

'Of course!' said Rita, looking startled. 'We'd better take William along too. It's a thing he probably ought to know about, and it will save time if he comes now.'

So in a few minutes six people were outside the drawing-room where the two headmistresses were sitting writing letters. Rita knocked.

'Come in,' said a quiet voice, and in they all went. Mr Johns was there too, and the three teachers looked surprised to see such a crowd of children appearing.

'Is anything the matter?' asked Miss Belle at once.

'There is, rather,' said Rita. 'Elizabeth, tell the story quickly.'

So Elizabeth told it all, and when she came to where Kathleen had packed a small case and gone down to the station, Mr Johns jumped up at once.

'I must go after her,' he said. 'I hope I shan't be too late.'

'But the train will have gone!' said Nora.

'They have been altered this month,' said Mr Johns. 'The one Kathleen went to catch doesn't run now – it's an hour later. If I go quickly, I can just get the child. Come with me, Rita.'

The two of them went out of the room, and in a moment or two the front door banged. They were gone. Elizabeth hoped and hoped that they would be able to catch poor Kathleen before she went home. Now that the heads knew everything she felt happier. Grown-ups always seemed to be able to put things right!

'Two things need to be put right, as far as I can see,' said Miss Best. 'The first thing is to put Kathleen right with herself, and make her see that running away never solves any difficulty at all, but only makes things worse. She thinks herself a failure, poor child, but no one need ever be that. If we can get that idea out of her head, things won't seem so bad to her.'

'And I know what the second thing is,' said Elizabeth in a low voice. 'It's to clear Robert of blame. I do hate to think I accused him unjustly – and he really has been decent about it. I feel terribly ashamed.'

'I am glad you feel ashamed, Elizabeth,' said Miss Best. 'We all know that you are just and honest by nature, but you will never do anything worthwhile if you rush at things impatiently and lose your temper.'

'No, I know. I'm doing my best to learn that,' said Elizabeth. 'But you've no idea how difficult it is, Miss Best.'

'Oh yes, I have!' said Miss Best. 'I once had a hot temper too!'

She smiled her lovely smile, and the four girls thought what a nice person she was. None of them could really believe that she had ever had a bad temper.

'Now what are we going to do with Kathleen if Mr Johns is able to bring her back?' said Miss Belle. 'I almost think that William and Rita would be the best people to deal with her. She would not be so much in awe of them as she would be of me or of Miss Best or Mr Johns.'

'She said she couldn't possibly face the school Meeting when they knew of her mean tricks,' said Elizabeth. 'She isn't very brave – though sometimes she argues in class in a way I simply wouldn't dare to do.'

'That isn't bravery,' said Miss Belle. 'It's a thing that weak, obstinate people do – they are always so afraid of being thought poor things that they like to draw attention to themselves in some way – by arguing or quarrelling or boasting – anything that will make people listen to them and take notice of them! You will never find strong, wise people quarrelling or boasting or trying to get attention – only the weak ones. It's a sign of weakness of some sort – and in Kathleen's case it meant that she thought herself a failure and was trying to hide it from herself and from the rest of you. Now she can't hide it any more and she has run away – just what you would expect a weak person to do.'

'Things seem sort of different when they are properly explained, don't they?' said Jenny. 'I'd never have mimicked Kathleen as I did if I'd known why she was behaving like that. Now I feel so sorry for her that I'd do anything to get things put right.'

'She's ashamed of her spots, even,' said Elizabeth. 'She's only got them because she eats so many sweets! She eats more than the whole form put together!'

'She looks nice when she smiles,' said Joan. 'I told her so.'

'Good!' said Miss Best. 'It seems to me that if only Kathleen would make herself neater and prettier, and get rid of her spots, poor child, that would be a good beginning. William, do you think you and Rita can manage to get some sense into her head? You have had some difficult problems this term, but I believe you will manage them all right!'

'And what about making her face the school Meeting?' asked William.

'You and Rita must decide that,' said Miss Belle. 'We leave that in your hands. If you think it best not to force her to be brave before she is ready, then you must just clear Robert of blame, and wait until Kathleen is brave enough to own up later on in the term. I am quite sure that if we handle her gently she will do the right thing in the future.'

It was surprising how much better everyone felt already, now that the matter had been plainly discussed and looked into. Kathleen's bad behaviour had grown from a very simple thing – the feeling that she was a failure. If that feeling could be put right, most of Kathleen's troubles would go. And that would be pleasant for everyone!

There came the sound of wheels in the school drive. Then the sound of a car door banging. Surely it must be a taxi! Everybody waited anxiously to see if Mr Johns and Rita had been able to bring back Kathleen – and everyone hoped they had.

Footsteps came down the passage to the drawing-room and the door opened. Only Mr Johns stood there! No Rita, no Kathleen!

'Didn't you find her?' asked Miss Best anxiously.

'Oh yes!' said Mr Johns. 'She was in the waiting-room, poor child, cold and miserable, wishing that she hadn't run away after all! When Rita went in and took her hand, she burst into tears, and came back with us quite willingly. Thank goodness the trains had been altered, and she had had time to think a little. If the train had come in as soon as she had arrived on the platform, she would certainly have gone.'

'Where is she?' asked William.

'Rita has taken her to her study,' said Mr Johns. 'You go too, William. I think you'll be able to help her – let her talk all she likes, and get everything off her chest.'

William went. The four other children got up to go too.

'I'm going to find Robert now,' said Elizabeth. 'That's something *I* must put right – but I'm not going to enjoy it one bit!'

17 Clearing up a few troubles

Elizabeth was angry with herself as she went to find Robert. 'I've done a really awful thing,' she thought. 'I've accused somebody in public of doing a whole lot of mean things and he didn't do one of them. I got him punished – just at a time when he began to try and turn over a new leaf too! Everybody has helped him – and I was the only one who must have made him feel angry and unhappy. I do feel disgusted with myself.'

She couldn't find Robert anywhere. Then she met Leonard and he told her that the boy was out in the stables.

'Bess was limping a bit today,' said Leonard, 'and Robert is out there attending to her with the stableman. I saw him just now when I came in from the cowshed. You know, Elizabeth, Fanny and I see him every morning, and we think he's jolly nice. He's doing all he can to make up to the youngsters for ill-treating them – I can't help admiring him.'

'I admire him too,' said Elizabeth. 'But he won't admire *me* when he hears what I've got to tell him!'

'Why, what's that?' asked Leonard. But Elizabeth wouldn't tell him.

It was dark outside. Elizabeth got her coat and put it on. She slipped out into the garden and went across to the stables. She heard Robert talking to the stableman, and she put her head round the door.

'Robert,' she said, 'can I speak to you?'

'Who is it?' said Robert in surprise. 'Oh, you, Elizabeth. What do you want?'

He came over to her, smelling of horses. It was a nice smell. His hair was untidy and his face was flushed, for he had been rubbing the horse's leg with oil, and it was hard work.

'Robert,' said Elizabeth, 'I made a dreadful mistake about you. It was somebody else who played those tricks, not you.'

'Well, I told you that,' said Robert. 'That isn't any surprise to me.'

'Yes – but, Robert, I told the whole school you'd done them,' said Elizabeth, her voice beginning to tremble, 'and I got you punished. I can't tell you how sorry I am. You've been mean to me, often, and I haven't liked you, but I've been much meaner to you. And I do think you're a brick, the way you came to watch the match and told me it was bad luck it rained. I – I – I think you've been big, and I've been very small.'

'Well, I think you have, rather,' said Robert, taking her hand. 'But *I* haven't been very big, Elizabeth – it was only that I was so happy to think I've been able to change myself, and to have the horses I love, and I really felt I hardly cared about the match – so you see it wasn't very difficult to come and watch, and tell you it was bad luck it rained. But I'm glad you've found out it wasn't my fault that those tricks were played. Who did them?'

'I can't tell you just at present,' said Elizabeth. 'But as soon as I knew, I came to find you to tell you I was dreadfully sorry for what I'd said about you. I'd like you to forgive me.'

'You needn't worry about that,' said Robert, with a laugh. 'People have had to forgive me a lot more than I shall ever have to forgive *you*. Don't let's be silly any more. It's fun being enemies at first, but it soon gets horrid. Let's be friends. Come and ride Captain tomorrow morning before breakfast. I'll ride Bess if her leg is better. And do cheer up – you look all funny!'

'I *feel* all funny,' said Elizabeth, swallowing a lump in her throat. 'I didn't think you'd be so awfully decent to me. I do get wrong ideas about people. Yes, Robert – I'd like to be friends. I'll be up early tomorrow morning.'

Robert smiled at her and went back to Bess. Elizabeth slipped away into the darkness. She stood in the cold wind and thought for a minute or two before she went in. How surprising people were! You thought some of them were so horrid, and believed all kinds of things about them – and then they turned out quite different and you wanted to be friends.

'Well, next time I'll give people a chance before I believe beastly things about them,' said Elizabeth to herself. 'I really must think twice, three times, *four* times before I lose my temper or accuse people of anything. It's so funny – I just hated Robert, and now I simply can't help liking him awfully – and yet he's the same person.'

But Robert wasn't quite the same person. He was different! He thought about Elizabeth too. It was brave of her to come and own up like that. She was a dreadful little spitfire, but he couldn't help liking her. It would be fun to ride with her and go galloping wildly over the hills in the early morning!

And meanwhile, what about Kathleen? Things had not been going too badly for her, for William and Rita had been wise and gentle, though quite firm and resolute. They had let the girl tell them every single thing.

'I felt awful when the train didn't come in,' said Kathleen, crying into her handkerchief, which was already soaking wet. 'I felt as if that was one more thing against me! I couldn't even run away because there wasn't a train!'

'It's a good thing you *couldn't* run away,' said William. 'It's not a very brave thing to do, is it? You can't get rid of troubles by running away from them, Kathleen. They go with you.'

'Well, what else can you do with troubles?' asked Kathleen, wiping her eyes.

'You can look them in the face and find out the best way to beat them,' said Rita. 'You were funny, Kathleen – you were really trying to run away from yourself! Nobody can ever do that!'

'Well, you'd want to, if you were like *me*,' said Kathleen. 'I'm so unlucky. Nothing nice ever happens to me, as it does to other children.'

'And nothing ever will as long as you think and talk like that,' said William. 'It isn't our luck that makes good or bad things happen, Kathleen, it's just ourselves. For instance, you might say that Jenny has plenty of friends, so she is lucky. But she doesn't have friends because she is *lucky* – she has them because she is kind and generous and happy. It is her own self that brings her lots of friends, not her luck.'

'Yes – I see that,' said Kathleen. 'I hadn't thought of that before. But I'm not pretty and happy and generous like Jenny.'

'Well, why not make the best of yourself?' said Rita. 'You have a sweet smile, and you have a dimple that goes in and out, though we don't see it very often. If you brushed your hair one hundred times each night and morning as Jenny does, it would look silky and shiny. If you stopped eating so many sweets, your spots would go; and if only you'd go out for more walks and try to play games a bit harder, you would soon get rosy cheeks and happy eyes!'

'Should I?' said Kathleen, beginning to look more cheerful.

Rita fetched a mirror from the mantelpiece and put it in front of Kathleen's sad, tear-stained face. 'Smile!' she said. 'Go on, smile, you silly girl! Quick! Let me see that dimple!'

Kathleen couldn't help smiling, and she saw her miserable face change in an instant to a much nicer one – and the dimple came in her left cheek.

'Yes,' she said, 'I do look much nicer. But I'm so dull and slow too – and think of the mean, horrid things I've done!'

'You're dull and slow because you're not as healthy as you might be, and you're not happy,' said William. 'Give yourself a chance, do! As for the mean, horrid things you've done – well, you can always make up for those. We all do mean things at times.'

'I'm quite sure you and Rita don't,' said Kathleen. 'And anyway, William and Rita – please, please don't make me stay at Whyteleafe, because I simply *couldn't* get up in front of the whole school at the next weekly Meeting and say what I'd done, even to clear Robert. I'm a coward. I know I am, so it's no good pretending that I'm not. I shall leave tomorrow morning if you make me do that.'

'We shan't make you do anything,' said William. 'It's no good *making* people do things like that! They must want to do them themselves, if it's to be any good. Well, listen, Kathleen – we'll get Elizabeth to clear Robert of blame, but she shall not say who *is* to blame; but maybe later on you will feel differently about things, and then you can talk to us again.'

'I shall never be brave enough to own up in front of everyone,' said Kathleen. 'But I'll stay at Whyteleafe if I don't need to do that. I've told Elizabeth and Jenny and that was hard enough.'

'It was a good thing you did that,' said William. 'We will see that those children who know that it was you will not tell anyone else. So you need not be afraid that anyone is despising you. Do as Robert has done – turn over a new leaf – and smile as much as you can!'

'I'll try,' said Kathleen putting her wet hanky away. 'I don't *feel* like smiling. I don't even feel like turning over a new leaf. But you've both been so kind to me that I'll try, just to please you.'

'Good!' said Rita and William. Rita looked at her watch. 'It's almost your bedtime,' she said. 'Have you had any supper – or did you miss it?'

'I missed it,' said Kathleen. 'But I'm not hungry.'

'Well, William and I are going to make ourselves some cocoa,' said Rita. 'We are allowed to have our own gas-ring, you know, as we are the head children of the school. Stay and have some cocoa with us – and we've got some good chocolate biscuits too. Even if you are not hungry you will like those!'

In ten minutes' time the three of them were drinking hot cocoa and nibbling chocolate biscuits. William was making jokes, and Kathleen was smiling, her dimple showing in her left cheek. When her bedtime bell went, she got up.

'You *are* kind,' she said, tears coming into her eyes again. 'I won't forget this evening. I'm glad you're the head boy and girl – I think you're fine!'

'Cheer up!' said William. 'You'll find things are never so bad as they seem. Goodnight!'

18 Things are better!

Elizabeth was up early, and went out to the stables. Robert was there, saddling the horses, whistling softly to himself. He was completely happy. He was looking after something he loved, caring for the horses, and getting back from them the affection he gave them.

'It's a lovely warm feeling,' he told Elizabeth. 'I never had it before, because I never had a pet – and anyway, I never much cared for any animal except horses. William and Rita couldn't possibly have thought of anything nicer! It seems strange, doesn't it, that instead of being punished for bullying, I get a marvellous treat like this! And yet it's stopped me from being beastly far more quickly than any punishment would. I just don't want to be horrid now.'

'You can't be horrid to anyone when you're feeling happy,' said Elizabeth wisely. 'I know I can't. I just want to be warm and generous then. Come on – let's go. Oh, Robert, isn't it strange to be friends after being such dreadful enemies!'

Robert laughed as he sprang on to Bess's back. The horse whinnied and tossed her head. She loved to know that Robert was riding her. The two children cantered down the grassy path and then galloped off over the hills. Elizabeth had ridden for years, and rode well. Robert rode well too, and the pair of them enjoyed their gallop tremendously.

They shouted to one another as they rode. Then Elizabeth had an idea.

'I say!' she yelled. 'Will you take Kathleen Peters with you sometimes? She might get red cheeks then!'

'Kathleen! I can't bear her!' shouted back Robert. 'She's an awful girl. Surely you aren't going to be friends with *her*!'

'Well, I am,' cried Elizabeth. 'I don't like her, Robert, any more than I liked you. But I've been so wrong about people lately that for all I know I may get to like her very much. Anyway, I'm going to give her a chance. So will you help?'

'All right,' said Robert. 'She doesn't ride badly. But come too. I really don't think I could bear to go galloping with her by myself. I should be bored stiff! There's one thing about *you* – nobody could ever be bored with you! You're either very, very nice, or very, very horrid!'

'Don't tease me about that,' said Elizabeth, slowing down her horse. 'I'm turning over a new leaf too! I want to be nice always. In fact, when I came back to Whyteleafe this term I had made up my mind to do my very, very best and be as nice as I could. And really, I've made the most awful muddles and mistakes! I know that I shall never be made a monitor!'

'You know, I'd rather like to be,' said Robert. 'It must be a lovely feeling to be trusted and looked up to, and to sit on the Jury's table. Still, we're neither of us ever likely to do that. I made a bad beginning this term – and you were the naughtiest girl in the school last term. My word, you *must* have been bad!'

Robert and Elizabeth were happy when they went in to breakfast that morning. Their cheeks were red with the cold wind, and their eyes sparkled. Elizabeth smiled at Kathleen, who was sitting in her usual place at the table, looking happier but rather nervous.

'Hallo, Kathleen!' said Elizabeth. 'Hallo, everybody! Gosh, I'm hungry! I could eat twenty sausages and twelve eggs!'

'Have you been riding?' asked Kathleen, pushing the toast towards Elizabeth. 'My goodness, you are red! The wind has made you look like a Red Indian!'

Elizabeth laughed. 'It was fun,' she said. 'You should get up early and come riding too.'

'Yes, do,' said Robert. 'You ride well, Kathleen. Why don't you come with Elizabeth and me sometimes? We could gallop for miles!'

Kathleen flushed with pleasure. She smiled warmly and everyone noticed at once how her dimple danced in and out. 'I'd love to,' she said. 'Thanks awfully. I like that horse called Bess best.'

'Do you really?' said Robert in surprise. 'How funny! So do I! She is a perfect darling, honestly she is. You know, she was limping yesterday and I was awfully worried.'

Soon he was telling Kathleen all about Bess and Captain, and Kathleen listened eagerly. She really knew quite a lot about horses, but for once she didn't boast, but listened humbly, glad that someone should speak to her in such a warm and friendly manner. She tried to remember not to let her mouth droop down at the corners in the way that made her so plain, but looked pleasant, and laughed at Robert's jokes.

She had been dreading that breakfast-time. It wasn't going to be easy to face Elizabeth, Jenny, Joan, and Nora, all of whom knew her poor, unhappy secrets. But after all it wasn't a bit difficult. Kathleen couldn't help feeling the warm generosity of the four girls near her, and it made her humble and happy instead of awkward and ashamed.

So breakfast was very pleasant, though some of the form were most astonished to see Robert and Elizabeth so friendly.

'You are a funny girl, Elizabeth,' said Kenneth. 'One day you are enemies and the next you are friends!'

'Last term Elizabeth was *my* bitterest enemy!' said Harry, with a laugh. 'I pinned a notice on her back, and on it was printed "I'm the Bold Bad Girl! I bark! I bite! Beware!" My goodness, how furious you were, Elizabeth!'

'Yes, I was,' said Elizabeth, remembering. 'But it seems rather a funny joke to me now. Let's go and look at the notice-board, Harry. I can see a new notice pinned up there.'

They went across to look at it. There *was* a new notice, rather an exciting one!

'Elizabeth Allen has been chosen to play in the match against Uphill School,' it said.

Elizabeth stared at the notice, her cheeks on fire.

'Goodness!' she cried. 'I've *really* been chosen this time! Last time Robert was chosen, and I was to take his place – but this time *I've* been chosen! I *am* pleased!'

'Yes – and this time it's an Away Match, not a Home Match,' said Harry. 'You'll have the fun of going off in the motorcoach to Uphill School. You *are* lucky!'

'Oh, it's marvellous!' cried Elizabeth, and she danced away to tell Joan and Jenny. Kathleen was with them, and the four were all smiles as they discussed the match.

'If only we could come and watch you shoot a goal!' said Joan, slipping her arm through her friend's. 'I do hope it won't rain this time, Elizabeth.'

'Oh, it couldn't be so unkind!' cried Elizabeth. 'Joan! Kathleen! Come and give me some practice at catching before dinner this morning, will you!'

Kathleen beamed. So few children ever asked her to do

anything. It was lovely to be wanted.

'You really *have* got a nice smile!' said Joan, looking at her. 'Come on – there's the bell. For goodness' sake hurry. I was half a second late yesterday morning and Miss Ranger nearly went up in flames about it!'

Kathleen found herself humming a tune as she ran to get her books. How decent the girls were! It was easy to smile when you were happy. Kathleen had smiled at herself once or twice in the mirror that morning, and really it was simply astonishing what a difference it made to her plain face! She had spoken sternly to herself.

'No more sweets for you! No more greediness! No more silliness at all! Smile and be nice, for goodness' sake!'

And the face in the mirror had smiled back at her, its dimple showing well. Who would have thought that a smile could have made so much difference to anyone?

When school was over that morning, Elizabeth rushed with Kathleen and Joan to get lacrosse sticks to practise catching and shooting. They bumped into Robert as they ran down the passage.

'Hey! What hurricanes!' said Robert. 'Whatever are you in such a hurry for?'

'We're going to give Elizabeth some practice at catching,' cried Joan. 'Didn't you know she has been chosen to play in the match against Uphill School on Saturday?'

'No – I didn't know,' cried Robert, his face falling for a moment, for he was bitterly disappointed. He had very much hoped that he would be chosen himself – for after all he *had* been chosen before, and Elizabeth had taken his place, though the match hadn't been played, as it happened. Now Elizabeth was chosen.

'Well, I mustn't be small about this,' he thought. 'I'll have plenty of chances to play in matches later on, I expect.' He shouted after Elizabeth:

'Good for you, Elizabeth! Wish I could watch you shoot a goal!'

He went off. Elizabeth turned to Joan. 'That was nice of Robert, wasn't it?' she said.

Joan looked at her. 'Did you see his face when he heard that you had been chosen?' she said.

'No, why?' asked Elizabeth in surprise.

'He looked awfully disappointed, that's all,' said Joan, getting out her lacrosse stick. 'I expect he hoped that he might get the chance this time, as he was prevented last time by the school Meeting.'

'Oh,' said Elizabeth. She got her lacrosse stick too, and the three girls went out in the playing-field. Soon they were throwing the ball to one another, and then Kathleen went into goal and let the other two shoot the ball at her.

But Elizabeth didn't enjoy the practice very much after all. She was thinking of Robert. She had prevented him from being able to play in the match last Saturday – and she couldn't help feeling that it wasn't very fair that she should be playing *this* Saturday. 'Though, of course, I didn't play last Saturday because of the rain,' she said to herself. She caught the ball and threw it to Joan.

'But I *would* have played if it hadn't rained, and then I would have played two Saturdays running, and Robert wouldn't have played once – though he really was chosen last week. I'm beginning to feel uncomfortable about it. I think I'll go and ask Nora what she thinks.'

So after dinner Elizabeth went to find Nora. The monitors were always ready to hear anyone's troubles, and the children went to them readily.

'Nora! Do you think I ought to let Robert play in the match on Saturday instead of me?' asked Elizabeth. 'You know it was because of me that he was told he mustn't play last Saturday. Well – I know he's disappointed about this. Shall I go to Eileen and tell her to let Robert play instead?'

'Yes,' said Nora at once. 'It's only fair, Elizabeth. Good for you! I'm glad you thought of that. There's one thing about you, you do like to be just, and that's a great thing!'

'I'll go and tell Eileen now,' said Elizabeth, and off she sped before she could change her mind. It was very disappointing for Elizabeth – but it would be a nice surprise for Robert!

19 A peaceful week

Eileen was in the gym. She was very good at gym and games of all kinds. She was busy doing some exercises, but she stopped when she saw that Elizabeth wanted to speak to her.

'What do you want, Elizabeth?' she asked.

'Eileen, would it be all right if Robert played in the match on Saturday instead of me?' asked Elizabeth. 'You see, I've discovered that he didn't do the things I accused him of at the last Meeting – so I think it would be only fair if I let him have the chance of playing this time.'

'Right!' said Eileen, taking out a notebook and writing something down in it. 'I'll see to that. As you say – it's only fair, Elizabeth. I'm sorry you can't play – but you've done the right thing!'

Elizabeth couldn't find Robert to tell him, and before she could do so, Eileen had taken down the first notice from the board and put up another.

'Robert Jones will play in the match against Uphill School on Saturday,' said the second notice.

Robert saw it as he came in to dinner. He stared at it in amazement. Surely Elizabeth had said *she* was playing! He stood frowning at the board, and Kenneth came up. 'Hallo!' said Kenneth, reading the notice. 'I wonder why that's altered. It said that Elizabeth was playing in the match, when I read it before breakfast!'

'Yes – that's what I thought,' said Robert, puzzled. 'Why

has it been altered? But I say – that's marvellous for me! I was jolly disappointed this morning!'

'I bet Elizabeth will be disappointed too,' said Kenneth. They went in to their dinner. Robert did not like to say anything to Elizabeth in front of the others, and she said nothing about the notice either.

It was Nora who told Robert about it. 'Did you see that you were playing in the match after all?' she asked.

'Yes – but why?' asked Robert. 'What made Eileen change?'

'It was because Elizabeth asked her to let you play instead,' said Nora. 'Elizabeth thought that would only be fair. And I must say I agreed with her.'

Robert went red. 'It's awfully sporting of her, but I can't let her do it,' he said. 'I know how badly she wants to play.' He went to find Elizabeth.

She was in the school garden, planting bulbs with John.

'Hi, Elizabeth!' called Robert. 'You're a sport – but I'd rather you played on Saturday, if you don't mind.'

'I shan't, Robert,' said Elizabeth. 'I've made up my mind. It's such a good way of trying to make up for the mistake I made. I should be ashamed of myself if I didn't do it.'

'But I don't mind whether you try to make up for your mistake or not,' said Robert.

'Yes, but *I* mind,' said Elizabeth. 'I shall think better of myself if I do this. Really I shall.'

'All right,' said Robert. 'Thanks. I only wish you were coming to watch, Elizabeth.'

'I hope you shoot lots of goals!' said Elizabeth, and went on with her planting. It was hard work. The crocus bulbs had come, and big patches of grass had to be lifted before the crocuses could be planted underneath. Then there were all the daffodil and tulip bulbs to plant too, though they were much easier to bury in the soil of the beds.

'There's so much to do and so little time to do it all!' sighed Elizabeth. 'I would like to ride oftener – and I would like to garden all day long – and I'd like to have more music lessons – and I'd like to spend more time with the rabbits – and I'd like to play games oftener. I wish I was like you, John – and only had one favourite thing to do, instead of about twenty!'

'Well, I dare say you have a more exciting time than I have,' said John seriously. 'Mr Johns is always saying I ought to do something else besides gardening in my spare time, because I shall become dull.'

'I don't think you're a bit dull!' cried Elizabeth. 'I love to hear you talk about gardening!'

'Yes – because you like gardening and understand it,' said John. 'But to those who don't, I expect I do seem dull! You think of something else for me to do, Elizabeth.'

'Well, what about riding?' said Elizabeth. 'I never see you on horseback. Get Robert to take you out on Captain sometimes – he'd like that, and you'd enjoy it.'

The week went by, and Friday came. The school Meeting was to be held again that night. The children filed in as usual, not so grave as last time, for there were no serious matters to be discussed tonight. They always enjoyed the Meetings. They liked ruling themselves, making their own laws, and seeing that they were kept.

The extra money was put into the box. Kenneth proudly put in a whole ten pound note from one of his uncles. Peter put in five pounds. Then the week's pocket-money was given out.

John Terry asked for money for the new crocus bulbs and

it was given him. He also asked for money for a new garden fork, a smaller one than the one he used.

'Peter is going to help with the digging,' he said, 'and our fork is too big for him. We've never had one suitable for the younger ones.'

That money was given out also. Richard asked for money to buy a record of a violin performance. He was anxious to play the same piece himself, and Mr Lewis had said that if he could get the record and hear how a great master played the piece it would help him. William granted the money at once. The whole School was becoming very proud of Richard, for he played both the piano and the violin beautifully. He sat down, pleased.

'Any complaints or grumbles?' asked William.

Leonard got up. He looked rather apologetic. 'This is rather a silly grumble,' he said. 'It's about Fred. He does snore so at night – and, you see, I have to get up early in the morning to milk the cows, so if I am kept awake by the snoring, I can't seem to make myself get up in time. We've all told Fred about it, but he can't help it. So what can we do?'

Fred stood up. 'I've had a bad cold,' he said. 'I think I'll be all right when it's quite gone. Shall I go and sleep in the Sanatorium by myself till Matron says I don't snore any more?'

'Yes, I should,' said William, smiling. 'It's about the funniest grumble we've ever had, I think. But Leonard *must* get his sleep or we shan't get our breakfast milk!'

Everyone laughed. William tapped on the table with his hammer.

'Before we dismiss,' he said, 'Elizabeth has something to say. Stand up, Elizabeth.'

Elizabeth stood up, red in the face. She had been thinking about what she had to say, and she said it straight out, without stammering or stopping.

'I want to say this,' she began. 'Last week I accused Robert of playing some mean tricks on me and on Jenny. You all believed me, and you said that Robert shouldn't play in the match as a punishment. Well, I was wrong. It wasn't Robert after all. It was somebody else.'

'Who was it? Tell us!' cried a dozen voices indignantly. William rapped on the table and everyone was quiet.

'Wait a minute, Elizabeth,' said William. '*I* want to say something. This is what I have to say: Rita and I, as Judges, have decided that for the present we shall not give you the name of the child who did the tricks. You know that in certain cases it is sometimes best not to refer the matter to the whole school. Well, this is one of them. I hope you will be satisfied that we are doing this for the best.'

'Of course!' cried half a dozen voices, for the head girl and boy were much liked and admired.

Poor Kathleen was sitting on her form with her knees shaking! She could not help thinking that the whole school must know it was she who had been so horrid. She looked down at the floor, and wished that a hole would come there so that she might go down into it and disappear! Jenny and Joan were sitting on each side of her, warm and comforting. They could feel Kathleen shaking and they were sorry. Well – it was a good thing that the Judges had decided to say no more about that!

Elizabeth was still standing up. She had a few more words to say. She waited for silence and then went on.

'I haven't got much more to say – except that I'm very sorry for what I said, and that in future I will always be careful to be quite sure before I accuse anybody. Robert was very nice about it indeed.'

She sat down. William was about to rap on the table to dismiss the Meeting, when Robert got up. He looked cheerful and bright, quite a different boy from the last Meeting!

'May I say something, William?' he asked. 'It's this. Elizabeth is letting me play in Saturday's match instead of her, to make up for saying wrong things about me. Well, I think that's very good of her, and I want the school to know about it!'

'Good old Elizabeth!' cried somebody. Everyone thought that Elizabeth had behaved justly and rightly. The girl could feel this, and she was happy.

Then the Meeting was dismissed, and the children filed out to do what they liked for the half-hour before supper.

Joan sat down to write to her mother. Jenny put on the gramophone and made up a dance in the middle of the floor, much to the amusement of the others. Elizabeth went to practise in one of the music-rooms. Robert began to read a book on horses.

Kathleen took up her sewing. She had spent all the money she had on two handkerchief-cases to embroider. One was to be for Jenny, and the other for Elizabeth. Rita had said that it was possible to make up for nasty things by doing something nice – so she was doing it!

'We learn a lot of things besides lessons at Whyteleafe School,' thought Kathleen, as she sewed. And she was right!

20 The great lacrosse match

Saturday came, marvellously bright and sunny. There was a frost in the morning, and the grass glittered white. But it disappeared in the sun, and everyone agreed that it was a perfect day for the match.

Elizabeth tried her very hardest to be glad that it was such a fine day. It was lucky for Robert; but she couldn't help feeling disappointed that she wasn't playing. She had missed playing the Saturday before because it rained and now that it was so fine, she couldn't play!

'Well,' she said to herself, 'it's your own fault, Elizabeth Allen; you shouldn't have been so foolish – then you would have been playing today!'

She went up to Robert when she saw him. 'I'm glad it's fine for you, Robert,' she said. Robert looked at her and knew what she was feeling.

'I wish you were playing too,' he said. 'Never mind – it will be your turn next time!'

The day kept fine. All the team who were going to play were in a great state of excitement. Nora was playing, and she told the others that Uphill School had never been beaten by Whyteleafe yet.

'If only we could beat them just this once!' she said. 'But I hear they've got an awfully good team. Eileen says they haven't lost a match yet this term. They really are frightfully good. All I hope is they let us get *one* goal!'

'Oh, Nora! We must get more than that!' cried Peter, a strong, wiry boy who was in the team. He was a marvellous runner and catcher. 'For goodness' sake let's put up a good show!'

'We'll do our best,' said Robert.

The morning went slowly by. Dinner-time came and the team could not eat very much, for they were all so excited. Elizabeth knew how she had felt the Saturday before. Oh, how she *did* wish she was going too! It was so terribly disappointing – but she was glad that she had been big enough to give up her place to Robert.

The sun shone in through the window. It was going to be a wonderful afternoon for a match. Elizabeth swallowed a lump in her throat. It was all very well to be big and brave and give up something because you thought it was right – but it didn't make the disappointment any less. Joan saw her face and squeezed her hand.

'Cheer up!' she said. So Elizabeth tried to cheer up and smile. And then she noticed something going on at the next table. People were getting up and talking – what was happening?

'It's Peter! He doesn't feel well,' said Joan. 'Isn't he white? I believe he's going to be sick. I didn't think he looked very well at breakfast this morning.'

Peter went out of the room, with Harry helping him. He did look very green. Mr Johns went out too. Mr Warlow looked at his watch. He hoped Peter would soon recover – because the coach was coming to fetch the team in twenty minutes.

Mr Johns came back in five minutes' time. He spoke to Mr Warlow, who looked disappointed. 'What's happened to Peter?' asked John, who was at the same table. 'Is he better?'

'He's got one of his tummy upsets,' said Mr Johns. 'Very bad luck. Matron is putting him to bed in the Sanatorium.'

'Golly!' said John. 'Won't he be able to play in the match then?'

'No,' said Mr Warlow. 'It's bad luck for our team. Peter was one of the best. We must choose someone else.'

The news spread round the tables, and everyone was sorry about Peter. He really was such a good player. And then one by one the children called out something:

'Let Elizabeth play!'

'What about Elizabeth?'

'Can't Elizabeth play? She gave up her place to Robert!'

'Well,' said Mr Warlow, looking at his notebook, 'I had planned to get someone else next time – but as Elizabeth really deserves a trial, she shall play!'

Elizabeth's heart jumped for joy. She could hardly believe the good news. Her face went bright red and her eyes danced. She was sorry for Peter – but after all Peter had played in dozens of matches, and would again. Oh, she was really, really going to play after all!

'Good for you, Elizabeth!' called her friends, all pleased to see her shining face. The whole school knew, of course, that Elizabeth had given up her place in the match to Robert, and now they were really glad that she had her reward so unexpectedly.

Elizabeth sat happily in her place. Joan clapped her on the back, and Jenny grinned at her. 'Things always happen to you, don't they, Elizabeth?' said Jenny. 'Well, you deserve this piece of luck!'

'Elizabeth! I'm so glad!' called Robert from the end of the table. 'We shall be playing in our first match together! That'll be fun!'

Elizabeth couldn't eat anything more. She pushed her pudding-plate away. 'I shall feel sick, like Peter, if I eat any more,' she said.

'Well, for goodness' sake, don't then!' cried Nora. 'We can't have another player going sick at the very last moment!'

Elizabeth rushed off to change with the others into her gym things. She found time to peep into the San with a book for Peter. 'I'm sorry, Peter, old thing,' she said. 'I hope you'll soon be all right. I'll come and tell you about the match when it's over.'

'Play up!' said Peter, who still looked rather green. 'Shoot a few goals! Goodbye and good luck!'

Elizabeth shot off, her heart singing. It was too marvellous for words. Everyone laughed at her face and everyone was glad for her. She found Robert and took his arm.

'Sit next to me in the coach,' she said. 'We are the only ones who have never played in a match before – and oh, Robert, though I'm awfully happy, I feel a bit nervous!'

'*You* nervous!' said Robert, with a laugh. 'I can't believe it. A fierce person like you can't be nervous!'

But Elizabeth was! She was very anxious to do her best in the match, to do her best for Whyteleafe School. Suppose she played badly! Suppose she didn't catch the ball but kept dropping it! It would be dreadful.

'Still, there won't be anyone from Whyteleafe watching to see if I play badly,' she comforted herself. She looked at Robert as he sat beside her in the coach, looking burly and stolid and not a bit nervous. It was nice to be playing with him after all.

'I simply can't imagine how I hated him so much,' thought Elizabeth. 'It seems to me that if we dislike people, we see all the worst side of them because we make them show that to us – but if we like them, then they smile at us and show their best side. I really must try to give people a chance and begin by liking them, so that they show their best side at once.'

The coach soon arrived at Uphill School, which, as its name showed, was at the top of a steep hill. It was a much bigger school than Whyteleafe, and had the choice of far more children for its lacrosse team than Whyteleafe had. The Whyteleafe children looked at the opposing team and thought that they seemed very big and strong.

The teams lined up in their places. The whistle blew, and the game began. The Uphill team were certainly strong but there were some fine runners in the Whyteleafe team. They missed Peter, who was the finest runner of all – but both Robert and Elizabeth seemed to have wings on their feet that afternoon. They had never run so fast in their lives before!

Both children felt honoured to play in the match, and were determined to do their very best. Elizabeth's nervousness went as soon as the game began. She forgot all about herself and thought only of the match.

She and Robert often threw the ball to one another. Both children had practised their catching every day for some weeks, and were very good at it. Neither of them dropped the ball, but passed it beautifully.

'Good, Robert! Good, Elizabeth!' cried Mr Warlow, who was with the team. 'Keep it up! Shoot, Elizabeth!'

Elizabeth saw the goal not far off. She shot the ball at it with all her might. It flew straight at the goal – but the goalkeeper was on guard and shot the ball out again at once.

'Well tried, Elizabeth!' cried Mr Warlow.

Then the Uphill team got the ball and sped off towards the other goal, passing gracefully to one another – and then the captain shot hard. The ball rolled right into the goal, though

Eileen, who was goalkeeper, did her best to stop it.

'One goal to Uphill!' said the umpire, and the whistle blew. The game began again, and both Robert and Elizabeth were determined not to let the Uphill team get the ball if they could help it.

Elizabeth got the ball in her lacrosse net and sped away with it. She was about to pass it to Robert, who was keeping near her, when another player ran straight at her. Elizabeth tripped over and fell. She was up again in a trice – but the ball had been taken by the Uphill girl. Down to the goal sped the girl, and passed the ball to someone else.

'Shoot!' yelled all the watching Uphill girls, and the ball was shot towards the goal. It rolled inside before Eileen could throw it out.

'Two goals to Uphill!' called the umpire. He blew the whistle for half-time, and the girls and boys greedily sucked the half-lemons that were brought out to them. Oh, how lovely and sour they tasted!

'Now play up, Whyteleafe,' said Mr Warlow, coming out on to the field to talk to his team. 'Robert, keep near Elizabeth – and, Elizabeth, pass more quickly to Robert when you are attacked. You two are running like the wind today. Shoot at goal whenever there's a chance. Nora, feed Elizabeth with the ball when you can – she may perhaps be quick enough to outpace the Uphill girl marking her.'

The children listened eagerly. The Whyteleafe team were feeling a little down-hearted. Two goals to none!

The whistle blew. The match began again. Nora got the ball and passed it at once to Elizabeth, remembering what Mr Warlow had said. Robert kept near to her and caught it when she passed it to him. He passed it back again, and the girl sped towards the goal.

She flung the ball with all her might. The goalkeeper put out her lacrosse net quickly – but the ball bounced off it and rolled into the goal.

'One goal to Whyteleafe!' said the umpire. 'Two to one.'

Elizabeth was thrilled. She couldn't keep still but danced up and down even when the ball was nowhere near her. Nora got the ball. She passed to Robert, Robert passed back, and Nora ran for goal. She shot – and once more the ball rolled right in! It was too good to be true!

'Two goals to Whyteleafe!' said the umpire. 'Two all, and ten minutes to play!'

The Uphill children, who were all watching the match eagerly, began to shout:

'Play up, Uphill! Shoot, Uphill! Go on, Uphill!'

And the Uphill team heard and played harder than ever. They got the ball – they raced for goal. They shot – and Eileen caught the ball neatly and threw it out again! Thank goodness for that!

Two goals all, and three minutes to play. Play up, Uphill! Play up, Whyteleafe! Three minutes left – only three minutes!

21 The end of the match

'Three minutes, Robert!' panted Elizabeth. 'For goodness' sake, let's play up. Oh, how I hope that Uphill School don't shoot another goal!'

The ball flew from one player to another. Elizabeth ran to tackle one of the Uphill girls, who was a very fast runner. She hit the girl's lacrosse stick and made the ball leap up into the air. Elizabeth tried to catch it but the ball fell to the ground. She picked it up in her lacrosse net, and tore off with it.

But another girl tackled her, and although Elizabeth tried to dodge, it was no use at all. She fell over and the ball flew into the air. The Uphill girl caught it neatly and raced off with it. She passed it to another Uphill girl who threw it vigorously down the field to the girl by the goal.

The girl caught it, and shot straight for goal. It looked as if the ball was flying straight for the goal-net – but Eileen saved it by flinging herself right out of goal! She fell over as she caught the ball, but somehow she managed to fling it to a waiting Whyteleafe boy. He caught it and was off up the field like the wind.

'Pass the ball, pass it!' yelled Elizabeth, dancing about. 'Look out! There's a girl behind you! PASS!'

The boy passed the ball just as the Uphill girl behind him tried to strike at his stick to get the ball. It flew straight through the air to Elizabeth. She caught it, and sped off, followed by a swift-running Uphill girl.

Elizabeth passed to Robert who was nearby. An Uphill girl ran at him – and he passed the ball back to Elizabeth, who ran for goal. Should she shoot from where she was? She might get a goal – and she would win the match for Whyteleafe!

But Robert had run down the field and was nearer the goal now – she ought really to pass to him! Without another moment's delay Elizabeth threw the ball straight to Robert.

He caught it – and flung it at the goal. It was a beautiful shot. The girl in goal tried her best to save the goal, but the ball flew past her stick and landed right in the corner of the net. Goal to Whyteleafe!

And almost at once the whistle blew for Time! The match was over!

'Three goals to Whyteleafe!' shouted the umpire. 'Three goals to two! Whyteleafe wins! Well played!'

Then all the watching Uphill girls cheered too, and clapped their hardest. It had been an excellent match and everyone had played well.

'Another second and the whistle would have blown for Time!' panted Elizabeth. 'Oh, Robert! You were marvellous to shoot the winning goal just in time!'

'Well, I couldn't have if you hadn't passed me the ball exactly when you did,' said Robert, his breath coming fast as he leaned on his lacrosse stick, his face flushed and wet. 'Well, Elizabeth – we've won! Think of that! We've never beaten Uphill before! Oh, I'm glad you shot a goal too!'

The two teams trooped off the field and went in to wash. It was nice to feel cold water, for they were all so hot! The two captains shook hands, and the Uphill girl clapped Eileen on the back.

'A jolly good match!' she said. 'It's the first we've lost this term. Good for you!'

Elizabeth hadn't been able to eat much dinner, but she made up for it at teatime. There was brown bread-and-butter and blackberry jam, currant buns and an enormous chocolate cake. The children ate hungrily, and the big plates of bread-and-butter and buns were soon emptied.

'I'm longing to get back to Whyteleafe to tell the good news,' said Robert to Elizabeth. 'Aren't you? Oh, Elizabeth, I *am* glad you played after all – and I can't tell you how glad I am that I was able to play! I hope we play in heaps more matches together. It was marvellous being able to pass the ball so well to one another!'

'You shot that winning goal well,' said Elizabeth happily. 'Oh, I'm so tired, but so happy. I feel as if I can't get up from this form! My legs won't work any more!'

All the children were tired, but their tongues still worked well. They chattered and laughed and joked together as they got ready to go back to the waiting motorcoach. Oh, what fun to tell the school that they had won!

They all got back into the coach. They waved goodbye to the cheering Uphill girls, and the coach rumbled off. The children sank back into their seats, their faces still red with all their running about, and their legs tired out.

But as soon as they got near Whyteleafe School they all sat up straight and looked eagerly to see the first glimpse of the Whyteleafe children, who would all be waiting to hear the result of the match.

Joan and Jenny and Kathleen had been looking out for the coach for the last half-hour. When they heard it coming they tore to the big school door. Dozens of other children ran with them. It was always the custom at Whyteleafe to welcome home the children who had been to an Away Match.

The lacrosse team waved their hands wildly as the coach rumbled up to the big school door.

'We won! We won! Three goals to two!'

'We've won the match. It was marvellous!'

'It's the first time Uphill have been beaten!'

'Three goals to two! Three to two!'

The Whyteleafe children cheered madly when they heard the news. They swarmed out round the coach and helped down the team, whose legs were still very wobbly from all the rushing about they had done.

'Jolly good! Oh, jolly good!' cried everyone. 'Come along in and tell us all about it!'

So into the gym went the team, and Miss Belle and Miss Best, and Mr Johns too, had to come along and hear all the excitements of the afternoon. Mr Warlow spoke for a while and told how well everyone had played. Then John shouted out:

'Who shot the goals?'

'Elizabeth, Nora – and Robert,' said Mr Warlow. 'Good goals all three. Robert's was the most exciting because he shot his almost as the whistle went for Time. Another second and it would have been too late!'

'Three cheers for Nora, Elizabeth, and Robert!' cried everyone, and they clapped them on the back. How pleased and proud those three children were! Elizabeth almost cried for joy. To think she had actually shot a goal for Whyteleafe in her very first match. It was too good to be true.

Nora had played in many matches and shot many goals, so she just grinned and said nothing. But Robert was as pleased and proud as Elizabeth, though he did not show it quite so much.

Elizabeth slipped her arm in his. 'I'm *so* glad we both had the chance to play together,' she said. 'And oh, Robert, you don't know how pleased I am that I've done something for Whyteleafe, even if it's only to shoot a goal! I hated Whyteleafe when I first came here – but now I love it. Wait till you have been here a term or two and you'll love it too.'

'I love it already, thank you,' said Robert. 'And what's more, I mean to do a whole lot more for it than just shoot a goal!'

There was a special supper that night for the winning team! Hot sausages appeared on the table, two for each one of the team. How delighted they were! And not only that, but anyone who had sweets or chocolates made a point of offering them to the team, so that by the time the bed-bell went, both Robert and Elizabeth felt that they couldn't eat anything more at all!

Kathleen was as delighted as anyone. Her face was beaming as she brought a tin of sweets along. Elizabeth took a good look at her.

'Golly, you don't look the same girl!' she said. 'Your eyes are all smiling and your hair is shiny! You walk as if you wanted to run, and you've already got rid of your awful spots!'

Kathleen laughed. She had kept her word to herself and hadn't eaten a single sweet. She had begun to forget herself, and to join in the chatter and jokes of the form. She held her head up and smiled gaily. Already when she thought of the horrid tricks she had played she could not imagine how she could have done them.

She had taken down Elizabeth's books from the top of the cupboard where she had put them, and had dusted them well. With scarlet cheeks she had given them back to

Elizabeth, who had taken them with a word of thanks. A few scornful words had almost come to Elizabeth's tongue when she remembered how Miss Ranger had scolded her for losing her books – but she had bitten them back and said nothing.

Kathleen worked hard at the two handkerchief-cases, and embroidered them carefully and well. Each had the word HANDKERCHIEF across it, and it was a long word to sew. There were blue forget-me-nots on Elizabeth's case and pink roses on Jenny's.

Just as Kathleen was finishing the very last stitch, Jenny came into the common-room.

'My goodness, I wish I'd played in the match too,' she said, flinging herself into a chair. 'What wouldn't I do for hot sausages for supper! Hallo, Kath! What are you so busy about? Let's see.'

She bent over Kathleen's work. 'My goodness!' she said. 'What tiny stitches – and how nicely you've worked the roses! I wish I could sew like that. I want a handkerchief-case.'

'Well, this is for you,' said Kathleen, delighted. 'I've done one for Elizabeth too.'

'But whatever for?' asked Jenny, in surprise.

'To make up just a little bit for other things I did which weren't quite so nice,' said Kathleen. 'Here you are, Jenny – take yours and use it. I'm so glad to give it to you.'

Jenny was very pleased indeed. She took the handkerchief-case at once. 'You *are* a pal!' she said. 'Thanks a lot. Here's Elizabeth! Look – hi, Elizabeth, come and see what you've got for an unbirthday present!'

Soon both girls were examining their new handkerchief-cases in delight, and other children came round to see them. Kathleen felt proud when she heard their remarks.

'It's much nicer to do something *for* people instead of *against* them,' she thought. 'But I'll never, never be brave enough to own up to the School that it was I who played those tricks! I *am* nicer – and kinder too – but I'm still just as much a coward!'

22 Elizabeth in trouble again

The term went on happily. Now that the quarrels between Robert and Elizabeth, and between Kathleen and the others, had been cleared up, things were much better.

Elizabeth worked well and shot to the top of her class. Robert was sometimes second and sometimes third, which pleased Miss Ranger very much, for it was by sheer hard work that the boy did so well. Kathleen, too, worked a great deal better, and had stopped arguing in the silly way she once had. Mam'zelle was pleased with her.

'The child in this class who has made the most improvement is the little Kathleen!' said Mam'zelle. 'Ah, how I thought she was stupid! How I scolded her! But now, see, her French essay is the best, and she rolls her r's in the right French way – not like you, R-r-r-r-robert, who will never get them right!'

Robert smiled – and Kathleen went red with pleasure. She had never been praised in class before, and it was very pleasant. She began to wonder if she was as stupid as she had always thought herself to be.

'My memory does seem to be better,' she thought, 'and I like working at my lessons now. I was bored before. Maybe I shan't always be at the bottom of the class now! How marvellous! Wouldn't Mother be pleased if I came out top in something!'

She worked especially hard for Mam'zelle, and this was a

great change for Kathleen, for ever since Mam'zelle had scolded her so badly she had disliked the French teacher and done her lessons carelessly. But now, somehow, things were different. For one thing the girl was healthier – she went out riding and walking with the others, and she even offered to help John, Elizabeth, and Peter in the school garden.

'Good gracious!' said John. 'You're the last person I would have thought wanted to help! Are you any good at gardening?'

'Well, no, not much,' said Kathleen honestly. Three weeks before she would have boasted untruthfully that she knew everything about gardening. 'But, John, I'd like to help a bit. Isn't there anything I can do?'

'You can wheel that rubbish over there to the rubbish heap,' said John. 'Then bring back the barrow and fork the next pile of rubbish in. It's really too heavy for Peter to wheel.'

Peter was very keen on gardening, and John was delighted to have him. Peter told John how Robert took him riding, and John grew quite interested in hearing about the horses.

'I'll really have to try riding myself,' he said. 'I've never much wanted to. I did when I first came to Whyteleafe, and then somehow I got so interested in gardening that I couldn't think of anything else. But perhaps I'll come tomorrow, Peter.'

Peter spoke to Robert, and it was arranged that John, Peter, Robert, Elizabeth, and Kathleen should all go riding together the next morning – and off they all went, galloping over the hills in the pale winter sunlight. John loved it.

'I must come again,' he said, when he jumped down from the saddle. 'That was fine. Goodness, Kathleen, what red cheeks you've got! You always used to look so pale! Coming to help me garden this weekend?'

'Yes, please,' said Kathleen, overjoyed at being asked to help someone. She was beginning to find how lovely it was to make friends, and to *be* a friend. If you offered to help other people, they offered to help you in return, and that was how friendships began – and surely it was the nicest thing in the world to have good friends round you!

'It was quite true what William and Rita said,' thought Kathleen to herself. 'I envied Jenny and said she was lucky because she had so many friends – and I thought that because I was an unlucky person none of those nice things happened to me. But now that I'm trying to be nicer, nice things happen to me too. It is our own selves that make us lucky or unlucky, it's our own selves that bring us friendship and kindness. I was always groaning and grumbling about everything and thinking I would always be unlucky and wouldn't be able to help it – but as soon as I changed myself, I changed the things that happened, too! What a pity that everyone doesn't know that!'

Elizabeth was working hard at her music, and Mr Lewis was very pleased with her. She and Richard were once again playing duets, and the big boy loved playing with the quick-fingered little girl. She looked up to Richard and thought he was wonderful.

'Can we play our duets at the school concert again?' asked Elizabeth. 'I do want to, Mr Lewis. Shall we be good enough?'

'Oh, yes,' said Mr Lewis. 'Richard is playing his violin, too. Have you heard him play the same piece that is on the gramophone record he got, Elizabeth?'

'No,' said Elizabeth. 'I haven't. But I'd like to. Please play it to me, Richard.'

So Richard was sent to fetch his violin, and the big, dreamy boy played a marvellous piece to his master and to Elizabeth. They both listened, enchanted.

'Oh, that's lovely,' sighed Elizabeth, when it was finished. 'Oh, I wish I could play like that. Can't I learn to play the violin too, Mr Lewis?'

'My dear child, you already fill your days too full!' laughed the music-master. 'No – stick to the piano.'

'But Richard plays the piano too,' said Elizabeth. '*And* the violin!'

'And he doesn't do anything else!' said Mr Lewis. 'But nobody can make him do anything else, so he might as well work hard at those. No one has ever made Richard pull a weed out of the garden, or ride a horse more than once, or keep even a harmless white mouse! He thinks of nothing but music.'

'I'll make him think of something else!' said Elizabeth. 'Come and practise with me at lacrosse tomorrow, Richard! You can't think how marvellous it feels to be good enough to play in a match!'

But Richard wouldn't come. He did play games sometimes, but so badly that he was worse than any child in the kindergarten. Not even determined little Elizabeth could make him leave his precious music, and she soon gave it up. Secretly she was very proud to play duets with him.

'One day Richard will be a famous musician and composer,' she told Jenny and Joan. 'Then I shall be very proud to think that once I played duets with him.'

There was to be a play at the school concert. The children in Elizabeth's form were to write one themselves, and they spent a long time thinking it out. When at last they had worked out the plot, there came the labour of writing it.

Jenny and Kathleen proved to be unexpectedly good at this. Jenny could manage conversation very well, and Kathleen had a good imagination and thought of all kinds of things. Before the week was out, the two were writing out the play together, with helpful and unhelpful remarks from the other members of the class.

It amused Elizabeth to see the two heads bent over the paper. 'It's just as funny to see Jenny and Kathleen like that as it was to see me and Robert,' she thought. 'How silly we are when we quarrel! Well – I'll never quarrel again!'

It was a pity she said that, for she broke her word to herself the very next day! She quarrelled with John!

They had built a big rubbish heap, and John had said they would light it the next time they had an hour or two to spare. But when Elizabeth went to find John in the garden to light the fire, he wasn't there.

'Oh, bother!' thought the little girl. 'I did so want to see the bonfire burning! Well – if John doesn't come in the next few minutes I'll light it myself. He won't mind.'

But she knew that he would mind, really, for although he trusted Elizabeth in a great many ways, things such as lighting bonfires he always did himself.

Elizabeth fetched a box of matches. She struck one and held it to some paper she had pushed into the heart of the rubbish heap. It caught fire – and in a trice the bonfire was burning furiously! What a blaze it made! Blue smoke streamed out from it and flew over the shed nearby.

Elizabeth danced round happily. This was marvellous! How silly John was to be late!

And then she suddenly noticed something! The wind was blowing the flames of the bonfire near the shed!

'Oh! I hope the shed won't catch fire!' cried Elizabeth in

alarm. 'Oh, my goodness – I believe it will! John! John! Quick, where are you?'

John was coming down the path at that moment. He saw the flames of the bonfire at the bottom of the garden, and hurried to see what was happening. When he saw that the red tongues were actually licking the woodshed, he had a terrible fright.

'Elizabeth! Get the hose out with me!' he cried. Together the two children unrolled the hose and hastily fitted it to the garden tap. John turned on the tap and the water gushed out of the hose. The boy turned it on the bonfire. In a few minutes the fire was out and only dense black smoke came from the very heart of it. John threw down the hose and turned off the tap.

'What in the world did you light the bonfire for?' he said angrily. 'What an idiot you are! Don't you know by now that I'm head of the school garden? You might have burnt down the shed!'

'Don't talk to me like that!' cried Elizabeth, firing up at once. 'You said *you* were going to light it – and it would have happened just the same if you had, wouldn't it?'

'My dear Elizabeth, I'm not *quite* so foolish as to light a bonfire just there, with the wind blowing the flames straight towards the shed,' said John furiously. 'Have a little sense! I didn't *dream* of lighting it today! And you've no business to. Now we've ruined the bonfire and I meant it to be such a beauty. You're a real nuisance, and I don't want you in the garden any more!'

'*Oh!*' cried Elizabeth, with tears in her eyes. 'You hateful boy! After all I've done in the garden and all the help I've given you!'

'You shouldn't have done it for me,' said John. 'You

should have done it for the garden and for the school. Go away, Elizabeth. I don't feel I want to talk to you any more.'

'Well, I'll certainly never come and help in the garden again!' shouted Elizabeth, and off she marched in a great rage.

But half an hour later a little voice spoke inside her head. 'You said you weren't going to quarrel with anyone any more. And you have already! After all, John was right to be cross. You might have burnt down the shed and all his precious tools and everything – and you've spoilt the lovely bonfire he wanted to light.'

And a voice was speaking inside John's head too. 'Elizabeth didn't mean it. She was just silly, not bad. She's as disappointed as you are about the bonfire. And you know you do want her help in the garden. Suppose she takes you at your word and doesn't come any more? That wouldn't be very nice!'

'I'll go and find her,' thought John. And the same thought came to Elizabeth. 'I'll go and find John.'

So they met round the corner of the garden path, each looking rather ashamed. They held out their hands.

'Sorry I was piggy to you,' said John.

'And I'm sorry I was too,' said Elizabeth. 'Oh, John, I said to myself yesterday that I'd never quarrel with anyone any more – and I've gone and done it again!'

'You always will!' said John, with a laugh. 'But it won't matter if only you will make it up quickly. Come on and do some digging. It will do us both good.'

Off they went together, the best of friends. It takes more than a quarrel to break up a real friendship, doesn't it?

23 A thrill for Joan

Two months of the Christmas term had already gone by. Seven school Meetings had been held, and the eighth was to be held on the next Friday night. A new monitor had to be chosen, because one of the old ones, a boy called George, had the flu, and was in the San for a week or two.

'How are new monitors chosen?' asked Robert. 'Nobody new has been chosen since I came at the beginning of the term. I thought monitors were only chosen for a month – but we've had the same ones for two months.'

'Yes, because they're so good we don't want to change them,' said Joan. 'We *can* change them at the end of each month if we want to – but there's no point in changing them if we are satisfied. I think all our monitors are awfully good.'

'So do I,' said Elizabeth. 'I once thought it must be awful to be a monitor and have to keep all the rules and see that the others did too – but now I've changed my mind. I think it's rather nice to be trusted so much, and to have people coming to you for help and advice.'

'Well, the people who matter in this world are the ones who can be really trusted and who are willing to help anyone in trouble,' said Jenny. 'We get good training for that at Whyteleafe! One day *I'd* like to be a monitor – but like you, Elizabeth, I know I never shall be!'

'Well, nobody's answered my question yet,' said Robert patiently.

'What *was* it?' asked Elizabeth.

'I asked how new monitors are chosen,' said Robert. 'Do we choose them – or do the Jury – or the Judges – or who?'

'Well, the whole school chooses them first,' said John. 'We each write down the name of one we think we would like as monitor, and then the slips of paper are folded and passed up to the Jury.'

'What next?' asked Robert.

'The Jury undo them and see which three children have the most votes,' said John. 'They vote for whichever of those three they think would be best. Then their votes are passed up to William and Rita – and the two Judges decide which child is to be made a new monitor.'

'I see,' said Robert. 'It seems very fair. Everyone has a say in the matter. That's what I like so much about Whyteleafe – we all have a say in things.'

'I can't quite think who to vote for,' said Jenny. 'I'll have to think hard.'

'So will I,' said Joan thoughtfully. 'It is such an honour to be chosen. The one we choose must really be worthy of it.'

'Can I walk with you when we go for our Nature ramble this afternoon?' asked Kathleen. 'Elizabeth can't go – she's got an extra music practice with Richard.'

'All right,' said Joan. 'But don't be late. I'm leading the ramble, you know, and you must be on time if you want to start off with me.'

Kathleen was very punctual, and the two set off together with their notebooks, followed by the rest of the children who were interested in Nature work. They were to find blossoming ivy, the last insect feast of the season, and to list and draw all the insects feasting on the nectar in the green blossoms.

It was fun to wander down the lanes together and over the fields. The pale winter sun shone down and the sky was the faint blue of a harebell. The trees were all bare except the firs and the pines, and the frost still glittered under the hedges.

Kathleen hummed a little song to herself as she looked about for the blossoms of the ivy. Joan looked at her.

'It's funny how people change,' she said. 'Last term I saw Elizabeth change from a horrid, naughty girl to a kind and good one. I felt myself change from somebody lonely and shy to somebody quite different. I've seen Robert change – and now you're changing too under my very eyes!'

'Yes, I know,' said Kathleen. 'But there's one way I haven't changed, Joan. I'm still a coward!'

'How do you mean?' asked Joan, surprised. 'Are you frightened of cows, or something?'

'No, of course not,' said Kathleen. 'I'm frightened of what people think! That's much worse than cows! Nobody but you and Jenny and Nora and Elizabeth know that it was I who played those horrid tricks – oh, and Rita and William, of course. And I know quite well that if it had been you or Jenny or Elizabeth you would all have been brave enough to get up in front of the whole school at a Meeting and say it was you!'

'Well, of course,' said Joan. 'Why not? You know quite well that the school would think well of you for owning up, and not so badly of you for doing the tricks. But if it leaks out that you *did* do them and didn't own up, why then, we should think much worse of you, and you'd think worse of yourself too! It's just a question of making up your mind to do it. Everybody has plenty of courage – only they don't always use it.'

'Have they really?' asked Kathleen. 'I mean, have I got

plenty of courage if I like to use it? I don't *have* to be a coward then?'

'You *are* an idiot!' said Joan, taking Kathleen's arm. 'I mean what I say. No one has to be a coward – anyone can draw on their courage the moment they make up their mind to! Try it at the next Meeting – you'll see what I mean then.'

They found a great stretch of blossoming ivy just then, so they said no more, but busied themselves in writing down the large list of insects hovering over the nectar. But Kathleen was thinking over Joan's words. It would be too marvellous if they were true. If everybody had courage deep down inside them, why then, nobody need be a coward – they only had to take hold of their courage and use it!

'I'll see if I can use mine at the next Meeting,' thought Kathleen, though her heart sank at the thought. 'It's tiresome to see all the other children standing up and saying things, and I hardly dare to open my mouth!'

So at the next Meeting, unknown to any of her friends, Kathleen sat with shaking knees, trying to take hold of her courage. The usual business was gone through – money put into the box – money given out – money granted or refused for several things. And then came the complaints and grumbles.

There was only one complaint and only one grumble, and they were quickly dealt with. Then, before the other business of choosing a monitor was put before the Meeting, William said a few words.

'I think the school would like to know that Fred is back in his dormitory, and doesn't snore any more.'

There was laughter at this, and a few cheers. Fred laughed too. William knocked on the table.

'I also want to say this – that the whole School has noticed and approved of the way that Robert has behaved for the last few weeks. Rita and I have had excellent reports from all the monitors. Also the stableman says that he really couldn't do without Robert now to help him with the horses.'

Robert flushed with pleasure. The school was pleased too – it was always good to hear that they had been right in their treatment of anyone.

And then Kathleen found her courage, took hold of it with two hands and stood up. Her knees no longer shook. Her voice was steady. She looked straight at the Judges and the Jury.

'I want to say something I should have said before,' she said. 'I want to say that I was the person who did all the things that Robert was accused of. I was afraid to own up before.'

There was complete silence. Everyone was most astonished. Those who hadn't known were surprised to hear the news – and those who had known were even more surprised to hear Kathleen owning up! Whatever had made her do it so suddenly?

Then Rita spoke. 'And what has made you able to own up now?' she asked.

'Well, it was really something Joan said,' explained Kathleen. 'She told me there was no need for *any*one to be a coward. She said we all had courage in us, only we had to take hold of it. So I took hold of mine this evening – and Joan was right. I wasn't afraid any more.'

'Thank you, Kathleen,' said Rita.

Kathleen sat down. Her heart was light. She had got rid of a heavy load. She had found her courage – and she wasn't going to lose it again!

'We won't say any more about what Kathleen has confessed to us,' said Rita. 'We are all glad she has been brave enough to own up. William and I knew it was she, of course – and we hoped that one day she would be able to tell you herself. Now she has – and we are pleased.'

'We had better get on with the business of choosing a new monitor,' said William. 'Give out slips of paper, please, Eileen.'

The slips were given out. Everyone wrote down the name of a girl or boy they thought fit to be a monitor. The papers were given to the Jury and opened. The Jury then chose out the three names that had most votes and voted on them themselves. Their papers were given to the two Judges.

William and Rita opened the twelve slips of paper from the Jury. They talked to one another in low voices whilst everyone waited eagerly to know who had been chosen.

Then William knocked on the table with his hammer, and everyone was perfectly quiet. 'There isn't much doubt as to who you want for a new monitor,' he said. 'Her name appears on almost everyone's paper. It is Joan Townsend!'

There were cheers and clappings, and Joan went as red as a beetroot. She had had no idea at all that the school would choose her! But everyone had heard with interest what Kathleen had said about Joan's wise word on courage – and now Joan's reward had come! She was to be the new monitor.

'We have had excellent reports of you from all the other monitors,' said Rita. 'We know that you are to be trusted, that you are kind and wise for your age, and that you will do your best for the whole school. Please come up and sit at the monitors' table, Joan – we are glad to welcome you on our Jury!'

Joan went up to the platform, proud and happy. Elizabeth

clapped madly – she was so proud of Joan, so pleased that she was honoured in this way.

'Joan deserves it!' she thought. 'She really does! My goodness, if only I could be a monitor too! But I'm not the right sort of girl, and never will be!'

24 A horrid adventure

The term slipped into December. The school was very busy planning and preparing plays and songs of all kinds. The weather was unkind, and many afternoons there were no games to be played out-of-doors.

'It's even too bad to garden,' groaned John, looking out of the window. 'The ground is so sticky that I can't dig.'

'Anyway, you'd get soaked through,' said Joan. 'It's a good chance for you to take an interest in something else! But I expect you'll get down one of your gardening books and pore over that!'

Joan was very happy to be a monitor. She took a great pride in her new honour, and did her duties well. She had to see that the children in her care did not break the rules of the school. She had to advise them when they came to her for help. She had to act wisely and kindly always – and this was not difficult for her because she was naturally a sensible and kindly child.

Elizabeth was very pleased that Joan was a monitor. She did not feel jealous, of course, but she longed to be one too. Still, Joan had been at Whyteleafe for far longer than Elizabeth – so she must wait her turn in patience. Though patience was not a thing that Elizabeth possessed very much of at present!

Elizabeth practised her music pieces hard and played the duets over and over again with Richard, for she was very anxious to do her best at the concert. Mr Lewis praised her.

'Elizabeth, you are working very hard. You are playing extremely well this term.'

Elizabeth felt proud. My goodness! She would show everyone at the concert how well she played! If her father and mother came to the concert they would be surprised to see Elizabeth playing such difficult duets with a big boy like Richard!

'You're getting conceited about your playing, Elizabeth,' said Richard one afternoon. Richard never thought twice about what he said, and he could be very hurtful. 'It's a pity. I like your playing – but I shan't like *you* if you get conceited.'

'Don't be so horrid, Richard,' said Elizabeth indignantly. 'I don't tell you *you're* conceited, do I!'

'No, because I'm not,' said Richard. 'I know quite well that my gift for music is nothing to do with *me* really – it's something that has been given to me – a real gift. I'm thankful for it and grateful for it and I'm going to use it for all I'm worth – but I'm not conceited about it and never shall be.'

Elizabeth was annoyed with Richard – especially as she knew that what he said was just a little bit true. She *was* getting conceited about her playing!

'But why shouldn't I be proud of it?' she thought. 'I haven't got a wonderful gift for it like Richard – so my playing is my own hard work, and I've every right to be proud of that!'

So she went on planning to show off at the school concert, and make everyone think what a wonderful pianist she was. But pride always comes before a fall – and poor Elizabeth was going to have a dreadful shock.

She and Robert, John and Kathleen, had arranged to go

out riding one afternoon before games. Peter came running up and begged Robert to let him go too.

'No, you can't, Peter,' said Robert. 'The horse you usually ride is limping – and I don't want you to have the other. It's a restive horse. Wait till your horse is all right.'

'Oh, please, do let me ride the other horse,' begged Peter. 'You know I'm a good rider!'

'Let him come, Robert,' said Elizabeth. 'You know he can ride Tinker.'

'Well, but Tinker really *is* a bit funny today,' said Robert. 'I'll see what he's like when two o'clock comes, Peter.'

When two o'clock came, Robert was not in the stables. The others were there. Elizabeth saddled the horses and looked for Robert. Still he didn't come.

'Oh bother!' said Elizabeth. 'It's ten-past two already. Wherever has Robert got to? We are wasting all our time.'

Peter sped off to look for Robert – but he came back in a few minutes to say that he couldn't find him.

'Well, if we're going for a ride we'd better go!' said Elizabeth. She called to the stableman.

'Hi, Tucker! Can I saddle Tinker? Is he all right?'

'Well, he's a bit upset about something,' said Tucker. 'You have a look at him, Miss.'

Elizabeth went to Tinker's stall. The horse, which was a small one, nuzzled into her hand. She stroked his long nose. 'He seems all right,' she said. 'I'll saddle him for you, Peter. I'm sure Robert would say you could ride him.'

She saddled him quickly. Peter leapt up on to his back, and the four children cantered out into the paddock. Then away they went down the grassy field path, the girls' hair streaming out in the wind.

'We shan't have time to go very far,' shouted Elizabeth.

'We've only got about twenty minutes. We'll go as far as Windy Hill and back!'

They cantered out into a lane leading to the hill. And then something happened!

As they trotted round a corner, a steam-roller started rumbling down the lane, which had just been mended. Tinker reared up in fright, and Peter held on with all his might.

Elizabeth cantered up beside him and put out her hand to hold the reins tightly – but the horse tossed its head, gave a loud whinny, and darted into an open gateway that led to a field.

And then it ran away! The three children stared in fright. Poor Peter! There he was on Tinker, holding on for dear life, whilst the horse galloped like mad across the stony field towards Windy Hill.

'I'm going after him!' cried Elizabeth. She swung her horse round and galloped through the gateway. She shouted to him, and smacked him on his broad back. He set off swiftly, knowing that he had to overtake the runaway horse.

Over the stony field went Elizabeth, whilst John and Kathleen watched in fright. Far away galloped Tinker, Peter still clinging fast.

Elizabeth's horse was bigger and faster than Peter's. He galloped eagerly, his heels kicking up the stones. Elizabeth urged him on, shouting loudly. It was a good thing that she was such a good rider and that she trusted her horse! On and on they went, gaining little by little on Tinker.

Peter's horse was panting painfully. He began to climb the steep Windy Hill and dropped to a trot. Peter tugged at the reins and tried to bring him to a stop, but the horse was still terribly frightened.

Elizabeth galloped her horse up Windy Hill and at last

overtook Tinker. But Tinker started in fright as soon as the other horse came up beside him. He stretched out his neck and began to gallop off again.

But Elizabeth had managed to get the reins, and when Tinker felt her strong little hand on them, he quietened down, and listened to her voice. Elizabeth was good with horses and knew how to speak to them. After the first tug to get rid of Elizabeth's hand, Tinker slowed down and then, trembling from head to foot, stopped still.

Peter was trembling too. He climbed down at once. Elizabeth leapt down and went round to Tinker's head. In a few minutes she had quieted the horse, but she did not dare to ride him.

'Peter, ride my horse and go back and join the others,' she said. 'I shall have to walk Tinker home. Tell the stableman what has happened, and take a message to Mr Warlow for me to tell him I shan't be back in time for games. Go on, now!'

Peter rode back to the others on Elizabeth's horse. He soon recovered himself, and began to boast about the runaway horse. The three children rode home and gave Elizabeth's message – whilst poor Elizabeth had to walk Tinker home for a very long way.

The little girl was tired and upset. Something dreadful might have happened – Peter might have fallen from the horse and been badly hurt! Why had she let him ride Tinker without first getting Robert to say he could? Well, it was Robert's fault for being late for the gallop!

Her left hand hurt her. She had got hold of Tinker's reins with it when she had tried to stop him, and somehow her wrist had been twisted. She tucked it into her coat, hoping it would soon be better. She was very miserable as she walked back over the fields and lanes, leading a tired and steaming horse.

The stableman was not pleased. Robert came running out when he saw Elizabeth coming back, and he was not pleased either.

'Elizabeth! I've heard all about it! How *could* you be so silly as to let Peter ride Tinker! I couldn't help being late. Mr Johns kept me to do something for him. You might have waited! This wouldn't have happened then, for I would never have let Peter ride Tinker in that state. You are always so impatient and cocksure of yourself!'

Elizabeth was tired and her hand was hurting her. She burst into tears.

'That's right! Be a baby now!' said Robert in disgust. 'I suppose you think that if you cry I'll be sorry for you and not say any more! That's just like a girl! It's a good thing for you that neither Tinker nor Peter have come to any harm!'

'Oh, Robert, don't be so unkind to me,' sobbed Elizabeth. 'I've hurt my hand, and I can't tell you how badly I feel about letting Peter ride Tinker.'

'Let's have a look at your hand,' said Robert, more kindly. He took a look at the swollen wrist. 'You'd better go right away to Matron. That looks pretty bad to me. Cheer up! It's no good crying over spilt milk!'

'I'm not!' said Elizabeth, wiping her eyes. 'I'm crying over a runaway horse and a hurt wrist!' And off she went to find Matron, nursing her hurt hand. Poor Elizabeth! Things always happened to her.

25 Elizabeth is very tiresome

Elizabeth went to find Matron. She was in the Sanatorium with two ill children there. She came out when Elizabeth knocked at the door.

'What is it?' she asked. 'You can't go in!'

'I know,' said Elizabeth. 'I've twisted my wrist and I thought perhaps you could do something for it.'

Matron looked at the swollen wrist. 'That must hurt you quite a lot,' she said. 'How did you do it?'

Elizabeth told her. Matron soaked a bandage in cold water and wrapped it tightly round the hurt wrist.

'Will it soon be better?' asked Elizabeth. 'It's a good thing it's not my right hand.'

'It will take a little time to get right,' said Matron. 'Now, keep it as still as possible, please. And look – I will make you a sling out of this old hanky – like that – round your shoulder. That will help a bit.'

It was past teatime by now. Matron took Elizabeth into her own room and made some toast. Elizabeth was tired and pale, and although she said she didn't want anything to eat, she couldn't help thinking that the buttered toast looked rather nice. So she soon ate it up and drank the cocoa that Matron put before her.

Then she went off to the common room. Everyone was waiting to hear what had happened. Joan ran to her at once.

'Elizabeth! Is your hand badly hurt?'

'Well, it hurts a bit now,' said Elizabeth, 'but it's not nearly as bad as it was, since Matron bandaged it. It's all my own fault, as usual! I was impatient because Robert was late and I saddled Tinker for Peter – and Tinker ran away.'

'Poor old Elizabeth!' said Jenny.

Robert said nothing. He sat reading a book. He still looked cross.

There came a knock at the common room door and small Peter poked his head in. 'Is Elizabeth here?' he asked. 'Oh, there you are, Elizabeth. I say – how's the wrist? I'm awfully sorry about it. I suppose you won't be able to play the piano for a little while now.'

Elizabeth hadn't thought of that for one moment. She stared in dismay at Peter. 'Oh, my goodness!' she said. 'I had forgotten that. Oh *dear* – and I so badly wanted to practise hard this week, and now I've only got one hand!'

Everyone was sorry for her. Robert raised his head and looked solemn. 'Bad luck, Elizabeth!' he said. 'I hope your hand will be well enough to play at the concert.'

Elizabeth was upset. She felt the tears coming into her eyes and she got up quickly. She hated people to see her crying. She went out of the room and went into one of the little music-rooms. She sat down at the piano and leaned her head against the music-rack. She was angry with herself for doing something silly that had ended, as usual, in bringing trouble on herself.

Richard came along humming. He didn't see Elizabeth at the piano, and switched on the light to practise. He was surprised to find her in the dark, all alone.

'What's the matter?' he asked. 'What are you crying for?'

'Because what you said has come true,' said Elizabeth sadly. 'You told me I was getting conceited about my playing

– and that pride comes before a fall. Well, you were right. I did something silly, and now I've hurt my wrist and I can't play the piano, so I don't expect I'll be able to play duets with you at the concert.'

'Oh, I *am* sorry!' said Richard, in dismay. 'Now I suppose I'll have to play them with Harry, and he's not nearly so good as you. Oh, Elizabeth – what bad luck for you!'

'You shouldn't have said pride comes before a fall!' wept Elizabeth. 'I feel as if you made this happen!'

'Oh, don't be so silly,' said Richard. 'No, really, that *is* silly, Elizabeth. Anyway, cheer up – it may not be as bad as you think. I'll play to you, if you like. Get up and let me come on the stool.'

Elizabeth got up. She went to the chair in the corner and sat down, tired and cross. She didn't like Richard. She didn't like Robert. She didn't like Peter and his runaway horse. She didn't like herself. She didn't like anybody at all! She was a cross, unhappy, tired girl who didn't want to be pleased with anything or anybody!

But Richard's music made things much better. The little girl's frown went away and she leaned back feeling happier as the soft notes of the piano fell into the silence of the little room. Richard knew exactly what music to play to comfort her.

She stole away in the middle of his playing and went back to the common room. Perhaps her wrist would be better by the next day. Perhaps she was making a fuss after all. The others looked up as she came in.

'Come and do this puzzle with me,' said Kathleen. 'I can't find the bits that go just here.'

Everyone was kind to her, and Elizabeth was grateful. But she was glad when bedtime came, for her legs ached and her wrist still hurt her. Matron had a look at it and bound it up again.

'Keep it in the sling,' she said. 'It won't hurt so much then.'

Elizabeth hoped it would be better when she awoke in the morning. But it was still swollen and tender, though it did not hurt quite so much. She couldn't possibly play the piano with it! It was too bad!

And then Elizabeth found how difficult it is to do even the most ordinary things with one hand instead of two! She couldn't tie her hair-ribbon! She couldn't tie her shoelaces! She couldn't wash herself properly. She couldn't do up a button. She couldn't even seem to blow her nose easily.

The others did what they could for her, but Elizabeth was not easy to do things for. She wouldn't stand still – she jerked her head about when Joan tried to do her hair. She stamped her foot when poor Kathleen tried her best to do up the buttons of her blouse and got them all wrong.

'Oh dear – you've gone back to being the little girl who had a little curl right down the middle of her forehead!' sighed Joan. 'And you're being very, very horrid!'

'Well, so would you be if this had happened to you!' said Elizabeth, in a rage. 'If it had been my right hand I could at least have missed all the exams next week – but as it is I'll be able to do the exams, and have to miss the things I really love, like gym and riding and music! Oh, it's just too bad!'

In a few days' time Matron said Elizabeth could use her hand again – but alas for Elizabeth, she seemed to have no strength in the hurt wrist, and did not dare to use it much. The doctor said she must do what she could with it, and that gradually it would be all right – but she must be patient.

Well, that was just the one thing that Elizabeth couldn't be. She was upset and she showed it. She was annoyed and everyone knew it. She was furious because Richard was now practising the duets with Harry. And when she found that she couldn't be in the play because her part, which was that of a soldier, meant doing some drilling and exercising with a wooden gun, which her wrist couldn't manage – well, that was just the last straw!

The form were worried about Elizabeth, and disappointed in her. They talked about it.

'She's just getting crosser and crosser,' said Jenny. 'Nobody can do anything with her. She can't help thinking about herself and the nice things she's missing all the time. It *is* bad luck that she can't even play games. She does love them so.'

'Let's think of some things for her to do,' said Joan sensibly. 'There's George in the San, getting better. Couldn't Elizabeth go and read to him? Then there's all the programmes to make out for our play. Elizabeth is awfully good at designing things like that. Let's ask her to help us. She can easily do it with her right hand. And there's those gold crowns we have got to make – Robert says he'll make them – and surely Elizabeth could paint them with gold paint?'

Everyone agreed that it would be a good thing to get Elizabeth to do a few things so that she might forget her crossness. So one by one they went to her and asked her for her help.

Now Elizabeth was sharp, and she soon guessed why the children were suddenly asking her to do things for them. At first she felt that she would refuse – why should she do things for them when she couldn't do anything nice for herself at all? Joan saw her face, and took hold of her arm.

'Come along with me,' she said. 'Let's have a talk,

Elizabeth. I'm a monitor now and I have a right to tell you a few things and to help you.'

Elizabeth went with her into the garden. 'I know all you're going to say,' she said. 'I know I'm behaving badly. I'll never be a monitor like you. I'll never be able to forget myself and not mind when things go wrong.'

'You're a goose, Elizabeth,' said Joan patiently. 'You don't know what you can do till you try. There are only two weeks left of the term. Don't make them miserable for yourself. We all like you and admire you – don't let a little thing like a hurt wrist spoil our liking and admiration for you. You really are being rather trying. Everyone has been as kind and patient as possible. You make things very hard for your friends.'

Elizabeth kicked a stone along the path. After all, why should she make things horrid for her friends when her hurt wrist was her own fault and nobody else's? It *was* rather feeble of her. She took Joan's arm.

'All right, Monitor!' she said. 'I'll help you all I can. I'll do the programmes – and read to George – and paint the gold crowns. If I can't be a sport for two weeks I'm not much good!'

'It's just because you're such a strong person really that we don't like to see you suddenly being awfully weak,' said Joan. 'All right – now do your best for us, Elizabeth!'

Once Elizabeth had really made up her mind to do something she could always do it. She could be just as patient as she could be impatient. She could be just as cheerful as she could be cross. And in the very next hour her friends saw the difference!

She set to work on the programmes. She could manage to hold the paper with her left hand, and it was quite easy then to draw and paint with her right. Soon she had done half a dozen excellent programmes and the whole form came to admire them. Elizabeth was pleased.

'Now I'm going to be a good girl and go and read to George,' she said, smiling cheerfully round. And off she went, leaving the others laughing.

'She can be a monkey but you can't help liking her!' said Jenny. And everyone agreed!

26 A marvellous surprise

The last week of the term came. Exams were held every day, and the children worked hard. Elizabeth, Robert, and Kathleen worked the hardest of all, for each of them wanted to do well. Elizabeth longed to be top of her form, and so did Robert. Kathleen wanted to be top in *something*, she didn't mind *what*!

'It would be so lovely to tell Mother I was top in something,' thought Kathleen. 'I'm always so near the bottom – and Mother has been so perfectly sweet about it. It really would be a marvellous surprise for her if I could do well in something.'

Elizabeth's wrist was much better, but she still could not use it for playing the piano, and neither was she allowed to go riding, to play games, to dig in the garden, or to do gym! It really was very hard luck indeed.

She was in the songs at the concert, but not in anything else. She was not in the play and she was not playing with Richard. Harry was taking her place.

She tried to be cheerful, and she did not let anyone see how miserable she sometimes felt. She had pulled herself together, and was doing all she could to help the others in every way. She had painted the crowns marvellously for the play, and had even painted some trees for the scenery. Everyone thought they were wonderful.

She had done twelve programmes, the best that had been

done in the school. Miss Belle was to have one and so were Miss Best and Mr Johns. Elizabeth was proud of that.

She had been to read to George and to play games with him every day till he had come out of the San. She had done lots of little jobs for Matron. She couldn't help John in the garden as she had been used to doing, but she wrote out lists of flower seeds for him, ready for the spring, and listened eagerly when he told her all he and Peter had been doing.

'She's really being a brick!' said Joan. 'There's good stuff in our Elizabeth! She can be the naughtiest girl in the school – but she can be the best girl too!'

Elizabeth went to watch the hockey and lacrosse matches, and cheered the players, though deep down in her heart she felt very sad because she too was not playing. It was awful not to be able to do any of the things she liked so much.

'You know how to grin and bear things, Elizabeth,' said Richard. 'I'll say that for you!'

Nothing that Elizabeth had ever done made the school admire her as much as they did the last weeks of the term. Everyone knew what a fiery, quick-tempered child she was, and they knew how hard it must be for her to be cheerful, patient, and helpful. They were proud of her.

The school concert came. It was a most exciting afternoon. All the parents who could come, came to hear it. Mr and Mrs Allen were there, and were going to stay at a hotel the next day so that they might take Elizabeth back with them. Elizabeth flew to meet them, and they hugged her in delight. They were sad to hear that her hurt wrist prevented her from taking any real part in the concert, but they loved the programme she presented to them.

'I did it for you,' said Elizabeth proudly. 'Do you like it? The heads have my programmes too. And Mummy, please notice the gold crowns in the play, because I painted them – and the trees too.'

The concert was a great success. The play was funny and made the audience laugh loudly. Jenny and Kathleen were thrilled, because it was they who had written it out for their form. Richard played the violin most beautifully, and he and Harry played the duets that Elizabeth had been going to play.

She felt sad when she heard them, but she made her face smile all the time, and clapped hard at the end. She saw Jenny, Joan, Robert, and Kathleen watching her, and she knew that they were proud of her for being able to smile and clap, when inside she was very disappointed.

At the end of the concert the results of the exams were given. Elizabeth listened with a beating heart. So did Robert and Kathleen. Jenny did not care much – so long as she was somewhere near the top, that was all she minded! Kathleen cared much more. She knew she had done her best, and she hoped she wouldn't be too near the bottom!

At last Miss Belle came to Elizabeth's form. 'Miss Ranger says that this form has done exceedingly good work,' she said. 'Some of the children have been surprisingly good. First comes Elizabeth Allen and . . .'

But Miss Belle couldn't go on, because a storm of clapping interrupted her. Everyone seemed to be delighted that Elizabeth was top! Robert clapped hard too. How he hoped that he might be second! He had half hoped he might be top – but never mind, he might be second!

Miss Belle held up her hand for silence. 'Wait a moment,' she said. 'Let me finish what I had to say. First come Elizabeth Allen and Robert Jones! They have tied for first place, so they are both top.'

Robert sat up straight, his face bright with surprise and delight. So he and Elizabeth were top together! That was almost better than being top by himself. Elizabeth was sitting just behind him and she bent forward and clapped him on the back.

'Robert,' she said, her face beaming, 'I'm *awfully* pleased! I'd rather be top with you than top by myself, honestly I would!'

Robert nodded and smiled. He couldn't speak because he was so pleased. He had not such good brains as Elizabeth, so he had had to work really hard to win his place – and how proud his father and mother looked!

Miss Belle read down the list. Jenny was fourth. Joan was fifth, and both girls were pleased. Kathleen was sixth, well away from the bottom and she had top marks in history! Her cheeks glowed as she heard Miss Belle read that out. She was fairly near the top – and she had the best marks in history. What would her mother say to that? Kathleen stole a look round the big gym, and saw her mother's face. One look at it satisfied Kathleen. Her mother was looking as happy as anyone in the room.

'I can't think what Whyteleafe has done to my little Kathleen,' her mother was thinking. 'She looks quite different. She was always such a plain child, poor little thing, but now she's really pretty when she smiles – and how happy and bright she looks with all her friends!'

It was a splendid afternoon – and in the evening the last school Meeting was to be held. There was a surprise for the school then, which William did not announce until after the usual business had been dealt with.

All the money was emptied out of the box and evenly divided between each girl and boy. This was always done at the end of term, and the children were pleased, because it meant that they started their holidays with a little money in their pockets.

Then William made his announcement. 'I am sorry to say that we are going to lose Kenneth this term,' he said. 'Kenneth's father and mother are going abroad and he is to go with them. So we shall not see him again until they come back, which will not be for six months.'

The school listened in silence. 'I should like to say that we thank Kenneth very much for being a wise and good monitor for many terms,' said William. 'He has done many kind and generous things that most of us know nothing about, and we shall miss him very much. We shall be very glad when you come back, Kenneth.'

'Thank you,' said Kenneth, going scarlet. He was a quiet, shy boy, liked by everyone. The School was sorry to say goodbye.

'Well, as Kenneth will not be here to be a monitor next term, we have to choose another new one,' said William. 'You may like to have George back again, of course, or you may like to give someone else a chance if you think there is anyone worthy of being tried as a monitor. Nora, give out slips of paper, please.'

Nora rose, and gave out the slips of paper to each boy and girl. They took them and sat, thinking hard. It was unexpected to have to choose a monitor without talking about it between themselves first. Elizabeth chewed her pencil. Whom should she put? She decided on John – though she half felt that John wouldn't be a *very* good monitor, because he only understood one thing really well, and that was gardening! Still, it might be good to give him a chance. So she wrote down his name – John Terry.

Soon everyone had written down a name. The papers were given to the Jury, who unfolded them and counted them. Then the Jury, too, considered the matter and at last handed in their own papers.

William and Rita undid them, said a few words to one another, and then William knocked on the table with his hammer.

'Three names have been given the most votes,' he said. 'One is John Terry – the second is Robert Jones, whom the younger ones have voted for (you should be pleased about that, Robert!) – and the third is – Elizabeth Allen.'

Elizabeth jumped. She had no idea at all that anyone would vote for her – or would even *think* her good enough to be a monitor. She had the surprise of her life!

'Now we have heard a great deal of Elizabeth this term,' said William. 'Some good, and some bad. But both Rita and I have noticed how well Elizabeth has tackled a big disappointment these last few weeks – and has tried to forget herself and to help her form in every way. So it is no wonder that so many people have voted for her.'

'We know that she brought disappointment on herself,' said Rita, 'but we mustn't forget that she hurt her wrist in trying to stop Peter's horse. It was a brave thing to do. Elizabeth, you are a real mixture! You can be foolish and you can be wise. You can be impatient and you can be patient. You can be unkind and you can be kind – and we all know that you try to be fair, just, and loyal.'

Rita paused. Elizabeth listened, her heart thumping. Was Rita going to say that she must try again and perhaps be made a monitor next term, if she did well?

No – Rita was not going to say that. She smiled down at Elizabeth and went on: 'Well, Elizabeth, both William and I know you well by now, and we are quite sure that if we make you a monitor we shall not be disappointed in you. You will always treat other people better than you treat yourself – so we feel that it is quite safe to call you up to the monitors' table, and ask you to do your best for the school next term.'

With burning cheeks and shining eyes Elizabeth marched up to the Jury's table. She had never in her life felt so proud or so pleased. Oh, she didn't mind now not playing in the school concert – she didn't mind missing games and matches and gym! Her ill-luck had turned into a piece of marvellous *good* luck – she was actually a monitor – yes, really and truly one.

She took her place beside Joan, who squeezed her hand in delight. 'Jolly good!' said Joan. 'I *am* glad!'

And there we will leave Elizabeth, sitting at the monitors' table, dreaming of all the marvellous things she would do next term. A monitor! Could it really be true that the naughtiest girl in the school had become a monitor?

'I shall still do silly things, I expect, even now I'm a monitor,' thought Elizabeth, 'but never mind – I've got my chance! I'll show everybody something next term!'

And I expect she will!

The Naughtiest Girl

Girl is a monitor

1 Arabella comes to stay

It was in the middle of the Christmas holidays that Mother sprang a surprise on Elizabeth. Christmas was over, and Elizabeth had been to the pantomime and the circus, and to three parties.

Now she was beginning to look forward to going back to boarding-school again. It was dull being an only child, now that she had got used to living with so many girls and boys at Whyteleafe School. She missed their laughter and their chatter, the fun and games they had together.

'Mother, I love being at home – but I do miss Kathleen and Belinda and Nora and Harry and John and Richard,' she said. 'Joan has been over here to see me once or twice, but she's got a cousin staying with her now, and I don't expect I'll see her any more these hols.'

Then Mother gave Elizabeth a surprise.

'Well,' she said, 'I knew you would be lonely – so I have arranged for someone to come and keep you company for the last two weeks of these holidays, Elizabeth.'

'Mother! Who?' cried Elizabeth. 'Somebody I know?'

'No,' said Mother. 'It is a girl who is to go to Whyteleafe School next term – a girl called Arabella Buckley. I am sure you will like her.'

'Tell me about her,' said Elizabeth, still very surprised. 'Why didn't you tell me this before, Mother?'

'Well, it has been decided in a hurry,' said Mother. 'You

know Mrs Peters, don't you? She has a sister who has to go to America, and she does not want to take Arabella with her. So she wanted to put the child into a boarding-school for a year, perhaps longer.'

'And she chose Whyteleafe School!' said Elizabeth. 'Well, it's the best school in the world, *I* think!'

'That's what I told Mrs Peters,' said Mother. 'And she told her sister – and Mrs Buckley at once went to see the headmistresses, Miss Belle and Miss Best . . .'

'The Beauty and the Beast,' said Elizabeth with a grin.

'And it was arranged that Arabella should go to Whyteleafe this term,' went on Mother. 'As Mrs Buckley had to leave for America almost at once, I offered to have Arabella here – partly as company for you, and partly so that you might be able to tell her a little about Whyteleafe.'

'Mother, I do hope she's a nice sort of girl,' said Elizabeth. 'It will be fun sharing hols with someone I like, but awful if it's someone I don't like.'

'I have seen Arabella,' said Mother. 'She was a very pretty girl with most beautiful manners and she was dressed very nicely too.'

'Oh,' said Elizabeth, who was often untidily dressed, and was sometimes too impatient to have very good manners. 'Mother – I don't think I like the sound of her *very* much. Usually beautifully dressed girls aren't much good at games and things like that.'

'Well – you'll see,' said Mother. 'Anyway, she is coming tomorrow – so give her a good welcome and tell her as much about Whyteleafe as you can. I am sure she will love it.'

Elizabeth couldn't help looking forward to Arabella coming, even if she did sound rather goody-goody. She put flowers into the room her new friend was to have, and put beside the bed some of her own favourite books.

'It will be rather fun to tell someone all about Whyteleafe School,' she thought. 'I'm so proud of Whyteleafe. I think it's marvellous. And oh – I'm to be a *monitor* next term!'

Impatient, hot-tempered Elizabeth had actually been chosen to be a monitor for the coming term. It had been a great surprise to her, and she had been happier about that than about anything else in her life. She had often thought about it in the holidays, and planned how good and trustworthy and wise she would be next term.

'No quarrels with anyone – no bad tempers – no silly flare-ups!' said Elizabeth to herself. She knew her own faults very well. Indeed, all the children at Whyteleafe knew their faults, for it was part of the rule of the school that every child should be helped with his faults – and how could anyone be helped if his faults were not known?

The next day Elizabeth watched from the window for Arabella to come. In the afternoon a rather grand car drew up at the front door. The chauffeur got out and opened the car door – and out stepped someone who looked more like a little princess than a school-girl!

'Golly!' said Elizabeth to herself, and thought of her own school tunic of navy blue with its bright yellow badge. 'Golly! I shall never be able to live up to Arabella!'

Arabella was dressed in a beautiful blue coat with a white fur collar. She wore white fur gloves and a round white fur hat on her fair curls. Her eyes were very blue indeed and had dark lashes that curled up. She had a rather haughty look on her pink and white face as she stepped out of the car.

She looked at Elizabeth's house as if she didn't like it very much. The chauffeur rang the bell, and put a trunk and a bag down on the step.

Elizabeth had meant to rush down and give Arabella a hearty welcome. She had decided to call her 'Bella' because she thought Arabella rather a stupid name – 'like a doll's name,' thought Elizabeth. But somehow she didn't feel like calling her 'Bella' now.

'Arabella suits her better after all,' thought Elizabeth. 'She *is* rather like a doll with her golden curls and blue eyes, and lovely coat and hat. I don't think I like her. In fact – I think I feel a bit afraid of her!'

This was strange, because Elizabeth was rarely afraid of anything or anyone. But she had never before met anyone quite like Arabella Buckley.

'Although she's not much older than I am, she looks rather grown-up, and she walks like a grown-up – all proper – and I'm sure she talks like a grown-up too!' thought Elizabeth. 'Oh dear, I don't want to go down and talk to her.'

So she didn't go down. The maid opened the door – and then Mrs Allen, Elizabeth's mother, came hurrying forward to welcome the visitor.

She kissed Arabella, and asked her if she had had a tiring journey.

'Oh no, thank you,' said Arabella, in a clear, smooth voice. 'Our car is very comfortable, and I had plenty of sandwiches to eat halfway here. It is so kind of you to have me here, Mrs Allen. I hear you have a girl about my age.'

'Yes,' said Mrs Allen. 'She ought to be down here giving you a welcome. She said she would be. Elizabeth! Elizabeth, where are you? Arabella is here.'

So Elizabeth had to go down. She ran down the stairs in her usual manner, two at a time, landing with a bump at the bottom. She held out her hand to Arabella, who seemed a little surprised at her very sudden appearance.

'Do come down the stairs properly,' said Mrs Allen. It was a thing she said at least twelve times a day. Elizabeth never seemed able to remember to go anywhere quietly. Mrs Allen hoped that this nice, well-mannered Arabella would teach Elizabeth some of her own quietness and politeness.

'Hallo,' said Elizabeth, and Arabella held out a limp hand for her to shake.

'Good afternoon,' she said. 'How do you do?'

'Gracious!' thought Elizabeth, 'I feel as if she's Princess High-and-Mighty come to pay a call on one of her poor subjects. In a minute she'll be offering me a bowl of hot soup or a warm shawl.'

Still – it might be that Arabella was only feeling shy. Some people did go all stiff and proper when they felt shy. Elizabeth thought she had better give Arabella a chance before making up her mind about her.

'After all, I'm always making up my mind about people – and then having to unmake it because I am wrong,' thought the little girl. 'I've made an awful lot of mistakes about people at Whyteleafe School in the last two terms. I'll be careful now.'

So she smiled at Arabella and took her up to her room to wash and have a talk.

'I expect you didn't like saying goodbye to your mother, when she went off to America,' said Elizabeth in a pleasant voice. 'That was bad luck. But it's good luck for you to be going to Whyteleafe School. I can tell you that!'

'I shall be able to judge whether it is or not when I get there,' said Arabella. 'I hope to goodness there are decent children there.'

'Of course there are – and if they are horrid when they

first come, we soon make them all right,' said Elizabeth. 'We had one or two boys who were awful – but now they are my best friends.'

'Boys! Did you say *boys*!' said Arabella in the greatest horror. 'I thought this was a girls' school I was going to. I hate boys!'

'It's a mixed school – boys and girls together,' said Elizabeth. 'It's fun. You won't hate boys after a bit. You soon get used to them.'

'If my mother had known there were boys at the school, I am sure she would not have sent me,' said Arabella in a tight, prim little voice. 'Rough, ill-mannered creatures – dirty and untidy, with shouting voices!'

'Oh, well – even the girls get dirty and untidy sometimes,' said Elizabeth patiently, 'and as for shouting – you should just hear *me* when I'm watching a school match!'

'It sounds a terrible school to me,' said Arabella. 'I had hoped Mother would send me to Grey Towers, where two of my friends had gone – it's such a nice school. They all have their own pretty bedrooms – and wonderful food. In fact, the girls are treated like princesses.'

'Well – if you think you'll be treated like a princess at Whyteleafe, you'll jolly well find out you're wrong!' said Elizabeth sharply. 'You'll be treated as what you are – a little girl like me, with lots of things to learn! And if you put on any airs there, you'll soon be sorry, let me tell you that, Miss High-and-Mighty!'

'I think you are very rude, considering that I am a visitor, and have only just come,' said Arabella, looking down her nose in a way that made Elizabeth feel very angry. 'If that's the sort of manners they teach you at Whyteleafe, I am quite sure I shan't want to stay there more than a term.'

'I jolly well hope you don't stay a week!' said hot-tempered Elizabeth at once. She was sorry the moment after.

'Oh dear!' she said to herself. 'What a bad beginning! I really must be careful!'

2 *Off to Whyteleafe School again*

Arabella and Elizabeth did not mix well at all. There was nothing that Elizabeth liked about Arabella, and it seemed that Elizabeth was everything that Arabella most despised and hated.

Unfortunately Mother liked Arabella – and certainly the little girl had most beautiful manners. She always stood up when Mrs Allen came into the room, she opened and shut the door for her, and fetched and carried for her in a very kind and polite manner.

The politer Arabella was, the noisier Elizabeth became. And then Mrs Allen began to say things that made Elizabeth cross.

'If only you had as nice manners as Arabella, dear! I do wish you would come into a room more quietly! And I wish you would wait till I have finished speaking before you interrupt . . .'

All this made Elizabeth rather sulky. Arabella saw it, and in her smooth, polite way, she enjoyed making the differences between her and Elizabeth show up very clearly.

A week went by. Everyone in the house by this time liked Arabella, even Mrs Jenks, the rather fierce cook.

'She only likes you because you suck up to her,' said Elizabeth, when Arabella came up from the kitchen to say that Mrs Jenks was making her very favourite cake for her that afternoon.

'I don't suck up to her,' said Arabella in her usual polite tones. 'And I do wish, Elizabeth, that you wouldn't use such unladylike words. *Suck up!* I think it's a very ugly saying.'

'Oh, shut up,' said Elizabeth rudely.

Arabella sighed. 'I wish I wasn't going to Whyteleafe. If you're the sort of girl they have there, I'm not going to like it at all.'

Elizabeth sat up. 'Look here, Arabella,' she said. 'I'm just going to tell you a bit about my school, then you'll know exactly what you're in for. You *won't* like it – and the school won't like you. So it's only fair to prepare you a bit, so that you don't feel too awful when you get there.'

'All right. Tell me,' said Arabella, looking rather scared.

'Well, what I'm going to tell you would please most children,' said Elizabeth. 'It's all so sensible and fair and kind. But I dare say a Miss High-and-Mighty like you will think it's all dreadful.'

'Don't call me that,' said Arabella crossly.

'Well, listen! At Whyteleafe we have a head boy and a head girl. They are called William and Rita, and they are fine,' said Elizabeth. 'Then there are twelve monitors.'

'Whatever are they?' asked Arabella, wrinkling up her nose as if monitors had a nasty smell.

'They are boys and girls chosen by the whole school as leaders,' said Elizabeth. 'They are chosen because we trust them, and know them to be kind and just and wise. They see that we keep the rules, they keep the rules themselves, and they help Rita and William to decide what punishments and rewards the children must have at each weekly Meeting.'

'What's the weekly Meeting?' asked Arabella, her blue eyes round with surprise.

'It's a kind of school Parliament,' said Elizabeth, enjoying telling Arabella all these things. 'At each meeting we put into the money-box any money we have had that week – that's the rule . . .'

'What! Put our own money into a school money-box!' said Arabella in horror. 'I have a lot of money. I shan't do that! What a mad idea.'

'It seems mad at first if you're not used to it,' said Elizabeth, remembering how she had hated the idea two terms ago. 'But actually it's a very good idea. You see, Arabella, it doesn't do for one or two of us to have pounds and pounds to spend at school – and the rest of us only a few. That's not fair.'

'I think it's quite fair,' said Arabella, knowing that she would be one of the few very rich ones.

'Well, it isn't,' said Elizabeth. 'What we do is – we all put our money in, and then we are each given two pounds out of the box, to spend as we like. So we all have the same.'

'Only two pounds!' said Arabella, looking quite horrified.

'Well, if you badly want some more, you have to tell the head boy and girl, and they will decide whether you can have it or not,' said Elizabeth.

'What else do you do at the Meeting?' asked Arabella. 'I think it all sounds dreadful. Don't the headmistresses have a say in anything?'

'Only if we ask them,' said Elizabeth. 'You see, they like us to make our own rules, plan our own punishments, and give our own rewards. For instance, Arabella, suppose you are too high-and-mighty for anything, well, we would try to cure you byó'

'You won't try to cure me of anything,' said Arabella in a very stiff tone. 'You're the one that ought to be cured of a lot of things. I wonder the monitors haven't tried to cure you before now. Perhaps they will this term.'

'I've been chosen to *be* a monitor,' said Elizabeth proudly. 'I shall be one of the twelve jurymen, sitting up on the platform. If a complaint is made about *you* by anyone, I shall have power to judge it and say what ought to be done with you.'

Arabella went very red. 'The very idea of a tomboy like you judging *me*!' she said. 'You don't know how to walk properly, you don't know your manners, and you laugh much too loudly.'

'Oh, be quiet,' said Elizabeth. 'I'm not prim and proper like you. I don't suck up to every grown-up I meet. I don't pretend, and put on airs and graces and try to look like a silly, beautifully dressed doll who says "Ma-ma" when you pull a string!'

'Elizabeth Allen, if I were like you, I'd throw something at your head for saying that!' said Arabella, standing up in a rage.

'Well, throw it, then,' said Elizabeth. 'Anything would be better than being such a good-little-girl, Mummy's-precious-darling!'

Arabella went out of the room, and so far forgot her manners as to slam the door, a thing she had never done in her life before. Elizabeth grinned. Then she looked thoughtful.

'Now,' she said to herself, 'you be careful, Elizabeth Allen. You're very good at making enemies, but you know quite well that leads to nothing but rows and unhappiness. Arabella's an idiot – a conceited, silly, empty-headed doll – you let Whyteleafe deal with her, and don't try to cure her all at once by yourself. Try to be friends and help her.'

So Elizabeth tried to forget how much she disliked vain little Arabella and her doll-like clothes and manners, and treated her in as friendly a manner as she could. But she was very glad indeed when the day came for her to return to school. It was dreadful to have no other companion but Arabella. At Whyteleafe she would have dozens of others round her, all talking and laughing. She need never speak to Arabella unless she wanted to.

'She's older than I am, and perhaps she will be in a higher form,' she thought, as she put on her school uniform with delight. It was a nice uniform. The coat was dark blue with a yellow edge to the collar and cuffs. The hat was also dark blue, and had a yellow band. On her legs Elizabeth wore long brown stockings, and brown laced shoes on her feet.

'How I hate these dark school clothes,' said Arabella in disgust. 'What a dreadful uniform! Now at Grey Towers, the school I wanted to go to, the girls are allowed to wear anything that suits them.'

'How silly,' said Elizabeth. She looked at Arabella. The girl seemed different now that she was in the ordinary school uniform, and not in her expensive, well-cut clothes. She looked more like a school-girl and less like a pink-faced doll.

'I like you better in your uniform,' said Elizabeth. 'You look more real, somehow.'

'Elizabeth, you do say extraordinary things,' said Arabella in surprise. 'I'm as real as you are.'

'I don't think you are,' said Elizabeth, looking hard at Arabella. 'You're all hidden away behind airs and graces, and good manners and sweet speeches, and I don't know if there is a real You at all!'

'I think you're silly,' said Arabella.

'Girls! Are you ready?' called Mrs Allen. 'The car is at the door.'

They went downstairs, carrying their small night-bags. Each girl had to take a small bag with the things in it that she would need for the first night, such as a nightdress, toothbrush and so on, for their big trunks were not unpacked till the next day.

They carried lacrosse and hockey sticks, though Arabella had said she hoped she wouldn't have to play either game. She hated games.

They caught the train up to London, and at the big station there they met the girls and boys returning to their school. Miss Ranger, Elizabeth's form-mistress, was there, and she welcomed Elizabeth.

'This is Arabella Buckley,' said Elizabeth. All the boys and girls turned round to look at Arabella. How new and spick and span she looked. Not a hair out of place, no wrinkles in her brown stockings, no smut on her cheek!

'Hallo, Elizabeth!' cried Joan, and put her arm through her friend's.

'Hallo, Elizabeth! Hallo, Elizabeth!'

One by one all her friends came up, smiling, delighted to see the girl who had once been the naughtiest in the school. Harry clapped her on the back and so did Robert. John asked her if she had done any gardening. Kathleen came up, rosy-cheeked and dimpled. Richard waved to her as he carried a violin-case to the train.

'Oh, it's lovely to be back with them all again,' thought Elizabeth. 'And this term – this term I'm to be a monitor! And won't I be a success! I'll make that stuck-up Arabella look up to me all right!'

'Get in the train quickly!' called Miss Ranger. 'Say goodbye, and get in.'

The guard blew his whistle. The train puffed out. They were off to Whyteleafe once more.

3 Four new children

One of the exciting things about a new term is – are there any new children? What are they like? Whose form will they be in?

All the old children looked to see who was new. Arabella was, of course. Then there were three more, two of them boys, and one a girl.

Elizabeth, as a monitor, made it her business to make the new children feel at home. As soon as they arrived at Whyteleafe she set things going.

'Kathleen, show Arabella her dormitory, and tell her the rules. I'll help the other three. Robert, will you give a hand too? You will have two new boys to see to today.'

'Right,' said Robert, grinning. He had grown in the holidays and was tall and burly now. He was glad to be back at school, for at Whyteleafe were the horses he loved so much. He hoped that he would be allowed to take charge of some of them, as he had been the term before.

Elizabeth turned to the new children. Arabella had already gone off with Kathleen, looking rather scared. The other three new ones stood together, one boy making rather a curious noise, like a hen clucking.

'That's just like a hen clucking,' said Elizabeth. 'You sound as if you've laid an egg!'

The boy grinned. 'I can imitate most animals,' he said. 'My name's Julian Holland. What's yours?'

'Elizabeth Allen,' said Elizabeth. She looked at the new boy with interest. He was the untidiest person she had ever seen. He had long black hair that fell in a wild lock over his forehead, and his eyes were deep green, and brilliant, like a cat's. 'He looks jolly clever,' said Elizabeth to herself. 'I bet he'll be top of the class if he's with Miss Ranger.'

The boy made a noise like a turkey gobbling. Mr Lewis, the music-master, was passing by, and looked round, startled. Julian at once made a noise like a violin being tuned, which made Mr Lewis hurry into the nearest music practice-room, thinking that someone must be there with a violin.

Elizabeth gave a squeal of laughter. 'Oh! You *are* clever! I hope you're in my form.'

The other boy, Martin, was quite different. He looked very clean and neat and tidy. His hair was well brushed back from his forehead, and his eyes were a very clear blue. They were set a little close together, but they had a very wide and innocent expression. Elizabeth liked him.

'I'm Martin Follett,' he said in a pleasant voice.

'And I'm Rosemary Wing,' said the new girl, rather shyly. She had a pretty little face, with a smiling mouth, but her eyes were rather small, and she did not seem to like to look anyone full in the face. Elizabeth thought she must feel very shy. Well, she would soon get over that.

'Robert, you take Julian and Martin to the boys' dormitories,' she said, 'and I'll take Rosemary to hers. Hang on to them till they know their way about, won't you, and show them where they have their meals and things like that.'

'Right, Monitor,' said Robert, with another grin. Elizabeth felt proud. It was grand to be a monitor.

'Oh, are you a monitor?' asked Rosemary, trotting after Elizabeth. 'That's something very special, isn't it?'

'It is rather,' said Elizabeth. 'I'm *your* monitor, Rosemary. So, if ever you are in any difficulty or trouble, you must come to me and tell me – and I'll try and help you.'

'I thought we had to bring our troubles or complaints to the weekly Meeting,' said Rosemary. She had heard about this in the train that day.

'Oh yes; but at first you had better tell *me* what you'd like to bring before the Meeting,' said Elizabeth, 'because, you see, we are only allowed to bring *proper* difficulties or complaints to the Meeting – not just tales. You might not know the difference between just telling tales and bringing a real complaint.'

'I see,' said Rosemary. 'That's a very good idea. I'll do that.'

'She's a nice little thing,' thought Elizabeth, as she showed Rosemary where to put her things and told her to put out her toothbrush, hairbrush and nightdress. 'By the way, Rosemary, we are only allowed to have six things out on our dressing-tables, not more. You can choose what you like.'

It was fun to give out the rules like this. Elizabeth remembered how Nora, her own monitor two terms ago, had told *her* the rules – and how she had disobeyed them at once by putting out eleven things! She wondered now how she could have been so silly – how she could have dared!

'Yes, Elizabeth,' said Rosemary obediently and she counted the things to put out.

In the next dormitory Kathleen was having trouble with Arabella, who was very scornful about all the rules told her.

'Well, there are not many,' said Kathleen, 'and after all, we make the rules ourselves, so we ought to obey them, Arabella. I'll fetch Elizabeth here, if you like – she is the monitor and can tell you the rules properly.'

'I don't want to see Elizabeth,' said Arabella at once. 'I saw her quite enough in the holidays. I only hope I'm not in the same form.'

Kathleen had a great admiration for Elizabeth, although she had hated her part of the term before. She spoke up at once.

'You'd better not say things like that about our monitors. We choose them ourselves because we like and admire them. Anyway, it's bad manners to talk like that about somebody whose guest you have just been.'

Arabella had never in her life been accused of bad manners before. She went quite pale and could think of nothing to say. She looked at Kathleen and decided that she didn't like her. In fact, she didn't think she liked anyone at all, so far, except that little pretty girl called Rosemary – the one who was new. Perhaps she could make friends with her. Arabella felt sure that Rosemary would be most impressed with her tales of wealth, rich clothes, and marvellous holidays.

The next few days everyone settled down. A few were homesick, but Whyteleafe was such a sensible school and the children were so jolly and friendly that even new boys and girls found it hard to miss their homes. There was laughter and chatter to be heard everywhere.

All the new children were in Elizabeth's class. Good! It was fun to have new children, and now that Elizabeth was a monitor, it was nice to impress Julian and the others. Joan had gone up into the next class, so Elizabeth was the only monitor in hers.

Miss Ranger, the form-mistress, soon sized up the new children, and talked them over with Mam'zelle.

'Julian is a lazy boy,' she said. 'A pity, because I'm sure he has a wonderful brain. He thinks of plenty of clever things to do *outside* lessons. He can make simply anything with his hands. I saw him showing the others a little aeroplane he had made – it flies beautifully. All his own ideas are in it, none of them copied. He'll spend hours thinking out things like that – but not one minute will he spend on learning his geography or history!'

'Ah, that Julian,' said Mam'zelle, in a tone of great disgust. 'I do not like him. Always he makes some extraordinary noise.'

'Noise?' said Miss Ranger in surprise. 'Well, I must say he hasn't tried out any extraordinary noises on me yet. But I dare say he will.'

'Yesterday, in my class, there was a noise like a lost kitten,' said Mam'zelle. 'Ah, the poor thing!' I said. 'It has come into our big classroom and got lost. And for ten minutes I looked for it. But it was that boy Julian doing his mews.'

'Really?' said Miss Ranger, making up her mind that Julian would not do any mews or barks or whines in *her* class. 'Well, thanks for the tip. I'll look out for Julian's noises!'

The talk passed on to Arabella. 'A silly, empty-headed doll,' said Miss Ranger. 'I hope we can make something out of her. She really ought to be in the next class, but she is rather backward, so I must push her on a bit before she goes up. She seems to have a very high opinion of herself! She is always doing her hair or smoothing down her dress – or else trying to show us what perfect manners she has!'

'She is not bad, that one,' said Mam'zelle, who was quite pleased with Arabella because the girl had lived for a year in France and could speak French well. 'In my country, Miss

Ranger, the children have better manners than the children here – and it is pleasant to see one with manners as good as Arabella's.'

'Hm,' said Miss Ranger, who knew that Mam'zelle would rarely have anything to say against children who spoke French well. 'What do you think of Martin – and Rosemary?'

'Oh, the sweet children!' said Mam'zelle, who loved Rosemary's willingness to please, and to obey her in everything. 'The little Martin now – he is so good, he tries so hard.'

'Well, I'm not so sure about him,' said Miss Ranger. 'Rosemary is all right, I think – but she's a weak little thing. I hope she'll make the right friends. I wish Elizabeth Allen or Jenny would make friends with her.'

So the teachers sized up their new children – and the old children sized them up too. Julian was an enormous success. He was a real dare-devil, with most extraordinary gifts which he used when he pleased. He had a wonderful brain, inventive and brilliant, and he could make all kinds of things, and think of all kinds of amusing tricks which he was quite prepared to perform in class as soon as he had settled down a bit.

'It's a shame you are so low in the form, Julian,' said Elizabeth at the end of a week. 'You've got such marvellous brains. You ought to be top!'

Julian looked at her with his brilliant green eyes. 'Can't be bothered,' he said in his slow, deep voice. 'Who wants to learn history dates? I'll forget them all when I'm grown. Who wants to learn the highest mountains in the world? I'll never climb them, so I don't care. Lessons are a bore.'

Elizabeth remembered that she was a monitor. She spoke earnestly to Julian.

'Julian, do work hard. Do try to be top.'

Julian laughed. 'You're just saying that because you've remembered you're a monitor! You can't catch *me* with goody-goody talk like that! You'll have to think of some jolly good reason for me to work hard before I do!'

Elizabeth went red. She didn't like being called goody-goody. She turned away.

But Julian came after her. 'It's all right, I'm only teasing,' he said. 'Listen, Elizabeth – Joan, your best friend, has gone up into the next form – so why can't *we* be friends? You've got the best brain in the form – after mine, of course – and you're fun. You be my friend.'

'All right,' said Elizabeth, rather proud that the brilliant and unusual Julian should ask her. 'All right. We'll be friends. It will be fun.'

It *was* fun – but it brought a lot of trouble too!

4 The school Meeting

Arabella and the other new children waited with much interest for the first Meeting. At none of their other schools had they had a kind of school Parliament, run by the children themselves. They wondered what it would be like.

'It sounds a good idea,' said Martin.

'I think so too,' said Rosemary, in her timid little voice. She always agreed with everyone, no matter what they said.

'Stupid idea, I think,' said Arabella. She made a point of running down everything at Whyteleafe if she could, because she had so badly wanted to go to the grand school her friends had gone to – and she looked down on Whyteleafe, with its sensible ideas.

Julian unexpectedly agreed with her, though he usually had no time for Arabella, with her silly airs and graces. 'I can't say *I* shall bother much about the school Meeting,' he said. 'I don't care what it says or does. It will never make any difference to me. As long as I can do what I like I am quite willing to let others do what *they* like too.'

'Oh, Julian – you say that, but you don't mean it,' said Kathleen. 'You'd hate it if someone broke one of the things you are always making, you know! Or told tales about you, or something like that. You'd go up in smoke!'

Julian did not like being argued with. He tossed his long black hair back, and screwed up his nose in the way he always did when he was annoyed. He was making a tiny boat out of an odd bit of wood. It was like magic to see it form under his hand.

'Anyone can tell tales of me as much as they like!' said Julian. 'I don't care about anything so long as I can do what I like.'

'You're a funny boy, I think,' said Jenny. 'You are either terribly stupid in class, or – just sometimes – terribly bright.'

'Why? What did he do that was so bright?' asked Joan, who was listening. She was in the next form, and so did not see Julian in class.

'We were having mental arithmetic,' said Jenny. 'And usually Julian gets every single thing wrong in maths. Well, for some reason or other – just because he wanted to show off, I think – he answered every single question right, straight off, almost before Miss Ranger had got them out of her mouth!'

'Yes, and Miss Ranger was so astonished,' said Belinda. 'She went on asking him harder and harder ones – things *we* would have to think about and work out in our heads for a minute or two – but Julian just answered them pat. It was funny.'

'It made Miss Ranger awfully cross with him next time, though,' said Kathleen, 'because at the next maths lesson, he seemed to go to sleep and wouldn't answer a thing.'

Julian grinned. He really was an extraordinary boy. The others couldn't help liking him. He was so exciting. They all begged and begged him to make some of his amazing noises in Miss Ranger's class, but he wouldn't.

'She's watching out for them, I know she is,' he said. 'It's no fun doing them if people know it's me. It's *really* fun when people honestly think there's a kitten in the room – or something like that – like Mam'zelle did the other day. You wait. I'll give you some fun one day soon – but I'd like to choose the person myself to try my tricks on.'

Elizabeth was longing for the first School Meeting. She wanted to go and sit up on the platform with the other monitors, in front of the whole school. She was not vain about being made a monitor, but she was rightly proud of it.

'It really is an honour,' she said to herself. 'It does mean that the school trusts me and thinks I'm worthwhile. Oh, I do hope this term will go well, without any upsets or troubles.'

The children filed into the big hall for the first Meeting. Then in came the twelve monitors, serious-faced. They took their places, and sat, like a thoughtful jury, in front of all the children. Arabella gazed at Elizabeth with dislike. Fancy that tomboy, with her bad manners, being made a monitor!

Then in came William and Rita, the head boy and girl, the Judges of the whole Meeting. All the children rose to their feet as they came in.

At the back sat Miss Belle and Miss Best, the two headmistresses, with Mr Johns, one of the masters. They were always interested in the Meetings, but unless the head-boy and girl asked them to, they did not enter into it in any way. This was the children's own Parliament, where they made their own laws, their own rules, and where they themselves rewarded or punished any child who deserved it.

There was very little to talk about at that first Meeting. Every child was told to put what money it had into the big school money-box. Elizabeth looked with interest at Arabella, when she was sent round with the box. Would Arabella do as she had said and refuse to put in her money?

Arabella sat looking as if butter would not melt in her mouth. When the box came to her, she put in a ten pound note and two separate pound coins. She did not look at Elizabeth.

Most of the children had quite a lot of money to put into the box at the beginning of term. Parents, uncles, and aunts had given them pounds, pennies, and even notes to go back to school with, and the box felt nice and heavy when Elizabeth took it back to William and Rita.

'Thank you,' said William. The children were all talking together, and William knocked on the table with his little hammer. At once there was silence – except for a curious bubbling noise, like a saucepan boiling over.

It seemed to come from somewhere near Jenny, Julian and Kathleen. William looked rather astonished. He knocked again with his hammer – but still the noise went on, a little louder, if anything.

Elizabeth knew at once that it was one of Julian's extraordinary noises. She looked at him. He sat on the form, his green eyes looking over the heads of the others, his mouth and throat perfectly still. How *could* he do noises like that? Elizabeth felt a tremendous giggle coming and she swallowed it down quickly.

'I mustn't giggle when I'm sitting up here as monitor,' she thought. 'Oh dear, I wish Julian would stop. It's just like a saucepan boiling over, but louder.'

By this time one or two children were giggling, and William knocked sharply with his hammer again. Elizabeth wondered if she ought to say that it was Julian who was making the noise and holding up the Meeting.

'But I can't. He's my friend. And I'm not going to get him into trouble, even if I *am* a monitor,' she thought. She tried to make Julian look at her, and he suddenly did. She glared at him, then frowned.

Julian made one last loud bubbling noise, and then stopped. William had no idea at all who had made the noise. He gazed round the Meeting.

'It may be funny to hold up the school Meeting *once*,' he said. 'But it would not be funny a second time. We will now get on with the money-sharing.'

Each child came up to take two pounds from the monitors, out of the school box. William had brought plenty of change with him, which he put into the box, taking out the notes instead.

When each child had its two pounds for spending, William spoke again.

'The new children probably know that out of this two pounds they must buy their own stamps, sweets, hair-ribbons, papers, and so on that they want. If any extra money is needed, it can be asked for. Does anyone want any extra this week?'

John Terry stood up. He was in charge of the school garden, and was a very hard and very good worker. He, with those other children who helped him, managed to supply the school with fine vegetables and flowers. Everyone was proud of John.

'William, we could do with a new small barrow,' he said. 'You see, there are one or two of the younger children who are helping in the garden this term, and the old barrow is really too heavy for them.'

'Well, how much would a smaller one cost?' asked William. 'We've got plenty of money in the box at the moment, but we don't want to spend too much money.'

John Terry had a price-list with him. He read out the prices of various barrows.

'They seem very expensive,' said William. 'I almost think we had better wait a bit to see if the younger children are going to go on being keen, John. You know what sometimes happens – they start so well, and then get tired of it. It would be a waste of a barrow if we bought it and then no one used it.'

John looked disappointed. 'Well,' he said, 'it's just as you like, William. But I do think the youngsters are keen. Peter is, anyway. He worked hard last term, and I really couldn't do without him in the garden now. He's got his two friends with him now, helping us.'

Small Peter glowed red with pleasure at hearing John say this. His two small friends at once made up their minds that they would work hard in the garden too, and make John as proud of them as he seemed to be of Peter.

'Has anyone anything to say about a new barrow?' asked Rita. Nobody spoke – until Julian suddenly opened his mouth and spoke in his deep voice.

'Yes. Let the youngsters have their barrow – but I'll make it for them. I can easily do that.'

Julian had not stood up to speak. He lolled on the form in his usual lazy fashion.

'Stand up when you speak,' said Rita. Julian looked as if he was not going to. But at last he did, and then repeated his offer.

'I'll make a barrow, a small one. If I can go into the sheds, I can easily find everything I want. You don't need to spend any money then.'

Everyone was interested. Elizabeth spoke up eagerly.

'Let Julian do it, William! He's awfully clever at making things. He can make *any*thing!'

'Very well. Thank you for your offer, Julian,' said William.

'Get on with the job as soon as you can. Now – any other business to discuss?'

There was not. William closed the Meeting and the children filed out.

'Good, Julian!' said Elizabeth, slipping her arm through his. 'I bet you'll make the finest barrow in the world!'

5 Arabella gets into trouble

All the new children settled down as the days went on. Julian set about making the new barrow in a very workmanlike way. He explored the various sheds, and brought out an old rubber wheel that had once belonged to somebody's tricycle. He found some odd bits of wood and other odds and ends, and took them all to the carpentering room.

The children heard him whistling there as he hammered away. Then they heard the creaking of a barrow being wheeled up and down.

'Golly! Has he finished it already?' said Harry in surprise. 'He's a marvel!'

But he hadn't, of course. He was only making one of his noises. His green eyes twinkled as the children peeped round the door. He loved a joke.

The boys and girls crowded round him, exclaiming in admiration.

'Julian! It's going to be a marvellous barrow! Julian, how clever you are!'

'No, I'm not,' said Julian, laughing. 'I was bottom of the form this week. Didn't you hear?'

'Well, the barrow is fine, anyway,' said Belinda. 'It's just as good as a real one.'

Julian cared for neither praise nor blame. He had not offered to make the barrow because he was sorry that the youngsters hadn't one. He had offered to make it simply because he knew he could, and he would enjoy making it.

Julian was very well liked, for all his don't-care ways. But Arabella was not. She would make friends with no one but the little meek Rosemary. Rosemary thought the lovely well-manncred girl was like a princess. She followed her everywhere, listened eagerly to all she said and agreed with everything.

'I think this is a stupid school,' Arabella said to Rosemary many times. 'Think of the silly rules it has – all the sillier because they are made by the children themselves.'

Up till then Rosemary had thought that the reason the rules were so good was because they *had* been made by the boys and girls. But now she agreed with Arabella at once.

'Yes. They *are* silly.'

'Especially the one about putting all our money into the school money-box,' said Arabella.

This had not mattered much to Rosemary, who had only had two pounds and fifty pence to put in. Her parents were not very well off, and she had not been given much money at any time. Still, she agreed with Arabella, of course.

'Yes, that's a very silly rule,' she said. 'Especially for people like you, Arabella, who have to give up so much money. It's a shame. I saw you put in the ten pound note and the two pound coins.'

Arabella looked at Rosemary and wondered if she could trust her – for Arabella had a secret. She had not put in all her money! She had kept a five pound note for herself, so that, with the two pounds she had been allowed, she had seven pounds. She was not going to give that up for anyone! It was hidden in her handkerchief-case, neatly folded up in a hanky.

'No,' she thought. 'I won't tell Rosemary yet. I don't

know her very well, and although she is my friend, she's a bit silly sometimes. I'll keep my own secret.'

So she told no one. But she and Rosemary went down to the town together that day to buy stamps, and a hair-grip for Rosemary – and Arabella could not help spending some of her money!

'You go to the post-office and buy your stamps, and I'll go and buy some chocolates at the sweet-shop,' she said to Rosemary. She did not want the other girl to see her buying expensive chocolates, and handing over two or three pounds for them.

So, while Rosemary was buying a stamp in the post-office, Arabella slipped into the big sweet-shop and bought a pound of peppermint chocolates, the kind she loved.

She saw a bottle of barley-sugar too, and bought that. Lovely! Then, as Rosemary didn't come, she went into the shop next door, and bought herself a book.

The two girls wandered round the town a little while, and then went back to school. 'You know,' said Arabella, linking her arm in Rosemary's, 'you know, that's another silly Whyteleafe rule – that no one is allowed to go down to the town alone unless she's a monitor or in the higher forms.'

'Awfully silly,' agreed Rosemary. Arabella undid the bag of chocolates. 'Have one?' she said.

'Oooh, Arabella – what a lovely lot of chocolates!' said Rosemary, her rather small eyes opening wide. 'Golly, you must have spent all your two pounds at once!'

They went in at the school gate, munching chocolates. They were really delicious. Arabella shut up the bag and stuffed it into her winter coat pocket. She did not want the others to see what a lot of chocolates she had, in case they might guess she had spent more than two pounds on them.

She went to take off her hat and coat. Jenny was putting hers on, and when Arabella put the book she had bought down on the bench between them, Jenny picked it up.

'Hallo! I always wanted to read this book. Lend it to me, will you, Arabella?'

'Well, I haven't read it myself yet,' said Arabella. 'I only bought it this afternoon.'

Jenny looked at the price inside the cover, and whistled. 'It's a three-pound book. How could you buy that with two pounds?'

'I got it cheap,' said Arabella, after a moment's pause. She went red as she said it, and sharp-eyed Jenny saw the blush. She said no more, but went off, thinking hard.

'The mean thing! She didn't put all her money into the box!' thought Jenny.

Rosemary annoyed Arabella very much that evening when they were in the common-room together, because she gave away the fact that Arabella had bought the chocolate peppermints! She did not mean to, of course – but she did it, all the same!

The children were talking about the sweet-shop, which they all loved, and where they all spent money each week.

'I think those boiled sweets are the best bargain,' said Jenny.

'Oh no – those clear gums last much the longest,' said Belinda.

'Not if you chew them,' said Harry. 'I bet if you sucked a boiled sweet properly, right to the end without crunching it up, and after that sucked a clear gum without chewing at all, there wouldn't be much to choose between them.'

'Let's have a competition and see,' said John.

'It's no good *me* trying,' said Jenny. 'I always crunch

everything, and it goes like lightning down my throat.'

'*I* think the best bargain of all is chocolate peppermints,' suddenly said Rosemary's meek little voice.

Everyone laughed scornfully. 'Idiot!' said Julian. 'You only get about five for fifty pence. They are most awfully expensive.'

'They're not,' said Rosemary, 'really they are not. Arabella, show them the enormous bagful you got today at the shop.'

This was the last thing that Arabella wanted to do. She frowned heavily at Rosemary.

'Don't be silly,' she said. 'I only got a few. They *are* expensive.'

Rosemary was amazed. Hadn't she taken one herself from an overflowing bag? She opened her mouth to say so, but caught sight of Arabella's warning face and stopped.

The others had listened to all this with much interest. They felt perfectly certain that Arabella had spent a lot of money on the chocolates, and Jenny remembered the book too. She looked sharply at Arabella.

But Arabella was now looking her usual calm self, rather haughty. 'You're a deceitful person, in spite of your grand, high-and-mighty ways,' thought Jenny to herself. 'I bet you've got those chocolates hidden away somewhere, so that no one shall know you spent a lot of money on them. I'll find them too – just see if I won't!'

Arabella got up in a few minutes and went out. She soon came back, carrying a small paper bag in which were six or seven chocolate peppermints. 'These are all I got for my money,' she said graciously. 'I'm afraid there isn't enough for one each – but we could divide them in half.'

But nobody wanted any. It was an unwritten rule at Whyteleafe that if you didn't like a person, you didn't accept things from them. So everyone except Rosemary said no. Rosemary took one, feeling puzzled and astonished. She *knew* she had seen a much bigger bag of chocolate peppermints before. Could she have been mistaken?

Jenny grinned to herself. Arabella must think they were all stupid if she thought she could make the other boys and girls believe she had only bought a few sweets – when that silly little Rosemary had given the secret away! She wondered where Arabella could have hidden the rest of the chocolates.

She thought she knew. Arabella learnt music and had a big music-case. Jenny had seen her go to it that afternoon, although she had neither lesson nor practice to do. Why?

'Because she wanted to put her chocs there,' thought Jenny. She slipped off to the music-room, where everyone kept their music. She took up Arabella's case and peeped inside it. The chocolate peppermints were there, where Arabella had hurriedly emptied them.

Richard came into the room whilst she was looking. 'See, Richard,' said Jenny, in a tone of disgust. 'Arabella has kept some money back – and bought heaps of chocs and a book – and told all kinds of lies.'

'Well, make a complaint at the Meeting, then,' said Richard, taking up his case and going out.

Jenny stood and thought for a moment. 'Would a complaint at the Meeting be thought a tale?' she wondered. She had better ask the others before saying anything. But she wouldn't tell Elizabeth – not yet, anyhow – because Arabella had been staying with Elizabeth, and it might be awkward for the new monitor if she knew about Arabella.

So Jenny told the others, when Elizabeth, Rosemary, and Arabella were not there. They were really disgusted.

'I'm sure it would be a proper complaint,' said Harry. 'All the same, it's rather awful to have your name brought up at the Meeting quite so soon in the term, just when you're still new. Let's just show Arabella that we think her jolly mean. She'll soon guess why – and at the next Meeting I bet she'll pop *all* her money into the box!'

Then poor Arabella was in for a bad time! For the first time in her life she knew what it was to be with children who didn't like her at all, and who showed it!

6 *Arabella makes a complaint*

Arabella had turned up her nose at the boys and girls of Whyteleafe School from the first day she had arrived. She had told Rosemary that she didn't care whether they liked her or whether they didn't.

But it was difficult not to mind when everyone seemed to turn up their noses at her! It gave Arabella a very important, superior sort of feeling to despise all her class except Rosemary. But it gave her quite a different kind of feeling when she felt *she* was despised!

The children would not have been so thorough about it if Arabella had not behaved so stupidly from the beginning. Now they couldn't help feeling they were getting a bit of their own back!

'They treat me as if I was a bad smell!' Arabella complained to the faithful Rosemary. 'Why, that horrid boy Julian actually holds his nose when he passes me.'

This was quite true. Julian did hold his nose with his finger and thumb every time he came near Arabella. It annoyed her dreadfully. She was so used to being looked up to and admired by children, and to being praised by grown-ups that she simply didn't understand this sort of behaviour. It made her very angry indeed.

Arabella did not guess why the children were treating her like this. She had no idea that it was because they thought she had been dishonest and deceitful over her money. She felt sure she had been so clever about that that no one knew about it. She did not know that Jenny had peeped into her music-case and seen the chocolates there.

Jenny entered into the fun of teasing Arabella too. Her way of teasing her was to talk in a very smooth, polite voice, exactly like Arabella's, of amazing riches and wonderful holidays, in the very same way that Arabella loved to talk.

Jenny was a very good mimic. She could imitate anyone's voice, and anyone's laugh. It made the children giggle to hear her talking just like Arabella, when Arabella was there.

'And, my dears,' Jenny would say, '*last* hols were the most marvellous of all. We actually took three cars with us when we went away – and the last one held nothing but my party clothes! Oh, and I really must tell you of the time when I went to stay with my grandmother. She allowed me to stay up to dinner *every* night, and we had fifteen different courses to eat, and four different sorts of – of – ginger beer!'

Shrieks of laughter followed all this. Only Arabella did not laugh. She did not think it was at all funny. She thought it was simply horrid. At her old school everyone had loved hearing her tales. Why did they make fun of them at this nasty school?

Another very annoying thing happened to Arabella, too. She would be sitting in the common room, sewing or writing, and suddenly Jenny or someone would say 'Oh, look – is that an aeroplane?' Or, 'I say – is that a moth?' pointing at the same time out of the window or up to the ceiling.

Everyone would at once turn their heads, Arabella as well – and when poor Arabella turned back to her sewing or her writing, she would find her pen gone, or her scissors. She would hunt on the floor for them until she suddenly heard a giggle.

Then she would know that someone had quickly snatched them up and put them on the window-sill or on a desk in the corner, just to tease her.

She told Rosemary about all the teasing, and the other girl listened with sympathy. 'It's too bad, Arabella,' she said. 'I don't know why they do it.'

'Well, you ask them, and find out,' said Arabella. 'See? Now, don't forget – and don't say I asked you to find out.'

So, when Arabella was next out of the room Rosemary found courage enough to speak to Jenny.

'Why are you so beastly to Arabella?'

'Because she deserves it,' said Jenny shortly.

'Why does she deserve it?' asked Rosemary.

'Well, don't you think she's a stuck-up, deceitful creature?' said Jenny. 'I know you're always hanging round her like a little dog, but you must surely know it's dishonest to keep back money from the school box and spend it on herself – and then tell lies about it.'

Jenny's sharp eyes were fixed on timid Rosemary. The other girl dropped her eyes and did not look at Jenny.

She was too weak to stick up for her friend, or even to say that she did not know that what Jenny said was true – though now that Jenny had said it, it did seem to Rosemary that Arabella *had* been deceitful.

'Yes. That was bad,' said Rosemary at last. 'Oh dear. Is that why you are so horrid to her?'

'Well, she must know why we are,' said Jenny impatiently. 'She's not so stupid as all that, surely.'

Rosemary did not like to say that Arabella had no idea why everyone was horrid to her. Neither did she like to tell Arabella why the others were annoying her so. She was like a leaf in the wind, blown this way and that – 'Shall I tell her?

I'd better. No. I can't, she'd be angry. Well, I won't tell her then. Oh, perhaps I'd better. No, I really can't.'

So, in the end Rosemary did not tell Arabella and when Arabella asked her what the others had said, she shook her head.

'They're – they're just teasing you because they think it's fun,' she said. 'Just because they're horrid.'

'Oh!' said Arabella, red with anger. 'Well – I shall complain to the Meeting. I just won't have this happen!'

'Oh, Arabella, don't do that,' said Rosemary in alarm. 'They might say it was telling tales – and you'd get into worse trouble! Tell your monitor first, and see if she thinks it would be telling tales to tell the Meeting.'

'I certainly shan't say anything to Elizabeth!' said Arabella. 'Go and ask advice from *her*? No, thank you!'

And so silly Arabella, not guessing the trouble that would come to her, boiled away inside all the week, hating the others and longing for the Meeting to come!

It came at last. Arabella's lips were tightly pressed together as she looked round at the children of her form. 'Just wait!' her eyes seemed to say. 'Just wait and see how I will show you up!'

The school money-box was handed round, but not very much was put in. Arabella put nothing in. Then the two pounds were handed to everyone, and the usual business began.

'Any requests?'

'Please can I have fifty pence extra, William?' asked Belinda, standing up. 'A letter came for me this week without a stamp on – so I had to pay double postage on it, and it cost me fifty pence. It was from one of my aunts. I expect she forgot to put a stamp on.'

'Fifty pence for Belinda,' ordered William. 'It wasn't her fault that she had to pay extra.'

Fifty pence was handed out to Belinda, and she sat down, pleased.

'Could I have sixty pence to buy a new ball, please?' said a small boy, standing up rather shyly. 'Mine rolled down the railway bank and we're not allowed to go on the line.'

'Go to Eileen, and she will sell you one of our old balls for twenty pence,' said William. 'You will have to pay it out of your own money.'

There were no more requests. The children were whispering between themselves and William knocked on his table with his little hammer. Everyone stopped talking.

'Any complaints?'

Arabella and another girl stood up almost at the same moment.

'Sit down, Arabella. We'll hear you next,' said Rita. 'What is it, Pamela?'

'It's a very silly complaint,' began Pamela, 'but it's an awful nuisance. You see, my cubicle is by the big window in my dormitory, and my monitor says it must be kept open when we are not there – and it must, of course – but on windy days all the things on my dressing-table blow out of the window and I'm always getting into trouble because they are found outside!'

Everyone laughed. Rita and William smiled. Joan, who was in Pamela's form, spoke to Rita. She was Pamela's monitor.

'Pamela is quite right,' she said. 'Anyone who has that cubicle has the same trouble. But we could move the dressing-table out of the window, if Matron wouldn't mind.'

'Ask her tomorrow,' said Rita. Matron was the one who

saw to things of that sort, and she would see that the table was moved.

'Now, Arabella,' said William, noticing the angry, flushed face of the little girl, waiting her turn. Arabella stood up gracefully, not forgetting her little airs even in her rage.

'Please, William,' she said, in her smooth polite voice, a little shaken now by nervousness and anger, 'please, I have a very serious complaint to make.'

Everyone sat up straight. This was interesting and exciting. Serious complaints were worth listening to. All the first form looked at one another and pulled faces. Was Arabella going to complain about them? Well – she was very silly then, because her own secret would be bound to come out!

'What is your complaint?' asked William.

'Well,' said Arabella, 'ever since I have come to this school the children in my class – all except Rosemary – have been absolutely horrid to me. I can't tell you the things they do to me!'

'I think you must tell me,' said William. 'It's no use making a complaint and not saying what it really is. I can't believe that the whole form have been horrid to you.'

'Well, they have,' said Arabella, almost in tears. 'Julian is the worst. He – he holds his nose whenever he comes near me!'

There were a few giggles at this. Julian laughed loudly too. Arabella glared at him. Elizabeth, up on the monitor's platform, looked most surprised. She was the only one who did not know the real reason for the first form's treatment of Arabella, and she thought it was very foolish of the girl to complain of ordinary teasing. She had not known there was a real reason behind it all. But now she guessed that there was.

Arabella went on with her complaints. 'Then there is Jenny. She mimics me and mocks me whenever she can. I'm a new girl and it's very unkind. I haven't done anything to make them so unkind to me. It makes me very unhappy. I shall write to my mother. I shall . . .'

'Be quiet,' said Rita, seeing that Arabella was working herself up in a real tantrum. 'Be quiet now, and sit down. We will go into this. You shall have another chance to speak later, if you want to. But wait a minute – have you told your monitor about this?'

'No,' said Arabella sulkily. 'She doesn't like me either.'

Elizabeth went red. That was true. She had *shown* that she didn't like Arabella too – and so Arabella hadn't come to her for help or advice before putting everything before the Meeting. Oh, dear – that was a pity!

'Oh,' said Rita, glancing at Elizabeth. 'Well, now, let me see. We'll hear Jenny first. Jenny, will you please explain your unkind behaviour, and tell us if you have any real reason for it?'

Jenny stood up. Well – Arabella had brought all this upon herself! She began to tell what she knew.

7 The Meeting deals with Arabella

'You see,' said Jenny, 'Arabella really brought all the trouble on herself. She didn't keep the rules, and we knew it, and so we didn't like her, and we teased her. That's all.'

'Oh, you storyteller!' said Arabella. 'I *have* kept the rules!'

'Arabella, be quiet,' said William. 'Who is Arabella's monitor? Oh – you are, Elizabeth Allen. Will you tell us, Elizabeth, if, in your opinion, Arabella has kept the rules?'

'Elizabeth doesn't know what we know,' said Jenny, interrupting. 'We know the deceitful and dishonest thing that Arabella did – but Elizabeth doesn't.'

Elizabeth looked very upset. How was it she hadn't known? She spoke to William.

'I'm afraid I don't know what Jenny is talking about, William,' she said. 'I know I ought to – because I'm a monitor and I should see all that goes on in the form – but I really don't know this.'

'Thank you,' said William gravely. He turned to Jenny. 'What have you to complain of about Arabella, Jenny?' he asked, with a glance at the fiery-red face of Arabella. The girl was full of horror now – whatever was Jenny going to say? She, Arabella, had meant to make a complaint, but she had never guessed that anyone else would complain about *her*.

Then, of course, it all came out.

'Arabella didn't put all her money into the Box last week. We know, because she bought a three pound book in the town and a lot of expensive chocolates,' said Jenny. 'She hid some in her music-case so that we wouldn't know. She told lies about it too. So, you see, William, we don't like her and we showed it. We thought perhaps she would be ashamed of herself if we teased her, and be honest next time and put all her money in.'

'I see,' said William. 'Sit down, Jenny.'

Everyone was now looking at Arabella. She didn't know what to say. How she wished she had never made her complaint! Whatever was she to do! This was simply dreadful.

'Arabella,' said Rita, 'what have you to say to this? Is it true?'

Arabella sat quite still and said nothing. Then a tear trickled down her cheek. She felt very very sorry for herself. Why had her mother sent her to this horrid school where they had Meetings like this every week, and where no fault could be kept hidden?

'Arabella,' said Rita, 'please stand up. Is this true?'

Arabella's knees were shaking, but she stood up. 'Yes,' she said in a low voice. 'Some of it is true. But not all. You see – I didn't quite understand about putting *all* my money in. I did put in most of it. I wanted to ask my monitor, Elizabeth, about lots of things, but she seems to dislike me too, and – and . . .'

Elizabeth felt angry. Arabella was trying to put some of the blame on to *her*. She scowled at the girl and disliked her all the more.

'That's nonsense,' said Rita briskly. 'Elizabeth would always tell you anything, even if she did dislike you. Now listen, Arabella – you have behaved very foolishly, and you have only yourself to blame for the others' treatment of you. You will have to put things right.'

The head girl turned to William and spoke in a low voice for a moment or two. He nodded. Rita spoke again. The whole school listened with interest.

'It is sometimes difficult for new children to understand and fall in with our rules,' said Rita in her clear voice. 'But after they have been here for a while, every boy and girl agrees that our rules are good. After all, we make them ourselves *for* ourselves, so it would be silly of us to make bad rules. We haven't very many, anyway. But what we have must be kept.'

'I see that,' said Arabella, who was still standing up. 'I'm sorry I broke that rule, Rita. If the others had told me I had broken the rule, and just scolded me and given me a chance to put *all* my money in next time, I'd have done it. But they didn't. They were just horrid and I didn't know why.'

'You will go to your monitor after this Meeting and give her all the money you have got, every penny. She will put it into the box. You will be allowed only fifty pence this week, for stamps, as you had so much extra last week.'

Arabella sat down, her cheeks flaming red again. Give her money to Elizabeth! Oh, dear, how she would hate that.

Rita had not quite finished with the matter. She spoke to the first form rather sternly.

'There is no need for you to take things in hand yourselves and do any punishing,' she said. 'After all, your monitors are there to give advice, and we have the Meeting each week to put anything right. You first-formers are not sensible enough to know how to treat a thing of this sort. You should have gone to Elizabeth.'

The first-formers looked uncomfortable and felt small.

'It is all rather a mountain made out of a molehill,' said William. 'Arabella is a new girl and didn't understand the importance of our rules. Now that she does she will keep them.'

A little more business was done at the Meeting and then the children filed out. Elizabeth went to Jenny.

'Why didn't you tell me about Arabella? It was mean of you not to. I did feel an idiot, sitting up there on the monitors' platform, hearing all this and not knowing a thing about it!'

'Yes – we ought to have told you,' said Jenny. 'I'm sorry. But, you see, we knew Arabella had been staying with you, and we thought it might be rather awkward, if she was a friend of yours.'

'Well, she's not,' said Elizabeth in a fierce tone, 'I can't bear her. She quite spoilt the last two weeks of my holidays for me.'

'Sh-sh, you idiot!' said Kathleen, giving her a nudge. Arabella was coming by, and must have overheard what was said.

'Arabella! You'd better get your money now and give it to me,' said Elizabeth hastily, hoping that Arabella hadn't overheard what she had just said. 'I'd like it now, whilst the school box is out.'

Arabella was rather white. She said nothing, but went to her dormitory. She took out all the money she had hidden in various places.

She went downstairs again and found Elizabeth. Elizabeth, feeling rather awkward, held out her hand. Arabella crashed all the money into her palm, making Elizabeth cry out in pain. Some of the money went on the floor.

'There you are, you horrid thing!' said Arabella, her voice full of anger and tears. 'I suppose you were pleased to see me made fun of at the Meeting! Well, you didn't come out of it so well yourself, did you – the only person who didn't know anything! I'm sorry I spoilt your holidays – you may as well know that you spoilt mine too! I hated your home and everything in it, you most of all!'

Elizabeth was shocked and angry. She stared at Arabella, and spoke sharply.

'Pick up the money you've dropped. Pull yourself together, and don't talk to your monitor like that. Even if we don't like one another, we can at least be civil.'

'I can't imagine why anyone made *you* a monitor!' said Arabella in a scornful voice. 'Ill-mannered tomboy! I hate you!'

Arabella went quickly to the door, went through it, and slammed it after her. Elizabeth was left alone to pick up the money and put it into the box. She was astonished at Arabella's fierceness, and worried too.

'Oh, dear, it's going to be very difficult to be a monitor in the first form if this sort of thing is going to happen,' thought Elizabeth, rattling the money into the box.

As she went down the passage Arabella met Rita. The head girl saw her tear-stained face and stopped her kindly.

'Arabella, we all make mistakes at first so don't take things too much to heart. And do go to your monitor for advice and help,' said Rita. 'Elizabeth is a very wise little person, and very fair and just. I am sure she can always help you.'

This was not at all what Arabella wanted to hear at that moment. She was glad to have Rita's kind word but she did not want to hear praise of Elizabeth. As for going to Elizabeth for advice – well, she would never, *never* do that!

Rita went on her way, rather worried about Arabella, for she did not really feel that she was sorry for her mistake. If a person was really sorry, it was all right – they did try to do better. But if they were not sorry, only angry at being found out, then things went from bad to worse.

Elizabeth went to find Julian. 'I say, *you* might have warned me about Arabella,' she said. 'You really might. Why didn't you?'

'Couldn't be bothered,' said Julian. 'I don't care whether she puts her money into the box or not – and I certainly don't care if she's teased or not. I like to do as I like – and I'm not interfering with other people. Let them do as *they* like.'

'But Julian,' said Elizabeth earnestly, 'you must see that we *can't* all do as we like, when we live so many together. We—'

'Now don't start that goody-goody monitor talk,' said Julian at once. 'That's the only thing I don't like about you, Elizabeth – that you're a monitor. You seem to think it gives you a right to lecture me and make me into a Good Boy, and put everything right the way *you* think it should be.'

Elizabeth stared at Julian in dismay. 'Julian! How horrid of you! I'm very *proud* of being a monitor. It's mean of you to say it's the one thing you don't like about me. It's the thing I'm proudest of.'

'I wish I'd known you when you were the Naughtiest Girl in the School,' said Julian. 'I'd have liked you better then, I'm sure.'

'You wouldn't,' said Elizabeth crossly. 'I was silly then. Anyway, I'm just the same girl now as I was then, only I'm more sensible, and a monitor.'

'There you go again!' said Julian, heaving an enormous sigh. 'You simply can't forget for one moment that you are one of those grand, marvellous, and altogether wonderful beings – a *monitor*!'

He stalked away and left Elizabeth looking after him

angrily. How stupid it was to have a friend who didn't like the thing you were proudest of! Really, Julian was most annoying at times!

8 Elizabeth lays a trap

School life went on its jolly way in that Easter term. Games were played and matches were won and lost. Many of the children who liked riding rode out every morning before breakfast. Robert always rode with Elizabeth, and the little girl chattered away to him as they rode.

'Do you like being a monitor, Elizabeth?' asked Robert one morning not long after the second Meeting of the school.

'Well,' said Elizabeth, and stopped to think. 'It's funny, Robert, I felt terribly proud when I was made a monitor – and I do still – but somehow it's set me a bit apart from the others, and I don't like that. And Julian will keep saying I'm goody-goody, and you know I'm not!'

'No, that's the very last thing you are,' said Robert with a grin. 'Well, I've never been a monitor or leader of any sort, Elizabeth, but I've often heard my uncle say that being set over others isn't altogether a happy thing at first – till you're used to it, and shake down into your new position.'

'I didn't like not being told about that Arabella business,' said Elizabeth. 'I felt left out. Last term I'd have been in the middle of it and heard everything. I think someone might have told me.'

'Well, we will, next time, I expect,' said Robert.

Elizabeth worked in the school garden as hard as ever with John Terry. The crocuses they had planted together came up by the hundred, and looked wonderful in the early spring. The yellow ones came out first, and opened out well in the sunshine. Then the purple ones and the white ones came out together.

Julian's barrow was a great success. It was strange-looking, but strong and well made. The smaller boys loved using it.

'Thanks, Julian,' said John, 'that has saved us quite a large amount of money. I shall come to you when I want anything else!'

There was a great deal to do in the garden that term. There always was in the spring term. There was a good deal of digging to finish, and many things to plant. The children, under John's direction, sowed rows and rows of broad beans.

'Oh, dear, *must* we sow so many thousands, John?' groaned small Peter, standing up to straighten his back.

'Well, the whole school likes broad beans,' said John. 'It's nice to grow what people like.'

The children could keep pets if they liked, although they were not allowed to have cats or dogs, because these could not be kept in cages. Any child who had a pet had to look after it, and look after it well. If he or she did not, the pet was taken away from them – but that rarely happened, because the children were fond of their guinea-pigs, mice, budgies, pigeons, and so on, and took a great pride in keeping them clean and happy.

Arabella did not give Elizabeth any trouble in the next week or two, but she did not speak to her or have any more to do with her than she could help. She and Rosemary went about together, sometimes with Martin Follett. Julian made friends with everyone – or rather, every-one made friends with him, for he did not seem to care whether people were nice to him or not – but the boys and girls thought him an exciting and very clever person.

His only real friend was Elizabeth, and the two laughed and joked together a great deal. He did not say any more about her being a goody-goody monitor, and slowly Elizabeth began to get used to the idea that she was set over the others. In fact she sometimes forgot it altogether.

She was reminded of it when Rosemary came to her in trouble. 'Elizabeth – can I speak to you about something?' said the girl timidly.

'Of course,' said Elizabeth, remembering at once that she was a monitor, and must help, and act wisely.

'Well – I keep missing money,' said Rosemary, looking upset.

'*Missing* money!' said Elizabeth. 'What do you mean? Losing it, do you mean?'

'Well, I did think I was losing it at first,' said Rosemary. 'I thought I must have a hole in my pocket – but I haven't. I missed fifty pence last week. And yesterday a whole pound went – and you know what a lot that is out of two pounds, Elizabeth. And today twenty pence has gone out of my desk.'

Elizabeth was very astonished. She stared at Rosemary, and could hardly believe her ears.

'But Rosemary,' she said at last, 'Rosemary, you don't think anybody *took* your money!'

'Well, I do,' said Rosemary. 'I hate to say anything, Elizabeth, really I do. But I haven't any money left now except thirty pence, and that has to last me till the next Meeting, and I really must buy some stamps.'

'This is awful,' said Elizabeth. 'It's – it's stealing, Rosemary. Are you quite, quite sure of what you say?'

'Yes,' said Rosemary. 'Shall I make a complaint at the next Meeting?'

'No,' said Elizabeth grandly. 'I may be able to settle it myself. Then we can bring it before the Meeting, and we can tell them we settled the matter between us.'

'All right,' said Rosemary, who had no wish to get up and say anything before the Meeting. She was far too timid and weak! 'How will you settle it?'

'We'll lay a trap,' said Elizabeth. 'I'll think about it, Rosemary, and tell you. Don't tell anyone else.'

'Well – I did tell Martin Follett,' said Rosemary. 'I couldn't very well help it, because I was looking all over the place for my pound yesterday, and feeling very miserable at losing it – and he came in and was awfully kind. He helped me hunt for ages, and he offered me fifty pence of his own. So then I told him that I couldn't understand what was happening to my money. But I haven't told anyone else.'

'Well, don't,' said Elizabeth. 'We don't want to put anyone on their guard. I must say it was kind of Martin to offer you fifty pence, though.'

'He's very generous,' said Rosemary. 'He bought John Terry a packet of very special dwarf beans for the garden, you know. He said he wasn't keen on gardening himself, so that was his only way of doing his bit.'

'I wonder – I do wonder who could possibly be mean enough to take anyone's money,' thought Elizabeth as Rosemary went out of the room. 'What a horrible thing to do! Now, this really is a problem for me, and I must think about it. I'm a monitor, and I must try to put it right.'

She sat down and thought hard. She must find out the thief. Then she could deal with her – or him – and prove to everyone what a fine, sensible monitor she was. But how could she catch him?

'I know what I'll do,' said Elizabeth to herself. 'I'll show everyone the fine new pound I got out of the school box last week, and then I'll put it in my desk – but I'll mark it first, so that I shall be able to know it again – and then watch to see if it disappears.'

So, the next day, when the children were playing in the gym at break, because it was raining out-of-doors, Elizabeth took out her brand-new pound and showed it round.

'Look,' she said. 'It must have come out of the mint only last week, I should think! Isn't it bright and new?'

Ruth had a new pound as bright as gold, and she brought that out of her purse too. Robert had a new fifty pence bit.

'I shan't keep my shiny pound in my pocket, in case I get a hole there,' said Elizabeth. 'I shall put it in my desk, just under the ink-hole. It will be safe there.'

Before she put it there she marked a little cross on it with black Indian ink. Then she placed it under the ink-hole, in front of everyone, just before Miss Ranger came to take the class.

She glanced at Rosemary. The girl nodded her head slightly to tell Elizabeth that she knew why she had shown off her pound and put it into a safe place in front of everyone.

'Now we'll just see,' thought Elizabeth glancing round the class and wondering for the hundredth time which boy or girl could possibly be mean enough to take it.

The children left the schoolroom after morning lessons were finished and went to have a quick run and play in the garden. Then they had to come in to wash before dinner.

Elizabeth ran into the classroom to see whether her pound was still in its place. She opened her desk. Yes – her pound was still there. She felt glad. Perhaps Rosemary was mistaken after all!

It was still there when afternoon school began. Rosemary

looked across at her and Elizabeth nodded her head to tell her that the money was still there. Suppose the thief did not take it? Elizabeth would have to think of something else.

The pound was still there after tea. Rosemary came up to Elizabeth. 'Don't leave your pound there any more,' she said. 'I don't want it to be taken. You might not get it back – and a whole pound lost would be dreadful.'

'I'll leave it there till tomorrow,' said Elizabeth. 'Just to see.'

In the morning, before school, the little girl slipped along to the classroom. She opened her desk and felt for the bright new pound.

It wasn't there. It was gone. Although she had half expected this, Elizabeth was really shocked. So there was a thief in the class – a mean, horrible thief. Who was it? Well – wait till she saw that marked pound – then she would know!

9 Elizabeth gets a shock

It was one thing to mark a coin so that she would know it again when she saw it, but another thing to make a plan to find it in someone's keeping! Elizabeth wondered and wondered how she could manage this.

After tea that day it was still raining and the children gathered together in their common-room. It was a cheerful room with wide windows, a big fireplace, a gramophone and a wireless, and lockers for all the children to keep their things in. It was the room the children liked best and felt to be really their own.

There was a merry noise that evening. The wireless was going, and the gramophone too, so that the one or two who wanted to read groaned aloud, and went to turn off either the wireless or the gramophone.

But as these were immediately turned on again by somebody else, it was a waste of time to turn them off!

'I say! Let's play a game of some sort,' said somebody. 'I've got a good race-game here. Let's all play it. There are twelve horses to race.'

'Right,' said the children, and watched Ruth put out the big game. It almost covered the table. There was a little squabbling over which horses to choose, and then the game began.

It was fun to be playing a game all together like this, and it was exciting to move the horses along the big board.

'Blow!' said Harry. 'I've landed in the middle of a ditch. I've got to go back six. One – two – three – four – five – six!'

The game was played to the end. Belinda won, and was presented with a bar of chocolate. Then Kathleen got out a game of her own. It was a spinning game. There were many little tops, all of different colours to be spun. They spun beautifully, making a tiny whirring sound as they did so.

Seeing the tops spinning gave Elizabeth an idea. She banged on the table.

'Let's all see if we can spin coins. Who is the best at it?'

The children put their hands into their pockets and brought out money. Some had pennies, some ten pences, some fifty pences, and one or two of them had pounds.

Julian had been far and away the best at spinning the tops. He could make them jump and hop across the table in a marvellous way. Now he showed how clever he was with coins.

'See my penny hop!' he cried, and spun it deftly on the polished table-top. It hopped and skipped as it spun in a marvellous way. Nobody else could do the trick.

'Watch me spin a pound on the top of a glass!' said Julian. 'It will make a peculiar noise. Fetch a glass, somebody.'

A glass appeared and was put on the table. Everyone watched Julian. His green eyes gleamed with pleasure as he saw the admiring looks around him. He spun the coin on the bottom of the upturned glass, and it made a very funny noise.

'Like singing a little song,' said Ruth. 'Let *me* try, Julian.'

The pound fell off the glass, and Ruth picked it up. She tried her best to spin it, but it hopped off the glass at once and rolled off the table beside Elizabeth. The little girl bent to pick it up.

It was a bright new one. Elizabeth glanced at it, thinking it was funny that there should be a second brand-new pound coin in the form – and then she saw something that gave her a terrible shock.

She saw the tiny black cross she had made on the coin! She stared at it in the greatest dismay. It was her own pound, her very own, the one she had shown everyone, the one she had marked and put into her desk.

'Come on, Elizabeth – hand over the pound!' said Ruth impatiently. 'Anyone would think you had never seen a pound before, the way you are staring at it!'

Elizabeth threw the coin across to Ruth. Her hand was trembling. Julian! *Julian* had her pound. But Julian was her friend. He couldn't have her pound. But he had – he had! He had taken it out of his pocket. Elizabeth herself had seen him. The little girl stared miserably across at Julian, who was watching Ruth with his deep-set eyes, a lock of black hair over his forehead as usual.

Rosemary had noticed Elizabeth's face. She had seen her staring at the pound. She knew that it must be the same one that the little girl had marked. She too looked in amazement at Julian.

Elizabeth was not going to say anything to Julian just then, but she could hardly wait for a chance to speak to him alone. She waited about that evening, hoping that she would find a chance. She thought and thought about the whole affair.

'Of course, I know Julian does just as he likes, and says so,' thought Elizabeth. 'He just doesn't care about anything or anybody. But after all, I am his friend, and he should care about what he does to *me*. He could have had my pound if he had asked me. How *could* he do such a thing?'

Then another thought came into her mind. 'I mustn't judge him till I hear what he says. Somebody may have lent it to him – or he may have given someone change for a pound. I must be careful what I say. I really must.'

Just before bedtime her chance came to speak to Julian alone. He went to get a book from the library, and Elizabeth met him in the passage as he came back.

'Julian,' she said, 'where did you get your nice bright pound from?'

'From the school box last week,' said Julian, at once. 'Why?'

'Are you sure?' said Elizabeth. 'Oh, Julian, are you quite, quite sure?'

'Of course I am, idiot. Where else can we get money from?' said Julian, puzzled. 'What are you looking so upset about? What's the matter with my pound?'

Elizabeth was about to say that it was *her* pound, when she stopped. No – she mustn't say that, or Julian would know she was accusing him of taking it from her. He was her friend. She couldn't accuse him of anything so dreadful. She must think about it.

'Nothing's the matter with the pound,' she answered at last, thinking that something must be dreadfully the matter with Julian.

'All right then, don't look so peculiar,' said Julian, getting impatient. 'It's *my* pound – out of the school box – and that's that.'

He stalked off, looking puzzled and annoyed. Elizabeth stared after him. Her mind was in a complete muddle. Of all the people in the form, the one she had never even thought of for one moment as the thief was Julian.

She slipped into a music-room by herself and began to

play a sad and gloomy piece on the piano. Richard, who was passing, looked in in surprise.

'Gracious, Elizabeth! Why are you playing like that? Anyone would think you had lost a pound and found a penny!'

This old saying was half true at the moment, and Elizabeth gave a choky laugh. 'Well – I *have* lost a pound – but I haven't found a penny,' she said.

'Golly, Elizabeth, you're not making yourself miserable over a pound, are you?' said Richard. 'I've never heard you playing so dolefully before. Cheer up.'

'Richard, listen – I'm not silly enough to be miserable over a pound,' said Elizabeth. 'It's something else.'

'Well, tell me then,' said Richard. 'I shan't tell anyone else, you know that.'

This was true. Elizabeth looked at Richard, and thought perhaps he could help her.

'Suppose you had a friend, and suppose he did something simply terribly mean to you – what would you do?' she asked.

Richard laughed. 'If it really was my friend – well, I wouldn't believe it!' he said. 'I'd know there was some mistake.'

'Oh, Richard, I think you're right,' said Elizabeth. 'I just won't believe it!'

She began to play the piano again, a happier tune. Richard grinned and left Elizabeth. He was used to her troubles by now. She was always getting into some difficulty or bother!

'Richard is right,' thought Elizabeth. 'I shan't believe it. It's some accident that Julian has got that pound. I'll have to begin all over again and find some way to catch the real thief.'

So she was just as friendly to Julian as ever, though Rosemary, who knew what had happened, was very puzzled to see it. She spoke to Elizabeth about it.

'It couldn't have been Julian,' said Elizabeth shortly. 'It must have been someone else. He got that pound out of the school box. He said he did, when I asked him. There is some mistake.'

The next day Rosemary came to Elizabeth again. 'Listen,' she said, 'what do you think has happened? *Arabella* has lost some money now! Do you suppose it's the thief at work again?'

'Oh, golly!' said Elizabeth. 'I was so hoping that nothing more would happen. How much has Arabella lost?'

'Fifty pence,' said Rosemary. 'She put it into her mac pocket, and left it there – and when she went to get it, it was gone. And, Elizabeth, Belinda left some chocolate in her desk – and that's gone too. Isn't it awful?'

'Yes – it is,' said Elizabeth. 'How hateful it all is! Well – I'm absolutely determined to find out who the thief is now – and I'll haul him or her in front of the Meeting at once!'

The next thing that disappeared was sweets out of Elizabeth's locker. She went to get them – and they were not there!

'Blow!' said Elizabeth, angry and shocked. 'This is getting worse. I wish I knew who had my sweets.'

She soon knew. In class that afternoon Julian screwed up his face as if he wanted to sneeze. He pulled a hanky out of his pocket quickly, and something fell out. It was a sweet.

'One of *my* sweets!' said Elizabeth angrily to herself. 'The beast! He's taken my sweets. Then he must have taken that pound too. And he calls himself my friend!'

10 A dreadful quarrel

The more Elizabeth thought about the stolen money and sweets, the angrier she felt with Julian. It must be Julian – but how could he do such a thing?

'He's always saying he does as he likes, so I suppose he takes other people's things if he wants them,' thought the little girl. 'He's bad. I know he's clever and amusing and jolly – but he's bad. I shall have to speak to him.'

She could hardly wait till the afternoon class was over. She paid no attention whatever to her lessons and Miss Ranger glanced at her sharply two or three times. Elizabeth did not seem to hear any questions at all, but simply gazed into space, with an angry look in her eyes.

'Elizabeth, I suppose you know you are in class?' said Miss Ranger at last. 'You have not answered a single question for the last half-hour.'

'I'm sorry, Miss Ranger,' said Elizabeth hastily. 'I – I was thinking of something else.'

'Well, will you kindly think of what you are supposed to be doing?' said Miss Ranger.

So Elizabeth had to try and forget Julian's misdeeds for a while, and think of Mary, Queen of Scots. But somehow her thoughts always slid away to Julian.

She looked at the boy, who sat in front of her. He was writing, his lock of black hair falling over his face. He brushed it impatiently away from time to time. Elizabeth wondered why he didn't have his hair cut shorter. Then it wouldn't worry him so. He looked round and grinned at her, his green eyes rather like a goblin's.

Elizabeth would not smile back. She bent her head down to her book, and Julian looked surprised. Elizabeth was usually ready with her smiles.

The class went rushing off at four o'clock – all except Elizabeth, who had to stay in and copy out some work for Miss Ranger. She was annoyed at this but not really surprised, for she knew she had not done any work at all that afternoon. So she raced through it, her mind still thinking of what she should say to Julian. She must get him alone somewhere.

It was teatime when she had finished. She went to have her tea, but because she was upset she could not eat much, and the others teased her.

'She's sickening for measles or something,' said Harry. 'I've never seen Elizabeth off her food before. There must be something wrong with her!'

'Don't be funny,' said Elizabeth crossly.

Harry looked surprised.

'What's the matter? Are you all right?'

Elizabeth nodded. Yes – *she* was all right, but something else was all wrong. Oh, dear. She didn't want to tackle Julian, and yet she wouldn't have any peace of mind till she did.

She went to Julian after tea. 'Julian, I want to talk to you. It's very important.'

'Can't it wait?' asked Julian. 'I want to finish a job I'm doing.'

'No. It can't wait,' said Elizabeth. 'It's really important.'

'All right,' said Julian. 'I'll come and hear this terribly important thing.'

'Come into the garden,' said Elizabeth. 'I want to talk to

you where we can't be overheard.'

'Well – I'll come to the stables,' said Julian. 'There won't be anybody about there now. You're very mysterious, Elizabeth.'

They walked together to the stables. No one was to be seen there at all. 'Now, what is it?' said Julian. 'Hurry up, because I want to get on with my job. I'm mending a spade for John.'

'Julian. Why did you take that money – and the chocolate and my sweets?' asked Elizabeth.

'What money – and what sweets?' said Julian.

'Oh, don't pretend you don't know!' cried Elizabeth losing her temper. 'You took my pound – and you must have taken Rosemary's money too – and I *saw* one of my sweets drop out of your pocket this afternoon when you pulled out your hanky to sneeze.'

'Elizabeth, how *dare* you say these things to me?' said Julian, his face going red, and his green eyes getting very deep in colour.

'I dare because I'm a monitor, and I know all about your meanness!' said Elizabeth in a low, angry voice. 'You called yourself my friend – and . . .'

'Well, I like that! *You* call yourself *my* friend – and yet you say these hateful things to me!' said Julian in a loud voice, also losing his temper. 'Just because you're a monitor you think you have the right to go round accusing innocent people of horrible tricks. You're not fit to be anyone's friend. You aren't mine any longer.'

He began to walk off, but Elizabeth ran after him, her eyes blazing. She caught hold of his coat-sleeve. Julian tried to shake her off.

'You've got to listen to me, Julian!' almost shouted

Elizabeth. 'You've got to! Do you want all this to be brought out at the next Meeting?'

'If you dare to say anything to anyone else, I'll pay you out in a way you won't like,' said Julian, between his teeth. 'All girls are the same – catty and dishonourable – making wild statements that aren't true – and not even believing people when they do tell the truth!'

'Julian! I don't want to bring it up at the Meeting,' cried Elizabeth. 'I don't – I don't. That's why I'm giving you this chance of telling me, so that I can help you and put things right. You always say you do as you like – so I suppose you thought you could take anything you wanted – and . . .'

'Elizabeth, I *do* do as I like – but there are many many things I don't like, and would never do,' said Julian, his green eyes flashing, and his black brows coming down low over them. 'I don't like stealing – I don't like lying – I don't like tale-telling. So I don't do those things. Now I'm going. You're my worst enemy now, not my best friend. I shall never, never like you again.'

'I'm not your worst enemy, I want to help you,' said Elizabeth. 'I saw my own marked pound, I tell you. I saw my own sweet come out of your pocket. I'm a monitor, so I . . .'

'So you thought you had the right to accuse me, and you thought I'd confess to something I don't happen to have done, and you thought I'd cry on your shoulder and promise my monitor to be a good little boy,' said Julian in a horrid voice. 'Well, you are mistaken, my dear Elizabeth. Why anyone made you a monitor I can't think!'

He walked away. Elizabeth by now was in a real temper, and she tried to pull him back once more. Julian turned in a rage, took hold of Elizabeth by the shoulders and shook her so hard that her teeth rattled in her head.

'If you were a boy I'd show you what I really think of you!' said Julian in a low, fierce voice. He suddenly let Elizabeth go and walked off, his hands deep in his pockets, his hair untidy, and his mouth in a straight, angry line.

Elizabeth felt rather weak. She leaned against the stable wall and tried to get back her breath. She tried to think clearly, but she couldn't. What a dreadful, dreadful thing to happen!

Footsteps nearby made her jump. Martin Follett came out of the stable, looking very white and scared.

'Elizabeth! I couldn't help hearing. I didn't like to come out and interrupt. Elizabeth, I'm so sorry for you. Julian had no right to be so beastly when you were trying your hardest to help him.'

Elizabeth felt grateful for Martin's friendly words, but she was sorry he had overheard everything.

'Martin, you're not to say a word to anyone about this,' she said, standing up straight again, and pushing back her curls. 'It's very private and secret. Do you promise?'

'Of course,' said Martin, 'but, Elizabeth, let me help a bit. I'll give you some of my sweets. And I'll give you a pound to make up for the one you lost. That will put things right, won't it? Then you needn't bother Julian any more, or quarrel with him. You needn't bring the matter up at the Meeting either.'

'Oh, Martin, it's all very kind of you,' said Elizabeth, feeling very tired suddenly, 'but you don't see the point. It's not my pound or my sweets I mind, silly – it's the fact that Julian has been taking them. You can't put *that* right, can you! Giving me a pound and your sweets won't help Julian to stop taking what isn't his. I should have thought you could have seen that.'

'Well – give him a chance,' said Martin earnestly. 'Don't report him at the Meeting. Just give him a chance.'

'I'll see,' said Elizabeth. 'I'll have to think it all out. Oh, dear, I wish I wasn't a monitor. I wish I could go to a monitor for help! I don't seem much use as a monitor myself. I can't even think what I ought to do.'

Martin slipped his arm through hers. 'Come and have a talk with John about the garden,' he said. 'That will do you good.'

'You're kind to me, Martin,' said Elizabeth gratefully. 'But I don't want to talk to John. I don't want to talk to anybody just now. I want to think by myself. So leave me, please, Martin. And, Martin, you do *promise* not to tell anyone about this, don't you? It's Julian's business and mine, not anybody else's.'

'Of course I promise,' said Martin, looking straight at Elizabeth. 'You can trust me, Elizabeth. I'll leave you now, but if I can help you any time, I will.'

He went, and Elizabeth thought how nice he was. 'I'm sure he won't tell anyone,' she thought. 'It would be so awful if the others got to know about this. I simply don't know what to do. Julian will really hate me now. If only things would blow over!'

But they didn't blow over. They got very much worse. Julian was not the kind of boy to forget and forgive easily, and he was certainly not going to make things easy for Elizabeth. She had been his best friend – now she was his worst enemy! Look out then, Elizabeth!

11 Julian plays a trick

Everyone soon noticed that Julian and Elizabeth were no longer friends. Elizabeth looked thoroughly miserable and upset, and Julian took no notice of her at all.

Arabella was pleased. She liked and admired Julian tremendously, for all his careless, untidy ways. She had been annoyed when he had chosen Elizabeth for his friend. She would have liked to have been chosen instead.

'He's got simply marvellous brains!' said Arabella to Rosemary, who, not having many herself, sincerely admired those who had. 'He could do anything, that boy! I think he will be a wonderful inventor when he grows up – really *do* something in the world!'

'Yes, I think so too,' said Rosemary, agreeing with Arabella, as she always did. 'Arabella, I wonder why Elizabeth and Julian have quarrelled. They haven't spoken a word to one another all day – and whenever Julian does take a look in Elizabeth's direction, it's really fierce!'

'Yes – I'd like to know too why they've quarrelled,' said Arabella, 'I think I'll ask Julian. Perhaps he would like to be friends with us, now that's he's quarrelled with Elizabeth.'

So Arabella asked Julian that afternoon. 'Julian, I'm sorry to see that you and Elizabeth have quarrelled,' she said in her sweetest voice. 'I'm sure it must have been Elizabeth's fault. Why did you quarrel?'

'Sorry, Arabella, but I'm afraid that's my own business,'

said Julian rather shortly.

'You might tell me,' said Arabella. 'I am on your side, not Elizabeth's. I never did like Elizabeth.'

'There aren't any "sides", as you call it,' said Julian.

And that was all that Arabella could get out of Julian. She felt cross about it and more curious than ever. Whatever could the matter be? It must be something serious or Elizabeth wouldn't look so worried.

'I do wish we could find out,' she said to Rosemary. 'I really do wish we could.'

'What do you want to find out?' asked Martin, coming up behind them.

'Why Elizabeth and Julian have quarrelled,' said Arabella. 'You haven't any idea, have you, Martin?'

'Well – I do know something,' said Martin. Arabella stared at him in excitement.

'Tell us,' she said.

'Well,' said Martin, 'it's a dead secret. You mustn't tell anyone at all. Promise?'

'Of course,' said Arabella, not meaning to keep the secret at all. 'Who told you, Martin?'

'Well – Elizabeth told me herself,' said Martin.

'Then you can quite well tell us,' said Arabella at once. 'If Elizabeth told *you*, she will be sure to tell the others too.'

So Martin told the secret – how Elizabeth had accused Julian of stealing money and sweets, and how he had denied it angrily. Arabella's big eyes nearly fell out of her head as she listened. Rosemary could hardly believe it either.

'Oh, how beastly of Elizabeth!' said Arabella. 'How could she, Martin? I'm sure that however don't-careish Julian is, he is honest!'

Soon the secret was out all over the form. Everyone knew

why Julian and Elizabeth had quarrelled. Everyone spoke about stolen money and sweets, Julian and Elizabeth.

'I think Julian ought to know that Elizabeth has spread the tale about him,' said Arabella to Rosemary. 'I really do. It's not fair.'

'But did she spread it?' asked Rosemary doubtfully. 'It was Martin that told us.'

'Well, he said Elizabeth told *him*, didn't she – and if she told him, she would probably have told others,' said Arabella. 'After all, everyone knows now, so I expect Elizabeth did a lot of the telling.'

Rosemary felt a little uncomfortable. She knew how much Arabella herself had told, and she knew too that Arabella had added a little to the story. But Rosemary was too weak to argue with her friend. So she said nothing.

Arabella spoke to Julian the next day. 'Julian,' she said, 'I do think it is mean of Elizabeth to spread that tale of you taking things – you know, money and sweets. I do really.'

Julian looked as if he could not believe his ears. 'What do you mean?' he asked at last.

'Well – it's all over the form now that you and Elizabeth quarrelled because she said you took things that belonged to other people, and you denied it,' said Arabella. She slipped her arm through Julian's. The boy had gone very pale.

'Don't worry, Julian,' she said. 'We all know what Elizabeth is! Goodness knows why she was made a monitor! Who would go to *her* for help, I'd like to know! She's not to be trusted at all.'

'You're right,' said Julian, 'but I thought she was. I never imagined for one moment she would spread such a story. A monitor, too! She's a little beast. I can't think why I ever liked her.'

'No, I'm sure you can't,' said Arabella, delighted. 'Fancy her going all round the form whispering these horrible things about you – and you haven't said a word about *her*!'

Of course, Elizabeth had not said a word either, but Julian did not know that. He had not known that Martin had overheard everything, and he thought that if the story got round, it could only have been told to the others by Elizabeth herself. He thought very bitterly of her indeed.

'I'll pay her back for that,' he said to Arabella.

'I should,' said Arabella eagerly. 'As I told you before, Julian, I'm on your side, and so is Rosemary. I expect lots of others are too.'

This time Julian did not say anything about there being no sides. He was hurt and angry, and the only thing he wanted to do was to get back at Elizabeth and hurt her.

And then many curious things began to happen to Elizabeth. Julian used all his clever brains to think out tricks that would get her into trouble – and when Julian really used his brains things began to happen!

Julian sat just in front of Elizabeth in class. In one lesson, history, the children had to have out a good many books, which they put in a neat pile on the back of their desks, so that they might refer quickly to them when they needed to.

Julian invented a curious little gadget like a spring. He twisted the spring up in a peculiar way so that it took a long time to untwist itself. He slipped it under Elizabeth's pile of books.

The lesson began. Miss Ranger was not in a good temper that day, for she had a headache, so the children were being rather careful not to make noises. Nobody let their desk-lids fall with a slam, nobody dropped anything.

Julian grinned to himself, as he worked quietly in front of

Elizabeth. He knew that the peculiar little spring was slowly untwisting itself under the bottom book. It was extremely strong, and when it reached a certain twist it would spring wide open and force the books off the desk.

Sure enough, this happened after about five minutes had gone by. The spring gave itself a final twist and the books moved. The top one fell, and then the others, all in a pile to the floor.

Miss Ranger jumped. 'Whose books fell then?' she said crossly. 'Elizabeth, don't be careless. How did that happen?'

'I don't know, Miss Ranger,' said Elizabeth, puzzled. 'I really don't.'

Julian bent to pick up the books, which had fallen just behind. He put another, twisted spring under the bottom one again, pocketing the first one, which had fallen to the floor with the books.

In five minutes' time that spring worked too. It was a stronger one, and the books shot off the desk in a hurry. Crash, crash, crash, crash, crash!

Miss Ranger jumped violently, and her fountain-pen, which she was using, made a blot on the book she was correcting.

'Elizabeth! Are you doing this on purpose?' she cried. 'If it happens again you will go out of the room. I will not have you disturbing the class like this.'

Elizabeth was extremely puzzled. 'I'm very sorry, Miss Ranger,' she said. 'Honestly, the books seemed to jump off my desk by themselves.'

'Don't be childish, Elizabeth,' said Miss Ranger. 'That's the kind of thing a child in the lower school might say to me.'

Julian picked up the books, grinning. Elizabeth gave him a furious look. She had no idea that he was playing a trick on her, but she didn't like the grin. Once more Julian placed one of his curious springs under the bottom book.

And once again all the books jumped off the desk in a hurry. This time Miss Ranger lost her temper.

'Go out of the room,' she snapped at Elizabeth. 'Once might have been an accident – even twice – but not three times. I'm ashamed of you. You're a monitor and should know how to behave.'

With scarlet cheeks Elizabeth went out of the room. In her first term she had *tried* to be sent out of the room – but now she felt it to be a great disgrace. She hated it. She stood outside the door, almost ready to cry for shame and anger.

'It wasn't my fault. My books really *did* seem to jump off by themselves. I never even touched the beastly things!' she thought.

And then, how dreadful! Who should come by but Rita, the head girl herself. She looked in the greatest surprise at Elizabeth, standing red-faced outside the door. 'Why are you here, Elizabeth?' she asked gravely.

12 Elizabeth in disgrace

'I was sent out of the room, Rita,' said Elizabeth, 'but it was for something that wasn't my fault. Please believe me.'

'Don't let it happen again, Elizabeth,' said Rita. 'You know that you are a monitor, and should set an example to the others. I am not very pleased with various things I have heard about you and the first form this term.'

She walked down the passage and Elizabeth stared after her, wondering what Rita knew. She felt suddenly very sad and gloomy. 'I looked forward to this term so much,' she thought, 'and now everything is going wrong.'

She was called back into the room at the end of the lesson, and Miss Ranger spoke a few stern words to her. Elizabeth knew that it was no good saying again that she had not made the books fall, so she said nothing.

The next trick that Julian thought of was most extraordinary. He grinned with delight when it came into his mind. He went into the laboratory, where the children did most of their science work, and mixed up various chemicals together. He made them into a few wet little pellets and put them into a box. Then, before afternoon school, he slipped into the empty classroom, moved Elizabeth's desk, and put a table in its place.

He stood a chair on top of the table and then climbed up and stood on it. He could reach the ceiling then. He arranged the little wet pellets close together on the white ceiling. He brushed them quickly over with a queer-smelling liquid. This would have the effect of making the little pellets gradually swell and burst, letting out a large drop of water which would fall straight downwards.

'This is a good trick,' thought Julian, as he jumped down from the chair, put it back in its place, and pulled the table away. He put Elizabeth's desk back, arranging it exactly under the pellets on the ceiling. They were white and hardly noticeable.

That afternoon Mam'zelle came to take French. Elizabeth and the others had learnt French verbs and some French poetry. Mam'zelle was to hear it. All the children gabbled it over to themselves just before the lesson, making sure they knew it. Mam'zelle was heard coming along the passage and Elizabeth sprang to hold open the door.

Mam'zelle was in a good temper. The children were glad. Miss Ranger didn't get cross unless there really was something to be cross about – but Mam'zelle often got cross about nothing. Still, this afternoon she looked very pleasant indeed.

'And now we will have a very nice afternoon,' she said, beaming round. 'You will all say your verbs without one single mistake, and you will say your poetry most beautifully. And I shall be very pleased with you.'

No one made any reply to this. It would be nice if nobody made any mistake, but that was too much to be hoped for! Someone always came to grief in the French class.

Julian chose that afternoon to use his brains in the proper way. He rattled off his verbs without a single mistake. He addressed Mam'zelle in excellent French, so that she beamed all over her face with pleasure.

'Ah, this Julian! Always he pretends he is so stupid, but he is very clever! Now we will see if he knows his poetry well! Speak it to me, Julian.'

Julian began reciting the French smoothly and well. But no sooner had he begun than there came an interruption. It was Elizabeth.

She had been sitting down, her head bent over her French book. And right on the top of her head had come a big drop of water! Elizabeth was most astonished. She gave a small cry and rubbed the top of her head. It was wet!

'What is the matter, Elizabeth?' asked Mam'zelle impatiently.

'A drop of water fell on my head,' said Elizabeth, puzzled. She looked up at the ceiling, but there did not seem anything to be seen there.

'You are silly, Elizabeth,' said Mam'zelle. 'You do not expect me to believe that.'

'But a drop of water *did* fall on my head,' said Elizabeth. 'I felt it.'

Jenny and Robert began to giggle. They thought Elizabeth was making it up in order to have a bit of fun. Mam'zelle rapped sharply on her desk.

'Silence!' she said. 'Julian, go on with your poetry. Begin again.'

Julian began again, knowing that another drop or two would fall on Elizabeth's head shortly. He wanted to laugh.

'Oh! Oh!' said Elizabeth suddenly from behind him! Two drops had fallen splash on to her hair. The little girl simply couldn't understand it. She rubbed her head.

'Elizabeth! Once more you interrupt!' said Mam'zelle angrily. 'Are you trying to spoil Julian's work? He is doing it so well. What is the matter now? Do not tell me again that it is raining on your head!'

'Well, Mam'zelle, it *is*,' said Elizabeth, and she rubbed her hand in her wet hair. Everyone roared with laughter. Mam'zelle began to get really angry.

'Silence, everybody!' she cried. 'I will not have this noise. Elizabeth, I am surprised at you. A monitor should not behave like this.'

'But Mam'zelle, honestly, it's very odd,' began Elizabeth again – and then another drop fell on her hair. She gave a jump and looked up at the ceiling. She really felt very puzzled indeed.

'Ah! You look at the ceiling as if it was the sky? You think it is raining on you! You think you will play me a silly joke!' cried Mam'zelle, her eyes beginning to flash. Everyone sat up, enjoying the fun. It was exciting when Mam'zelle lost her temper.

'Well, can I sit somewhere else?' asked Elizabeth in despair. 'Something does keep dropping on my head and I don't like it.'

'You can go and sit outside the room,' said Mam'zelle sternly. 'This is the silliest joke I have ever heard of. You will ask next if you can bring an umbrella into my class and sit with it over your head.'

The whole class squealed with laughter at the thought of this. But Mam'zelle had not meant to be funny, and she banged angrily on her desk.

'Silence! I do not make a joke. I am very angry. Elizabeth, leave my class.'

'Oh, please, Mam'zelle, no,' said poor Elizabeth. 'Please don't send me out of the room. I won't interrupt again. But, honestly, it's very strange.'

Another drop fell on her head, but she said nothing this time. She could not bear to be sent out of the room a second time, she really couldn't! She would rather get soaked through than that!

'Well – one more word from you and you will go,' threatened Mam'zelle. Elizabeth thankfully sat down, and made up her mind not even to jump if another of those unexpected drops landed on her hair.

But there was no more to come. Soon Elizabeth's hair was dry again, and nothing fell to wet it. She recited her verbs and poetry in her turn, and was allowed to remain in the room for the rest of the lesson.

Afterwards most of the children crowded round her. 'Elizabeth! How did you dare to act like that? Let's feel your head!'

But it was now dry, and no one would believe Elizabeth when she said over and over again that drops of water *had* fallen on her. They rubbed their hands over her hair, but not a bit of wetness was left.

'Why don't you own up to us and say it was a good joke?' asked Harry. 'You might just as well.'

'Because it *wasn't* a joke, it was real,' answered Elizabeth angrily.

The children went off. They all thought Elizabeth had played a joke, but they also thought it wasn't right not to own up to it afterwards.

'She's telling untruths,' said Arabella to Rosemary. 'Well, all I can say is – she's a funny sort of monitor to have!'

One or two of the others agreed. They had enjoyed the joke – but they really did think that Elizabeth had made up the story of the falling drops, and they felt rather disgusted with her when she denied it.

Mam'zelle related the story to Miss Ranger in the mistresses' common-room that day. 'It is not like Elizabeth to be so silly,' she said.

Miss Ranger looked puzzled. 'I don't understand her,' she said. 'She is not behaving like herself lately. She was very stupid in my class too – kept pushing piles of books over! So childish.'

'I really thought she would make a good monitor,' said Mam'zelle. 'I am disappointed in Elizabeth.'

Arabella spoke against Elizabeth whenever she could, and some of the children listened. Arabella was clever in the way she spoke.

'Of course,' she said, 'I like a joke as much as anyone, and it's fun to play a trick in a dull lesson. But honestly I don't think a *monitor* should do that. I mean, I don't see why any of us shouldn't play the fool a bit if we like – but not a monitor. You do expect a monitor to behave – or why make them monitors?'

'She was called the Naughtiest Girl in the School two terms ago, wasn't she?' said Martin. 'Well, it must be difficult to stop being that, really. I think it was silly to make her a monitor. She couldn't have been ready to be one.'

'Look at the beastly stories she spread about poor Julian too,' said Arabella. 'A monitor should be the first to stop a thing like that, not start it. Well, I always did say I couldn't imagine why Elizabeth was a monitor.'

'Perhaps she won't be for long!' said Martin. 'I don't see why we should put up with someone who behaves like Elizabeth. How can we look up to her or go to her for advice? She oughtn't to *be* a monitor!'

Poor Elizabeth. She knew the children were whispering about her – and she couldn't do anything about it.

13 Arabella's secret

The next school Meeting came and went without anything being said by Elizabeth. The girl was so miserable and so puzzled as to what she should do for the best that she had made up her mind to say nothing, at least for the present.

Meanwhile Arabella was soon going to have a birthday. Her mother had promised to send her a big birthday cake, and whatever else she liked to ask for to eat or drink. Mrs Buckley was now in America, but Arabella could order what she liked from one of the big London stores.

Arabella talked about it a good deal. She loved to boast, and she talked of all the good things she would order.

Then she had an idea. She told it to Rosemary. 'What about a midnight feast, Rosemary? We had one once at my old school and it was such fun. We should have plenty to eat and drink – and think how exciting it would be to have it in the middle of the night!'

Rosemary agreed. 'Should we have it at midnight?' she asked. 'We couldn't very well have it earlier, because some of the mistresses and masters might be up.'

'Yes – we'll have it just after midnight,' said Arabella. 'But we won't ask Elizabeth! She's such a horrid thing she might give the secret away and spoil the feast!'

'All right,' said Rosemary. 'Well – who will you ask, then?'

'Everyone – except just a few who are Elizabeth's old friends,' said Arabella. 'We won't ask Kathleen – or Harry –

or Robert. They still stick up for Elizabeth. Anyway, I suppose Elizabeth wouldn't come, even if we did ask her, because she might think a midnight feast was against the silly rules, and she's a monitor.'

So the first form once more had a secret that was whispered from one to the other. Elizabeth heard the talking, and noticed that it died down when she passed. She thought they must be whispering about her again, and she was angry and sad.

Julian was asked, of course, and Martin. Julian's green eyes gleamed when he heard of the midnight feast. This was just the sort of daring thing he liked.

The children discussed where they should hide the food and drink. They did not want the mistresses to guess what they were going to do.

'We'll show the birthday cake round, and have some of it for tea,' said Arabella, 'but we won't say anything about the other things.'

'Hide the ginger beers in one of the garden sheds,' said Martin. 'I know a good place. I'll put them there. I can fetch them on the night.'

'And put the biscuits in the old games locker in the passage,' said Julian. 'It's never used, and no one will see it there. I'll take them along.

So the goodies were hidden here and there, and the children began to feel most excited. The few that were left out did not know what was happening. They only knew that it was Arabella's secret, and that a great fuss was being made of it.

Arabella always made a point of talking in a low voice about the party whenever she saw Elizabeth coming near. Then she would give a jump when she looked up and saw

Elizabeth, nudge the person she was talking to and change the subject quickly and loudly.

This annoyed Elizabeth very much. 'You need not think I want to hear your stupid secret,' she said to Arabella. 'I don't. So talk all you like about it – I'll shut my ears!'

All the same, it was not pleasant to be left out. Neither was it pleasant to see Julian talking and laughing to Arabella and Rosemary. She did not know that he did it sometimes to annoy her. He could not bring himself to like the boastful, vain little Arabella very much. But if his friendship with her annoyed Elizabeth, then he would certainly go on with it!

Arabella's birthday came. The children wished her many happy returns of the day and gave her little presents, which she accepted graciously, with pretty words of thanks. There was no doubt that Arabella knew how to behave when she was getting her own way!

Elizabeth gave Arabella nothing – neither did she wish her a happy birthday. She saw Julian give her a beautiful little brooch he had made with his own clever hands. Arabella pinned it on joyfully.

'Oh, Julian!' she said loudly, knowing that Elizabeth could hear. 'You *are* a good friend! Thank you ever so much.'

The midnight feast was to be held in the common room. This room was well away from any of the mistresses' bedrooms, and the children felt they would be safe there. They all felt excited that day, and Miss Ranger wondered what could be the matter with her class.

Quite by chance Elizabeth opened the old games locker in the passage. She was hunting for a ball to practise catching with on the lacrosse field, and she thought there might possibly be one there. She stared in surprise at the bag of biscuits.

'I suppose Miss Ranger put them there,' she thought. 'Perhaps she has forgotten them. I must tell her. She may want them for the biscuits to give out at break.'

But Elizabeth forgot all about them and didn't say anything to Miss Ranger. She had no idea that they belonged to Arabella, and were going to be eaten at the feast.

Arabella's secret was well kept. The children who had been asked really were afraid that if Elizabeth got to know it she might try to stop it, as she was a monitor. So they carefully said nothing at all to her. She and a few others were quite in the dark about it.

When midnight came all the children but Arabella were asleep. She had said she would keep awake and tell everyone when it was time. She was so excited that she had no difficulty at all in keeping her eyes wide open until she heard the school clock strike midnight from its tower.

She sat up in bed and groped for her dressing-gown. She put on her slippers. Then, taking a small torch she went to wake her friends, giving them little nudges.

They awoke with jumps. 'Sh!' whispered Arabella to each one. 'Don't make a noise! It's time for the midnight feast.'

Elizabeth was sound asleep, and so was Kathleen. They did not wake when the others padded out of their room to meet the boys, who were now coming from their own part of the school to the common room. There was a lot of whispering, and choked-back giggles could be heard all the way down the passages.

The children crowded into the common room and lighted candles. They were afraid to put on the electric light in case the strong light showed through the blinds.

'Anyway, it's more fun to have candles!' said Arabella gleefully. This was the kind of thing she liked. She was queen of the party! She wore a beautiful silk dressing-gown and blue silk slippers to match. She really looked lovely, and she knew it.

The children set out the food and drink. What a lovely lot there was!

'Sardines! I love those!' said Ruth.

'Tinned peaches! Oooh! How lovely!'

'Bags I some of those chocolate buns! They look as if they would melt in my mouth!'

'Pass that spoon, someone. I'll ladle out the peaches.'

'Don't make such a noise, Belinda. That's twice you've dropped a fork! You'll have Miss Ranger here if you don't look out.'

Pop! A ginger-beer bottle was opened and another and another. Pop! Pop! The children looked at one another, delighted. This was really fun. It was past midnight – and here they were eating and drinking all kinds of lovely things!

'Where are the biscuits?' said Arabella. 'I feel as if I'd like a biscuit to eat with these peaches. I can't see the biscuits. Where are they?'

'Oh – I forgot to get them,' said Julian, getting up. 'I'll fetch them now, Arabella. I won't be a minute. They are in that games locker.'

He went out to fetch the biscuits, groping his way along the passage, then up the stairs to where the locker stood in a corner.

He had no torch and it was dark. He stumbled along, trying to be as quiet as possible. He walked into a chair, and knocked it over with a crash. He stood still, wondering if anyone had heard.

He was not far from the room where Elizabeth slept. When the chair went over, the little girl awoke with a jump.

She sat up in bed, wondering what the noise was.

'I'd better go and see,' she thought. She slipped out of bed and put on her dressing-gown. She did not notice that half the beds were empty in the dormitory. She put on her slippers and crept to the door with her torch not yet switched on.

She went into the passage and stood there. She walked along a little way and thought she heard the noise of someone not very far in front of her. She padded softly down the passage.

The Someone went to the old games locker. Elizabeth distinctly heard the creak as it was opened. Who could it be? And what were they doing at that time of night?

Elizabeth walked softly up to the locker. She switched on her torch very suddenly, and made Julian almost jump out of his skin.

'Julian! What are you doing here? Oh – you rotten thief – you're stealing *biscuits* now! I think you're too disgusting for words! Put them back at once!'

'Sh!' hissed Julian. 'You'll wake everyone, you idiot.'

He did not attempt to put back the bag of biscuits. He meant to take them to the feast. But Elizabeth did not know that, of course. She honestly thought he had come there to steal the biscuits in the middle of the night.

'Well – I've really caught you this time!' she cried. 'Caught you with the stolen goods in your hand! You can't deny *that*! Give them to me!'

Julian snatched them away. The lid of the locker fell with a terrific bang that echoed all up and down the passage.

'Idiot!' said Julian, in despair. 'Now you've woken everyone!'

14 Sneezing powder

The crash of the locker lid certainly had awakened a good many people. There came the sound of footsteps and of doors being opened. The mistresses would soon be on the scene.

Julian fled to warn the others, giving Elizabeth a furious push as he passed her. She almost fell over. She did not know where he had gone, so she ran back to her own dormitory, excited to think that she really had caught Julian in the very act of stealing the biscuits.

'Now I'll report him!' she thought, as she climbed into bed. 'I jolly well will!'

Julian ran to the common room and opened the door. 'Quick!' he said. 'Get back to your beds. Elizabeth caught me as I was getting the biscuits, and made an awful noise. If you don't get back quickly, we'll all be caught.'

Hastily the children stuffed everything into their lockers round the wall, or into empty desks. Then they blew out the candles and fled, hoping that they had not left too many crumbs about.

The boys raced for their own dormitories. The girls rushed to theirs.

'Blow Elizabeth!' panted Arabella as she took off her dressing-gown and slipped into bed. 'We were just in the middle of everything. Now it's all spoilt!'

The mistresses had been asking one another what the noise was. Mam'zelle, who slept nearest to the first-form dormitories, was a sound sleeper, and had heard nothing at all. She was surprised when Miss Ranger opened the door and woke her.

'Perhaps it is the girls in the first-form dormitories playing tricks on one another,' said Mam'zelle sleepily. 'You go and see, Miss Ranger.'

But, by the time that Miss Ranger went into the dormitories and switched on the lights, not a sound was to be heard. All the children seemed to be sleeping most peacefully. Too peacefully really, Miss Ranger thought!

Elizabeth saw the light switched on, and out of the corner of her eye she watched Miss Ranger. Should she tell her what had happened? No – she wouldn't. She would spring it on the School Meeting tomorrow, and make everyone sit up and take notice!

Miss Ranger switched off the light and went quietly back to bed. She couldn't imagine what the noise had been. Perhaps the school cat had been chasing about and upset something. Miss Ranger got into bed and fell asleep.

Elizabeth lay awake a long time, thinking of Julian and the biscuits. She was quite, quite sure now that Julian was a disgusting thief. All that talk about doing what he liked and letting others do what *they* liked! It was just a way of excusing himself for his bad ways.

'He'll get a shock when I stand up at the Meeting and report him,' thought Elizabeth.

The children were angry that Elizabeth should have brought their fun to such a sudden end. 'Shall we give her a good scolding?' said Arabella primly.

'Well – she doesn't know about the feast,' said Julian, 'though she must have wondered what you had all been up to when you crept back to bed so suddenly.'

Elizabeth *had* wondered – but she knew that Arabella had had a birthday and she had simply thought that the girls had visited her that night, and had a few games. She had not thought of a feast.

'Don't let's tell her,' said Julian. 'We could finish the feast tonight – and she might stop it if she guessed.'

So no one told Elizabeth that she had spoilt the feast, but they gave her many black looks which puzzled her very much.

Julian thought of a way to pay back Elizabeth for spoiling the fun of the night before. He told the others.

'Look,' he said, 'I've made some sneezing powder. I'll scatter some between the pages of Elizabeth's French book – and we'll all watch her get a sneezing fit in Mam'zelle's class.'

'Ooh yes!' said everyone in delight. This was a joke after their own hearts.

Julian slipped into the classroom before afternoon school. He went to Elizabeth's desk and opened it. He found her French book, and lightly scattered the curious sneezing powder over it. He had discovered it when he was inventing something else, and had found himself suddenly sneezing. Julian was always inventing something new, thinking of something that no one had thought of before!

He scattered the pages full of the white powder, then shut the book carefully and put it back. He slipped out of the classroom, grinning. Elizabeth would get a surprise in the French class. So would Mam'zelle.

The children went to their form-rooms when the bell rang for afternoon school. 'French!' groaned Jenny. 'Oh dear. I'm sure I shall forget everything if Mam'zelle is in a bad temper.'

'I feel so sleepy,' whispered Arabella to Rosemary, who also looked tired, after the midnight feast. 'I hope Mam'zelle doesn't pick on me if she wants to be cross. I hope she'll pick Elizabeth. Won't it be fun if she *does* start sneezing!'

There was oral French for the first ten minutes. Then Mam'zelle told the class to get out their French reading books. Elizabeth got out hers and opened it.

It was not long before the sneezing powder did its work. As the little girl turned over the pages, some of the fine white powder flew up her nose and tickled it. She felt a sneeze coming and got out her hanky.

'A-tish-oo!' she said. Mam'zelle took no notice.

'*A-tish-oo!*' said Elizabeth, wondering if she had got a cold. 'A-TISH-OOOOOO!'

Mam'zelle looked up. Elizabeth hastily tried to smother the next sneeze. There was a pause, in which Jenny read out loud from her French book. She came to the end of the page, and turned over. Everyone did the same.

The turning of the page sent more of the powder up Elizabeth's nose. She felt another sneeze coming and hurriedly put up her hanky. But she couldn't stop it.

'A-TISH-OOOOOO! A-TISH-OOOOOO!' The sneezes were quite loud enough to drown Jenny's reading. One or two of the children began to choke back giggles. They waited for Elizabeth's next sneeze. It came. It was such a loud one that it made Mam'zelle jump.

'Enough, Elizabeth,' she said. 'You will sneeze no more. It is not necessary. Do not disturb the class like this.'

'I can't – *a-tish-ooo* – help it,' said poor Elizabeth, with tears streaming down her cheeks, for the powder was very strong. 'A-tish-tish-tish-oooo!'

Mam'zelle became angry. 'Elizabeth! Last week it was

drops falling on your head – this week it is sneezes. I will not have it.'

'A-tish-ish-ish-ooo-ooo,' said poor Elizabeth. The class began to laugh helplessly. Mam'zelle flew into a temper and banged on the desk.

'Elizabeth! You are a monitor and you behave like this! I will not have it. You will stop this sneezing game at once.'

'A-tish-OOOOOO!' said Elizabeth. The children laughed till the tears ran down their cheeks. This was the funniest thing they had ever seen.

'Leave the room, and do not come back,' ordered Mam'zelle sternly. 'I will not have you in my class.'

'But oh, Mam'zelle, please – tishoo, tishoo – tishoo – oh Mam'zelle,' began Elizabeth. But Mam'zelle came over to her, took her firmly by the shoulders, and walked her to the door.

She shut it behind Elizabeth and turned to face the class sternly.

'This is not funny,' she said. 'Not at all funny.'

The boys and girls thought it was. They tried their hardest to swallow down their giggles, but every now and again someone would choke, and that would set the whole class giggling again.

Mam'zelle was very angry indeed. She set them a page of poetry to copy out that evening as a punishment, but even that did not make the class stop giggling.

Elizabeth stood outside the door, upset and puzzled. 'Whatever made me sneeze like that?' she wondered. 'I'm not sneezing at all, out here. Am I starting a very bad cold? I simply could *not* stop sneezing in the classroom. It was mean of Mam'zelle to send me out here.'

And then, to Elizabeth's horror, William, the head boy,

came along, talking to Mr Lewis, the music-master. Elizabeth tried to look as if she wasn't there at all. But it was no use. William knew at once she had been sent out of the room.

'Elizabeth!' he said. 'Surely you haven't been sent out of the room *again*! Rita told me you had, last week. Are you forgetting you are a monitor?'

'No,' said Elizabeth miserably. 'I'm not. Mam'zelle sent me out because I couldn't stop sneezing, William. She thought I was doing it on purpose. But I wasn't.'

'Well, you are not sneezing now,' said William.

'I know. I stopped as soon as I came out here,' said Elizabeth.

William walked on, thinking that Elizabeth must have been playing a silly joke. He would have to speak to Rita about it. They could not have monitors being sent out of the room like that. It was not right to have monitors setting a bad example.

Elizabeth had no idea that Julian had played a joke on her. She really thought she had been sneezing because she was beginning a cold. She was surprised when no cold came.

'Well, I shall go to the Meeting tonight,' she thought. 'And it will serve Julian right to be shown up in front of everyone. I know they will believe me, because I am a monitor.'

15 A stormy Meeting

The children filed into the big hall for the usual school Meeting that night. Elizabeth was excited and strung-up. She longed to get the Meeting over, and have everything settled.

'Any money for the box?' said William, as usual. Ten pounds came in from a boy who had had a postal order from an uncle. Arabella put in two pounds – her birthday money. She had learnt her lesson about that! She was not going to be reported for keeping back money again.

Two pounds was given to everyone. Then William and Rita dealt with requests for more money. Elizabeth could hardly keep still. She felt nervous. She glanced at Julian. He sat as usual on the bench, a lock of hair falling into his eyes. He brushed it back impatiently.

'Any complaints?' The familiar question came from William, and a small boy sprang up before Elizabeth could speak.

'Please, William! The other children in my class are always calling me a dunce because I'm bottom. It isn't fair.'

'Have you spoken to your monitor about it?' asked William.

'Yes,' said the small boy.

'Who is your monitor?' asked William.

A bigger boy stood up. 'I am,' he said. 'Yes – the others do tease James. He has missed a lot of school through illness, so he doesn't know as much as the others. But I spoke to his teacher, and she says he could really try harder than he does, because he has good brains. He doesn't need to be bottom very long.'

'Thank you,' said William. The monitor sat down.

'Well, James, you heard what your monitor said. You yourself can soon stop the others teasing you, by using your good brains and not being bottom! You may have got so used always to being at the bottom that it didn't occur to you you could be anything else. But it seems that you can!'

'Oh,' said James, looking pleased and rather surprised. He sat down with a bump. His form looked at him, not quite knowing whether to be cross with him or amused. They suddenly nudged one another and grinned. James looked round, smiling too.

'Any more complaints?' asked Rita.

'Yes, Rita!' said Elizabeth, and jumped up so suddenly that she almost upset her chair. 'I have a very serious complaint to make.'

A ripple of whispering ran through the school. Everyone sat up straight. What was Elizabeth going to say? Arabella went rather pale. She hoped Elizabeth was not going to complain about *her* again. Julian glanced sharply at Elizabeth. Surely – surely she wasn't going to speak about him!

But she was, of course. She began to make her complaint, her words almost falling over one another.

'Rita, William! It's about Julian,' she began. 'I have thought for some time that he was taking things that didn't belong to him – and yesterday I caught him at it! I caught him with the things in his hand! He was taking them out of the old games locker in the passage.'

'Elizabeth, you must explain better,' said Rita, looking grave and serious. 'This is a terrible charge you are making.

We shall have to go deeply into it, and unless you really have proof you had better say no more, but come to me and William afterwards.'

'I *have* got proof!' said Elizabeth. 'I saw Julian take the biscuits out of the locker. I don't know who they belonged to – Miss Ranger, I suppose. Anyway, Julian must have found them there, and when he thought we were all asleep at night he went to take them. And I heard him and saw him.'

The whole school was quite silent. The first-formers looked at one another, their hearts beating fast. Now their midnight feast would have to be found out! Julian would have to give away their secret.

William looked at Julian. He was sitting with his hands in his pockets, looking amused.

'Stand up, Julian, and tell us your side of the story,' said William.

Julian stood up, his hands still in his pockets. 'Take your hands out of your pockets,' ordered William. Julian did so. He looked untidy and careless as he stood there, his green eyes twinkling like a gnome's.

'I'm sorry, William,' he said, 'but I can't give any explanation, because I should give away a secret belonging to others. All I can say is – I was not stealing the biscuits. I was certainly *taking* them – but not stealing them!'

He sat down. Elizabeth jumped up, like a jack-in-the-box. 'You see, William!' she said, 'he can't give you a proper explanation!'

'Sit down, Elizabeth,' said William sternly. He looked at the first-formers, who all sat silent and uncomfortable, not daring to glance at one another. How good of Julian not to give them away! How awful all this was!

'First-formers,' said William gravely, 'I hope that if any

one of you can help to clear Julian of this very serious charge, you will do so, whether it means giving away some secret or not. If Julian, out of loyalty to one or more of you, cannot stick up for himself, then you must be loyal to him, and tell what you know.'

There was a silence after this. Rosemary sat trembling, not daring to move. Belinda half got up then sat down again. Martin looked straight ahead, rather pale.

It was Arabella who gave the first form a great surprise. She suddenly stood up, and spoke in a low voice.

'William, I'd better say something, I think. We *did* have a secret, and it's decent of Julian not to give it away. You see – it was my birthday yesterday – and we thought we'd have a – a – a midnight feast.'

She stopped, so nervous that she could hardly go on. The whole school was listening with the greatest interest.

'Go on,' said Rita gently.

'Well – well, you see, we had to hide the things here and there,' said Arabella. 'It was all such fun. We didn't tell Elizabeth – because she's a monitor and might have tried to stop us. Well, Julian hid my biscuits in the old games locker – and he went to get them after midnight, when the feast had begun. I suppose that's when Elizabeth means. But they were *my* biscuits, and I asked him to get them, and he brought them back to the common room where we were. And I think it's unfair of Elizabeth to accuse Julian of stealing them. She's done that before. The whole form knows she's been saying that he takes money and sweets that don't belong to him.'

This was a very long speech. Arabella finished it suddenly, and sat down, almost panting. Julian looked at her gratefully. He knew that she would not at all like telling the secret of the midnight party – but she had done it to save him. His opinion of the vain little girl went up sky-high – and so did everyone else's.

William and Rita had listened closely to all that Arabella had said. So had Elizabeth. When she had heard the explanation of Julian's midnight wanderings she went very white, and her knees shook. She knew in a moment that in that one thing, at any rate, she had made a terrible mistake. William turned to Elizabeth, and his eyes were very sharp and stern.

'Elizabeth, it seems that you have done a most unforgivable thing – you have accused Julian publicly of something he hasn't done. I suppose you did not even ask him to explain his action to you, but just took it for granted that he was doing wrong.'

Elizabeth sat glued to her seat. She could not say a word.

'Arabella says that this is not the only time you have accused Julian. There have been other times too. As this last accusation of yours has been proved to be wrong, it is likely that the other complaints you have made to the first form are wrong too. So we will not hear them in public. But Rita and I will want you to come to us privately and explain everything.'

'Yes, William,' said Elizabeth in a low voice. 'I'm – I'm very, very sorry about what I said just now. I didn't know.'

'That isn't any excuse,' said William sternly. 'I can't think what has happened to you this term, Elizabeth. We made you a monitor at the end of last term because we all thought you should be – but this term you have let us all down. I am afraid that already many of us are thinking that you should no longer be a monitor.'

Several boys and girls agreed. They stamped on the floor with their feet.

'Twice you have been sent out of your classroom,' said William. 'And for the same reason – disturbing the class by playing foolish tricks. That is not the behaviour of a monitor, Elizabeth. I am afraid that we can no longer ask you to help us as a monitor. You must step down and leave us to choose someone else in your place.'

This was too much for Elizabeth. She gave an enormous sob, jumped down from the platform and rushed out of the room. She was a failure. She was no good as a monitor. And oh, she had been *so* proud of it too!

William did not attempt to stop her rushing from the room. He looked gravely round the well-filled benches. 'We must now choose another monitor,' he said. 'Will you please begin thinking who will best take Elizabeth's place?'

The children sat still, thinking. The Meeting had been rather dreadful in some ways – but to every child there had come a great lesson. They must never, never accuse anyone of wrong-doing unless they were absolutely certain. Every child had clearly seen the misery that might have been caused, and they knew that Elizabeth's punishment was just.

Poor Elizabeth! Always rushing into trouble. What would she do now?

16 Elizabeth sees William and Rita

A new monitor was chosen in place of Elizabeth. It was a girl in the second form, called Susan. Not one child outside the first form had chosen a first-former. It was clear that most people felt that the first form would do better to have an older girl or boy for a monitor.

'Arabella, it *was* brave of you to own up about the midnight feast,' said Rosemary admiringly. All the others thought so too. Arabella felt pleased with herself. She really had done it unselfishly, and she was rather surprised at herself for doing such a thing. It was nice to feel that the rest of the form admired her for something.

One person was feeling rather uncomfortable. It was Julian. He felt very angry with Elizabeth for making such an untruthful and horrible complaint about him – but he did know that it was because of his tricks she had been sent out of the room twice, and not because of her own foolishness. Partly because of his tricks and their results, Elizabeth had lost the honour of being a monitor.

'Of course, William and Rita might have said she couldn't be because she complained wrongly about me,' said Julian to himself. 'But it sounded as if it was because of her being sent out of the room. Well, she doesn't deserve to be a monitor anyway – so why should I worry?'

But he did worry a little, because, like Elizabeth, he was really very fair-minded, and although he did not like the little girl, he knew that dislike was no excuse at all for being unfair. He had come very well out of the whole affair, thanks to Arabella. But Elizabeth had not. Even Harry, Robert, and Kathleen, her own good friends, had nothing nice to say of her at the moment.

The meeting broke up after choosing the new monitor. The children went out, talking over what had happened. You never knew what would come out at a school Meeting.

'Nothing can be hidden at Whyteleafe School!' said Eileen, one of the older girls. 'Sooner or later everyone's faults come to light, and are put right. Sooner or later our good points are seen and rewarded. And we do it all ourselves. It's very good for us, I think.'

Miss Belle and Miss Best had been present at the Meeting, and had listened with great interest to all that had happened. William and Rita stayed behind to have a word with them.

'Did we do right, Miss Belle?' asked William.

'I think so,' said Miss Belle, and Miss Best nodded too. 'But, William, have Elizabeth along as soon as ever you can, and let her get off her chest all that she has been thinking about Julian – there is clearly something puzzling there. Elizabeth does not get such fixed ideas into her head without *some* reason. There is still something we don't know.'

'Yes. We'll send for Elizabeth now,' said Rita. 'I wonder where she is.'

She was out in the stables in the dark, sobbing against the horse she rode each morning. The horse nuzzled up to her, wondering what was upsetting his little mistress. Soon she dried her eyes, and sat down on an upturned pail in a corner.

She was puzzled, deeply sorry for what she had said about Julian, very much ashamed of herself, and horrified at losing the honour of being a monitor. She felt that she could never face the others again. But she knew she would have to.

'What is the matter with me?' she wondered. 'I make up my mind to be so good and helpful and everything and then I go and do just the opposite! I lose my temper. I say dreadful things – and now everyone hates me. Especially Julian. It's funny about Julian. I did see that he had my marked pound. I did see that one of my sweets fell out of his pocket. So that's why I thought he was stealing the biscuits, and he wasn't. But did he take the other things?'

Someone came by calling loudly. 'Elizabeth! Where are you?'

Messengers had been sent to find her, to tell her to go to Rita and William. She could not be found in the school, so Nora had come outside to look for her with a torch.

At first Elizabeth thought she would not answer. She simply could not go in and face the others just yet. Then a little courage came to her, and she stood up.

'I'm not a coward,' she thought. 'William and Rita have punished me partly for something I *haven't* done – because I really *didn't* play about in class – but the other thing I *did* do – I did make an untruthful complaint about Julian, though I thought at the time it was true. So I must just face up to it and not be silly.'

'Elizabeth, are you out here?' came Nora's voice again.

This time the little girl answered. 'Yes. I'm coming.'

She came out of the stables, rubbing her eyes. Nora flashed her torch at her. 'I've been looking everywhere for you, idiot,' she said. 'William and Rita want you. Hurry up.'

'All right,' said Elizabeth, feeling her heart sink. Was she going to be scolded again? Wasn't it enough that she should have been disgraced in public without being scolded in private?

She rubbed her hanky over her face and ran to the school. She made her way to William's study. She knocked at the door.

'Come in!' said William's voice. She went in and saw the head boy and girl sitting in armchairs. They both looked up gravely as she came in.

'Sit there,' said Rita in a kindly voice. She felt sorry for the headstrong little girl who was so often in trouble. Elizabeth felt glad to hear the kindness in Rita's voice. She sat down.

'Rita,' she said, 'I'm terribly sorry for being wrong about Julian. I did think I was right. I honestly did.'

'That's what we want to see you about,' said Rita. 'We couldn't allow you to say any more about Julian in public, in case you were wrong again. But we want you to tell us now all that has happened to make you feel so strongly against Julian.'

Elizabeth told the head boy and girl everything – all about Rosemary's money going and Arabella's; how her own marked pound had gone – and had appeared in Julian's hand, when he was spinning coins; and how her own sweet had fallen from his pocket.

'You are quite, quite sure about these things?' asked William, looking worried. It was quite clear to him that there was a thief about – somebody in the first form – but he was not so sure as Elizabeth that it was Julian! He and Rita both thought that whatever the boy's faults were, however careless and don't-careish he was, dishonesty was not one of his failings.

'So you see, William and Rita,' finished Elizabeth earnestly, 'because of all these things I jumped to the idea that Julian was stealing the biscuits last night. It was terribly wrong of me – but it was the other things that made me think it.'

'Elizabeth, why did you think you could put matters right yourself, when the money first began to disappear?' asked Rita. 'It was not your business. You should not have laid a trap. You should have come straight to us, and let us deal with it. You, as a monitor, should report these things to us, and let us think out the right way of dealing with them.'

'Oh,' said Elizabeth, surprised. 'Oh. I somehow thought that as I was a monitor I could settle things myself – and I thought it would be nice to put things right without worrying you or the Meeting.'

'Elizabeth, you must learn to see the difference between big things and little things,' said Rita. 'Monitors can settle such matters as seeing that no one talks after lights out, giving advice in silly little quarrels, and things like that. But when a big thing crops up we expect our monitors to come to us and report it. See what you have done by trying to settle the matter yourself. You have brought a terrible complaint against Julian, you have made Arabella give away the secret she wanted to keep, and you have lost the honour of being made a monitor.'

'I felt so grand and important, being a monitor,' said Elizabeth, wiping away two tears that ran down her cheek.

'Yes – you felt *too* grand and important,' said Rita. 'So grand that you thought you could settle a matter that even Miss Belle and Miss Best might find difficult! Well, there is a lot you have to learn, Elizabeth – but you do make things as hard for yourself as possible, don't you!'

'Yes, I do,' said Elizabeth. 'I don't think enough. I just go rushing along, losing my temper – and my friends – and everything!' She gave a heavy sigh.

'Well,' said William, 'there is one thing about you, Elizabeth – you *have* got the courage to see your own faults, and that is the first step to curing them. Don't worry too much. You may get back all you have lost if only you are sensible.'

'I think we had better get Julian here and tell him all that Elizabeth has said,' said Rita. 'Perhaps he can throw some light on that marked pound – and the sweet. I feel certain he didn't take them.'

'Oh – let me go before he comes,' begged Elizabeth, who felt that Julian was the very last person she wanted to meet just then. She pictured his green eyes looking scornfully at her. No – she couldn't bear to meet him just then.

'No – you must stay and hear what he has to say,' said Rita firmly. 'If Julian didn't take these things, there is something peculiar about the matter. We must find out what it is.'

So Elizabeth had to sit in William's study, waiting for Julian to come. Oh dear, what a perfectly horrid day this was!

17 Good at heart!

Julian came at once. He was surprised to see Elizabeth in the study too. He gave her a look, and then turned politely to William and Rita.

'Julian, we have heard a lot of puzzling things from Elizabeth,' said William. 'We are sure you have an explanation of them. Will you listen to me, whilst I tell you them – and then you can tell us what you think.'

Julian listened whilst William told all that Elizabeth had poured out to him and Rita. Julian looked surprised and puzzled.

'I see now why Elizabeth thought I was the thief,' he said. 'It did look very odd, I must say. Did I really have the marked pound? And did a sweet of Elizabeth's really fall out of my pocket? I heard something fall, but as the sweet wasn't mine, I didn't pick it up. I saw it on the floor, but I didn't even know it had fallen from my pocket. I certainly never put it there.'

'How did it get there then?' said Rita, puzzled.

'I believe I've got that pound now,' said Julian suddenly. He felt in his pockets and took out a brand-new coin. He looked at it closely. In one place a tiny black cross could still be seen. 'It's the same pound,' said Julian.

'That's the cross I marked,' said Elizabeth, pointing to it. Julian stared at it thoughtfully.

'You know, I'm sure, now I come to think of it, that I

didn't have a bright new pound like this out of the box that week,' he said. 'I'd have noticed it. I'm sure I got two old pounds. So someone must have put this new coin into my pocket – and taken out an old one. Why?'

'And someone must have put one of Elizabeth's sweets into your pocket too,' said William. 'Does any boy or girl dislike you very much, Julian?'

Julian thought hard. 'Well, no – except, of course, Elizabeth,' he said.

Elizabeth suddenly felt dreadfully upset when she heard this. All her dislike for Julian had gone, now that she felt, with Rita and William, that Julian hadn't taken the money or sweets, but that someone had played a horrible trick on him.

'Elizabeth just hates me,' said Julian, 'but I'm sure she wouldn't do a thing like that!'

'Oh, Julian – of course I wouldn't,' said poor Elizabeth, almost in tears again. 'Julian, I don't hate you. I'm more sorry than I can say about everything that has happened. I feel so ashamed of myself. I'm always doing things like this. You'll never forgive me, I know.'

Julian looked gravely at her out of his curious green eyes. 'I have forgiven you,' he said unexpectedly. 'I never bear malice. But I don't like you very much and I can't be good friends with you any more, Elizabeth. But there is something I'd like to own up to now.'

He turned to William and Rita. 'You said, at the Meeting, that Elizabeth had twice been sent out of the room for misbehaving herself,' he said. 'Well, it wasn't her fault.' He turned to Elizabeth. 'Elizabeth, I played a trick on you over those books. I put springs under the bottom ones and they fell over when the springs had untwisted themselves. And I stuck pellets on the ceiling just above your chair, so that drops fell on your head when the chemicals in them changed to water. And I put sneezing powder in the pages of your French book.'

William and Rita listened to all this in the greatest astonishment. They hardly knew what Julian was talking about. But Elizabeth, of course, knew very well indeed. She gaped at Julian in the greatest surprise.

Springs under her books! Pellets on the ceiling that turned to water! Sneezing powder in her books! The little girl could hardly believe her ears. She stared at Julian in amazement, quite forgetting her tears.

And then, very suddenly, she laughed. She couldn't help it. She thought of her books jumping off her desk in that peculiar manner. She thought of those puzzling drops of water splashing down – and that fit of sneezing. It all seemed to her very funny, even though it had brought her scoldings and punishments.

How she laughed. She threw back her head and roared. William, Rita, and Julian could not have been more surprised. They stared at the laughing girl, and then they began to laugh too. Elizabeth had a very infectious laugh that always made everyone else want to join in.

At last Elizabeth wiped her eyes and stopped. 'Oh, dear,' she said, 'I can't imagine how I could laugh like that when I felt so unhappy. But I couldn't help it, it all seemed so funny when I looked back and remembered what happened and how puzzled I was.'

Julian suddenly put out his hand and took Elizabeth's. 'You're a little sport,' he said. 'I never for one moment thought you'd laugh when I told you what I'd done to pay you out. I thought you might cry – or fly into a temper – or sulk – but I never thought you'd laugh. You're a real little sport, Elizabeth, and I like you all over again!'

'Oh,' said Elizabeth, hardly believing her ears. 'Oh, Julian! You *are* nice. But oh, what a funny thing to like me again just because I laughed.'

'It isn't really funny,' said William. 'People who can laugh like that, when the joke has been against them, are, as Julian says, good sports, and very lovable. That laugh of yours has made things a lot better, Elizabeth. Now we understand one another a good deal more.'

Julian squeezed Elizabeth's hand. 'I don't mind the silly things you said about me, and you don't mind the silly things I did against you,' he said. 'So we're quits and we can begin all over again. Will you be my friend?'

'Oh *yes*, Julian!' said Elizabeth happily. 'Yes, I'd love to. And I don't care if you make hail or snow fall on my head, or put any powder you like into my books now. Oh, I do feel happy again.'

William and Rita looked at one another and smiled. Elizabeth seemed to fall in and out of trouble as easily as a duck splashed in and out of water. She could be very foolish and do silly, hot-tempered, wrong things – but she was all right at heart.

'Well,' said William, 'we have cleared up a lot of things – but we still don't know who the real thief was – or is, for he or she may still be taking other things. We can only hope to find out soon, before any other trouble is made. By the way, Elizabeth, if your first accusation of Julian was made privately and secretly, as you said, how was it that all the first form knew? Surely you did not tell them yourself?'

'No, I didn't say a word,' said Elizabeth at once. 'I said I wouldn't, and I didn't.'

'Well, I didn't say anything,' said Julian. 'And yet the

whole form knew and came to tell me about it.'

'Only one other person knew,' said Elizabeth, looking troubled. 'And that was Martin Follett. He was in the stables, Julian, whilst we were outside. He came out when you had walked off, and he offered me a pound in place of mine that had gone. I thought it was very nice of him. He promised not to say a word of what he had heard.'

'Well, he must have told pretty well everyone, the little sneak,' said Julian, who, for some reason, had never liked Martin as much as the others had. 'Anyway, it doesn't matter. Well – thanks, William and Rita, for having us along and making us see sense.'

He gave his sudden, goblin-like grin, and his green eyes shone. Elizabeth looked at him with a warm liking. How could she *ever* have thought that Julian would do a really mean thing? How awful she was! She never gave anyone a chance.

'He's always saying he does as he likes, and he's not going to bother to work if he doesn't want to, and he doesn't care what trouble he gets into, and he plays the most awful tricks – but I'm certain as certain could be that he's good at heart,' said Elizabeth to herself.

And Julian grinned at her and thought: 'She flies into the most awful tempers, and says the silliest things, and makes enemies right and left – but I'm certain as certain can be that she's good at heart!'

'Well, goodnight, you two troublemakers,' said William, and he gave them a friendly push. 'Elizabeth, I'm sorry about you not being a monitor any more, but I think you see yourself that you want to get a bit more common sense before the children will trust you again. You do fly off the handle so when you get an idea into your head.'

'Yes, I know,' said Elizabeth. 'I've failed this time but I'll have another shot and do it properly, you see if I don't!'

The two went out, and William and Rita looked at one another.

'Good stuff in both those kids,' said William. 'Let's make some cocoa, Rita. It's getting late. Golly, I wonder who's the nasty little thief in the first form. It must be somebody there. He's not only a nasty little thief, but somebody very double-faced, trying to make someone else bear the blame for his own misdeeds by putting the marked pound into Julian's pocket!'

'Yes, it must be someone really bad at heart,' said Rita. 'Someone it will be very difficult to deal with. It might be a girl or a boy – I wonder which.'

Julian and Elizabeth went down the passage to their own common-room. It was almost time for bed. There was about a quarter of an hour left.

'I'm coming into the common room with you,' said Julian, and Elizabeth squeezed his arm gratefully. He had sensed that she did not want

to appear alone in front of all the first form. It was going to be hard to face everyone, now that she had been disgraced, and was no longer a monitor.

'Thank you, Julian,' she said, and opened the door to go in.

18 Julian is very funny

The first-formers had been talking about Elizabeth most of the time, wondering where she was, and saying that it served her right to be punished. Everyone was on Julian's side, there was no doubt about that.

'I shall tell Julian just what I think of Elizabeth,' said Arabella. 'I never did like her, not even when I stayed with her in the hols.'

'I must say I think it was a pity that Elizabeth accused Julian without being certain,' said Jenny.

'I suppose she was feeling annoyed because she had been left out of my party,' said Arabella spitefully. 'So she got back at Julian like that.'

'No. That wouldn't be like Elizabeth,' said Robert. 'She does do silly things, but she isn't spiteful.'

'Well, I shan't speak a word to her!' said Martin. 'I think she's been mean to Julian.'

'Sh. Here she comes,' suddenly said Belinda. The door opened, and Elizabeth came in. She expected to see scornful looks and even to hear scornful words, and she did. Some of the children turned their backs on her.

Close behind her came Julian. He saw at once that the first-formers were going to make things difficult for Elizabeth.

'Julian,' said Arabella, turning towards him. 'We all feel sorry to think of what you had to face at the Meeting tonight. It was too bad.'

'You must feel very sorry about it,' said Martin. 'I should.'

'I did,' said Julian in his deep and pleasant voice, 'but I don't now. Come on, Elizabeth – we've still got about ten minutes before bedtime. I'll play a game of double-patience with you. Where are the cards?'

'In my locker,' said Elizabeth gratefully. It had been dreadful coming into the room and facing everyone – but how good it was to have Julian sticking up for her like this – her friend once more. She fumbled about for the cards in her locker.

Every boy and girl stared in the greatest astonishment at Julian. Had he gone mad? Was he being friendly to the person, the very person, who had said such awful things about him? It was impossible. It couldn't be true.

But clearly it was true. Julian dealt the cards, and soon he and Elizabeth were in the middle of the game. The others were so surprised that they watched silently, not finding a word to say. Arabella was the most surprised, and it was she who found her tongue first.

'Well!' she said, 'what's come over you, Julian? Don't you know that Elizabeth is your worst enemy?'

'You're wrong, Arabella,' said Julian in an amiable voice. 'She's my best friend. Everything was a silly mistake.'

There was something in Julian's voice that warned the others to say nothing. They turned to their own games, and left Julian and Elizabeth alone.

'Thanks, Julian,' whispered Elizabeth.

His green eyes looked at her with amusement. 'That's all right,' he said. 'Count on me if you want any help, Worst Enemy!'

'Oh, Julian!' said Elizabeth, half laughing and half crying. Then the bell went for bedtime and everyone cleared away books and games and went upstairs.

Things were not very easy for Elizabeth the next few days. The other children did not forgive and forget as easily as Julian did, and they treated her coldly. One or two were nice to her – Kathleen was, and Robert, and Harry. But most of them took no notice of her, and seemed to be glad she was no longer monitor.

Joan, of the second form, who had been Elizabeth's friend in the first term, came to find her. She took Elizabeth's hand and squeezed it. 'I don't quite know the rights and wrongs of it all,' she said, 'but I do know this, Elizabeth – that you wouldn't have said what you did if you hadn't really thought it was true. It will all blow over and you'll be made monitor again, you'll see!'

Elizabeth was glad of the kind words that her real friends gave her. 'Now I know what it is like when people are kind to others in trouble,' she thought. 'I shall remember how much I like kindness now, when things have gone wrong – and I shall be the same to others if *they* get into trouble.'

Elizabeth looked very serious these days. She worked very hard, was very quiet, and her merry laugh did not sound nearly so often. Julian teased her about it.

'You've gone all quiet, like Rosemary,' he said. 'Come on – laugh a bit, Elizabeth. I don't want a gloomy friend.' But Elizabeth had had a shock and had to get over it. Julian wondered what he could do to make her her old happy self. He began to think out a few jokes.

He told the children what he was going to do. 'Listen,' he said, 'when Mr Leslie, the science-master, takes us for science in the laboratory, I shall make some of my noises. But you must none of you make out that you hear them. See? Pretend that you hear nothing, and we'll have a bit of fun.'

Science was a bit dull that term. Mr Leslie was rather boring, and very strict. The children did not like him much, so they looked forward with the greatest glee to Julian's idea. They rushed to the lab that morning with much eagerness.

'What noises will you make?' asked Belinda.

'Wait and see,' said Julian, grinning. 'We will have a bit of fun – and Mr Leslie will get a few surprises.'

He certainly did. He walked stiffly into the room, nodded to the children, and told them to take their places.

'Now, this morning,' he said, 'we are going to test potato slices for starch. I have here . . .'

He went on talking for a while, and then handed out small slices of potato. Soon all the children's heads were bent over their experiment.

A curious noise gradually made itself heard. It was like a very high whistle, so high that it might have been the continual squeak of a bat, or of a bow drawn over a very highly strung violin-string.

'Eeeeeeeeee,' went the noise. 'Eeeeeeeeee.'

All the boys and girls stole a look at Julian. He was bending over his work, and there was not a single movement of mouth, lips, or throat to be seen. Yet they all knew he must be making that weird noise.

Mr Leslie looked up sharply. 'What is that noise!' he asked at once.

'Noise?' said Jenny, with an innocent stare. 'What noise, Mr Leslie?'

'That high, squeaking noise,' said Mr Leslie impatiently.

Jenny put her head on one side like a bird, pretending to listen. All the other children did the same. From outside the window there came the sound of an aeroplane in the sky, and in a moment the plane came in sight.

'Oh. It was the aeroplane you heard, Mr Leslie,' said Jenny brightly. Everyone giggled.

Mr Leslie frowned. 'Don't be absurd, Jenny. Aeroplanes do not make a high, squeaking noise. There it is again!'

'Eeeeeeeeeee!' Everyone heard the noise, but pretended not to. They bent their heads over their work, badly wanting to giggle.

Julian changed his noise. Into the room came a deep, growling noise. Mr Leslie looked startled.

'Is there a dog in the room?' he asked.

'A dog, Mr Leslie?' said Belinda, looking all round. 'I can't see one.'

Elizabeth exploded into a giggle which she tried to turn into a cough. The growling noise went on, sometimes hardly to be heard, sometimes very loud. Mr Leslie couldn't understand it.

'Can't you hear that noise?' he said to the nearest children. 'Like a growl.'

'You said it was a squeak just now, sir,' said Harry, looking surprised. 'Is it a squeaky growl, or a growly squeak?'

Elizabeth exploded again, and Jenny stuffed her hanky into her mouth. Mr Leslie grew very cross.

'There is nothing funny to laugh at,' he snapped. 'My goodness – what's that now?'

Julian had changed his noise, and a curious, muffled boom-boom-boom sound could be heard. It did not seem to come from anywhere particular, least of all from Julian!

Mr Leslie felt scared. He glanced at the children. Not one of them seemed to be hearing this new boom-boom noise. How strange! It must be his ears going wrong. He put his hands up to them. Perhaps he wasn't well. People had noises in their ears then.

Boom-boom-boom went the strange muffled sound. 'Can you hear a boom-boom noise?' said Mr Leslie in a low voice to Harry. Harry put his head on one side and listened. He listened with his hand behind one ear. He listened with it behind the other. He listened with both hands behind both ears.

Elizabeth gave a loud giggle. She really couldn't help it. Jenny giggled too. Mr Leslie glared at them. Then he turned to Harry.

'Well, if you can't hear it, it must be something wrong with my ears,' he said. 'Get on with your work, everyone. Stop giggling, Jenny.'

The next noise was like a creaking gate. It was too much for poor Mr Leslie. Muttering something about not feeling very well, he fled out of the classroom, telling the children to get on with their work till he came back.

Get on with their work? That was quite impossible! Peals of laughter, roars of mirth, squeals and giggles filled the room from end to end. Tears poured down Jenny's cheeks. Harry rolled on the floor, holding his aching sides. Elizabeth sent out peal after peal of infectious laughter. Julian stood in the middle of it and grinned.

'Oh, that *has* done me good!' said Elizabeth, wiping the tears from her eyes. 'I've never laughed so much in my life. Oh, Julian, you're marvellous! You *must* do it again. Oh, it was gorgeous!'

It did everyone good. Those gusts of laughter had cleared the air of all spitefulness, scorn, and enmity. Everyone suddenly felt friendly and warm. It was good to be together to laugh and to play, to be friends. The first form was suddenly a much nicer place altogether!

19 Julian has some shocks

Julian's success in Mr Leslie's class rather went to his head. He tried several other noises in Mam'zelle's class, and in the art class too. He tried a mooing noise in Mam'zelle's class, not knowing how terrified she was of cows.

Poor Mam'zelle honestly thought that a cow was wandering about in the passage outside, and she stood trembling in horror. 'A cow!' she said. 'It is nothing but a cow that makes that noise.'

'Moo-ooo-oo,' said the cow, and Mam'zelle shuddered. She could not bear cows, and would never go into a field where there was one.

'I'll go and shoo the cow away, Mam'zelle,' said Jenny, enjoying herself. She rushed to the door and there began a great shooing, mooing noise which sent the class into fits of laughter. Then Mam'zelle suddenly came to the conclusion that cows do not usually wander about school passages, and she looked sharply at Julian. Could that dreadful boy be making one of his famous noises?

The first form had a wonderful time with Julian's noises and tricks. There seemed no end
to them. His brilliant brains invented trick after trick, and they were so clever that no mistress or master seemed able to guess that they were tricks until it was too late.

Julian used the sneezing powder again, this time on Mr Lewis, the music-master, when he was taking a singing lesson. He took two or three forms together for singing, and the lesson quickly became a gale of laughter as poor Mr Lewis sneezed time after time, trying in vain to stop himself. Julian was quite a hero in the school for his many extraordinary jokes and tricks.

But he was not a hero to the teachers. They often talked of him, sometimes angrily, sometimes sadly.

'He's the cleverest boy we've ever had at Whyteleafe,' said Miss Ranger. 'Far and away the cleverest. If only he would work he would win every scholarship there is. His brains are marvellous if only he would use them.'

'He thinks of nothing but jokes,' said Mr Leslie angrily. He was now firmly convinced that the extraordinary noises he had heard in the science lesson had been made by Julian, and he was angry every time he thought of it. And yet that boy, as if to make up for playing such a trick, had written out a really brilliant essay for Mr Leslie, an essay that he himself would have been proud to write. He was an odd fellow, there was no doubt about it.

At the school Meeting following the one in which Elizabeth had lost her position as monitor, the little girl, now no longer on the platform with the 'Jury', but down in the hall with the others, had got up to speak.

'I just want to say that I know now I was completely wrong about Julian,' she said humbly. 'I have said so to him, and he has been very nice about it – and we are good friends again, so that shows you how nice he has been. I'm sorry I was such a bad monitor. If ever I am a monitor again I will do better.'

'Thank you, Elizabeth,' said William, as the little girl sat down. 'We are very glad to have Julian absolutely cleared of the charge against him – and glad to know that he has been big enough to forgive you and to be friends so quickly.'

There was a pause. Julian grinned at Elizabeth, and she smiled back. It was good to be friends once more. Then William spoke again, and a graver note was in his voice.

'But I have something else to say to Julian,' he said. 'Something not quite so pleasant, Julian. All your teachers are displeased with you. It is not so much that you play the fool in class, and play tricks and jokes, but that you only use your brains for those things and for nothing else. According to everyone you have really wonderful brains, inventive and original – brains that could do something for the world later on – but you only use them for nonsense and rubbish, and never for worthwhile work.'

He stopped. Julian flushed and put his hands deeper into his pockets. He didn't like this at all.

'It's all very well to keep your class in fits of laughter, and to be a hero because of your jokes,' said William, 'but it would be much better to work hard also, and later on become a hero in the world of science, or in the world of inventions.'

'Oh, I don't care whether I'm famous or not when I'm grown-up,' said Julian rather rudely. He was always rude when he felt awkward. 'I just want to have a good time, do what I like and let others do what *they* like. Hard work is silly, and—'

'Stand up when you speak to us, and take your hands out of your pockets,' said William.

Julian frowned, stood up, and took his hands out of his pockets.

'Sorry, William,' he said, his green eyes looking rather angry. 'I haven't any more to say – only that they're *my* brains, and I can choose how to use them myself, thank you. All this goody-goody talk doesn't mean a thing to me.'

'I can see that,' said William. 'It's a pity. It seems you only care for yourself and what you want yourself. One day you will learn differently – but what will teach you, I don't know. I am afraid it will be something that will hurt you badly.'

Julian sat down, still red. Use his brains for hard work when he could have a good time and laze around, playing tricks and jokes to make his friends laugh! No, thank you. Time enough to use his brains when he had to go out into the world and earn his living.

Elizabeth said nothing to him about William's talk. It was a little like she herself had once said to him when she was a monitor. It wasn't goody-goody talk. It was common sense. Julian was silly not to work. He could win marvellous scholarships, and do all kinds of fine things when he grew up. It was odd that he didn't want to.

The only effect that William's talk had on Julian was to make him even lower in the form than before! He was nearly always bottom, but the next week his marks were so poor that even Julian himself was surprised when they were read out. He grinned round cheerfully. *He* didn't care if he was bottom or not!

The week went on, and soon half-term came near. The children began to talk about their parents coming to see them. Elizabeth spoke to Julian about it.

'Will your parents come, Julian?'

'I hope so,' said the boy. 'I'd like you to see my mother. She's simply lovely. She really is – and so pretty and merry and sweet.'

Julian's eyes shone as he spoke of his mother. It was clear that he loved her better than anything on earth. He loved his father too, but it was his pretty, happy mother who had his heart.

'It's because of Mother I wear my hair too long,' he said to Elizabeth with a laugh. 'She likes this silly haircut of mine, with this annoying lock of hair always tumbling over my forehead. So I keep it like that to please her. And she loves my jokes and tricks and noises.'

'But isn't she disappointed when she knows you are always bottom of the form?' asked Elizabeth curiously. 'My mother would be ashamed of me.'

'Oh, mine likes me to have a good time,' said Julian. 'She doesn't mind about places in class, or whether I'm top of exams or not.'

Elizabeth thought that Julian's mother must be rather odd. But then Julian was odd too – very lovable and exciting, but odd.

Half-term came at last – and with it came most of the children's parents, eager to see them. Mrs Allen came and Elizabeth gave her a great hug.

'You're looking well, darling,' said Mrs Allen. 'Now, we must ask Arabella to come with us, mustn't we – because no one is here to see her.'

'Oh,' said Elizabeth, '*must* we, Mother?'

She caught sight of Julian, and called to him. 'Julian, here's my mother. Has yours come yet?'

'No,' said Julian, looking a little worried. 'She hasn't – and she said she would be here early. I wonder if the car has broken down.'

Just then the telephone bell rang loudly in the hall. Mr Johns went to answer it. He beckoned to Julian and took the boy into the nearest room. Elizabeth wondered if anything had happened.

'Mother, I must just wait for Julian to come out before I go and get ready to come with you,' she said. She hadn't long to wait. The door opened, and Julian came out. But what a different Julian!

His face was quite white, and his eyes were full of such pain that Elizabeth could hardly bear to look at them. She ran to him.

'Julian! What's the matter? What has happened?'

'Go away,' said Julian, pushing her away blindly, as if he could hardly see. He went into the garden by himself. Elizabeth ran after Mr Johns.

'Mr Johns! Mr Johns! What's the matter with Julian? Please – please tell me.'

'It's his mother,' said Mr Johns, 'she's very ill – desperately ill. His father is a doctor, you know, and he is with her, and some other very clever doctors too. She is too ill for him even to see her. It's rather a blow for him, as you can see. Maybe you can help him, Elizabeth. You're his friend, aren't you?'

'Yes,' said Elizabeth, all her warm heart longing to comfort the boy. He was so proud of his mother – he loved her so much. She was the most wonderful person on earth to him. Oh, surely, surely she would get better!

She ran to her mother. 'Mother, listen. I can't come out today. I'm so sorry – but Julian's mother is desperately ill – and I'm his friend, so I must stay with him. Could you just take Arabella out, do you think? I think I really must stay with Julian.'

'Very well,' said her mother, and she went to find Arabella. Elizabeth herself went to hunt for Julian. Goodness knew where he would hide himself. He would be like a wounded animal, going to some hole. Poor, poor Julian – what could she say to comfort him?

20 *Julian makes a solemn promise*

Julian was nowhere to be seen. Wherever had he gone? Elizabeth called to Harry. 'Harry! have you seen Julian anywhere?'

'Yes – I saw him tearing down to the gates,' said Harry. 'What's the matter with him?'

Elizabeth didn't answer. She rushed down to the big school gates too. She wondered if Julian had thought of catching a train and going to his mother. She ran out of the gates and stood looking down the road.

Some distance away, hurrying fast, was a boy. It must be Julian. Elizabeth tore after him, panting. She must get hold of him somehow. He was in trouble, and she might be able to help him.

She ran down the country lane and turned the corner. There was no one in sight. How could Julian have gone so far in such a short time! He couldn't possibly have turned the next corner yet! Elizabeth hurried along, feeling worried.

She came to the next corner. There was no one in sight on the main road either. Where could Julian have gone? She went back some way, thinking that he might have gone into a field through a gate a little way back. She passed a red telephone kiosk without thinking of looking inside it – and she was very startled when she suddenly heard the click of the kiosk door, and heard Julian's voice calling her urgently.

'Elizabeth! Oh, Elizabeth! Have you got any change on you?'

Elizabeth turned, and saw that Julian was in the telephone-box. She ran to him eagerly, fumbling in her pocket for her money.

'Yes – here is a fifty pence – and some tens,' she said. 'What are you doing?'

'Telephoning my father,' said Julian. 'Mr Johns said I wasn't to, at school – he said my father wouldn't want to be worried by phone calls – and I dare say he's right – but I've *got* to ask him a few questions myself. But I haven't got the right money to put in the box for the call.'

He took the money Elizabeth offered, and shut himself in the telephone-box again. Elizabeth waited outside. She had to wait for a long time.

It was a quarter of an hour before Julian could get through to his father, and the boy was almost in despair with the delay. He kept brushing his long lock of hair back, and he looked so white and forlorn that it was all Elizabeth could do not to open the kiosk door and go in beside him.

But at last he got through to his father, and Elizabeth could see him asking urgent questions, though she could hear nothing. He spoke to his father for about five minutes, and then put down the receiver. He came out, looking very white.

'I think I'm going to be sick,' he said and went pale green. He took Elizabeth's hand, and went through the nearby gate into the field. He sat down, still looking green. But he wasn't sick. He slowly lost his green look, and a little colour came back to his cheeks.

'I'm an idiot,' he said to Elizabeth, not looking at her, 'but I can't help it. Nobody knows how much I love my mother – or how sweet and loving she is.'

Elizabeth saw that he was making a great effort not to cry, and she wanted to cry herself. She didn't know what to do or say. There didn't seem any words that were any use at all. So she just sat close to Julian and squeezed his hand.

At last she spoke in a low voice. 'What did your father say?'

'He said – he said – Mother had just got a tiny chance,' said Julian, and he bit his lip hard. 'Only a tiny chance. I can't bear to think of it, Elizabeth.'

'Julian – doctors are so clever nowadays,' said Elizabeth. 'She will get better. They'll do something to save her – you'll see!'

'My father said they're trying a new drug, a new medicine on her,' said Julian restlessly, pulling up the grass that grew beside him. 'He said that he and two other doctors have been working on it for years – and it's almost ready. He's getting some today, to try it on Mother. He says it's the last hope – it will give her a tiny chance.'

'Julian, your father must be very clever,' said Elizabeth. 'Oh, Julian, it must be marvellous to be as clever as that, and to be able to discover things that can save people's lives. Fancy – just fancy – if your father's clever work should save your mother's life. You must take after him in brains, I think, Julian. You're very clever too. Oh, Julian, one day *you* might be able to save the life of someone you love by using a great invention of your own.'

Elizabeth had said these words in order to comfort Julian – but to her dismay and horror the boy turned over on to the grass and began to sob.

'What's the matter? Don't do that,' begged Elizabeth. But Julian took no notice. After a while he sat up again, looked for a hanky which he hadn't got, and rubbed his hands over his dirty face. Elizabeth offered him her hanky. He took it and wiped his face.

'If my father's new drug *does* save my mother's life, it will be because of his years of hard work, it will be because he's used his brains to the utmost,' said Julian, almost as if he were speaking to himself. 'I thought he was silly to work so hard as he did, and hardly ever have a good time or take long holidays.'

He rubbed his eyes again. Elizabeth listened, not daring to interrupt. Julian was terribly in earnest. This was perhaps the biggest moment in his life – the moment when he decided which road he was going to tread – the easy, happy-go-lucky road, or the hard, tiring road his father had taken – the road of hard work, of unselfish labour, always for others.

Julian went on speaking, still as if he were thinking aloud.

'*I've* been given brains too – and I've wasted them. I deserve to have this happen to me. There's my father using his brains all these years – and maybe he can save my mother because of that. It's the finest reward he could have. Oh, if only I could still have my mother, how hard I'd work! It's a punishment for me. William said something would teach me sooner or later – and it might be something that would hurt me badly.' Julian brushed back his hair, and bit his trembling lip.

'You have got the most wonderful brain, Ju,' said Elizabeth in a low voice. 'I've heard the teachers talking about you. They said you could do anything you liked, anything in the world. And, you know, I do think if you've got a gift of any sort, or good brains, you can be very, very happy using them, and you can bring happiness to other people too. This isn't goody-goody talk, Julian, really it isn't.'

'I know,' said Julian. 'It's wise and sensible talk. Oh, why didn't I show Mother what I could do, when I had the chance? She would have been so proud of me! She always said she didn't mind what I did, or how I fooled about – but she would have been so proud if I'd really *done* something. Now it's too late.'

'It isn't – it isn't,' said Elizabeth. 'You know your mother has a chance. Your father said so. Anyway, whatever happens, Julian, you can still work hard and use your brains and do something in the world. You could be anything you liked!'

'I shall be a surgeon,' said Julian, his green eyes gleaming. 'I shall find new ways of curing ill people. I shall make experiments, and discover things that will give millions of people their health again.'

'You will, Julian, you will!' said Elizabeth. 'I know you will.'

'But Mother won't be there to see me,' said Julian, and he got up suddenly and went to the gate. 'Oh, Elizabeth, I see why this has happened to me now. It's about the only thing that could have made me really see myself, and be ashamed. I wish – oh I wish . . .'

He stopped. Elizabeth knew what he wished. He wished that such a dreadful lesson need not have come to him. But things happened like that. The little girl got up and went through the gate with him.

They walked back to the school, and on the way they passed a small country church. The door was open.

'I'm going in for a minute,' said Julian. 'I've got a very solemn promise to make, and I'd better make it here. It's a promise that's going to last all my life. You stay outside, Elizabeth.'

He went inside the little, dim church. Elizabeth sat down

on the wooden bench outside, looking at the early daffodils blowing in the wind.

'I'd better pray too,' she thought. 'If only Julian's mother would get better! But I don't somehow think she will. I think poor Julian will have to work hard and do brilliantly without his mother to be proud of him, and love him for his big promise.'

After a short while Julian came out again, looking more at peace. He had a very steadfast look in his green eyes, and Elizabeth knew that, whatever happened, his promise of a minute ago would never be broken. Julian's brains would no longer be used only to amuse himself. Now, all his life long, he would do as his father had done, and use them for other people. Perhaps, as he had said, he would be a great surgeon, a wonderful doctor.

They walked back to the school in silence. There were no boys or girls there, for they all had gone out with friends or parents. Julian gave Elizabeth back her dirty hanky.

'Sorry you've had to miss your outing,' he said with a crooked little smile, 'but I couldn't have done without you.'

'Let's take some food and go for a picnic,' said Elizabeth.

Julian shook his head. 'No,' he said, 'I want to be here – in case there's any news. There may not be, today, my father said – or even for a day or two. But there might be, you see.'

'Yes,' said Elizabeth. 'All right, we'll stay here. Let's go and do some gardening. John won't be there, but I know what to do. There are some lettuces to plant, and there is still a bit of digging to be done. Could you do that, do you think?'

Julian nodded. They went out together, and were soon working in the wind and the sun. How good it was to work in the wind and the sun! How good it was to have a friend, and stick by him in times of trouble!

21 Martin gives Elizabeth a surprise

No news came for Julian that day, except a message to say that his mother was about the same, no worse and no better. The other children were upset to hear of the boy's trouble, and everyone did their best to comfort him, in their various ways.

Strangely enough, Martin seemed the most upset. This was odd, Elizabeth thought, because Julian had never liked Martin very much, and had not troubled to hide it. Martin went to Elizabeth, looking very distressed.

'Can I do anything to help Julian?' he said. 'Isn't there anything I can do?'

'I don't think so,' said Elizabeth. 'It's kind of you to want to help, Martin – but even I can't do very much, you know.'

'Do you think his mother will get better soon?' asked Martin.

'I don't somehow think so,' said Elizabeth. 'It's going to be awful for him when the news comes. I wouldn't bother him at all if I were you, Martin.'

Martin shuffled about, fidgeting with books and pencils, and Elizabeth grew impatient.

'What's the matter with you, Martin? You are awfully fidgety!' she said. 'You keep shaking the table, and I want to write.'

There was only one person in the common-room besides Elizabeth and Martin, and that was Belinda. She finished what she was doing, and then went out. Martin shut the door after her and came back to Elizabeth.

'I want to ask your advice about something, Elizabeth,' he said nervously.

'Well, don't,' said Elizabeth at once. 'I'm not a monitor any more. I'm not the right person to ask for advice now. You go to our new monitor. She's sensible.'

'I don't know Susan, and I do know you,' said Martin. 'There's something worrying me awfully, Elizabeth – and now that Julian is in trouble, it's worrying me still more. I love my own mother very much too, so I know what Julian must be feeling. Please let me tell you what I want to, Elizabeth.'

'Martin, don't tell me,' said Elizabeth. 'Honestly, I shan't be able to help you. I'm not sure of myself any more – I keep doing the wrong things. Look how I accused poor Julian of stealing. I shall be ashamed of that all my life. He was so decent about it too. You go and tell Susan.'

'I can't tell someone I don't know,' said Martin in despair. 'I don't want you to help me. I just want to get it off my chest.'

'All right – tell me then,' said Elizabeth. 'Have you done something wrong? For goodness' sake stop shuffling about, Martin. Whatever's the matter with you?'

Martin sat down at the table, and put his face in his hands. Elizabeth saw that his face was getting red, and she wondered curiously what was up with him. He spoke in a muffled voice through his fingers.

'I took that money – quite a lot of it – from Arabella – and Rosemary – and you – and other people too. And I took the sweets and the chocolate – and I took biscuits too and cake once,' said Martin, in a funny dull voice.

Elizabeth sat staring at him, startled and shocked.

'You thief!' she said. 'You horrid, beastly thief. And yet you always seemed so kind and generous. Why, you even offered me a pound in place of the one I lost – and all the time *you* had taken it! And you offered Rosemary money too, and she liked you awfully for it. Martin Follett, you are a very wicked boy, and a horrid pretender too, because you made yourself out to be so kind and generous and all the time you were a deceitful thief.'

Martin said nothing. He just sat there with his face in his hands. Elizabeth felt angry and disgusted.

'What did you tell *me* for? I didn't want to hear. I accused poor, unhappy Julian of doing what *you* did, you beast. And oh, Martin – was it *you* who put the marked pound into Julian's pocket – and the sweet too – to make me think it was he who had taken them? Could you be so mean as that?'

Martin nodded. His face was still hidden. 'Yes. I did all that. I was afraid when I found that pound was marked – and I never liked Julian because he didn't like me. I was afraid that if I was found out, none of you would like me. And I so badly wanted to be liked. Hardly anyone ever likes me.'

'I don't wonder,' said Elizabeth scornfully. 'Good gracious! It was mean enough to take the money and the other things – but it was much, much meaner to try and put the blame on somebody else. That's not only mean, but cowardly. I can't imagine why you've told me all this. It's a thing to tell William and Rita, not me.'

'I can't,' said Martin with a groan.

'Think of all the damage you've done!' said Elizabeth, growing very angry as she thought of it. 'You made me think poor Julian stole – and I accused him – and he got back at me by getting me turned out of class – and I lost my position as monitor. Martin Follett, I think you're the nastiest, most hateful boy I've ever met. I wish to goodness you hadn't told me.'

'Well – I can't bear to think that I got Julian into trouble, now that he's so – so desperately unhappy,' said Martin. 'That's why I told you. I had to get it off my chest. It seemed about the only thing I could do for Julian.'

'Well, I wish you'd confessed to somebody else,' said Elizabeth, getting up. 'I can't help you and I don't want to. You're mean and cowardly and horrible. You oughtn't to be at Whyteleafe. You're not fit to be. Anyway, I'm too worried about Julian just now to bother my head about *you*!'

The little girl gave Martin a scornful glance, got up and went out of the room. How disgusting! Fancy behaving like that – stealing, and then putting the blame on to others – and letting them bear it too!

Rosemary went into the common-room as Elizabeth walked out. Elizabeth went to a music-room, got out her music, and began to practise, thinking of Julian and Martin and herself, as she played.

After a short while the door of the practice-room opened and Rosemary looked in. Her pretty, weak little face looked rather scared as Elizabeth frowned at her. But for once in a way Rosemary was strong, and in spite of Elizabeth's frown she went into the music-room and shut the door.

'What do you want?' said Elizabeth.

'What's the matter with Martin?' asked Rosemary. 'Is he ill? He looked awful when I went into the common room just now.'

'Good,' said Elizabeth, beginning to play again. 'Serves him right!'

'Why?' asked Rosemary in surprise.

Elizabeth would not tell her. 'I don't like Martin,' she said, and went on playing.

'But Elizabeth, why not?' said Rosemary. 'He's really awfully kind. You know, he's always giving away sweets and things. And if ever anyone loses their money, he offers to give them some. I really think he's the most generous boy I know. He never eats any sweets himself – he only keeps them to give away. I think he's most unselfish.'

'Go away, Rosemary, please. I'm practising,' said Elizabeth, who didn't want to hear Martin praised just then.

'But, Elizabeth, what *is* the matter with poor Martin?' said Rosemary, overcoming her timidity for once. 'He really did look dreadful. Have you been saying anything unkind to him. You know how unkind you were to poor Julian. You never give anyone a chance, do you?'

Elizabeth did not answer, and Rosemary went out of the room, going so far as to bang the door because she really felt cross with Elizabeth. She did not like to go back to Martin because he had turned his back on her, and told her to go away. It was all very puzzling.

'I suppose Elizabeth has quarrelled with *him* now!' she thought. 'Well – I haven't done any good by going to her.'

But she had. As soon as she had gone, Elizabeth began to remember the things that Rosemary had said about Martin – and they suddenly seemed very strange to her.

'She said he was the most generous boy she knew,' said Elizabeth to herself. 'She said he never ate sweets himself but always gave them away. And when anyone loses their money he always offers them some. And it's quite true he offered *me* sweets and money. How odd to steal things and then give them away! I've never heard of that before.'

Elizabeth stopped practising, and began to think hard.

How could Martin be mean and yet generous? How could he make people unhappy by taking their things, and make others happy by giving them things? It didn't seem to make sense. And yet he did – there was no doubt about it.

'He doesn't steal for himself,' thought Elizabeth. 'I do think it's odd. I wish I could ask someone about it. But I'm not going to Susan, and I'm certainly not going to William and Rita again just now. I don't want them to think I'm interfering again – and anyway I'm not a monitor now. It was tiresome of Martin to tell me.'

She thought about it all for some time, and then something happened that made her forget. It was in the middle of the arithmetic class.

The children heard the telephone bell ring shrilly in the hall. It rang two or three times and then someone went to answer it. Then footsteps came down the passage, and a knock came at the classroom door.

A maid came in and spoke to Miss Ranger. 'If you please, Miss, there's someone urgently wanting Master Julian on the telephone. It's a long-distance call, so I didn't go to tell Miss Belle, in case the call was cut off before Master Julian got to the phone.'

Julian was out of his seat almost before the maid had finished. With a face as white as a sheet he half ran out of the room and down the hall. Elizabeth's heart almost stopped beating. At last news had come for Julian. But was it good or bad? The whole class was silent, waiting.

'Let the news be good – let the news be good,' said Elizabeth to herself over and over again, and didn't even notice that she had made blots all across her book.

22 Martin really is a puzzle!

There came the faint tinkle of the telephone bell as the receiver was put down. Then came the sound of footsteps down the passage, back to the schoolroom – hurrying footsteps. The door was flung open, and Julian came in, a radiant Julian, with sparkling eyes and a smiling mouth.

'It's all right,' he said. 'It's good news. It's all right.'

'Hurrah!' said Elizabeth, most absurdly wanting to cry. She banged on her desk for joy.

'Good, oh good!' cried Jenny.

'I'm so glad!' shouted Harry, and he drummed with his feet on the floor. It seemed as if the children had to make some sort of noise to express their delight. Some of them clapped. Jenny smacked Belinda hard on the back, she didn't know why. Everyone was full of joy.

'I'm very glad for you, Julian,' said Miss Ranger. 'It has been a great worry. Now it's over. Is your mother much better?'

'Much – much better,' said Julian, his face glowing. 'And it was all because of that wonderful new medicine my father and his two friends have been working on for so many years. It gave my mother a chance, just a chance – and this morning she suddenly turned the corner, and she's going to be all right. Gosh – I don't know how I'm going to do any more lessons this morning!'

Miss Ranger laughed. 'Well – there are only five minutes

left of this lesson before break. You had better all clear away your books and have five minutes' extra break, just to work off your high spirits. Everyone is glad for you, Julian!'

So the first form put away their books, chattering gaily, and rushed out into the garden early. The other forms were surprised to hear them playing there before the bell had gone. Elizabeth dragged Julian to a quiet corner.

'Julian, isn't it marvellous? Are you happy again now?'

'Happier than I've ever felt before,' said the boy. 'I feel as if I've been given another chance – one more chance to show my mother she's got someone to be proud of. I'm going to work now! I'm going to take all my exams with top marks, I'm going to win any scholarship I can, I'm going to take my medical exams as young as possible, I'm going to use my brains in a way they've never been used before!'

'You'll be top of the form in a week,' laughed Elizabeth. 'But, Julian, don't give up being funny, will you?'

'Well – I don't know about that,' said Julian. 'I'll perhaps think of jokes and tricks in my spare time – but I shan't waste my time or anybody else's now by being too silly. I'll see. I'm turning over a new leaf – going all goody-goody, like you wanted me to be!'

'No – I didn't want that,' said Elizabeth. 'I like good people, but not goody-goody. Save up some noises and jokes for us, Julian – you'll want a bit of rest from hard work sometimes!'

Julian laughed, and they went off to play with the others. The boy was quite mad with delight. All his fears were gone – his mother was better – he would see her again soon – there was time this term to work hard for her, and let her see what he could do.

For a time Elizabeth forgot about Martin. Then she

noticed him now and again, looking, as Rosemary had said, very forlorn. He hung round Julian in an irritating way, and Julian, who didn't like him, had difficulty in shaking him off.

'Oh blow – I'd forgotten about Martin,' thought Elizabeth to herself. 'Well, I shan't tell Julian what he told me. He's so happy today and I won't let Martin's meanness spoil his day. Anyway, I've been ticked off enough for trying to manage things my own way. I shan't bother about this. I should only get into trouble again.'

So she tried not to think any more about Martin. But soon he stopped trying to hang round Julian and began to hang round Elizabeth instead. He seemed completely lost somehow. Elizabeth was glad when bedtime came and she could get rid of him.

The excitements of the day were a bit too much for Elizabeth. She lay in bed that night and could not get to sleep. She turned this way, she turned that way, she punched her pillow, she threw off her eiderdown, she pulled it on again – but she couldn't go to sleep, no matter what she did!

She began to think about the puzzle of Martin. Again and again she thought: 'How can a person be two different things at one and the same time? How can you be selfish and unselfish, mean and generous, kind and unkind? I wish I knew.'

She lay and remembered all the School Meetings she had been to. She thought of the odd things some children did, and how, when the reason for their actions was found, they could be cured.

'There was Harry – he was a cheat – but it was only because he was afraid of being bottom of the form and letting his father down,' thought Elizabeth. 'And there was Robert – he was a bully last term – but it was only because he had once been dreadfully jealous of his small brothers, so he got rid of his jealousy by being beastly to other small children. And there's me – I was awful, but I *am* better now, even though I've been in disgrace this term.'

She remembered the Big Book in which William and Rita wrote down the accounts of every School Meeting. In it were the stories of many bad or difficult children who, through many a year at Whyteleafe, had had their faults and wrong-doings shown up, discussed kindly and firmly, and, in the end, been helped to cure themselves.

'I don't believe there's any cure for Martin, anyway,' thought Elizabeth. 'I wonder if there's anything in William's Big Book that would explain Martin's funny behaviour. I'd like to see. Oh dear, I wish it was morning, then I could go and see.'

The children were allowed to refer to 'William's Big Book', as they called it, when they liked. There was so much sound common sense in it.

'I'll go and read it now,' thought Elizabeth suddenly. 'I shall never go to sleep tonight. There won't be anyone about now, so I'll just pop on my dressing-gown, go down to the hall, and find the Book. It will be something to do anyway.'

She put on her dressing-gown and slippers. She crept out of the dormitory, where everyone was sound asleep, and went downstairs to the hall. On the platform was a table, and in the drawer of the table the Big Book was kept.

Elizabeth had a torch with her, for she dared not switch on the light. She opened the drawer and took out the Book. It was filled with writing – different writing, for three or four head-boys and head-girls had kept the Book throughout the time that Whyteleafe School had been running.

Elizabeth dipped here and there. *She* was in the Book too

– here it was, 'The Bold Bad Girl' – that was what Harry had
called her two terms ago, when she was the Naughtiest Girl
in the School. And here she was again, made a monitor
because of fine behaviour – and oh dear, oh dear, here she
was again, disgraced because of bad behaviour!

'Elizabeth Allen lost her position as monitor because she
accused one of her form wrongly of stealing, and because her
behaviour in class showed that she was unsuited to be a
monitor,' she read in William's neat, small handwriting.

'I seem to appear in this Book rather a lot,' said Elizabeth.
She turned to the beginning pages of the Book and read with
interest of other children who had been good or bad, difficult
or admirable – children who had left the school long ago.
Then the story of a girl began to interest her. It seemed very
much like Martin's story.

She read it through, then shut the Book and thought hard.
'What a peculiar story!' she thought. 'Very like Martin's
really. That girl – Tessie – she took money too – but *she*
didn't spend any of it on herself – she gave it away as fast as
she stole it. And she took flowers from the school garden,
pretended she had bought them, and gave them to the
teachers. And it was all because nobody ever liked her, so she
tried to buy their liking and their friendship by giving them
things. She stole so that she might appear kind and generous.
I do wonder if Martin does the same.'

She went back to her bed, thinking. 'How awful to be so
friendless that you've got to do something like that to get
friends,' she thought. 'I wonder if I'd better say something to
Martin tomorrow. He did look pretty miserable today.
Anyway, I've had enough with interfering with other people.
I'll just ask him a few questions, and then leave it. He can do
what he likes about himself. I don't care.'

She went to sleep after that, and was so tired in the morning that she could hardly wake up. She went yawning down to breakfast, grinned at Julian, and sat down to eat her porridge. What had she been worrying about the night before? Her French? No – she knew that all right, thank goodness. Julian? No – that worry was gone now.

Of course – it was Martin she had been thinking about. She took a look at his pale face, and thought that he looked rather small and thin.

'He's a horrid boy,' she thought. 'Really horrid. Nobody *really* likes him, not even Rosemary, though they say he's kind and all that. It's funny he hasn't a single real friend. Horrid as I have sometimes been, I've always had real friends – somebody has always liked me.'

A chance came for Elizabeth to speak to Martin soon after breakfast. Elizabeth had rabbits to feed, and Martin had a guinea-pig. The cages were side by side and the two children were soon busy.

'Martin,' said Elizabeth, going straight to the point, as she always did. 'Martin, why do you give away the sweets and money and things you steal, instead of keeping them for yourself? Why steal them if you don't want them?'

'Only because I want people to like me, and you can't make people like you unless you're kind and generous,' said Martin in a low voice. 'My mother has always told me that. It's not *really* stealing, Elizabeth – don't say that – I give the things away at once. It's – it's the same sort of thing that Robin Hood did.'

'No, it isn't,' said Elizabeth. 'Not a bit. It's stealing, and you know it is. How can you bear to know that you are so dishonest and mean, Martin? I should die of shame!'

'Well, I feel as if I'm dying of shame too, ever since you

called me all those awful names yesterday,' said Martin in a trembling voice. 'I simply don't know what to do!'

'There's only one thing to do – and a little coward like you would never do it,' said Elizabeth. 'You ought to own up at the next Meeting that you took the things, and say that you put the blame on Julian! *That's* what you ought to do!'

23 A school match – and other things

School went happily on. A lacrosse match was played, and Elizabeth was in it. It was a home match, not an away match, so the whole school turned out to watch. Elizabeth felt most excited.

Julian was playing in the match too, and so was Robert. Julian was good at all games. He could run swiftly and catch deftly.

'We ought to put up a good show today,' said Eileen, when she took the team out on to the field. 'We've got some strong first-form players this term. Now, Elizabeth, keep your head, pass when you can, and for goodness' sake don't go up in smoke if one of your enemies kicks you on the ankle! Julian, keep by Elizabeth if you can, and let her pass to you. You catch better than anyone else.'

It was an exciting match. The other school had brought a strong team, and the two schools were very evenly matched. Elizabeth got a whack on the hand from someone else's lacrosse stick, that gave her so much pain she thought she would have to go off the field.

Julian saw her screwed-up face. 'Bad luck!' he called. 'You're doing well, Elizabeth. Keep it up! We'll shoot a goal soon, see if we don't!'

Elizabeth grinned. The pain got better and she played well. The other school shot three goals, and Whyteleafe also shot three. The children who were looking on anxiously consulted their watches – only one minute more to go!

Then Elizabeth got the ball and tore for the goal. 'Pass, pass!' yelled Julian. 'There's someone behind you!'

Elizabeth threw the ball deftly to him, and he caught it. But another enemy was on him at once, trying to knock the ball out of his net. He passed it back quickly to Elizabeth. She saw yet another enemy coming to tackle her, and in despair she flung the ball hard at the goal.

It was a wild shot – but somehow or other it got there! It bounced on a tuft of grass, and just avoided the waiting lacrosse net of the goal-keeper. It rolled into the corner of the goal-net and lay still.

Whyteleafe School went quite mad. The whistle blew for Time, and the two teams trooped off the field. Julian gave Elizabeth such a thump on the back that she choked.

'Good for you, Elizabeth!' said Julian, beaming. 'Just in the nick of time. Jolly good!'

'Well – it was really a fluke,' said Elizabeth honestly. 'I couldn't see where I was throwing. I just threw wildly, and by a fluke it went into the goal!'

The first-formers crowded round her, cheering her and patting her on the back. It was very pleasant. Then the two teams went in and had a most enormous tea. It was all great fun.

'I think you ought to be a monitor all over again!' said Rosemary. 'I never felt so thrilled and proud in my life as when you shot that last goal, Elizabeth, just as the whistle blew. I almost forgot to breathe!'

Elizabeth laughed. 'Golly – if people were made monitors just for shooting goals, how easy it would be!'

Nobody felt like doing prep that night. Julian longed to make a few noises. The others looked at him, trying to make him start something. Mr Leslie was taking prep and it would be fun to have a bit of excitement.

Julian wanted to please the others. He wondered what to do. Should he make a noise like a sewing-machine? Or what about a noise like bees humming?

He looked down at his book. He hadn't begun to learn his French yet. He remembered his promise, made so solemnly in the little country church a few days back. He was never going to forget that.

Julian put his hands over his ears and began to work. Maybe if there were a few minutes left at the end of prep he would do something funny – but he was going to do his work first!

Work was easy to Julian. He had a quick mind, and an unusual memory. He had already read a great deal, and knew a tremendous lot. He could easily beat the others if he tried. But it was not so easy to try at first, when he had let his mind be lazy for so long.

But at the end of the first week of trying, Julian was top of the form! He was one mark ahead of Elizabeth, who was also trying hard. Everyone was amazed, especially Miss Ranger.

'Julian, it seems that you must either be top or bottom,' she said, when she read out the marks. 'Last week you were so far at the bottom that I am surprised there were any marks to read out at all. This week you are a mark ahead of Elizabeth, who has been working extremely well. I am proud of you both.'

Elizabeth flushed with pleasure. Julian looked as if he didn't care a rap, but Miss Ranger knew that was only a pose. Something had changed him, and he cared now – he wanted to use his brains for the right things, not only for silly jokes and tricks.

'I think perhaps his mother's illness must have had something to do with it,' thought Miss Ranger. 'I do hope this great change lasts! Julian is a joy to teach when he really works. I hope he won't be bottom again next week.'

But Julian would never be bottom again. He was going to keep that promise all his life. He was not going to waste his brains any more.

Only Martin did badly that week – even worse than Arabella usually did! He was right at the bottom and Miss Ranger spoke sharply to him.

'You can do better than this, Martin. You have not been bottom before. You seem very dreamy this week.'

Martin was not really dreamy. He was worried. He wished he had not told Elizabeth his secret now. She had said such hard things to him, things he couldn't forget. And she hadn't helped him at all.

Miss Ranger had a few words to say to Arabella also. 'Arabella, I am getting tired of seeing you so low in the form. You are one of the oldest – the very oldest in fact. I think if you gave a little more attention to your work and a little less to whether your hair is looking nice, or whether your collar is straight or your nails perfect, we might see a little better work.'

Arabella went red. She thought Miss Ranger was very unkind. 'She speaks more sharply to me than to anyone else in the form,' she complained to Rosemary.

This was quite true – but Miss Ranger knew that she could only get at thick-skinned Arabella by plain speaking. The vain little girl hated to feel small, hated to be scolded or put to shame in front of anyone. Whyteleafe School was very good for her. There was plenty of plain speaking there.

Arabella decided not to be bottom the next week. She

stopped fussing about her hair and her dress – at least she stopped fussing in class.

'You'll soon be quite passably nice, Arabella,' said Robert, who hadn't much time for the vain little girl. 'I haven't heard you ask Rosemary once today if your hair is tidy. It's simply marvellous!'

And, for once in a way, Arabella laughed at the joke against herself, instead of sulking. Yes, she really was getting 'passably nice' in some ways!

The next school Meeting came. 'It won't last long,' said Elizabeth to Julian. 'There won't be much business done at it, Julian. Let's slip out quickly afterwards and bag the little table in the common-room. I've got a big new jigsaw we can do.'

'Right,' said Julian.

But there was more 'business' to be done at that Meeting than Elizabeth thought, and there was no time for a jigsaw puzzle that night. It was all quite unexpected, and nobody was more surprised than Elizabeth when it happened.

The Meeting opened as usual. There was very little money to be put into the box, though a few children had postal orders. Then the money was given out.

'Any requests?'

'Please, William,' said one small boy, Quentin, 'the cage I keep my guinea-pig in fell over yesterday, and one side of it broke in. Could I have the money for another cage?'

'Well, that's rather expensive,' said William. 'There isn't a great deal of money in the box at the moment. Can't you mend the cage?'

'I have tried – but I'm not very good at it,' said Quentin. 'I thought I'd done it all right, but I hadn't, and my guinea-pig got out. I was late for school because I had to catch it. It's in with Martin's guinea-pig now, but they fight.'

'I'll mend it for Quentin,' said Julian, actually remembering to stand up and take his hands out of his pockets. 'It won't take me long.'

'Thank you, Julian,' said William. 'There really isn't a great deal of money in the box at the moment. But I believe there are quite a lot of birthdays next week, so maybe we shall have a full box again soon. Any more requests?'

Nobody quite liked to ask for any more money as there wasn't much to spare.

'Any complaints?' said William. There was a dead silence. It was clear there were none.

'Well, there's nothing much to say this week – except that I am sure the whole school will like to know that Julian is top of his form, instead of bottom, this week,' said William with a sudden smile. 'Keep it up, Julian!'

'That is the nice part about Whyteleafe School,' thought Elizabeth. 'You get blamed – but you do get praised too, and that's lovely!'

'You may go,' said William, and the children got up to go. But, in the middle of the noise of feet, there came a voice.

'Please, William! I've got something to say!'

'Sit down again,' ordered William, and everyone sat in surprise. Who had spoken? Only one boy was on his feet – and that was Martin Follett, looking very green and shaky. 'What do you want to say, Martin?' asked William. 'Speak up!'

24 Martin gets a chance

Elizabeth looked in astonishment at Martin. Surely he could not be going to tell his own secret – that it was he who had stolen the money and tried to put the blame on to Julian!

'He's such a mean, deceitful, horrid boy,' she thought, 'and a real coward. Whatever is he going to say?'

Martin swallowed once or twice. He seemed to find it difficult to say a word now. William saw that he was dreadfully nervous and he spoke more kindly to him.

'What is it you want to say, Martin? Don't be afraid of saying it. We are always ready to hear anything at the school Meeting, as you know.'

'Yes. I know,' said Martin in rather a loud voice, as if he was trying to get all his courage together at once. 'I know. Well – I took that money – and all the other things – and I put that pound into Julian's pocket, and the sweet too, so that nobody would think it was me – they would think it was Julian.'

He stopped speaking, but he didn't sit down. Nobody said a word. Martin suddenly spoke again. 'I know it's awful. I dare say I'd never have owned up except for two things. I couldn't bear it when Julian's mother was ill – I mean, it was awful to think I'd done a mean trick to someone who was miserable. And the other thing that made me speak was – someone said I was a coward, and I'm not.'

'You certainly are not,' said Rita. 'It is a courageous thing to do – to stand up and confess to something mean. But why did you steal, Martin?'

'I don't really know,' said Martin. 'I know there's no excuse.'

Elizabeth had sat and listened to all this in the greatest surprise. Fancy Martin being brave enough to say all that in front of everyone! Now Julian was completely cleared of any blame. She looked at Martin and felt suddenly sorry for him.

'He so badly wanted people to like him, and they don't,' she thought, 'and now he has had to own up to something that will make them dislike him all the more! Well – that was a brave thing to do.'

William and Rita were talking to one another. So were the monitors. What was to be done with Martin? How was this to be tackled? Elizabeth suddenly remembered what she had read in the Big Book the night before. She stood up.

'William! Rita! I understand about Martin! He hasn't got any excuse for what he did, but there's a real reason, it wasn't just badness. It wasn't the usual sort of stealing.'

'What do you mean, Elizabeth?' asked William, in surprise. 'Stealing is always stealing.'

'Yes, I know,' said Elizabeth, 'but Martin's sort was strange. He only took things from other people so that he might give them away! He never kept them himself.'

'Yes, that's quite true,' said Rosemary, most surprisingly forgetting her timidity, and standing up beside Elizabeth. 'He gave me money whenever I lost mine, and he is always giving away sweets. He never keeps any for himself.'

'William, there's a bit about the same sort of thing in our Big Book – the one on the table in front of you,' said Elizabeth eagerly. 'I couldn't help wondering why Martin seemed such a funny person – you know, kind and unkind, mean and generous – it seemed so odd to be opposite things at once – and there's a bit about a girl in our Book who was just the same.'

'Where?' asked William, opening the Book. Elizabeth walked up to the platform, bent over the Book, turned the pages, and found the place. 'There you are!' she said, pointing.

'How did you know it was here?' asked Rita.

'Well – Martin told me all he'd done, and I was disgusted,' said Elizabeth, 'but all the same I was puzzled about him – and I wondered if there was anything about that kind of thing in our Book – so I looked, and there was.'

William read the piece and passed it to Rita. They spoke together. Elizabeth went back to her place. Martin was looking very miserable, wishing heartily that he had never said a word now. He felt that everyone's eyes were on him, and it was not at all a nice feeling.

William spoke again, and everyone listened intently. 'Stealing is always wrong,' said William, in his clear, pleasant voice. 'Always. People do it for many reasons – greed – envy – dishonesty. All bad reasons. But Martin did it for a different reason. He did it because he wanted to buy friendship. He did it because he wanted to buy people's liking and admiration.'

William paused. 'He took things in order to give them away to someone else. He may have thought to himself that because it is good to give to others, it was therefore not bad to take them away from someone else. But they were not his to give. It was stealing just the same.'

A tear trickled down Martin's cheek and fell on the floor. 'I want to go away from Whyteleafe,' he said in a low voice, without standing up. 'I shall never do any good here now. I've never done any good anywhere.'

'You can't run away like that,' said William. 'What's the good of trying to run away from yourself? You've got courage or you wouldn't have stood up and said what you did. We all make silly mistakes, we all have bad faults – but what really matters is – are we decent enough to try and put them right? You did have a reason for what you did, a silly reason. Now you see it was silly, and you see that what you did was bad. All right – that's the end of it.'

'What do you mean – that's the end of it!' said Martin in surprise.

'The end of your silly habit of taking what doesn't belong to you in order to buy friendship!' said William. 'You know quite well you *can't* buy it. People like you for what you are, not for what you give them. Well – if the reason for that bad habit is gone, the habit goes too, doesn't it? You'll never steal any more.'

'Well – I don't think I shall,' said Martin, and he sat up a little straighter. 'I've felt so guilty and so ashamed. I'll take another chance.'

'Good,' said William. 'Come and see me this evening and we'll get things a bit straighter. But I think you must pay back each week any money you have taken from different children, and you must also buy sweets to give back to those you took them from. That's only fair.'

'Yes, I will,' said Martin.

'And we'll give him a chance and be friendly,' suddenly said Elizabeth, eager to do her bit to help. How she had disliked Martin! Now she wanted to help him! What was there about Whyteleafe School that made you see things so differently all of a sudden? It was odd.

'It seems to me,' said Rita, in her slow distinct voice, 'it seems to me as if Elizabeth is a much better monitor when she isn't one than when she *is*!'

The children laughed loudly at this. Elizabeth smiled too. 'Rita is right,' she thought, surprised. 'I do seem to be wiser when I'm not a monitor than when I am! Oh, how topsy-turvy I am!'

The Meeting broke up at last. Martin went to Julian. 'I'm sorry, Julian,' he muttered, not looking at the boy at all.

'Look at me,' commanded Julian. 'Don't get into the habit of not looking at people when you speak to them, Martin. Look at me, and say you're sorry properly.'

Martin raised his eyes and looked rather fearfully into Julian's green ones, expecting to see scorn and anger. But he saw only friendliness there. And he said he was sorry properly.

'I am sorry. I was a beast. I've learnt my lesson and I'll never be two-faced again,' he said, looking straight into Julian's eyes.

'That's all right,' said Julian. 'I like you better now than I did before, if that's any comfort to you. Look, William is wanting you.'

Martin went off with William. What William said to him nobody ever heard, but Rosemary, who saw him coming from the study later, said that Martin looked much happier.

'I'm going to be really friendly to him,' she said. 'He'll want a friend. I never thought he was bad, I always thought he was nice. So I shall go on thinking it.'

Elizabeth looked in surprise at the timid Rosemary. Good gracious – that was another person changing! Who would have thought that Rosemary, who agreed with everyone, would say straight out that she was going to be friends with someone like Martin!

'You simply never know about people,' thought Elizabeth. 'You think because they're timid they'll always be timid, or because they're mean they'll always be mean. But they can change awfully quickly if they are treated right. Golly, Arabella will be changing and forget to be vain and boastful! No – that could never happen!'

There was no time to do the jigsaw – only just time to clear away the things left out, and have some supper and go to bed.

'Things do happen here, don't they?' said Julian, with a grin. 'Come on down to supper.'

At supper Miss Ranger was continually annoyed by the buzzing of a bluebottle. She looked all down the table for it, but could see it nowhere.

'Where *is* that fly?' she said. 'It's very early in the year for a bluebottle, surely! Kill it somebody. We can't have it laying eggs in our meat.'

The bluebottle buzzed violently, and Mr Leslie, at the next table, looked all round for it. It really was becoming a nuisance.

Elizabeth looked suddenly at Julian. He grinned at her and nodded. 'Oh – it's one of Julian's noises!' she thought, and exploded into a giggle. Then everyone knew – and how they laughed, even Miss Ranger.

'I thought it was a good time to play a joke,' said Julian when he said goodnight to Elizabeth. 'We had all had such a very serious evening. Goodnight, Elizzzzzzzzzzzzzabeth!'

25 An adventure for Elizabeth

The days went swiftly by, days of work and play, riding and gardening, looking after pets, going for nature rambles – it was extraordinary the way the weeks flew by.

'Once the beginning of the term is past, the end seems to appear so quickly!' said Elizabeth. 'There doesn't seem to be much middle to a term!'

'Let's go for a nature walk this afternoon,' said Julian. 'We've got an hour and a half quite free. Don't garden with John – he's got plenty of helpers at the moment with that tribe of youngsters – we'll go over the hills and down to the lake.'

'All right,' said Elizabeth, looking out of the window at the brilliant April sunshine. 'It will be lovely on the hills – we might find primroses on our way.'

So, that afternoon, the two set off together. They carried nature-tins on their backs, for they meant to bring back many things for the nature class. 'We'll find frog-spawn in the lake,' said Julian. 'I bet there's plenty there, and tadpoles too.'

They went over the hills together. 'We must be back by tea-time,' said Elizabeth. 'That's the rule, unless we have permission to stay out later. My watch is right. I don't want to get into trouble again for anything just at present. I've not been too bad this last week or two!'

Julian grinned. He thought that of all the children in the

form Elizabeth probably tried hardest to be good, and yet walked into trouble more often than anyone else. You never knew what was going to happen to Elizabeth.

'She seems to make things happen, somehow,' thought Julian. 'She's such a fierce little person, so downright and sincere. Well – we've both had our ups and downs this term. Let's hope we'll have a little peace till the end of term.'

They went over the hills, picking primroses in the more sheltered corners. The sun shone down quite fiercely, and Elizabeth took off her blazer and carried it.

'This is lovely,' she said. 'Julian, look, there's the lake. Isn't it beautiful?'

It was. It lay smooth and blue in the April sunshine. There seemed to be nobody there at all. The children were pleased to think they would have it all to themselves.

They began to look for frog-spawn. There was none to be found – but there were plenty of tadpoles. They caught some and put them into their jars.

'I feel a bit tired now,' said Elizabeth. 'Let's sit down.'

'I'm going up the hill a bit,' said Julian. 'I want to find some special sort of moss. You sit here and wait for me.'

Julian disappeared. After a while Elizabeth thought she heard him coming back – but it was someone else. It was a child of about six, nicely dressed, with big blue eyes and very red cheeks. He was panting as if he had been running.

Elizabeth was surprised to see him all alone. He seemed rather small to be allowed near the lake by himself. She lay back and shut her eyes, letting the sun soak into her.

She heard the little boy playing about – and then she heard a loud splash. At the same moment she heard a terrified scream, and she sat up suddenly.

The little boy had disappeared. But a little way out on the

lake some ripples showed, and then a small hand was flung up.

'Golly! That boy has fallen in!' said Elizabeth in dismay. 'He must have crawled out on that low tree-branch, and tumbled off. I thought he oughtn't to be here by himself.'

Then a woman appeared, running. 'Where's Michael? Did I hear him scream?' she called anxiously. 'He ran away from me. Have you seen a little boy anywhere?'

'He has fallen into the water,' said Elizabeth. 'Can he swim?'

'No, oh no! Oh, he'll be drowned,' cried the woman. 'Oh, let's get help quickly.'

There was no help to be got. Elizabeth quickly undid her shoes. 'I'll wade in and get him,' she said. 'If the water is too deep, I'll have to swim.'

She waded out, feeling the sand of the lake-bottom just under her stockinged feet. Suddenly the sandy bottom fell away, and Elizabeth was out of her depth. She had to swim.

She was a good swimmer, and she struck out at once – but it was not easy to swim in clothes. They weighed her down dreadfully. Still, she managed somehow, and it was only a few strokes that she had to swim. Her quick mind remembered all she had learnt about life-saving.

She caught hold of the sinking child and pulled him towards her. At once he clung to her, almost pulling her under too.

'Leave go!' ordered Elizabeth. 'Leave go! I will hold *you*, not you me.'

But the child was too frightened to leave go. He pulled poor Elizabeth right under, and she gasped and spluttered. Somehow she undid his arms from round her neck, turned him over on his back, put her hands under his armpits, and swam on her back to the shore, pulling the kicking child along.

Soon she felt the sandy bottom under her feet and she struggled to stand. The child slipped from her hands and went under again. He got caught in some weeds and did not float up to the top. Elizabeth was in despair. She went under the water herself to look for him, and caught sight of a leg. She got hold of it and pulled hard.

The child came out of the weeds. He was no longer struggling. 'Oh dear – I believe he is drowned,' thought Elizabeth in horror. She dragged him to the shore. He was quite limp, and lay still.

The nurse bent over him, moaning, and quite terrified. Elizabeth thought she was silly. 'Look, we must work his arms up and down, up and down, like this,' she said. 'That will bring air into his lungs and make him breathe again. Look – work his arms well.'

The girl was tired, and she let the nurse do the life-saving work, then she took her turn – and suddenly the child gave a big sigh and opened his eyes.

'Oh, he's alive – he's alive!' cried the nurse. 'Oh, Michael, Michael – why did you run away from me?'

'You'd better get him home as soon as he can walk,' said Elizabeth. 'He's wet through. He'll catch an awful chill.'

The nurse took the child off in her arms, weeping over him, forgetting even to say thank you to the little girl who had saved him. Elizabeth took off her dress and squeezed it dry. She began to shiver.

Suddenly Julian appeared down the hill. He stared in the greatest astonishment at Elizabeth. 'Whatever *have* you been doing?' he asked. 'You're wet through.'

'I had to pull a kid out of the water,' said Elizabeth. 'I

couldn't help getting wet. I hope Matron won't be angry with me. Good thing I took my blazer off – I've got one dry thing to put on at any rate.'

'Come on home, quick,' said Julian, helping her on with her blazer. 'We're late anyway – and now you'll have to change all your clothes. Oh, Elizabeth – you can't even go out for a walk without doing something like this!'

'Well, I couldn't leave the child to drown, could I?' said Elizabeth. 'He ran away from his nurse.'

They went home as quickly as they could. The tea-bell went as they reached the school. 'I'll slip in to tea and say you are coming in a minute,' said Julian. 'Hurry up.'

Elizabeth hurried up – but she was cold and shivery, and wet clothes are not easy to take off. She put them in the hot-air cupboard to dry hoping that Matron would not see them there before she herself had time to take them out.

'I don't see how I could help it, all the same,' said Elizabeth, drying herself on a towel. 'I just had to pull that child out of the water. I bet he would have drowned if I hadn't.'

Matron didn't notice the wet clothes. Elizabeth was able to take them out of the cupboard before she saw them. She had a sharp word from Miss Ranger for being late for tea, but otherwise it seemed as if things were all right.

'Oh, Julian – I left my jar of tadpoles by the lake,' said Elizabeth in dismay, after tea. 'Aren't I an idiot?'

'Well – you must share mine,' said Julian. 'I've got plenty. I suppose if you go about dashing into lakes rescuing silly kids, you are bound to forget something or other.'

Elizabeth laughed. 'Don't tell anyone, please,' she said.

'Matron doesn't know my clothes were wet, and the others would only tease me if they knew I'd dashed into the lake like that.'

So Julian said nothing. He hadn't seen Elizabeth swim to the child's rescue, he hadn't known what a hard task it had been to get him safely to shore, or how Elizabeth had brought him back from death by showing the nurse how to work his arms up and down to make him breathe again. He just thought she had waded into the water, slipped and got wet, and pulled the child out.

So nobody knew, and Elizabeth forgot about it. She was working very hard indeed, trying to keep pace with Julian, who, now that he was using his brains properly, seemed likely to beat her easily every single week.

'It's most annoying!' said Elizabeth, giving him a friendly punch. 'I do my best to make you use your brains and work hard and what happens? I lose my place at the top of the form! I shall complain about you at the Meeting tonight, Julian. I shall say that you are robbing me of my rightful place at the top of the form. So be careful!'

'There'll be no excitement at the Meeting tonight, old thing,' said Julian. 'We've all been as good as gold lately.'

But he was wrong. There was plenty of excitement!

26 Happy ending

The children always enjoyed the weekly school Meetings, even if there was not much business to be done. It was good to meet all together, good to share their money, good to see their head boy and girl on the platform, with the serious monitors near by.

'You feel how much you belong to the school then,' said Jenny. 'You really feel part of it, and you know that what you are and do really matters to the whole school. It's a nice feeling.'

There were only two weeks to go till the end of the term. No one had any money at all to put into the Box. But there had been several birthdays two or three weeks before, so there was still plenty of money to share.

It was given out as usual, and then William allowed ten pounds to go to John to buy two big new watering-cans.

'One of ours has two holes in it and they can't be mended,' said John. 'The water drips out on to our feet and wets them all the time. And the other can is so small. Last summer we lost a lot of plants because we didn't do enough watering, and this time I want plenty of water if the weather's dry. So I'd be awfully glad to have two new cans.'

The garden had looked lovely that early spring. Crocuses had blazed on the school bank, daffodils were out everywhere, wallflowers were filling the air with their delicious scent, and polyanthus had flowered along the edges of the beds. John and his helpers had done really well. The whole school was willing to buy him cans, barrows, spades – anything he wanted. They were very proud of John and his hard work.

Nobody else wanted any money. There were no complaints either. It looked as if it was going to be a short and rather dull Meeting. But no – what was this? Miss Belle and Miss Best were actually walking up from the back of the big hall! *They* had something to say, they had business to discuss! Mr Johns came with them.

In surprise William and Rita gave them chairs, wondering what was happening. The school looked up to the platform, wondering too. It couldn't be anything awful, because Miss Belle and Miss Best were smiling.

The headmistresses sat down. Mr Johns sat beside them. They spoke a little and then Miss Belle got up.

'Children,' she said, 'it is not often that Miss Best, Mr Johns, and I come up here to speak to you at a school Meeting – unless, of course, you ask us. But this time we have something to say – something very pleasant – and I want to say it in front of the whole school.'

Everyone listened eagerly. Whatever could it be? Nobody had the least idea.

Miss Belle took a letter from her bag and opened it. 'I have had a letter,' she said. 'It is from a Colonel Helston, who lives not far from here. This is what he says.'

Miss Belle read the letter and everyone listened with interest and excitement.

'Dear Madam – Four days ago my little son, Michael, ran away from his nurse. He fell into the lake near your school, and would have been drowned if it had not been for a girl from Whyteleafe. This girl waded into the water, then swam to Michael. Michael struggled hard and pulled her under the water. She got him on his back, and swam towards the shore with him. He slipped from her hands and became entangled in some weeds. He was without any doubt drowning at that moment. The girl dived into the weeds and pulled him out. When she got him to shore she showed the nurse how to bring him back to life again, and herself helped to do this, with the result that he lived, and is now safe and well with me at home.

I was away at the time, and only came back today, to hear this amazing story. I do not know which girl it was. All I know is that the nurse saw she had a Whyteleafe school blazer on the ground near by, and I would like you, please, to tell me the name of the child so that I may thank her myself, and give her some reward for her very plucky action. She saved the life of my little boy – he is my only child – and I can never be grateful enough to the little girl from Whyteleafe School, whoever she may be.

Yours sincerely,

Edward Helston.'

The children listened in amazement. Who could it be? Nobody knew. But then, whoever it was must have come home with wet clothes – surely they would have been seen. The children looked from one to the other. Julian nudged Elizabeth. His green eyes shone with pride in his friend. Elizabeth was as red as a beetroot. 'What a fuss about nothing!' she thought.

'Well,' said Miss Belle, folding up the letter, 'this surprising letter gave me and Miss Best very great pride and pleasure. We do not know who this girl is. We asked Matron if anyone had given her wet clothes to dry, but no one had. So it is a complete mystery.'

There was a silence. Elizabeth said nothing at all. Everyone waited.

'I should like to know who it is,' said Miss Belle. 'I should like to give her my heartiest congratulations on a brave deed that she said nothing about. The whole school should be proud of her.'

Elizabeth sat quite still. She simply could *not* stand up and say anything. For the first time in her life she really felt shy. She hadn't done anything much – only just pulled that child out of the water – oh dear, what a fuss about it all!

Julian got to his feet. 'It was Elizabeth!' he said, so loudly that it sounded almost like a shout. 'Of course it was Elizabeth! Who else could it be? It's exactly like her, isn't it? It was our Elizabeth!'

The children craned their necks to look at Elizabeth. She sat on the floor, still very red, with Julian patting her on the shoulder.

Then the clapping and cheering began! It nearly brought the roof down. Elizabeth might be naughty and hot-tempered and often do silly, wrong things – but she was as sound and sweet as an apple in her character, and all the children knew it.

Clap, clap, clap, hurrah, hurrah, bang, bang, clap, clap! The noise went on for ages, until Miss Belle held up her hand. The sounds died down.

'Well – so it was Elizabeth!' she said. 'I might have guessed it. Things always happen to Elizabeth, don't they? Come up here on the platform, please, Elizabeth.'

Elizabeth went up, flaming red again. Miss Belle, Miss Best, and Mr Johns actually shook hands with her solemnly and said they were very proud of her.

'You are bringing honour to the name of Whyteleafe,' said Miss Belle, her eyes very bright. 'And you bring honour to yourself at the same time. We would like to give you a reward ourselves, Elizabeth, for your brave deed. Is there anything you would like?'

'Well . . .' said Elizabeth, and paused. 'Well . . .' she said again. Julian wondered what she was going to say. Was she going to ask if she might be made a monitor again?

'I'd like you to give the school a whole holiday, please,' said Elizabeth, in a rush, thinking that she was asking rather a big thing. 'You see – there's a big fair on at the next town soon – and it would be such fun if you would give us a whole holiday, so that we could go to it. We've all been talking about it, and I know everyone would like to go. Do you think we could?'

There was another outburst of cheering and clapping. 'Good old Elizabeth!' shouted somebody. 'Trust her to ask something for the school, and not for herself!'

Miss Belle smiled and nodded. 'I think we might say yes to what Elizabeth wants, don't you?' she said, and Miss Best nodded too. Elizabeth smiled, very pleased. She might have been in great disgrace, and made the children think bad things of her that term – but anyway she had made up for it now by getting them a whole holiday to go to the fair.

She turned to go down into the hall again. But somebody was standing up, waiting to speak. It was Julian.

'What is it, Julian?' asked Miss Belle.

'I am speaking for the whole of the first form,' said Julian. 'We want to know if Elizabeth can be made a monitor again, now, this very night? We think *she* ought to have some reward. And we want her for our monitor. We all trust her and like her.'

'Yes, we do, we do!' cried Jenny, and a few others. Elizabeth's eyes shone like stars. How marvellous! To be made a monitor because the whole form wanted it, and wanted it so badly! Oh, things were wonderful!

'Wait, Elizabeth,' said Miss Belle, stretching out her hand and pulling the little girl to her. 'Do you want to be made a monitor again?'

'Oh yes, please,' said Elizabeth happily. 'I can do better now. I know I can. Let me try. I won't let anyone down again. I'll be sensible and wise, really I will.'

'Yes, I think you will,' said Miss Belle. 'We won't pass round bits of paper and vote for you, Elizabeth, as we usually do – you shall be monitor from this very minute. Susan shall still be monitor too. For once in a way we must have an extra one! A very special extra one!'

So Elizabeth went to sit at the monitors' table, proud and pleased. Everyone was glad, even Arabella. How could anyone not be glad, when Elizabeth had so generously asked for something for the whole school, instead of asking for something for herself alone, as she might so easily have done?

'Well, that was a good Meeting, wasn't it?' said Julian, when the children at last filed out of the hall, chattering and laughing in excitement. 'This has been a thrilling term, I must say. I'm glad I came to Whyteleafe School. It's the best school in the world!'

'Yes, it is,' said Elizabeth. 'Oh, I do feel so happy, Julian.'

'You've a right to,' said Julian. 'Funny person, aren't you? Naughtiest girl in the school – and best girl in the school! Worst enemy – and best friend! Well, whichever you are, you're always our Elizabeth, and we're proud of you!'

Turn the page to read about other classic series by Enid Blyton . . .

CELEBRATE 70 YEARS OF

The Famous Five

These special edition jackets of the first five books have been brought to you by Quentin Blake and friends in support of the House of Illustration.

CHRIS RIDDELL

Helen Oxenbury

Quentin Blake

OLIVER JEFFERS

emma chichester clark

www.famousfivebooks.com
www.houseofillustration.org.uk

House of Illustration

Hodder Children's Books

The Complete Famous Five

Have you read them all?

More classic stories from the world of

Enid Blyton

The Secret Seven

Join Peter, Janet, Jack, Barbara, Pam, Colin, George
and Scamper as they solve puzzles and mysteries,
foil baddies, and rescue people from danger – all without
help from the grown-ups. Enid Blyton wrote fifteen
stories about the Secret Seven. These editions contain
brilliant illustrations by Tony Ross, plus extra
fun facts and stories to read and share.

The Complete Secret Seven

Have you got them all?